THE SHROUD OF HADES

By Andy McDermott and available from Headline

Featuring Nina Wilde and Eddie Chase
The Hunt for Atlantis
The Tomb of Hercules
The Secret of Excalibur
The Covenant of Genesis
The Cult of Osiris
The Sacred Vault
Empire of Gold
Temple of the Gods
The Valhalla Prophecy
Kingdom of Darkness
The Last Survivor (A Digital Short Story)
The Revelation Code
The Midas Legacy
King Solomon's Curse
The Spear of Atlantis
The Resurrection Key
The Temple of Skulls
The Knights of Atlantis
The Shroud of Hades

Featuring Alex Reeve
Operative 66
Rogue Asset
Ghost Target
Final Traitor

Standalone Thriller
The Persona Protocol

ANDY McDERMOTT
THE SHROUD OF HADES

HEADLINE

Copyright © 2025 Andy McDermott

The right of Andy McDermott to be identified as the Author of the Work has been asserted by him in accordance with the Copyright, Designs and Patents Act 1988.

First published in 2025 by
Headline Publishing Group Limited

1

Apart from any use permitted under UK copyright law, this publication may only be reproduced, stored, or transmitted, in any form, or by any means, with prior permission in writing of the publishers or, in the case of reprographic production, in accordance with the terms of licences issued by the Copyright Licensing Agency.

All characters in this publication are fictitious and any resemblance to real persons, living or dead, is purely coincidental.

Cataloguing in Publication Data is available from the British Library

Hardback ISBN 978 1 0354 0093 5
Trade Paperback ISBN 978 1 0354 0094 2

Typeset in 12/15.5pt Aldine 401 BT by Jouve (UK), Milton Keynes

Printed and bound in Great Britain by Clays Ltd, Elcograf S.p.A.

Headline's policy is to use papers that are natural, renewable and recyclable products and made from wood grown in well-managed forests and other controlled sources. The logging and manufacturing processes are expected to conform to the environmental regulations of the country of origin.

Headline Publishing Group Limited
An Hachette UK Company
Carmelite House
50 Victoria Embankment
London EC4Y 0DZ

The authorised representative in the EEA is Hachette Ireland,
8 Castlecourt Centre, Dublin 15, D15 XTP3, Ireland (email: info@hbgi.ie)

www.headline.co.uk
www.hachette.co.uk

For Kat and Sebastian

Prologue

The Shetland Islands

In early winter, the Shetlands, far to the north of Scotland, are a harsh place to be on the best of days. This year, following a summer of record-breaking heat across the Northern Hemisphere, nature had with an ironic smile flicked the switch to an unseasonal cold. Frost coated the ground, and a stiff wind sliced across the rolling lowlands, seeking targets to cut with its icy edge.

One small island on the archipelago's eastern periphery would not normally present the wind with any victims. From the sea it appeared unremarkable and inhospitable, a treeless swathe of grass-topped rock some four hundred metres long. The only evidence that humans had ever set foot on the desolate land was a single structure, a low concrete blockhouse poking up from a hillock near its southern shore. It had the utilitarian, weathered look of something built in haste during wartime, which was indeed the case; it had been constructed in 1943 to house facilities for Britain's secretive Special Operations Executive.

Now, ninety years later, it served an equally clandestine purpose for another intelligence agency: MI6.

The blockhouse's door slid open, stark light beyond silhouetting a man in a heavy coat. Stuart Collins drew in a breath as the wind hit him. It was past dawn, but heavy clouds reduced the daylight to a mournful grey. Even so, he was glad of the sight despite the cold and gloom. Any break from the unrelenting fluorescent glare below ground was welcome.

There was another reason he had chosen to brave the elements. Even the most trusted guards at the United Kingdom's highest-security prison had their addictions. He lowered his head to shield his face from the wind, then lit a cigarette. A deep draw, the cigarette's tip blazing as he brought the reassuring warmth of the smoke into his lungs, then he ascended the few concrete steps and emerged into the open.

Christ, it was cold! Still, there were others who had it worse. A boat, a small trawler or some similar working vessel, rocked on the slate sea about a mile offshore. With the wind kicking up whitecaps, he was happy to remain on land, however bleak.

He ambled away from the entrance, booted feet crunching the tough, frosted grass as he climbed a shallow slope. The view from the summit was far from inspiring, but he still turned to take in the panorama. From here he could see most of the island, for all it was worth. Nothing but scrubby vegetation and scattered boulders, surrounded by unwelcoming waters. His home for two months on, one month off. If only it were the other way round, he thought with a mental sigh. Still, it was good money, and being a prison guard was much easier when the prisoners were never allowed to leave their cells.

He turned his back to the wind and took another drag on his cigarette. The boat was still there in the distance. It didn't seem to have moved since he first saw it.

On the boat, someone was watching Collins.

The Russian, smoking a cigarette of his own, was called Ossovich. His country had trained him as a soldier, but he had no remaining loyalty to that corrupt, collapsing nation. He now worked as a mercenary for the highest bidder. And nobody could bid higher than his current employer. He briefly looked away from his powerful telescope to pick up a radio handset. 'Someone's outside,' he reported.

'Have you identified them?' came the reply over the radio. The man speaking had a German accent.

'Yes. Collins.' The gyro-stabilised telescope had an attachment on its eyepiece that fed the image to a laptop. Facial recognition software had already done its work.

'Where is he?'

'On the rise west of the entrance. About fifty metres from you.'

'Facing?'

'Towards the boat. He's smoking.' A tiny red dot glowed in the muted greys of the magnified view.

'A bad habit. For him.' It could have been a joke, but there was no humour behind the words. 'Are we clear to move in?'

Ossovich stared intently at the figure on the island. Collins took one last look around, then started down the slope, wind whipping away the smoke as he exhaled. 'Yes. He's going back to the door.'

'Okay. Then we are *go*.'

On land, six figures rose from behind boulders and rapidly closed on Collins.

They had arrived in the dead of night, dropping from the boat wearing drysuits and scuba tanks and swimming underwater to the isolated island's northern end. From there, they had patiently crawled the length of the barren landscape, following a path that avoided the prison's surveillance systems. A tower bearing cameras or a radar would have given away that the blockhouse was not as abandoned as it appeared, but it was still far from blind. Its electronic eyes were focused upon the surrounding sea, though; this close, the intruders could finally move freely.

The leader of the team was called Steinitz. He gave silent hand signals, telling his companions to spread out. Whichever path Collins took to return to the blockhouse, at least one of them would be able to intercept him. But the guard was following the easiest route, retracing his steps. With the wind whistling in his ears, he didn't hear the approaching men until they were almost upon him. He hesitated, turned—

And was tackled to the ground.

The man who had brought him down was a tall, beaky-nosed Austrian named Duger, his lank blond hair skittering in the wind. He delivered a brutal kidney-punch to Collins, making him convulse, then rolled him onto his back and pressed an elbow against his throat with crushing force. Steinitz stood behind him, looking down at his prisoner. 'Mr Collins,' said the German. He was older than the other mercenaries, hair greying, skin weathered by conflict. Even through his pain, Collins reacted with surprise at being addressed by name. Steinitz held up a tablet. 'We have your sister. If you do not cooperate, we will kill her.'

A tap, and the device's screen came to life. Surprise became shock as Collins saw his sister gagged and bound to a chair, a man wearing a balaclava mask holding a large knife to her throat. The trapped woman squirmed; the video was a live feed.

Or so it appeared. In fact, it was an AI-generated fake. There was one for every guard on the island, an appropriate family member – wife, child, parent, sibling – under threat. But Collins would not have time to examine it for the telltale discrepancies of synthesised video. Steinitz gave him just long enough for recognition and fear to cross his face, then the tablet was withdrawn. 'You are going to get us into the prison. Do as you are told, and you will live. Do not, and you will die, and so will your sister. Do you understand?'

Collins managed to nod. Steinitz had expected nothing else. No matter how loyal to their country someone professed to be, in his experience prioritising it over the life of a loved one was the preserve of the sociopathic or stupid. 'Good. Now, stand.'

The other mercenaries had by now joined him. All held guns. Collins saw the weapons and involuntarily sagged in defeat. Duger withdrew, and the guard struggled upright, gasping for breath. Steinitz gestured with his own sidearm towards the nearby concrete structure. 'Go to the door,' he ordered. 'I will be right behind you. If you make any attempt to warn the men inside, I will kill you. Move.'

Duger shoved Collins down the slope. Steinitz took up position behind him, gun aimed at his back. The guard reached the bunker, glancing around nervously. 'Move!' Steinitz repeated, jabbing him with his weapon.

Collins helplessly walked on as ordered. A camera on the top of the blockhouse overlooked the beach, but from its position could not see anything directly below. There was another camera by the metal door at the bottom of the steps, but Steinitz was prepared for it. He dropped low, using Collins to shield himself from view as the guard reached the entrance.

Security was lax, the German saw. There should have been a challenge, a confirmation of identity required before entrance was permitted. But the door opened almost immediately. The guards inside recognised Collins, letting him in at once. As far as they knew there was nobody else on the island, no threat.

They were wrong.

'Go in,' Steinitz growled. Collins stepped through the doorway. He tensed, ready to warn of the danger—

But Steinitz had expected it. He leapt up and grabbed the other man with his free hand, forcefully shoving him forwards to use as a human shield. Duger and two other mercenaries were already rushing up behind him. 'Trigger!' Steinitz barked into his throat mic.

The command was not for his companions, but Ossovich on the boat. He was still watching through the telescope. In one hand he held a remote-control unit, thumb poised over a red button.

He pressed it.

He was not the only mercenary on the boat. Two other men, Craine and Vikram, had dived down into the chill waters. An undersea cable linked the MI6 facility to the telecommunications network on the Shetland mainland; again, a visible radio mast would have drawn unwanted attention. But the cable was the only direct link to the outside world. If it were damaged, the secret prison would be completely cut off.

The fibre optics at the cable's core were shielded by multiple layers of plastic and steel wire. They were no protection against almost a kilogram of high explosive. The cable was severed in a millisecond by the underwater blast.

The guards on the island were now on their own.

Steinitz looked past Collins as he forced the other man deeper into the room. It was a blank-walled, claustrophobic hall, lit by stark overhead fluorescent tubes. A windowed booth stood against a wall to one side, a startled man within looking up at the unexpected flurry of action. Two more guards were in the main space, one seated at a desk, the other standing. The latter was the first to react, grabbing for his holstered sidearm—

Steinitz was faster. He fired over the shoulder of Collins, who screamed as the noise of the gunshot blew out his eardrum. A ragged bullet wound exploded in the standing guard's upper chest. He fell. Steinitz changed direction, driving Collins with him to block the second guard's firing angle as he too drew his weapon.

Duger, following Steinitz, had him covered. The guard was only halfway out of his chair as bullets punched into his chest and neck. He toppled backwards as blood and gobbets of shredded flesh splattered the desk.

The man in the booth slammed his hand down on a control panel. An alarm wailed. Steinitz didn't fire at him. There was no point; the booth's windows were bulletproof. Instead he sought new targets. He spotted them where the walls met the low ceiling. CCTV cameras. A door at the booth's rear led to another section of the prison: the guardhouse. Living areas, storage – and a security station.

His gun cracked, darting between targets with mechanical accuracy. The cameras shattered. Behind him, two more mercenaries entered. The first, Bakst, a heavy-set Belarussian, held a sub-machine gun. Palancio, the second, carried an assault rifle – with a grenade launcher beneath its barrel.

Collins had completed his purpose. Steinitz fired a round through his heart, then quickly backed away from the booth. Bakst and Duger did the same, retreating to the cover of the desk as Palancio readied his secondary weapon. The man in the booth saw him and frantically ducked. With the security cameras destroyed, the other guards now had no idea what was happening in the lobby. Someone would be trying – and failing – to call the mainland for help, while their comrades grabbed weapons to defend the facility—

The door in the booth opened. Steinitz saw armed figures beyond. They were well trained, reacting quickly. But the guards would need a split-second to take in the scene, locate their attackers, take up positions . . .

Palancio didn't give them that moment. The Italian fired. The grenade exploded on impact, mere bulletproofing unable to withstand the blast. The booth disintegrated in a storm of wood and metal. One guard was flung from its side to crash against the lobby's rear wall, clothes and skin shredded. Another flew backwards through the open door.

Debris and shrapnel showered across the room. Steinitz waited a moment for the storm to cease, then rose. The booth was a smoking ruin, pieces of at least two corpses amongst the wreckage. The German glanced back as the last three mercenaries ran in. 'Clean up,' he ordered, indicating the door. 'There should only be five guards left. Find them and kill them.'

His team hurried to the door, preparing for the next stage of their assault. A flashbang grenade was tossed into the guardhouse. 'Flash out!' a bearded American named Flagg warned. Everyone covered their ears. A moment later came a piercing detonation and a dazzling burst of light, then the two remaining men, a Frenchman called Lannard and the Iranian Hassani, rushed in with guns clattering savagely. Screams echoed through the concrete rooms.

Steinitz ignored them. He marched to the remains of the booth. The control panel inside had been destroyed. No matter: there was a backup. 'Someone go to the security room,' he ordered over the intermittent gunfire. 'Open the door to the cells.'

He and Duger crossed to the lobby's rear. A heavy metal door awaited them. It had no handle. They stood at it for several seconds as more shots rang from the guardhouse – then a harsh buzzer sounded and the door opened.

Steinitz and Duger went through. A bleak concrete corridor was beyond, doors on each side. 'Number six,' said Duger.

'I know.' Steinitz stopped at the third door on the left. 'Open it.'

Dugan placed a shaped explosive charge on the lock mechanism, then retreated, winding out a length of wire. Steinitz banged a balled fist on the door. 'I would recommend you take cover,' he called out to the cell's occupant, before following Duger to a safe distance. 'Three, two, one – fire!'

Duger flicked a switch. There was a sharp retort, and shattered metal fragments pelted the opposite wall like a shotgun blast. As soon as the echoes faded, the two men returned to the door. A fist-sized hole had been punched through it. Duger pushed the door. It slowly swung open. They entered the cell.

At first, there was no sign of its occupant. Then a mattress that had been hastily pulled into the corner behind the steel toilet bowl moved. A figure slowly rose from behind it.

John Brice had once been an officer of MI6. Now, he was one of its prisoners, a man who was officially dead in a facility that did not officially exist. He had attempted a coup on his own government, toppling the clock tower housing Big Ben onto the Commons chamber in the Houses of Parliament. Over a third of the country's politicians had been killed in the attack. Since his capture and incarceration, he had never left this cell.

He had not been idle, though. Always tall and athletic, he was now a hulk of a man, nothing else to do but work out until exhaustion took him, recover, then work out some more. He wore a plain pale grey shirt and dark blue trousers, muscles bulging visibly beneath the garments.

Brice regarded his visitors. A hint of madness swirled in his eyes. Both his rescuers subtly shifted to show they were ready for any dangerous moves he might make. He stood straighter, rising to his full height. The movement revealed his throat. It was scarred, once torn open by a bullet. During its repair a slotted metal disc had been surgically implanted – a mechanical larynx, replacing his ruined voice box. The reason for its permanence was simple: the more common external type could potentially have been used by him as a weapon or escape tool.

He spoke. 'So, to what do I owe the pleasure?' His voice was a flat, robotic buzz.

'You are John Brice,' said Steinitz. Not a question; he knew his face from files that had been covertly hacked from MI6's records. 'My employer wants to hire you.'

'And who might that be?'

'Nobody you would have heard of before coming here.'

Brice narrowed his eyes. 'What's the date?'

'The second of November.'

'What *year*?'

'Twenty thirty-three.'

The mad eyes widened in disbelief. 'Twenty thir—' His fists clenched, every muscle in his body tightening. 'Thirteen years. I've been here for *thirteen years*?' He looked around at the cell that had been his world for all that time. 'I thought nine, perhaps ten. Thirteen years!'

'You are now a free man,' said Steinitz, unmoved. 'If you accept my employer's offer.'

Brice stepped forward to loom before the two mercenaries. Duger's hand tightened around his gun. Brice noticed the movement. He halted. 'I'd like to meet your employer.'

'You can't.'

'Why not?'

'He's dead.'

Brice's eyebrows rose. Steinitz handed him the tablet. 'Watch this. It will explain everything.' The big man tapped play.

The video he watched was only a few minutes long. Brice took in every word with rapt attention. At certain points his body tightened again with barely contained anger, but he remained fixated on the person on the screen. At last, it ended.

Steinitz regarded him warily, putting his own hand on his sidearm. 'Well?' he asked. 'What is your decision?'

Brice smiled. It was not a reassuring sight, rage and insanity behind his stretched lips. 'Count me in.'

1

New York City

Two Weeks Later

Eddie Chase paused at the door of his daughter's room and sighed. The sound was not loud, but in her nearby study, his wife heard it. 'What's wrong?' asked Nina Wilde.

The bald Englishman came to her open doorway. 'It's finally sinking in, I suppose. Macy's gone.'

Nina looked up from her laptop. 'It's not as if she won't come back.'

'Only to visit. She doesn't live here any more.' He glanced back at the other door. Their now-adult daughter's bedroom contained the same furniture it always had, and on the surface seemed unchanged from how it had looked that summer. But there were small but significant gaps where items of importance, whether practical or sentimental, were absent. 'It's weird. I keep expecting her to come out of there.'

'Or for us to go in and tell her to turn her music down.'

He snorted. 'That bell-end downstairs took over that job.' A new neighbour had moved into the apartment building a couple of months earlier, and his habit of demonstrating his expensive sound system at late hours had led to friction. 'Bloody typical, isn't it? I go part-deaf from all the gunshots and explosions I've been close to, but I can still hear his bass speaker perfectly.'

'He did turn it down after you went and threatened him.'

'I didn't *threaten* him. Just used . . . forceful language, that's all.' Eddie seemed about to speak again, but instead stood silently, deep in thought.

Nina gave him a quizzical look. '*Is* something wrong? It seems like something's bothering you.'

Eddie shook his head. 'No, no,' he said. 'I'm fine. Just at a bit of a loose end.' He gestured at Nina's laptop and the various papers beside it. 'I need to do what you've done and find something to keep myself busy.'

The redhead tapped on a stack of folders. 'If you want to help me out by going through these photocopies Macy sent and highlighting mythological places or artefacts that the Knights of Atlantis thought were real . . .'

He raised his hands. 'I'm good, thanks. It's not my idea of holiday fun.'

'I'm on sabbatical, not vacation,' Nina insisted. 'That's the great thing about having tenure at the university, I can take time out for research. And I think this research is more important right now than teaching.'

'It's the IHA's job,' said Eddie. 'Let them handle it.' The International Heritage Agency was their former employer, Nina once the director of the United Nations-funded organisation dedicated to locating and securing potentially dangerous historical artefacts.

It was Nina's turn to snort. 'I can't trust them any more,' she said bluntly. 'Not after what John Hoffman said in Portugal.' Hoffman was the IHA's current director, and not a man Nina held in high regard. 'He was absolutely open about the IHA's primary function now being exploitation and even weaponisation of the discoveries they're meant to be protecting. I'm totally opposed to that.'

'So are the Knights of Atlantis.' The secret society had sought to recruit Macy earlier that year; its members were direct descendants of the lost civilisation's high priestesses. 'Let Macy and her new mates take care of this stuff, then. They're the ones who have the power to use it, after all.' Nina said nothing, but after twenty-five years together Eddie knew when his wife's silence said as much as her words. 'Wait, you've still got a problem with them?'

'I don't like the idea of some self-appointed group laying claim to every Atlantean relic they find,' she said carefully. 'The artefacts they already have are dangerous – you've seen what they can do. They have weapons, they have armour – they can *fly*, for God's sake.'

Eddie nodded, a half-smile on his lips. 'That was pretty cool, I have to admit. Our daughter, the superhero.'

'It's not Macy I'm worried about. What if the artefacts they're *protecting*,' she didn't quite add air-quotes, but her intonation was clear enough, 'fall into the wrong hands? Or the *Knights* become the wrong hands? That almost happened already!'

'The guy who tried it's dead. And Macy's in charge now. I mean, she's given you all this stuff.' He indicated the piled folders. 'Between the Knights and the Brotherhood, you should have enough info to find out if these things really exist.'

'At least the Brotherhood email me their information,' said Nina. The Brotherhood of Selasphoros was another secret society with a very long history, one that a quarter of a century earlier had tried to kill her to stop her from locating the remains of Atlantis. Once she did so despite the organisation's best efforts, time – and heavy pressure from the IHA and international law enforcement – had brought it around to begrudging cooperation. 'The Knights' archives are still entirely physical. It's a pain in the ass. Macy can't even take phone pictures of what I need and email *those* to me in case someone intercepts them and uses them to find the Knights' new headquarters.'

Not knowing to where the Knights of Atlantis had relocated meant also not knowing where their daughter was. The thought darkened Eddie's mood. 'But have you found anything?' he asked, trying to divert his mind from that particular subject.

'I've found *out* plenty,' she replied, with a hint of exasperation.

'But that's not the same as *physically* finding anything. There's a whole slew of supposedly mythological things that both the Knights and the Brotherhood make reference to as if they're historically real. The Sword of Goliath, Pandora's Jar—'

Eddie cocked his head. 'Don't you mean Pandora's Box?'

'"Box" is a Renaissance mistranslation, it drives me nuts. But that, the Shroud of Hades, the underground city of Agartha... those are just the ones I've been researching the last few days. There are plenty more. And we know that if both the Knights and the Brotherhood say something in their records is real, there's a good chance it actually is.'

'Like the Iron Palace.' They had located the vast underground redoubt of the Turanian king Afrasiab in the depths of Turkmenistan's Karakum desert earlier that year. 'So you haven't actually figured out where any of these things are?'

'Not yet.' She frowned, taking off her reading glasses. 'Depending who wrote it and when, the records contradict each other far too often. Like the Sword of Goliath – is it four feet long, or six, or ten? Or the Shroud of Hades, which supposedly makes the wearer invisible – the Knights' records clearly call it a shroud. But the Brotherhood describe it as a piece of armour, which fits Greek mythology, but even then it can be a cap, or a helmet. Again, every account has its own take.'

'I'd rather fight wearing a helmet than a cap,' said Eddie. 'But they can't all be true.'

'Exactly. But we both know from experience that even myths which seem contradictory can be real. And if they are real, and powerful enough to become part of legend, then I don't want the IHA to get hold of them.'

'Or the Brotherhood.' Eddie waited until Nina nodded in reply, then added, slightly pointedly, 'Or the Knights?'

This time, she did not respond at all. 'You don't trust your own daughter?' he went on.

'Of course I do!' she exclaimed, affronted – and to Eddie's mind, over-defensively. 'But apart from Rain and MacDuff, we don't know any of the other members, or the new people they've started recruiting. Until I can be sure I can trust them all, I'd rather be safe than sorry.'

Eddie conceded the point with a nod of his own. But he wasn't finished. 'Does Macy know you're dealing with the Brotherhood as well?'

'I'm keeping anything that might give away information about the Knights secure, if that's what you're asking. The Brotherhood doesn't know I'm cross-referencing their records with the Knights'.'

'That *wasn't* what I was asking.'

His wife gave him a brief, guarded look. 'Anyway, what time are we meeting Holly?'

It was a blunt attempt to change the subject. Eddie sighed inwardly, then said, 'Quarter to one. She said she'll meet us by the Alice in Wonderland statue.'

She checked her laptop's clock. 'Okay, give me fifteen minutes.' She donned her glasses and turned back to her work.

'All right.' There was a time when the Yorkshireman would have taken some degree of offence at what seemed like a curt dismissal, but he was long used to her eccentricities. Once Professor Nina Wilde became focused on her archaeological work, he reflected, that was it: everything else faded into the background. Macy had sometimes been infuriated by her mother's obsessive nature, and probably justifiably so, but to him it was simply the price of love. His wife was . . . how best to put it? *Unique.*

Amused, he left her alone and went to the living room. To kill time, he turned on the television and stretched out on an armchair with his feet on the coffee table. The current topic on a news channel was what he'd expected. 'And with less than an hour before the space station of the late trillionaire Rafael Loost burns up in the atmosphere,' said the perky blonde presenter, 'people are gathering to watch the spectacle.'

THE SHROUD OF HADES

The picture cut to Central Park. A scattered crowd was braving the unseasonal chill, some observers carrying binoculars for a better view. Another cut, this to a beaming young man holding a stack of cheap yellow plastic helmets labelled OFFICIAL SPACE STATION SHIELD. A sign showed he was selling each for twenty dollars. 'Some enterprising people may be offering protection,' the presenter continued chirpily, 'but the experts at NASA assure us there's no danger of being hit by debris. The space station will pass directly over New York City at an altitude of forty miles, and any pieces large enough not to burn up will splash down in the Atlantic Ocean.'

'The twat deserves to splash down in a fucking cesspit,' Eddie muttered. His personal dislike of the world's richest man had only intensified after actually dealing with Loost some months prior, and he was actively pleased that he was dead. In fact, he had assisted in his demise.

Brief interviews with people in the park followed, expressing varying degrees of regret at the loss of the 'tech visionary'. One young man in particular seemed genuinely upset. 'He was going to save the Earth, then take us to the stars,' he proclaimed. 'Who's going to replace him? There's nobody else like him!'

Eddie shook his head. For all Loost's claims to the contrary, ultimately he had wanted the same as every other ultra-wealthy person in history – more money and more power for himself at the expense of everyone else. Even his private space station, supposedly a new frontier of exploration, was in the end a means of dodging tax. Yet here were his followers weeping and wailing like cult members. 'Bloody morons.'

'But not everyone held Rafael Loost in such high regard,' said the presenter. 'One of his former nurses has very strong feelings against him.'

Another cut, this to a woman in her early thirties. Her hair was brown with blonde streaks, slightly untidy as it grew out of what had been a short cut. A caption read NATALIE BACHAND: RAFAEL

LOOST'S NURSE, but Eddie already knew who she was. She had been doing the media rounds quite extensively in advance of the station's splashdown.

'Everyone thinks of Rafael as this genius who was going to save the planet,' she said, her accent softly French-Canadian. The screen showed a photo of a smiling Natalie floating in zero gravity aboard the orbiting habitat, wearing a sleek white catsuit-style uniform. 'But to me, he's the man who got me pregnant and then left me with nothing, even though he knew I was having his baby. He—' The interview returned, a twinge of anger crossing her face. 'He doesn't deserve anyone's love. All he cared about was money, not people. I hope his fans remember that.'

Back in the studio, the blonde presenter nodded. 'Whatever your opinions on Rafael Loost, his final act will be spectacular. We'll have full coverage as it happens, in less than an hour. But now, here are the other headlines from around the world.'

Dramatic music cued in clips of politicians and wars, floods and blizzards. Eddie watched with only half-attention, waiting for Nina to finish what she was doing. Finally she entered. 'Okay, shall we go?' she asked. Eddie turned off the television and stood as she peered out of the window. The sky was blue with only patchy cloud, but the people on the street below were all wearing heavy clothing. 'Looks cold. I need to find my gloves.'

Her husband had already donned the garment he usually wore in rain or shine, his black leather jacket. Nina rooted through a small chest of drawers near the door for her gloves. 'Is my hat in there?' he asked.

She pulled out a black woollen beanie cap. 'This one?'

'Yeah, thanks.' She gave it to him. He donned it, then unlocked the door as she put on her weatherproof winter coat. 'Let's go and watch the toasting trillionaire.'

The couple lived in Manhattan's Upper East Side, not far from Central Park. Many other people had also turned out to watch the impending fireworks, the open areas of the great green space now hosting a multitude of skywatchers. The event could hardly have been better timed, coming when many workers were on their lunch breaks.

There had obviously, Nina thought as she held Eddie's gloved hand, been some amount of planning behind the space station's fiery demise. Rafael Loost had died over two months prior due to complications from beta thalassemia intermedia, a congenital blood disorder. A transfusion would have saved his life, and in fact one had been scheduled to launch aboard a supply rocket. Unfortunately for Loost, it never left the ground, exploding on the pad in what an official investigation had classified as a freak weather occurrence.

The truth was closer to home. Loost had been manipulating both Macy and a member of the Knights of Atlantis via his social media app Uzz in an attempt to locate and obtain an ancient artefact: the Staff of Afrasiab. According to legend, Afrasiab had the power to control the weather . . . which had turned out to be true. The staff was a conductor for the still little-understood force of earth energy, generated by and flowing through the planet itself. People of a certain, very specific genetic heritage had the ability to focus and control that energy through such a conductor. People whose ancestors had been high priestesses of Atlantis.

People like Macy. And her mother.

Nina had found the staff first, only to lose it – to her own daughter. But the family was reunited when Loost's plot was exposed. The trillionaire had intended to use it to control the weather worldwide to his personal benefit: ending droughts, or causing them, providing the ideal conditions to grow crops, or to obliterate them, all depending on who was willing to give him the most money or control. Nina's last communication with Loost had seen him threaten to use his effectively infinite resources to destroy her and her family.

So they destroyed him first.

Macy still possessed the Staff of Afrasiab – and used it. A

lightning storm of inconceivable force turned Loost's supply ship into a fireball, followed by the giant crawler needed to transport his rockets to the launch pad. Despite Loost's belief in the reality-bending power of his sheer wealth, his commercial rivals had been unwilling to bump their scheduled cargoes in favour of Loost's medical supplies, all the more so after a video of Loost threatening to have Nina, Eddie and Macy murdered went public. The world's richest man died soon after, a sickly shell trapped in orbit by his own hubris.

He'd had time enough to make sure his funeral was like none ever seen before, though. While his nurses were eventually brought safely back to Earth, his body was left on the space station, which his ground controllers had programmed for a slow decay of its orbit before finally plunging to its end. That it would flash directly above the hometown of the people who had brought about his demise hadn't escaped Nina's notice. But if that was deliberate on Loost's part, it was a gesture, nothing more, a final impotent shake of the fist by an already defeated foe. The station's course had been tracked, analysed, predicted. It would not – could not – hit New York. Loost could do nothing more to harm her, or her family.

Another family member awaited them in Central Park. Holly Bennett, Eddie's niece, stood by the bronze statue of Alice and her companions at the Mad Hatter's tea party. Though born in England, Holly had emigrated to the United States over a decade before; unlike her uncle, she had taken on full American citizenship. 'Hi, guys,' she said, her accent retaining only a vestige of its original British tones. 'How are you?'

'We're good, thanks,' said Eddie, hugging her.

Holly greeted Nina, then glanced past her as if expecting to see someone else. 'It's so weird, Macy moving out. And going to Europe too! How are you handling it?'

'Coping,' was Eddie's curt reply. 'How about you? We haven't seen you for a while.'

'I've been super-busy. We took over another company, so I've been trying to integrate their operations with ours, and ugh, you don't want to know.' She made a face. 'It's good to have a break. Plus, it's not every day you see a space station fly over the city.'

'It's not like it's coming in to land at JFK,' Eddie said with a grin. 'It'll be pretty high up. Forty miles, the news said.'

Holly shrugged. 'Should still be a hell of a display.'

'The most expensive Viking funeral in history,' Nina remarked as they set off through the park. 'God, the *ego* of the man.'

'Well, he's dead now, and good riddance,' added Eddie.

Holly eyed them with amusement. 'Sounds like you two had a personal issue with him.'

'We had some dealings, yeah,' said Nina. 'Let's just say he's not the world-saving philanthropist he liked to make out.'

The younger woman chuckled. 'It's amazing, the number of rich and powerful people you've pissed off.'

'How's your mum?' Eddie asked. 'I haven't spoken to her for a bit.'

Holly hesitated before replying. 'She's . . . been better.'

He was immediately filled with concern for his sister. 'What's wrong?'

'I'm not sure. She said she's been really tired all the time. She's going for a scan in a couple of weeks. It might just be the menopause.' She drew in a breath. 'I'm sure she'll be fine. She always is.'

'I'll give her a call later,' Eddie promised.

They made their way to the Great Lawn, a flat, treeless oval expanse of grass near the Metropolitan Museum of Art. It had an uninterrupted view of the sky, so had drawn quite a number of observers. The trio found a spot, Eddie checking the time. 'It's almost one. Should be visible soon.' The heavens were largely clear, with patchy cloud to the north.

'Which way is it coming from?' Holly asked.

Nina faced roughly north-west. 'That way, I think.' She looked into the sky. Nothing out of the ordinary was visible, but it couldn't be too long.

A couple of minutes passed. Then someone cried out, 'There, there!'

Heads turned to see where the speaker was pointing. Nina followed their gaze – and saw, high in the far distance, a point of light. She would at first have taken it for an aircraft catching the sun, but as she watched she saw it was flickering. She realised why: the deorbiting space station was already ablaze, atmospheric drag tearing pieces from it. 'Shee-it,' a nearby woman said in dismay. 'It's not gonna hit us, is it?'

Nina trusted the scientists at NASA to know their jobs, but still couldn't help feeling a chill of alarm. It really did seem as if the shimmering dot of fire was coming straight at her. But it gradually began to move, beginning a long arc over the dome of the sky that would, she realised, pass directly overhead. Somebody behind her was watching live news coverage on their phone. 'The station is now fifty miles up, somewhere above Pennsylvania,' a commentator noted. That gave a hint of how fast it was travelling; the state was over forty miles away in that direction, but the point – now streak – of light would be overhead in under a minute.

She kept watching. Gasps of awe and surprise rose as the line of flame suddenly split into several parts. The station was breaking up. People cheered as if watching a fireworks display. Nina felt brief annoyance; she had no love for Loost, but his body was somewhere amidst the inferno. But she appeared alone in thinking the cheer was disrespectful. Phones were raised high to record the event as it cut across the firmament, the burning streaks now right above—

Dozens of chimes sounded simultaneously around her.

People reacted in surprise as message alerts came through on their phones. 'What the hell?' said Holly, fumbling in her coat for her own device. 'I always have it on mute in the office.' Hers too was signalling an incoming message – at full volume.

Nina recognised the chime. Not from her phone, but it had been almost omnipresent on Macy's at one time. It was the default jingle of the social media network Uzz.

The company that had made Rafael Loost's fortune.

Neither Nina nor Eddie had the app on their phones. It had not appealed even before their dealings with Loost, and after learning the extent to which both Uzz and the artificial intelligences of his quantum computing company spied on its users, they had all the more reason to avoid it. But even after Loost's death and Uzz's purchase by another corporation, it was still the world's most popular social media network.

And now it was making a call. To everyone who used it.

Holly looked at her screen, which displayed the Uzz logo on a colourful swirling background. Before she could even touch a button to accept or ignore the message, the logo vanished; her phone's camera had recognised her face and taken the call without any action from her. From the startled exclamations around her, Nina guessed others were experiencing the same thing.

A face appeared on Holly's screen. Nina felt a cold shock.

It was Rafael Loost.

'Hello, Holly,' he said. Similar greetings came from other phones in earshot, Holly's name replaced by that of each device's owner. 'This is Rafael Loost.' A cold smile. 'I'm back from the dead.'

2

Nina and Eddie stared in shock at Holly's phone. It *was* Loost, just as they remembered him. Late thirties, dark spiky hair, pale and thin features. 'What the fuck is this?' Eddie exclaimed.

'It's a recording, it *has* to be,' Nina said.

Loost spoke again. 'I'm sure you know who I am – and that I died not long ago. But my quantum computing company had been secretly working on a way to record the human consciousness; to digitise the mind. Well . . .' He gestured with both hands to indicate himself. 'It worked. Before I died, I uploaded myself – because I have some unfinished business.'

He smiled. Again, there was no humour behind it, more like a hungry wolf baring its teeth. 'I didn't die of natural causes. I was killed, *murdered*, when the supply rocket carrying my blood transfusion was destroyed. I hold one specific person responsible. And here she is.'

Nina gasped as her own face replaced Loost's. It was the picture from her New York State driver's licence. 'Say hello to Professor Nina Wilde,' Loost went on. The image changed to the publicity portrait used in her books. 'You might have heard of her too. She's the world's most famous archaeologist, discoverer of Atlantis, yadda yadda.' Other pictures flashed by: television appearances, newspaper photos, even CCTV images. 'But she caused my death. Deliberately, calculatedly. Nina, I know you don't use Uzz, but if you're hearing this, I should be right above you about . . . now.'

She glanced skywards. The burning space station, forgotten by all, was indeed directly overhead. She and Eddie exchanged worried looks. What the hell was going on – and where was it leading?

'I considered deorbiting my station straight onto your apartment building,' said Loost. 'But the collateral damage would have been kind of excessive. So I came up with something more personal. We're going to play a game.' He paused for effect, then announced: 'I have placed a bounty of one billion US dollars in an untraceable digital currency account. It will be given to the person who kills Professor Nina Wilde live on Uzz.'

Nina clutched Eddie's hand in fear. This was insane – some kind of demented nightmare!

But she wasn't dreaming it. It was happening.

Loost continued. 'Anyone who tags her using Uzz will not only receive a large amount of kudos,' Uzz's virtual currency, 'but also reveal her location to the world. So even if you don't want to kill her, you can still benefit by helping out. A good place to start looking for her would be her home, apartment 805 at 65 East 78th Street, New York City.' A picture of her building taken from the street appeared. 'Or you could try her office in the Columbia Center for Archaeology at 1200 Amsterdam Avenue, NYC.' Another photo, from the winter clothing of the pedestrians taken recently. 'Once you catch her, use Uzz to tag her face in close-up; I want to talk to her before she dies. Then kill her, to the satisfaction of my adjudicator, and one billion dollars is yours. Remember, you don't get the money until *after* I talk to her on Uzz. That's very important.' He smiled again. This time, it was genuine, filled with a malevolent glee. 'The hunt starts now. Good luck. And Nina, if you are hearing this? I'll see you soon.'

The call ended, the screen going dark. Holly regarded Nina and Eddie in wide-mouthed dismay. 'Oh, my God! What – what are you going to do?'

Eddie looked around. A few people nearby, then a few more, and more, were turning to stare in dawning recognition at them – more specifically, at Nina. A woman hesitantly raised her phone as if to take a photo of her. Eddie moved to obscure her view, but it was too late. Another chime came from Holly's phone – and numerous others within earshot.

'We have our first sighting of Nina Wilde!' crowed Loost, reappearing on all the phones. 'She's in Central Park, New York City, GPS coordinates forty point seven-eight-zero-three, minus seventy-three point nine-six-six-six. Go get her!'

'Let's move,' Eddie growled. The trio hurried towards the park's eastern side. Nina saw two other people track her with their phones as she went. Loost didn't pop up on Holly's phone to provide any updates.

At least, not immediately. They reached Fifth Avenue, where a man whipped up his phone when he recognised her. 'Nina Wilde is now at Fifth Avenue and 79th Street in New York City,' Loost reported a few seconds later, rattling out the exact coordinates. 'Keep on her!'

'He must only tell everyone where you are when you've moved a bit,' said Eddie as they ran diagonally across the intersection, weaving between cars.

'I don't think staying in one place will help me much!' Nina complained. Uzz had, at a conservative estimate, almost three billion users worldwide, about a third of the entire global population, and in New York it seemed a much higher proportion of people had the app on their phones. All around her, she saw eyes widen: *Hey, wait, isn't that—*

Holly was still with them. 'This is crazy! What can I do to help?'

'Not much,' said Eddie. Nina knew from his stony tone that he had gone into combat mode; her husband was a former British SAS soldier, and was more than capable of defending himself and his loved ones – with deadly force if necessary. 'You don't have a car, and we've got to get out of the city. Nina, we need to go home first.'

'Will that be safe?' Nina asked as they rounded the corner of East 78th Street. 'Loost told everyone where we live.'

'We need some stuff. I'll call Amy – she can drive us somewhere.'

'Where?'

'Fucked if I know! Holly, you need to go in case anything kicks off.' He gave a threatening glare to a man who was fumbling for his phone as they passed.

'Are you sure?' Holly protested.

'Yeah. Go, go.'

Holly reluctantly slowed. 'Stay safe, please,' she called after them. Eddie shot a grimace back at her, then he and his wife hurried on.

They reached their building. A few people were waiting outside, reacting when they saw Nina. None seemed openly hostile – but they were still happy to claim some extra kudos as their phones came up. By the time the couple reached the entrance, Loost was reporting her new location.

'Fuck off out of the way,' Eddie snarled, shoving one man back to reach the doors. They ran inside. Nobody followed them, but Nina was sure they hadn't gone away either.

They took the elevator up to their apartment. 'Grab our passports,' Eddie said as he entered, taking out his phone.

'We're leaving the country?'

'I don't know *what* we're doing, but I want to be prepared for anything.' Their passports were in a drawer; Nina collected them. 'Go into our wardrobe – my blue sports bag's at the bottom. There's a rolled-up rugby shirt inside it with some cash.'

'Is there now?' said Nina as she headed for their bedroom. It was the first she had heard of it.

'My just-in-case stash. Amy? It's Eddie.' He continued his urgent conversation as Nina went to the wardrobe.

There was the bag; there was an old blue-and-orange-striped rugby shirt. She unrolled it, and was startled when a Ziplock bag containing a wad of banknotes dropped out. A rapid inspection revealed a mixture of twenties, fifties and hundreds, totalling at least three thousand dollars. She returned to the living room, brandishing the bag. 'Eddie, how long have—'

He held up a hand to shush her. 'Okay, great,' he said into the phone. 'See you soon.' He ended the call. 'We're lucky; Amy's on duty, and she's not that far away. You got the money?'

'Yes, and why didn't you tell me you were squirrelling this away?'

'Didn't want to worry you. I hoped we'd never need it. But if we use a card to get cash from an ATM, it might be tracked.' He took the bag and tucked it inside his leather jacket, then dug through another drawer. 'Our phones might be as well, but I don't want to get rid of them just yet.' He found a compact charger bank and pocketed that too, then started towards the kitchen. 'I'll grab the first-aid kit in case—'

Someone knocked on the door.

They both whirled at the sound. 'Who is it?' Nina called nervously.

'It's Armand,' a man replied. 'From downstairs?'

Eddie frowned. 'What the fuck does he want?' Armand Carlson was the new neighbour with the overbearing sound system.

'What is it?' Nina echoed, more politely. 'We're, ah, kinda busy.'

'I know, I heard. I can't believe it! Look, I know we've had some issues, but this . . . this is insane. I want to help. Do you need anything? I can drive you out of the city if you need to get somewhere safer.'

'We're good,' said Nina. 'Someone's coming to pick us up.'

'But my car's right outside, I just got back. You won't have to wait.'

Exasperated, Eddie went to the door. 'I'll get rid of him,' he muttered. 'Nina, you get the—'

He opened the door – and was hit in the face by a jet of pepper spray.

3

Eddie reeled back, blinded and choking. The door was kicked open. Armand Carlson charged in and body-slammed the Englishman to the floor.

He rounded on Nina. Carlson was in his late twenties, half Eddie's age and somewhat taller. He had a neatly trimmed beard of a style at the crest of the tech-bro fashion wave and wore expensively scruffy clothing to match. He also had a dripping canister of pepper spray in one hand – and a large kitchen knife in the other.

Eddie groaned, trying to get up. Carlson paused to kick him, two firm blows slamming into the Yorkshireman's gut. He let out a choked yell. 'Hey, keep the noise down,' the younger man sneered. 'Or as you put it, "keep the *fucking* noise down"!' Another kick, then he turned back to Nina.

She was already running for the nearest exit – the hallway to the bedrooms and her study. Carlson darted after her. The first door she reached was to Macy's room. She rushed in and slammed it, holding it closed with her body. It jolted violently behind her as the invader threw himself against it. Her boots ground over the carpet, creasing it as she struggled for grip. She braced herself as another impact shook the door. A muffled curse came from the other side. Nina leaned forward as far as she could, looking for anything she could use to defend herself – then shrieked as Carlson's knife punched through the door with a bang, the tip of the blade close enough to catch her hair.

The knife squirmed, then clumsily withdrew as her attacker pulled it back out. She realised another strike was about to come and slid sidelong towards the handle. A second later came another crack of splintering wood as the knife stabbed through the barrier again, this time lower. If she hadn't moved, it would have speared into her lower back.

The blade started to retreat – then stuck. She heard Carlson shift and grunt with exertion, jerking it free—

Nina jumped up and spun, kicking the disappearing knife and knocking it sideways. The unexpected blow wrenched it from Carlson's grip. It fell to the hall floor. She whirled again. Macy's small desk had a chair tucked beneath it. She grabbed the latter.

The door burst open, splinters flying from the frame as Carlson kicked it. He still had a weapon in each hand. He recovered his balance, looking for Nina—

The chair slammed into his face and chest. He stumbled backwards as pieces scattered around him. Nina dropped her broken weapon and shoved past him. His left hand flailed towards her as she ran back into the living room. The pepper spray! She jerked her head away, closing her eyes as he squeezed the trigger – but still caught the incapacitant's vaporous edge.

It was only a fraction of the amount Eddie had received, but was enough to set her eyes and nostrils ablaze. She cried out as tears filled her vision. Blinking frantically, water streaming down her cheeks, she tried to get her bearings. 'Eddie!' she gasped. 'Where are you?'

'Here!' came the strained reply. He was still near the apartment's door. Another blink, and a dark shape on the floor partially resolved itself into her husband. 'I can't fucking see!'

A thud of footsteps from behind warned that Carlson had recovered. She looked back. The bearded man dropped the spray and lunged at her. Nina jinked away, but he managed to catch her coat's sleeve. He hauled at her, his greater weight sending her tumbling onto the couch.

Carlson straightened, looming over her. '*You* killed Rafael Loost?' he almost screamed. 'Don't you realise what you've done? You extinctionist bastards! He was our best hope for survival – for the whole human race! I'm not just doing this for the money, it's for all the people who will never be born because of you!'

The knife came down – but Nina rolled just as his rant ended. The blade stabbed into the cushion beside her. She kicked, squarely hitting his kneecap. He lurched back with a pained gasp. She righted herself and made a scrambling jump over the back of the couch—

He slashed the knife at her. It was a furious, almost unthinking move – but it worked. The blade's tip caught the back of her thigh, cutting through her trousers and opening a gash in her skin. Pain shot through her leg – and it buckled before she fully cleared the couch, pitching her heavily to the floor.

Carlson followed. He dropped to his knees beside her and, face twisted in anger, brought the knife down at her chest. She snapped up both hands to catch his wrist, arresting the attack barely an inch from her body. But he was stronger than her, shifting his weight to push it down harder. 'Eddie!' she wailed.

Eddie had managed to crawl away from the door and pull himself to his feet, using a shelf for support, but his eyes were still screwed shut by the pepper spray's searing sting. He turned towards his wife's desperate cry – and his hand brushed against something smooth and heavy. His mental map of their apartment told him instantly what his eyes couldn't; it was one of Nina's awards, a glass bowl on a heavy wooden base. 'Nina!' he called as he picked it up. 'Where is he – to your left or your right?'

'Left!' came her strained reply. Eddie hurled the trophy with full force. All he heard was an explosive burst of shattering glass as it hit a wall. 'No, *my* left – your right!' Nina frantically corrected.

The pressure bearing down on her eased slightly as Carlson looked around, realising Eddie was still a threat – then it abruptly vanished as the bearded man was hit in the face by another trophy, this one metal. He yelled, clutching instinctively at his broken nose. Nina kicked him in the chest, knocking him back, and twisted to jump up and run clear—

A burning flash of pain from her wounded leg sent her back down to the floor. She held in a cry and awkwardly scrabbled behind an armchair.

Carlson wiped blood from his face and stood, searching for his enemies. Nina was retreating around the chair – but Eddie was fumbling along the shelf to find another missile. The younger man started towards the greater threat.

'Eddie!' Nina called. 'He's coming for you!'

Her husband immediately switched to a defensive posture, both hands raised. 'From where?'

'Around the couch – left side.'

'My left or your left?'

'Yours!'

Eddie turned to face the approaching man, his streaming eyes still clenched shut. He waited, barely moving.

Carlson advanced. Against a blinded target, he had every possible advantage. No way he could lose. The knife stabbed out—

Strong fingers clamped around his hand, stopping it dead.

Carlson flinched, shocked. How—

A brutal haymaker slammed into his head. Sound – and decades of fighting experience – had told the former SAS man where his opponent was and what he was doing, *feeling* the incoming attack. Carlson almost fell, reeling around as Eddie tried to twist the knife from his hand, but managed to yank his arm free of the Yorkshireman's grip. He backed unsteadily away as he recovered from the bone-rattling punch, spitting out blood. Then he tensed, taking a couple of deep breaths to fuel his fury before raising the knife again.

Nina pulled herself upright on the armchair's back, adrenalin overpowering pain. 'Eddie, he's still up!'

'Tell me when he moves,' Eddie ordered. He took up his ready stance again, listening for his attacker.

Now more cautious, Carlson moved again. 'Going to your left,' Nina reported. Her path to the apartment's open door was now clear.

She could escape. But she couldn't leave Eddie, not when he couldn't see to defend himself. 'About eight feet away.'

Eddie faced him. Carlson paused, then edged a little closer, shifting sideways. Nina gave an update. 'He's gone slightly right. Six feet away.' She looked for anything she could use as a weapon, but nothing presented itself.

Breathing heavily, Carlson rocked on the balls of his feet, psyching himself up – then moved. Eddie responded—

The bearded man jinked, arresting his motion for a split-second before slashing his blade. Eddie was caught out by the brief decoy. The knife cut across his forearm. His leather jacket's sleeve took most of the strike – but not all. He let out a sharp exclamation as the steel bit into his flesh, then jerked back. 'Eddie!' Nina cried in horror.

Carlson pressed his advantage. A couple of rapid steps from side to side, Eddie blindly trying to follow his movements – then he darted forward. The Englishman's hands snapped out to intercept his knife hand—

But he wasn't attacking with the knife. One foot pounded into Eddie's groin. He folded and toppled backwards to the floor.

Carlson gripped the knife in both hands, about to plunge it down—

Nina found a weapon – the coffee table. She smashed it against Carlson's back with all the strength she could summon. He was thrown forwards, tripping over Eddie – and landed on his front with his hands beneath him. A brief shriek became a more drawn-out gurgling moan, the bearded man convulsing for a few seconds before sagging into the stillness of death.

She caught her breath, then went to assist Eddie, grimacing at the pain from her leg. 'Are you okay?'

His reply came through clenched teeth. 'Yeah,' he rasped. 'Bastard cut my arm.'

She looked at the tear in his sleeve. A bloodied line was visible on his skin, but the wound appeared less deep than her own. 'It doesn't look too bad.'

'What happened to him?'

'He's dead.'

Eddie managed a thin, impressed smile. 'Nice work.'

'I didn't do it! He fell onto his own knife.'

A half-laugh. 'Fucking amateurs.'

Nina pushed at Carlson's upper body, briefly rolling him onto his side. The knife was embedded to its hilt in his heart, blood flowing out. She had seen death far too often to feel much more than mild shock; exasperation was higher on her emotional list. 'Oh, great. The carpet's ruined and we've got a corpse in our living room. The landlord'll be pissed.'

Another faint laugh. 'Priorities, love. Help me up, I need to clean this stuff out of my eyes.'

She did so, guiding him into the kitchen. 'Do you want milk? That's supposed to get rid of it, isn't it?'

'Just cold water and soap are better. Trust me, I tried all the different methods in training.' He felt his way to the sink and ran the cold tap, using both hands to scoop copious amounts of water onto his eyes. Nina found him some soap, which he carefully began to use. 'We need to get moving. It's only been maybe ten minutes since Loost put up his bounty, and one person's tried to kill you already. For a billion dollars, Christ knows how many more might take a pop.'

The throb from her leg reminded Nina that she had been about to find the first-aid kit when Carlson arrived. She took it from a cupboard. Eddie rinsed away soap suds and risked opening his eyes slightly. 'Ow, shit. That fucking burns.'

'Have you got all of it off?'

'I'll have to manage. We can't stick around here. Besides, Amy should arrive soon.' He blinked repeatedly. The skin around his eyes was red and swollen. He looked as if he had been punched. 'Where did he get you?'

She showed him the knife wound. He muttered a curse. 'I can

patch it up for now, but there won't be time to stitch it. Have to do that later.'

'If we get a chance,' Nina noted glumly.

He opened the first-aid kit and handed her some painkillers, which she gratefully took. 'I've had an idea where we can hide out for a while. Charlie – you remember Charlie Brooks?' She nodded. 'He's got a cabin in the mountains upstate. Nearest house is literally two miles away. I don't think anyone'll bother us there.'

'Getting away from it all sounds appealing right now,' she said, clenching her jaw as he quickly applied butterfly bandages to hold the wound closed before using a large Band-Aid to cover it. 'Ah, damn. That stings.'

'It should be okay once I sort it properly. Right, let's go.'

He led Nina out, leaving the first-aid kit behind. 'We're not taking it?' she asked as she fastened her hair into a ponytail.

'Charlie'll have everything we need at his cabin. He's ex-army, like me. He's always prepared.'

'Good to know.' They reached the door, Nina taking a last look back into their apartment – trying to ignore the corpse on the floor – before shutting it. She wondered if she would ever return home.

There were potentially nine billion people who might try to prevent her.

4

Eddie's phone rang while they were waiting for the lift. 'Amy's outside,' he announced with relief after taking the brief call.

They rode the elevator downwards. More people were now outside the building, but a path to a black Ford Police Interceptor had been cleared by the undercover police vehicle's occupants. 'Eddie!' said Amy Martin. 'Nina, are you both okay?'

'Been better,' Eddie replied as they hurried to the SUV. 'Someone tried to kill Nina in our apartment.'

'Jesus,' she gasped. 'And let me guess, they're dead?' Neither of the couple needed to say a word to provide an answer. 'Goddamn it, Eddie. There's always a stiff involved whenever you ask me for help.'

'Better them than us,' he said as he and Nina got into the back seats.

'Yeah, I suppose. Come on, people, back, get back!' the dark-haired detective shouted at the onlookers as she opened the driver's door.

Her partner, a wiry, hard-faced man of around fifty, added his own encouragement. 'Hey! Move your asses, if you don't want to spend the night in a cell.' He took the front passenger seat. Amy sent a sharp warning *whoop-whoop* from the siren, then pulled away and headed east.

Eddie exhaled, glad to be on the move. The car was warm; he took off his hat. 'Thanks for this, Amy.'

'No problem,' she answered. 'Lou and I – oh, you haven't met my partner, have you? Lou, this is Eddie Chase, and his wife, Nina Wilde.'

'Lou Novak,' added the other detective, turning to nod at the passengers. Eddie and Nina returned the greeting.

'Anyway,' Amy continued, 'we were getting a coffee when both our phones went off at once – and a lot of other people around us. Thought it was the emergency warning system, and that World War Three was about to break out! But then the message from that guy Loost came through, and *then* it turned out he had some beef against Nina, so I figured you'd probably want my help. I was already on the way uptown when you called.'

'Thank you,' said Nina, with genuine gratitude.

'Don't mention it. So where we going?'

'Queens,' Eddie told Amy.

'Why?'

''Cause it's where you live, and we need to borrow your car.'

She let out a mocking laugh. 'I should have guessed. And I suppose you're not gonna tell me where you're going in it?'

'That'd be safer for everyone, yeah.'

She sighed. 'Man, the things I do . . . Okay, okay. So long as you bring it back in one piece and fully gassed up. Deal?'

Eddie grinned. 'Deal.'

'Great.' Amy turned the Interceptor southwards on Second Avenue, heading for the Queensboro Bridge. 'But what the hell have you two gotten yourselves into *this* time? I mean, Loost's dead, but now he's saying he stuck his brain inside a computer . . .'

'That's bull,' Nina said firmly. 'He can't have done that. The technology simply doesn't exist. It's a deepfake, or pre-recorded before he died.'

'He called me by name in his message, though,' Amy pointed out. 'And the same for Lou. He can't have pre-recorded *everybody's* names.'

'Then it's a computer using his voice. I refuse to accept that he zapped his mind into a mainframe like . . .' She struggled to think of a comparison. 'Like some kind of *Tron* crap,' she managed.

'No, *Tron* was where his whole body got zapped into a computer,' Eddie corrected. 'You're thinking of *The Lawnmower Man*.'

'What-*ever*! Some sci-fi nonsense, either way. And Loost living on as a digital ghost is nonsense too. It's a trick.'

'His bounty's real, though,' said Novak. 'Someone already tried to kill you. A billion dollars? You better believe I see fifty people every day who'd be happy to do the job for one per cent of that. Hell, one per cent of one per cent.'

'That's only a hundred thousand dollars,' Nina told him, instantly performing the mental calculation.

'That much? Christ, some'd do it for one per cent of *that*. Money makes people go crazy. I guess the richest guy in history was the craziest of them all.'

They soon reached the on-ramp for the bridge. 'So what did you guys do to piss off Loost?' Amy asked as she turned onto it.

Nina and Eddie exchanged glances. 'It's a long story,' said the former. 'But it boils down to, we stopped him from doing something that would have been very bad for the world, and he got very mad about it.'

'He said you killed him by blowing up his rocket,' Novak remarked.

'We weren't even in the same *country* as his rocket,' said Nina carefully. 'It was a freak accident, but I suppose he couldn't accept that.' She couldn't help but feel a twinge of guilt at the lie. No, she and Eddie and Macy hadn't *directly* killed Rafael Loost . . . but they had certainly ensured his death would be inevitable.

The feeling evaporated as Eddie spoke. 'He tried to kill us, and he tried to hurt Macy,' he said, anger entering his voice at the mere thought of someone trying to harm his daughter. 'The bastard got what he deserved, far as I'm concerned. Fuck him.'

The outburst brought silence to the SUV for a while. Nina looked outside as Amy drove on. They were on the lower roadway of the Queensboro Bridge, the wood and concrete and metal of the upper deck blocking out the sky, and a sense of claustrophobia suddenly hit her. She tried to lower her window to let in air, but nothing happened when she pushed the switch. Of course: even if it was an undercover vehicle, it was still a police car, and people riding in the back seat might often have every reason to want to get out. The rear doors were probably child-locked too. The thought did not brighten her mood. She needed to run, but already felt trapped.

Amy finally turned off the elevated highway and guided the Interceptor southwards. Nina didn't know exactly where the policewoman lived, but her route was taking them through Hunters Point and Long Island City. A lifelong Manhattanite, she found the comparatively low-rise buildings of Queens faintly wasteful, as if their occupants weren't taking full advantage of the empty space above them. Apartment blocks gave way to larger, anonymous industrial buildings and warehouses. Cranes marked where new developments were being built. She hoped Amy lived somewhere nicer on the far side—

Novak broke her reverie. 'A billion dollars, damn. That guy really had it in for you, I guess.'

'You could say that,' Eddie replied.

'And in digital currency, too. Y'know, the older kinds of that stuff weren't as untraceable as the people using it thought – the feds got pretty good at tracking it down. But the new AI-powered ones? Nobody's figured it out yet. Whoever gets that bounty really would have a billion dollars they could access from their phone any time they wanted, and the feds and IRS wouldn't have a clue.'

Amy glanced at him. 'Nobody's gonna *get* the bounty, Lou. We're making sure of that right now.'

Her partner grinned. 'Yeah, yeah. But still, it didn't cross your mind? Split it two ways, half a bill each, retire to the Caribbean?' He looked back at Nina and Eddie as if to assure them he was joking. Eddie responded with a cold frown.

Amy shared his view. 'Not funny. I don't sell out my friends, Lou.'

'Yeah, I know.' Novak sighed – then pulled out his Glock 19 service pistol. He twisted in his seat to cover both Amy and Eddie. 'It's a shame.'

'What the fuck?' Amy said, startled. Her right hand started for her own holstered gun inside her coat, but Novak's weapon twitched towards her, freezing her movement.

'Don't,' he said, voice cold as stone. 'I woulda settled for the half-billion, but I got no problem with taking the full amount. Your choice if you wanna share or not. Now, remember the warehouse where the Calloway girl was found last year? It's only a couple of blocks away. Drive there.'

'Lou, this is fucking crazy,' insisted Amy.

'Well, yeah, I said money does that to people. Now dri—'

Amy's right hand was still raised across her chest. She suddenly snatched for her gun, managing to pull it from her coat—

Novak fired. The noise was almost deafening inside the SUV's confines. Amy lurched sideways against her door, blood spurting from a ragged hole in her clothing below her right shoulder. She screamed. The Interceptor swerved, slowing as her foot came off the accelerator. Novak seized the wheel with his free hand and pulled it around to avoid an oncoming car.

Eddie lunged forward to grab the distracted Novak—

His seat belt was still fastened. The tension lock clunked, jerking him to a halt. He stabbed at the release. The delay had cost him less than a second.

But it was enough. Novak's still-smoking Glock snapped around to point at his face. Eddie froze. There was nothing stopping the cop from pulling the trigger, no reason to keep him alive . . .

Amy screamed again, flailing in agony. But even through her pain, she still had some sense of what was happening. She kicked down, hitting the accelerator. The Interceptor surged forward towards the unyielding pole of a streetlight—

A second ear-splitting detonation, a flash of fire – and another hollowpoint bullet punched into Amy's chest. She jerked . . . then slumped in her seat, dead.

Novak swerved the wheel again, fumbling with the gear selector to put the SUV in neutral before pulling the parking brake's switch.

The car came to a halt at an angle near the roadside. Before Eddie could make another attempt to attack him, he had released his seat belt and shifted forward, gun aimed at the Englishman. 'Shit!' he said, glancing at his partner's corpse. 'Shit! Why the fuck you have to do that, Amy?'

Eddie's expression was one of pure rage and hate. 'You *fucker*! I'll fucking kill you.'

'The fuck you will,' Novak growled. He looked at the street outside. They were still amongst industrial buildings, traffic minimal. The only pedestrians were over a hundred metres distant, heading away. 'Okay, you, Chase – get out. Move Amy across to my seat, then you're gonna drive. I'll be in the back with your wife. Try anything, I shoot her in the leg, then you in the head. I need her alive. You, not so much.' He retrieved Amy's gun, then got out to round the car. He opened Eddie's door, then backed away to keep him covered as he emerged. 'We're going for a little drive.'

As Novak had said, their destination was not far away. The warehouse was derelict, a half-roofless shell on a block where the majority of properties were marked with signs saying ACQUIRED FOR DEVELOPMENT. A gate fastened by a padlock and chain blocked its entrance, but it proved a feeble security measure; on their captor's order, Eddie drove into the gate, the chain snapping. He continued inside.

'Over there,' said Novak, indicating a far corner. Eddie did as he was told, though he was scanning the building's interior for anything he could use against the cop. He saw nothing. The floor was strewn with trash and rubble, but the best he could do with any of it would be drive over it to jolt the SUV. That wouldn't be enough to throw Novak off for long enough to overpower him. And with his gun aimed at Nina, there was a chance of an accidental shot. He couldn't risk it.

He still brought the car along a course that would leave it close to a pile of debris with rusted metal rods poking out of it. He might be able to snatch one up when he got out of the car before Novak could react...

But the opportunity never came. 'Stop here,' the other man barked. Eddie reluctantly halted, several metres short of his potential weapons. Beyond them were the remains of the building's offices, crumbling drywall and breezeblock sectioning off a corner of the interior. The ceiling was mostly intact here, dropping everything into gloom. 'Turn off the engine.'

Eddie put the vehicle into Park and did so. 'So what now?' he said sarcastically. 'You going to kill us like you did Amy? How long were you partners? A year?'

'Almost two,' Novak replied. For a moment he seemed shaken, as if only just noticing Amy's body in the passenger seat. Then he composed himself, stiffening with renewed resolution. 'But I've kinda passed the point of no return, so yeah, I am going to kill you. I don't have a choice now, do I?'

'You actually do,' said Nina, eyes fixed in fear on the gun. 'You could just leave us here, and run.'

He gave her a mocking look. 'They'd find me. That's kinda what we do as cops. And it's not like I have a lot of resources; most of my pay goes in alimony. But if I had a billion dollars... well now, that makes things easier.'

'How far do you think you'll get?' said Eddie.

'Further than you.' He lashed out with his gun hand and cracked Eddie on the back of his skull, drawing blood. Eddie cried out. Another savage strike, and the Yorkshireman slumped limply, head dropping down to his chest. Nina gasped.

'Stay there,' Novak warned her. He had disabled the child lock on his rear door when he got in, now backing out with his Glock still pointed at her. He opened the driver's door, then produced a set of handcuffs. Still with the gun raised, he clumsily used one hand to cuff the unconscious Eddie's wrists to the bottom of the steering wheel. Once both bracelets were locked, he tugged the wheel to engage the steering lock. 'Okay,' he said, turning his attention back to Nina. 'Now, get out.'

Hands raised, she hesitantly slid across the rear seat. She cringed at the sight of the cuts on the back of Eddie's head as she passed him. 'I thought you were going to kill him,' she said, breathing heavily.

'You do as I say and your kid won't be an orphan,' was Novak's reply as she got out. He looked around, spotting a bright patch near the offices where daylight came through a hole in the roof. 'Go over there, in the light. I wanna be sure he can see you.'

'Who?'

'Loost, obviously. Or whatever the fuck he is. Come on, move it.'

Nina traipsed across the dirty concrete to the illuminated area. She stopped and turned. Novak had taken out his phone, holding it in his left hand as he kept the gun in his right. 'Sit down,' he told her. She reluctantly did so. 'Okay, I don't know if I'm supposed to open Uzz to do this, or what . . .' he said, half to himself, as he aimed the phone's main camera at Nina. Nothing happened for a few seconds – then the Uzz fanfare sounded. She could tell from the glow on Novak's face that his phone's screen had come to life.

An unpleasantly familiar voice reached her: Loost's. 'Congratulations, Lou,' he said. 'It looks like you've found Nina Wilde! I just need to confirm that it's really her. Can you move a bit closer?' Surprised at being addressed by a dead man, Novak did so, extending his arm closer to Nina. She drew back and turned her head away from him in disgust.

'Thank you,' said Loost. 'That's a biometric match; it really is her. Well done. Now, Lou, before we move on to what you need to do, I want to talk to Professor Wilde. Can you turn the phone so she can see me?'

Still slightly unsettled, Novak did so. He held the phone up to Nina, keeping it just out of her reach. But she could see the person on the screen clearly enough.

Rafael Loost.

Or so it claimed to be. But Loost was dead. This was nothing more than a facsimile, a digital shade. However realistic it appeared to be, it was merely a computer-generated head, either animated by software or mapped as a deepfake onto a collaborator's face.

But it *did* seem realistic, Nina had to admit. There were none of the dead-eyed imperfections that often marred digital replicas in movies. Of course, the trillionaire could have put enough money to pay for an entire series of blockbuster movies into lifting his simulacrum out of the uncanny valley.

His reaction to seeing her certainly appeared flawless. A tiny flicker of recognition in his eyes, then an unpleasant, gloating smile. 'Nina,' he said. 'I bet you didn't expect to see me again.'

'I'm *not* seeing you,' she replied. 'The real Rafael Loost died months ago. This is just some creepy CGI copy. How about whoever's controlling it drops the pretence and talks to me in person?'

Loost's nostrils widened as he blew out a small huff of amusement, exactly as they would for a living person. The imitation was very good indeed. 'There *is* no pretence, Nina. My physical body may be dead, but the important part of me lives on: my mind. I gave my quantum computing company the challenge of devising a means to record and store the human mind a few years ago. Thanks to you, they suddenly had a deadline and a very strong incentive to perfect it. Which they did. Everything that makes me who I am, what I am, was uploaded to a quantum matrix.'

'What you are is an asshole,' Nina cut in, having already had enough. 'A bitter, petulant, overgrown child with a chip on your shoulder and too much money. And you're full of crap. Quantum matrix, my ass! You may as well have said you'd uploaded yourself to the holodeck.'

She wondered how Loost – or rather, his representation – would respond to the insults. A human might be taken aback, then fumble to come up with a rejoinder. A computer, on the other hand, would determine what she had said, then run through its preprogrammed decision tree to deliver a suitable answer . . . or a boilerplate non-response if nothing was found. She waited to see which it would be.

To her surprise, it was neither. A moment as he processed her words, then Loost's eyes narrowed with all-too-believable anger. 'Still dismissing my achievements, Nina,' he said, voice low. 'When yours are nothing to be proud of. I changed the world for billions of people, while you stole trinkets from graves!'

He closed his eyes for a moment, drawing in a slow, calming breath. Then they snapped open again, focused on her with chilling clarity. 'Speaking of graves, it's time you went to yours. I just wanted to enjoy your realising that I *beat* you. That I'm *smarter* than you. And I'm disappointed in you,' he added, almost in mockery. 'It hasn't even been an hour since I issued the bounty, and someone's already claiming it!' He laughed. There was a hollowness to it, the first time Loost's digital recreation had appeared less than perfect. 'Lou, I need to speak to you again.'

Novak turned the phone so its screen faced him. He kept his gun trained on Nina. 'What?'

'This is what you need to do to claim the bounty. Keep Nina in view of the main camera – and kill her.' The chilling command was delivered in an almost casual tone. Nina felt a cold rush of fear as Novak glanced at her over his phone, knowing he would do it. 'My adjudicator will confirm her death. Then, you'll receive a message via Uzz with the details of the digital currency wallet and the passcode to access it. It's a self-deleting message that can't be traced, so make sure you can take notes before you read it. Use it, and one billion dollars is yours.' A short pause, then Loost went on: 'Goodbye, Nina.' Even though she couldn't see the screen, she knew Loost was smirking.

Novak hesitated, the weight of knowing he was about to commit cold-blooded murder a great one even after what he had already done. But then he straightened – and aimed his gun at Nina's face.

5

Eddie woke, and regretted it.

The first thing he felt was a piercing pain through his skull. The second was a swirling nausea. Any blow hard enough to knock someone unconscious risked a concussion, or worse. But he forced his eyes open – seeing Amy's body slumped in the passenger seat. Horror and anger surged through him as memory returned.

Where was Nina? He had to save her—

She was directly ahead, sitting on the concrete floor with Novak standing before her, back to him. He tried to move, only to find his hands cuffed to the steering wheel. The cop had secured his wrists on either side of the wheel's lower spoke to prevent his reaching any of the Ford's controls. Not that he could start the car; Novak had taken the keys. Nor were the radio or onboard computer terminal any more accessible.

Novak had a gun aimed at Nina, but was also holding his phone out to her. She was watching something on its screen. A message from Loost? The trillionaire was dead, but he would still have wanted to gloat, even if only through a recording. Eddie had time to intervene.

But how?

He leaned back in the seat and pulled with full force, muscles straining. The wheel creaked as he hauled at it. The cuffs cut into his wrists, but the chain held. 'Bollocks!' he muttered—

Wait. He couldn't break the *cuffs*, but maybe . . .

Eddie changed tack, gripping the bottom of the wheel as firmly as he could. Soles against the footwell's bulkhead for leverage, he pulled again. The creaking returned, louder. 'Come on,' he rasped, teeth clenched. 'Come on, you bugger . . .' He jerked at it, making the SUV rock on its suspension. He paused until it subsided. If Novak saw he was awake and trying to escape, he might kill Nina before coming to the car to deal with him too.

A glance at his wife. Her expression told him she was giving Loost a verbal thrashing. The corners of his mouth twitched into a brief smile. The redhead had never been shy about expressing her opinion. But how long before Loost lost his patience and ordered her killed?

The fear galvanised him. Every muscle burning, he pulled at the wheel, and pulled—

The creak became a crack, something shearing apart – and suddenly it broke away from the steering column. He fell back hard into the seat, the Interceptor rocking again. Luckily Novak's attention was fully on Nina and Loost's exchange. He was free!

Sort of. His hands were still cuffed to the wheel, wires connecting it to the decapitated column. He yanked it to snap their connections, then rapidly assessed his situation. Could he reach Novak undetected?

Probably not. The old warehouse was littered with debris and junk. Any accidental noise from his footsteps would alert the cop. He would be caught in the open, a sitting duck. There was nothing he could use as cover between the SUV and his target.

Unless he could use the SUV itself . . .

No keys, so he couldn't start it. He tugged at the gear selector stalk on the steering column, but it wouldn't move. Again, without the key, the Interceptor was immobilised.

But there were ways around that.

He regarded the centre console. This being a police-specification vehicle, the space where a civilian model would have the gear selector and cupholders was replaced by a flat panel for mounting equipment – in this case, a control console for the lights and siren. But the underpinnings were the same on both versions. There would be a manual release for the shifter so it could be put into neutral, for when a dead vehicle had to be towed . . .

He dug his fingernails into the thin panel gap along the transmission tunnel's side and pulled at it. Plastic crackled as the panel's clips popped out of their holders. A nail split, pain stabbing through his fingertip, but he ignored it. One final wrench, and the panel came off, exposing metal framework and mechanical parts within.

The police model's shifter might be on the steering column, but he doubted the designers would have gone to the trouble and expense of creating two completely different systems. It would be interlinked with the transmission in the same place as on a civilian vehicle. So the release should be—

There! A small sprung button inside the frame. He pushed it. A solid *chunk* came from the tunnel. He sat up and shoved the gear selector. This time, it moved. He put it in neutral. The SUV could now roll freely.

Novak had turned his phone around to see its screen. Even from this distance, Eddie recognised Loost on it. Still with the broken steering wheel hanging from the handcuff chain, he pulled the door latch and quietly slipped out. Loost's voice reached him as he left the cabin. 'My adjudicator will confirm her death.' Shit! He was out of time!

He darted to the Interceptor's rear and started to push. His feet slipped on the dirty floor, but sheer desperation drove him on. The SUV picked up speed, walking pace, faster. The distance to Nina and Novak closed rapidly. The cop would hear at any moment—

'Goodbye, Nina,' said Loost.

One last straining shove, bringing the hefty police vehicle to the pace of a brisk jog – and its tyres crunched over debris. Novak, focused on Loost's message, finally heard the approaching vehicle. He spun – seeing it just a few metres away. His gun locked onto the driver's-side windscreen and fired, bullets punching holes in the glass and the seat behind it. But there was nobody at the wheel, no wheel even—

Novak hurriedly jumped clear as the Interceptor reached him. Nina had already leapt up and run for the nearby offices. Novak glanced after her as if about to follow, but then ran around the back of the rolling police car to locate Eddie, gun raised.

But the Yorkshireman was prepared for him.

The wheel was still attached to his cuffed hands – and he swung it up and around as Novak appeared. It caught his gun hand, snagging his Glock and yanking it from his grip. The pistol spun into the shadows, a sharp bang of metal on concrete echoing through the warehouse.

The attack took Novak by surprise. Eddie took advantage by shoulder-barging him, knocking him backwards, then whirling to smash the steering wheel's metal hub into his face. Novak almost fell, his mouth bloodied. His phone dropped to the floor. Eddie delivered a couple of brutal kicks to his legs before swinging the wheel again.

This time Novak was ready. He ducked sideways, the improvised weapon whistling past his head – then caught its trailing edge with his free hand and pulled backwards, twisting it hard. The rim caught Eddie's wrists. The cop wrenched harder, forcing the bald man's arms downwards as the handcuffs bit into his flesh – then kicked out, catching Eddie in the stomach.

The Englishman gasped, pained and winded. Before he could recover, Novak whirled around, dragging him with him – then hacked at Eddie's legs. He caught an ankle, knocking Eddie's foot backwards. He fell hard onto his front.

Novak pounded another kick into his side, then dropped knees-first onto his opponent's back, driving his remaining breath from his lungs. The cop still had hold of the steering wheel. A savage twist and the steel cuffs gnawed ever deeper into Eddie's flesh, drawing blood—

A gunshot echoed through the derelict building.

Novak's head whipped around – to see Nina standing twenty feet away, holding his gun. The shot had been a warning, fired at the ceiling. Now, though, the Glock was aimed squarely at him. 'Let him go,' she said, voice low and dangerous.

He carefully released the steering wheel and raised his hands to chest height. 'Okay, let's take it easy. Put the gun down. Nobody else has to get hurt here.'

It was straight out of police de-escalation training, and Nina knew it. 'Bullshit,' she replied. 'You were just about to execute me!'

'Think about this. You really gonna kill a cop?'

Nina's glaze flicked towards Amy's body in the SUV. 'It didn't bother you. Get off him, *now*.'

Still with his hands up, Novak slid off Eddie and stood. The Yorkshireman groaned as the pressure on his chest and arms was released. The cop took a wary step closer to Nina. 'Maybe there's a way we can fix this, okay? We *fake* your death.' Another step. 'He's looking at you through a phone – he can't check your pulse or anything like that. We split the money, pretend this never happened.' Closer still. Nina's eyes narrowed, hands gripping the Glock more tightly. 'We can all come out of this winners.'

Behind him Eddie rolled painfully onto his side. 'Nina? Just fucking *shoot* this arsehole!'

Novak tensed at the words, his eyes meeting Nina's. Realisation came that she was fully prepared to do so – and he rushed at her—

She fired. The bullet hit his right shoulder, smashing the clavicle and ripping a bloody chunk of torn meat from his trapezius muscle. Novak screamed, staggering back as he clutched at the ragged wound.

He came to an abrupt stop against something solid and unmoving.

Eddie Chase.

The Yorkshireman spun him around, yanking his hand from the injury – then punched the shattered bone. Novak's scream was even louder this time, the agony so overwhelming that he collapsed on his back at Eddie's feet.

Eddie wasn't finished with him. He dropped and drove the lower edge of the steering wheel against Novak's throat, putting his entire weight on the top. Novak choked and thrashed as his breath and blood supply were cut off. Eddie snarled and pushed down harder. A grotesque wet crunch came from inside the cop's neck. 'This is for Amy!'

A final snap – and Novak went limp, bulging eyes staring lifelessly at the hole in the roof. Breathing heavily, Eddie levered himself off the corpse. 'See if you can find his handcuff keys,' he wheezed to Nina.

She hurried to him. 'Jesus, are you okay?'

'No, I'm fucking not,' he said, anger clear. Knowing it wasn't aimed at her, Nina rifled through Novak's pockets, finding a set of small keys. 'Here.' She unlocked the cuffs, which sprang off and clinked to the floor.

Eddie dropped the steering wheel and rubbed gratefully at his wrists. The bracelets had cut deeply into his skin, drawing lines of blood. 'Ow, shit,' he gasped. 'I thought that bastard was going to break my wrists.'

'He was going to kill me,' Nina pointed out. 'You stopped him just in time. Thank you.'

'What are husbands for?' His smile was weak, but genuine. 'Okay, we need to get out of here. Cop cars have trackers; sooner or later, someone from the NYPD'll wonder why it's here.'

'Where can we go?'

'Amy's place is about a mile away. She said we could borrow her car.' He looked towards the SUV, face falling. 'Oh, Christ. Amy . . .'

'It wasn't your fault,' Nina assured him. 'It was Loost's.'

He stood, anger returning. 'Yeah, and he's dead, so there's nothing I can do to make him pay for it.'

Nina gripped his hand. 'We can stay alive,' she said firmly. 'We make sure he loses this sick game he's created, okay? No matter what, we can't let him win.'

'You're right,' said Eddie after a moment. 'You're right. He's not going to win.' He squeezed her hand in return. 'So let's make sure of that by getting out of the city before anyone else tags you.'

He went to the Interceptor. 'What are you doing?' Nina asked.

'I'll need Amy's car keys. I'll get her gun as well. You keep that shithead's, just in case. I'll leave a note for the cops, saying what happened.' He opened the front passenger door. Amy's body was still slumped in the seat. His fists clenched. 'I'm sorry,' he whispered as he reluctantly searched her. 'This shouldn't have happened. I'm sorry.' Nina watched him in mournful silence.

He quickly did what he needed to, then turned to Nina. 'Okay. Let's go.'

They started for the street – only to halt as the Uzz fanfare reached them in stereo. One source was Novak's phone on the floor, the other Amy's in the police car. It was followed by Loost's voice. 'We have another sighting of Nina Wilde!' he crowed. The street address of the warehouse and its GPS coordinates followed.

'What?' Eddie snapped in disbelief. 'How do they know you're here?'

Nina regarded Novak's phone in dismay. 'Lou tagged me. They must have realised he wasn't going to kill me and restarted the hunt.'

'Shit. Then we'd better run. There could be people here any minute.'

They hurried away, leaving Eddie's dead friend behind them.

6

Amy's car was a six-year-old Kia Seltos SUV. It had been parked outside her house in Ridgewood, Queens; there was a subway station a few blocks away that she used to travel to her precinct in Manhattan.

Had used, Eddie angrily corrected himself as he drove northwards. Amy had helped him and Nina – and paid the price. Something that had happened to far too many of his friends over the years. His fingers clenched more tightly around the wheel.

Nina noticed. 'Are you okay?' she asked softly.

'No,' was his curt reply.

'I'm so sorry about Amy. I didn't know her that well, but she always seemed like a good person.'

'She was.' He clenched his jaw, lips tight. 'But I don't want to talk about it right now. We need to get to somewhere safe.' He took out his phone, passing it to Nina. 'Hook this up to the car's Bluetooth. I'll call Charlie.'

It took only a minute for Nina to do so. Once the link was made, Eddie used a voice command to phone his friend and occasional employer. 'Charlie, it's Eddie.'

'Eddie, Christ.' The voice was English, gravelly Cockney tones softened with a mid-Atlantic twang after years of living in the United States. 'What the fuck's going on, mate? I was having lunch with some clients and nearly every phone in the restaurant went off at the same time with a message from that dead trillionaire geezer, and I thought, "Hang on, Nina Wilde? That's Eddie's missus!" What have you gone and got yourself into now?'

'Trouble, as usual,' Eddie replied. 'Listen, we need your help.'

'You got it, mate. You know it.'

'Great. Is your cabin empty at the moment?' The Yorkshireman knew he sometimes rented out his mountain retreat. 'We need somewhere we can hide out for a while.'

'Yeah, it's free. Stocked up, too – I was up there just last week. Keys are in the usual place. Turn on the generator and light the wood-burner, and you'll be sorted. You want anything else?'

'Whatever you can give us. We've got a couple of handguns, but might need something bigger if anyone comes calling.'

'I'll see what I can scrounge up. I'm down in DC at the moment on business, but I'll get up to the cabin as soon as I can. Tomorrow morning, most likely. But you know my place: once the generator's on and the security systems are up, nobody'll get within two hundred metres without you knowing.'

'Cheers, mate. That's fantastic. I knew I could rely on you.'

'No problem. You stay safe, okay? I'll see you soon.'

'Thanks, Charlie. Bye.' He ended the call. 'Okay, we've got somewhere to go. Let's just hope we can get there without any hassle.'

'We should call Macy,' Nina said. 'Let her know we're okay.'

He nodded, and issued another voice command to the phone. The connection, when it was made, was crackly and distorted. 'Dad?' came Macy's surprised but pleased voice. 'Hi, what's up?'

'She doesn't know,' Nina whispered. Macy no longer used Uzz now that she knew the social media app's potential for intrusive surveillance and tracking. 'Hi, honey, I'm here too.'

'Hey, Mom! Are you both okay?'

'We're . . . fine,' Eddie said. 'We just wanted to check in on you, see what you were up to.'

'Rain and I are in Romania, in the Carpathians,' replied Macy. 'Looking for new friends, if you know what I mean.'

'We know,' said Nina. The Knights of Atlantis had suffered many casualties at the hands of Loost's mercenaries, and now that she was at its helm, Macy had decided rebuilding it should be her priority. 'How's that going?'

'Pretty well! Mr MacDuff is using his genetic database to find more people descended from the Atlanteans. We've got three potential candidates already – that's why we're in Romania, we're checking one of them out. So, what are you guys up to?'

'Oh, nothing much,' said Eddie, in what he hoped was a light tone. 'We're taking a trip to Charlie Brooks's cabin upstate. Spur-of-the-moment thing. We thought, why not? Get out of the city, have a mini-break in the mountains.'

There was a pause. When Macy spoke again, there was a distinctly probing edge to her words. 'Mom, is everything okay?'

'Of course it is, honey,' Nina told her, with a concerned glance at her husband. 'Why?'

'It's just that . . . well, the only time you two *ever* do anything on the spur of the moment is if you're rushing off to hunt for some archaeological thing. And Mom, you don't like leaving Manhattan unless it's for work. You get itchy without skyscrapers in your field of vision.'

'No, we're fine, love,' insisted Eddie, again trying to sound unconcerned. 'Nothing for you to worry about.'

His daughter knew him too well. 'Now I'm *definitely* worried!' Macy cried. 'What's going on?'

The couple exchanged looks, Nina touching her forehead in dismay. 'O-kaaay. Well, if you're in the Carpathians, I suppose you haven't exactly been surrounded by people using Uzz.'

'What's Uzz got to do with it?'

'Wasn't that a Tina Turner song?' said Eddie, with a brief flicker of his usual humour.

Nina rolled her eyes. 'You remember that Rafael Loost's space station was going to burn up over New York?'

'That was today?' asked Macy. 'I guess we *have* been out of touch.'

'It turns out . . .' Nina took a breath before launching into an explanation. 'That was a warning from Loost to us – personally. I don't know how, but he took over Uzz and sent a message to every single person with the app, putting a bounty on my head. One billion dollars to the person who kills me. And two people have already tried.'

There was a shocked silence before Macy managed to reply. 'Oh, my God! Are you all right?'

'I'm okay. So's your father.'

'But – but how could Loost do this? He's dead!'

'He arranged it before he died. It's his revenge.'

'Okay, that's absolutely insane. And what we're doing here can wait. I'm coming back home, and I'll bring Rain with me. With our armour.'

'No, absolutely not,' Nina said firmly. Eddie looked at her in surprise.

Macy was equally bewildered. 'Why not?'

'Because there's a chance that Loost set this up to get to you, and all the Knights of Atlantis, through me. He knows you went into hiding – but he also knows you used the Staff of Afrasiab to blow up his supply rocket. Your coming out into the open might be exactly what he was hoping for. Yes, he's dead, but he must still have people working for him to have set this up. They could be waiting to carry out the rest of his plans.'

'But we can protect you! You know what I can do now.'

'I do, yes. But I also know that your armour doesn't make you invincible. Sure, you can stop bullets . . . but not for long. Whoever created these artefacts never expected them to have to deal with modern weapons. That's how the Nephilim were defeated, remember?'

'Yeah, I remember.' For a moment Macy sounded almost pouty, returning to her pre-adulthood attitude. 'Are you absolutely sure about this?'

'It's still our job to look after you, love,' said Eddie adamantly.

'Just because you're not a kid any more doesn't mean we stop being your parents. Whatever we have to do to make sure you're safe, we'll do. Even if that means we have to look after ourselves.'

'Okay.' Macy expressed her unhappiness clearly in the single word. 'But if that changes, you call me, all right? We can be on a plane to New York in a few hours.'

'You make sure you stay safe,' Nina told her. 'And Rain and everyone else, too. If the artefacts in the Knights' vaults get into the wrong hands . . . well, we already know what happens. It almost got us all killed.'

'Yeah.' There was now resigned reluctance in her daughter's voice. 'I can't believe this is even happening. I thought another company bought Uzz after Loost died! How did he manage to take control of it?'

'I don't know. But it doesn't matter right now. Look, we'll call you again when we have any kind of news, okay? I love you. We both love you.'

'I love you too. And I'd better see you soon, okay?'

'You will,' Eddie assured her. 'Bye, love. Stay safe.'

'And you.' The call ended.

Nina sagged back in her seat. 'Well, we warned her. Although I can't help wondering if she would have been better off not knowing.'

'She would have found out sooner or later,' said Eddie.

'I suppose.' She let out a deflated breath. 'Okay, so all we can do now is stay out of sight and wait for Charlie to reach us. You think he'll be able to help?'

He nodded. 'People come to him because they need protection. If he can't sort it out personally, he'll know someone who can.'

'Like you.' Eddie had acted in various roles for Charlie Brooks, from physical bodyguarding work to acting as a military consultant using his SAS experience.

'Yeah. Never expected I'd be the one needing his help, though!'

'How far away is his cabin?'

'From here?' They were now close to the northern limits of New York City proper, heading along an expressway through the Bronx. 'Three hours, about.' He checked the instruments. 'We'll need to stop for fuel somewhere. Should get most of the way, though.'

'There are gas stations here,' Nina pointed out. They had passed one only a few minutes before.

'The further out of the city we are, the quieter they'll be. Can't risk anyone tagging you again.'

'Good point.' Suddenly self-conscious, she dropped lower and turned her head away from the side window to reduce the chances of anyone in another car recognising her.

Once clear of New York City and its satellite towns, the journey became straightforward, if tedious. Places with familiar names rolled by; Tarrytown, Poughkeepsie, Albany. Eventually, the terrain began to rise beyond the rolling forests as they entered the Adirondack Mountains. Patches of snow appeared on the ground as they drove higher, many peaks already white even early in the winter season. Some cars on the highway had skis on their roof-racks, heading for the various resorts. Trailers with snowmobiles aboard also started to make appearances the further north they went.

Eddie eventually turned off the freeway onto a lesser road. 'It's all uphill from here,' he remarked. 'Should only be about half an hour now. If the road's clear.'

Nina stretched and stifled a yawn as she surveyed their surroundings. Forest on both sides, the conifers dusted with snow. The ground beyond the road was covered to a depth of perhaps an inch. The highways department had, however, kept the asphalt clear. 'Looks cold.' The clear sky above Manhattan had given way to cloud cover, with some ominously dark patches that suggested more snow was on the way. 'And you haven't got any gloves.'

'I'm hoping Charlie's got some spares at his cabin. Otherwise, there's a ski resort about five miles away. I can drive there and buy stuff if we need it.'

'His place sounds pretty isolated.'

'It is. It should be perfect for us. Hopefully.'

The snow on the trees gradually became thicker, weighing down their branches, as the Kia ascended. The road began to twist back and forth. A sign at its side read GAS: 1 MILE. 'We'd better stop there,' said Eddie. 'I don't think there's another one before the cabin.'

'Get me something to eat while you're in there, will you?' Nina took out her phone, checking the signal indicator at the top of its screen. It had phone and data connections, though both were low.

'What are you doing?' Eddie asked.

'Seeing what the news is saying – and if anyone tagged me after we left the warehouse.' She hadn't seen anyone doing so, but that didn't mean someone hadn't caught a snapshot.

The news was slow to load. Cellular reception in the mountains was patchy at best, and she imagined whole swathes of the Adirondacks were communication blackspots. But the page finally came up as they neared the gas station. She was, as she'd expected, one of the day's top stories. Speed-reading, she reported a summary to Eddie. 'Okay, they found Amy and Novak, but the NYPD hasn't given out any more information than two officers being killed. The news is being cagey about giving details of places I've been tagged, but it doesn't look like anyone else has seen me. And Uzz says it hasn't been able to block Loost's messages, but is still trying.'

'They should bloody try harder, then,' Eddie rumbled. He slowed to turn the Kia into the gas station. It was small and anonymous, a canopy over its four pumps outside a glass-fronted brick cabin that also served as a convenience store. A single electric charging point stood alone at one side of the forecourt. Business was slow; a car with a ski-rack was parked beside the cabin, and a large pickup truck towing a trailer carrying a snowmobile took up two spaces at the pumps.

Eddie brought their car to the furthest empty pump from the

truck. 'I'll fill up,' he said, opening his door. 'I'll pay in cash in case anyone's trying to trace our cards.'

'Okay,' Nina replied, her attention still on her phone. How could Uzz not be able to block Loost? Surely it would be straightforward to trace his messages, especially as they were taking over the entire social media network . . .

There was a rattle behind her as Eddie inserted the fuel hose and started pumping gas, but she ignored it, searching for information as an idea came to her. Who was the new boss of Uzz? And how could she get hold of him? The slow connection meant it took frustratingly long to find what she needed, but as soon as she had it, she tapped the link to phone Uzz's public relations department.

The call was quickly answered. 'Hi, this is Aisha at Uzz, how can I help you?' said a woman. Her voice was tinny and distorted, the signal weak.

'Hi, Aisha,' said Nina. 'This is Professor Nina Wilde. You might have heard my name in all the messages from Rafael Loost inviting people to kill me!' Pent-up anger came out with the words. 'I want to talk to your boss, Newton Pahl. And I want to talk to him right now. Otherwise, if I survive this, your company will be facing the mother of all lawsuits, okay?'

The unfortunate Aisha clearly had heard of her. 'I, ah – let me talk to my supervisor, I'll get right back to you.'

'Make it quick,' the redhead told her coldly.

The nightmare scenario the company was experiencing had apparently lit fires under its employees' behinds. Nina was passed up the chain of command in short order, and by the time Eddie had filled the Kia's tank and gone into the cabin to pay, she was through to Uzz's CEO, Newton Pahl. 'Professor Wilde,' he said. 'Thank you for your patience. I want to offer my deepest apologies for what's happening—'

'That's great, but what I really want from you is to *stop* what's happening! What are you doing about it?'

'We're trying our hardest to stop it, of course.' The reception was deteriorating, Pahl's voice glitching briefly. Nina glanced outside, wondering if the metal canopy above was causing interference. 'But so far we haven't even figured out *how* these messages are being sent to everybody simultaneously, never mind block them. And the log files are being deleted the moment they finish, so we can't trace them.'

'Why can't you stop them from being deleted?'

'We don't know. All we can think is that somebody put a backdoor into the system before we took over the company. It would have to be someone with very high-level access, but we don't know who. Not yet, at least. We're inves-a-ng.'

That last word broke up with a crackle, stuttering digital static echoing in Nina's ear. 'Hello? I didn't hear that. Hello?' No answer. Annoyed, she got out of the car and strode out from beneath the canopy in the hope of finding better reception. 'Can you hear me?'

'Yes, yes,' Pahl replied. The signal was no better than at the beginning of the call, but at least it wasn't incomprehensible. 'I said, we're investigating.'

'There can't be many people who would have that level of access, surely?'

She knew from his intake of breath that she was about to be patronised. 'Professor Wilde, we currently employ over fifteen thousand software engineers around the world. When we bought Uzz, that headcount was almost double. There are probably five hundred employees or ex-employees who could have made that deep an intrusion into our codebase if they decided to act against us. We don't know if whoever is responsible planted this backdoor before they were let go, or is still within the company.'

'Well, I suggest you pull your thumb out of your ass and find out,' she snapped. 'Your company is directly responsible for people trying to kill me – two people have tried already! It's got to be someone who was close to Loost, someone he trusted and who was completely invested in his personality cult. Start from the top and work down.

Whoever did this would have been in contact with Loost a lot to have set up something this complex.'

'We are doing everything we can to find and close the backdoor and identify who placed it,' said Pahl, in an officious tone that suggested *we're done talking, now go away*. 'Until then, I recommend that you let the authorities protect you.'

'The authorities were one of the people who already tried to kill me, but thanks for the advice. Just shut this thing down, and fast.' Nina irritably ended the call. She didn't like Uzz's new boss much more than its old one.

'What're you doing?' Eddie asked as he emerged from the cabin, carrying a bag of provisions. 'Why'd you get out of the car?'

'Bad reception,' she replied as she returned to the Kia. 'I called the boss of Uzz to ask what he was doing about this whole thing. Turns out, not much.' She opened the door – noticing as she did that the pickup truck's owner, a large man with a red baseball cap and a big beard of the kind favoured by US special forces members, and people who liked to pretend they were, was regarding her sidelong as he came back to his own vehicle.

Had he recognised her? Sudden fear hit, and she hurriedly ducked back into the SUV. The man continued to his truck, surreptitiously glancing at her. But he entered the pickup without taking out a phone to tag her.

Eddie noticed her concern. 'What's wrong?'

'That guy was giving me the eye. I thought he might have recognised me.'

'Time to shift, then.' He started the car and set off, keeping a wary watch on the pickup as he returned to the road.

Nina was also watching in the mirror. 'Shit, he's following us,' she said, seeing the truck and trailer pull out of the gas station and start after them.

'He's got a snowmobile. He might just be going to a ski resort.' All the same, Eddie did not sound convinced. He increased speed.

The pickup dropped back, but every so often reappeared in the mirrors as if holding a watching brief.

Eventually Eddie slowed. By now, the snow was quite thick on the ground, and the road itself had patches of dirty slush where it had not been fully cleared. 'This is the road up to Charlie's,' he said, making the turn. 'We'll see where he goes.' He headed up the steeper and narrower new route. About thirty seconds later, the pickup passed the turning, continuing on out of sight behind the snowy trees.

'He's gone,' said Nina with relief.

Eddie made a noncommittal sound, still with an eye on the mirror as he continued uphill. But by the time the road's turns took the junction beyond view, the truck had not returned. 'Looks like it. Once we get there, I'll start up the security system, though. There's a sensor covering the track to the cabin; we'll know if anyone drives up it.'

'Okay.' Nina turned her attention to the road ahead, hoping they had found a respite from the nightmare.

But she couldn't shake a sense of foreboding.

7

It took longer than Eddie expected to reach the isolated cabin. A mile beyond the main road, asphalt gave way to dirt track, seemingly the limit of responsibility for whoever kept the route ploughed. The SUV had four-wheel drive, but only normal road tyres, making traversing the path increasingly difficult. The former SAS man had to use all his off-road experience to keep the Kia moving, and by the time they finally arrived at their destination, he was tired and tetchy.

A gate blocked their path. Nina looked around. 'So he literally lives at the end of the road?' The last property they had passed was about two miles back.

'Yeah,' said Eddie as he opened his door. 'One way in, one way out. By car, anyway. He's got a couple of snowbikes for going into the forest.' He climbed out. Cold air took his place. Nina shivered as he closed the door again and went to the gate. It was padlocked, a large red sign on it saying PRIVATE PROPERTY, NO TRESPASSING.

He followed the wooden fence to its left for some thirty feet, tramping through snow, and crouched at a fencepost. A few moments of rummaging around to clear the white covering, then he lifted up a plate-sized stone. Something was attached to its underside – a small, flat box. He slid it open and took out a set of keys, then put the stone back in its place and kicked snow over it. A short trudge to the gate, and it was unlocked. He opened it, then got back into the car. 'Bloody hell, it's nippy,' he exclaimed through his teeth.

'I hope this cabin has good heating,' said Nina. She looked uphill as Eddie carefully guided the car through the gate. The cabin was about a hundred metres away across a cleared area of forest. It was a wooden structure with two floors, the upper about half the size of the one below.

'Don't worry, it warms up pretty quick once the wood-burner's going.' He halted again once clear of the gate and hopped back out to close it. 'Just in case anyone does drop by,' he explained once he'd returned to his seat. 'No point letting 'em drive right up to the door.'

'I don't think it'll stop them from getting in.' The fence was hardly an impenetrable obstacle, easily climbable and even with a few gaps that people could squeeze through if they turned sideways.

'No, but we'll know they're here. The whole place has got motion sensors and stuff. Charlie likes his privacy.'

He brought the SUV to the cabin's front. They got out. The cold immediately wrapped itself spikily around Nina despite her coat. Eddie would feel even colder in only his leather jacket, she imagined, but as usual he was toughing it out. She surveyed her darkening surroundings. White-capped peaks were visible over the trees, the forest stretching out endlessly all around. Behind the cabin, the ground rose sharply to become nearly a cliff, standing a little taller than the structure itself, bare rock poking through the snow. It was almost impossibly quiet, sound muted by the pines and the soft covering on the ground. She had to listen carefully even to pick out the calls of distant birds. As a Manhattanite, the silence was faintly unnerving. She had to admit it was beautiful, though, and she understood why Eddie's friend had chosen it as a place for solitude.

Rather than go to the front door on the raised porch, Eddie rounded the wooden building to a lean-to extension. 'The generator's in here,' he said. 'I'll start it, then we can go inside.'

Nina went with him, as much out of curiosity as a desire to be out of the cold. Another padlock was released with the keys. Inside, the only light came through the open door. As Eddie went to a large, red-painted metal box that she assumed was the generator, she checked out the room's other contents. A rack of firewood and unchopped logs, numerous tools like axes and saws and shovels, canisters of fuel – and most prominently, the snowbikes Eddie had mentioned. They were considerably smaller than a snowmobile, narrow, single-seater machines with a rear track for propulsion and a single front ski for steering. The cables connected to their boxy frames told her they were electric rather than gasoline-powered.

Eddie examined the generator's control panel, flicked a couple of switches, then pushed a button. A strained, rhythmic whining filled the room as it woke from its slumber, then the engine caught with a diesel clatter and it rumbled to full life. It was surprisingly quiet. A ceiling light came on, providing more illumination. LEDs also lit up on the bikes' handlebars, showing they were charging. 'There we go,' said Eddie, pleased. 'I'll grab some logs and get a fire going.'

He collected an armful of wood, then the couple went to the cabin's door. It had multiple locks. While Eddie released each in turn, Nina noticed a dish antenna attached to the roof. 'Is that a satellite link?'

'Buggeration and fuckery!' he said, annoyed, as he looked up. 'Yeah, it is – and I forgot to get the passcode off Charlie. Arse!'

'Can't you just phone him?' She answered her own question a moment later. 'There's no phone signal up here, is there? That's why he has a satellite link. Duh.'

'Yeah. Can't believe I forgot to ask him.' He undid the last lock and opened the door. 'Bloody idiot.'

'We were in kind of a rush,' Nina reminded him, following him inside.

Eddie turned on the light. Most of the cabin's lower floor was a single room, a combined living area and kitchen dominated by a large cylindrical wood-burner with a metal chimney pipe going through the ceiling. The upper floor, stairs in one corner leading to it, would be warmed by the rising heat as well. A door led to what Nina guessed was a bathroom. Couches and chairs covered in heavy blankets filled much of the space, with numerous cupboards against the walls. The whole place was functionally rustic, a small box with blinking lights on a shelf, presumably the satellite link, the only modern technology visible. 'Cosy,' she said. Her breath steamed as she spoke.

He went to the wood-burner. 'Once this gets going, you'll start thinking it's too hot.' A metal bucket beside it contained old newspapers, pokers and a gas torch. He opened the hatch, crumpling up some paper and putting it inside, then laid the firewood on it as if settling it in a nest. The gas torch, a fat six-inch cylinder with a long stainless-steel nozzle, lit at the click of a button, an intense blue flame hissing from its end. He played it over the newspapers, which instantly ignited, flames surging up over the wood. A few taps with a poker to make sure that everything was properly spread, then he closed the metal door. 'Give it a few minutes and everything should warm up.'

Nina sat on a couch, huddled in her coat. 'So, we made it here. How long do we stay? How long *can* we stay?'

Eddie went to check on the cupboards. 'Charlie said he'd stocked up recently, so there should be food for a week or two. There's survival stuff as well in case the place gets snowed in.'

The idea did not appeal. 'I suppose that'd be one way to make sure nobody finds us here.'

'It shouldn't come to that. Charlie's a smart guy. He'll probably come up with a way to sort this out by the time he arrives.' He finished his survey. 'Plenty of food, so we won't starve. I need to go out to get some water, though.'

Nina eyed the kitchen area; there was a small sink with a single faucet. 'There's no plumbing?'

He gave her a faint grin. 'We're in the middle of nowhere, love. There's a well out the back.' He opened a cabinet and took out a large, flat-bottomed metal pan. 'I'll go up to the well. You scoop up some snow in this and put it on top of the wood-burner. It'll melt, and we'll have some hot water. Well, warm. Ish.'

'All the comforts of home,' she said with a sardonic sigh.

They both went back outside, Nina carrying the pan and Eddie two large plastic jerry cans. As Nina filled her container with snow, the Yorkshireman marched around the cabin towards the steep rise behind it. She had expected the well to be at its foot, but instead he started to ascend, picking his way carefully up a rocky, zigzagging path.

She brought the pan back inside and placed it on the wood-burner, which to her relief was already putting out heat. Curious to see what Eddie was doing, she went to a window. Her husband was now at the summit. He lifted a snow-caked wooden cover off the well's top, then picked up a bucket attached to a rope and started to lower it down. From the time it took him, the water was quite some way below, possibly even beneath the cabin's ground level. Funny, having to go all the way up there to get—

The thought was instantly banished. A seemingly contradictory statement in her recent archaeological notes suddenly made sense. What was the exact wording, and what did it describe? Something like 'Climb to the sky to reach the Underworld below' – that was from the information she'd collated about the Shroud of Hades. If the Underworld, the domain of the god Hades, was real, which both the Knights of Atlantis and the Brotherhood of Selasphoros believed, could its entrance be at the top of a hill or mountain? According to mythology it was a wet and swampy place, which would fit with its being underground at the level of the local water table . . .

By the time Eddie returned, bearing the two now-heavy containers, her mind was a whirl of possibilities. 'Eddie, Eddie,' she said excitedly as he came in, 'I think I figured out something about the Shroud of Hades! You going all the way up the cliff to get water from underground made me realise what it meant. So I went through everything else I could remember about it. The Knights' records said it's somewhere in western Thessaly in Greece, in a place where hermits live in caves, and you have to climb up high to find a way down to the Underworld. The Brotherhood say it's where the fingers of

Hades reach into the sky, and the entrance is at the knuckle of the longest, marked by a dark narcissus. Now, I still don't know exactly what all that means when it's put together, but wherever the Underworld is, the way into it is near the top of some tall geological feature.' She had found notepaper and a pen in a drawer, waving her notes at him. 'If I had internet access, I could narrow down the possibilities right now!'

While she was speaking, Eddie had lugged the jerry cans into the small bathroom, used a folding footstool to reach a water tank mounted above the toilet, opened a flap on its top and started to pour the cold water into it. His response was far from enthused. 'Don't take this the wrong way, love,' he said, tone tired and grumpy, 'but I couldn't really give a shit right now. We've got other things to worry about than some archaeological bollocks.'

Nina's hackles rose, instantly feeling defensive at his dismissal of her work, but she forced herself not to snap back at him. 'Okay, point taken. But if we're going to be here for a while, I'm not just going to stare at the wall the whole time.' He didn't reply, the only sound from the bathroom the rhythmic gurgle of water pouring into the tank. She went to the door, seeing pent-up anger on his face. 'What's wrong?' she asked gently.

'Amy,' he admitted after a moment. 'She died trying to help me – to help you. I should have seen it coming. But I didn't, and now she's dead.'

'You couldn't have known,' she insisted. 'He was her partner; Amy probably trusted him with her life. She never expected him to turn on her, so how could you?'

The first container was now empty. Eddie dropped it on the floor, the loud clunk of plastic hitting wood making Nina flinch, then descended the steps to collect the second one. 'You were right, earlier on.'

'About what?'

He resumed filling the tank. 'At the flat, about not trusting anyone.

Anybody we meet could suddenly try to kill you like we're in the fucking Matrix.'

'I was talking about the IHA. I didn't mean we literally can't trust anyone in the world.'

'It's the only way to be safe. Lou said it himself: there are plenty of people who'd be willing to kill a stranger for a lot less than a billion dollars.'

'Twenty thousand pounds,' Nina said, almost without realising why.

He looked down at her, not understanding. 'What?'

'It's a line from *The Third Man*. Orson Welles is at the top of a Ferris wheel with the main character, and he asks him if he'd be willing to take twenty thousand pounds to make one of the little dots of the people on the ground stop moving, for ever. He wouldn't.'

'That was a movie, though,' Eddie pointed out. 'And there's a bit of difference between twenty grand and a billion.' The last of the water sloshed into the tank, and he closed the flap and descended. 'I think we need to go on the basis of: if you don't know 'em, don't trust 'em.'

'Yeah,' she reluctantly agreed. 'Let's just hope we can figure out some way to end this that *doesn't* involve my being killed.'

'It won't happen if I can help it, love.' A brief smile of reassurance, then he picked up both the empty jerry cans. 'I'll stick these back in the garage, then do any first aid we need. After that, I'll make us some food. Okay?'

She smiled back. 'All right.'

Night came, and with it a shower of snow. Nina watched the falling flakes swirl outside the window, then retreated and drew the thick curtain. The cabin had by now fully warmed up – Eddie's prediction that she might actually find it excessively hot had come true, forcing her to take off not only her coat but her sweater beneath – but she imagined that by morning, every bit of insulation to trap the heat inside would be essential.

The upper floor comprised a single bedroom, but the couple opted to stay in the main room below. Two of the couches were sofa beds. Eddie came down the stairs bearing an armful of blankets as Nina unfolded one. 'This lot should do us,' he said.

'Thanks.' She glanced towards the bathroom. 'I don't suppose Charlie's supplies included any spare toothbrushes?'

He dropped the blankets onto the bed. 'I'll check.' He went into the bathroom and rummaged through a cabinet. 'Well, bloody hell, there are some! Toothpaste too. He really does think of everything.'

'I'm kinda getting the feeling he thinks of this place as a survivalist holdout as much as a vacation retreat.'

Eddie returned from the bathroom with two toothbrushes, still in their packaging. 'Nah, if he did he'd have a proper bunker, and he doesn't. Or if he does, he doesn't want the likes of me knowing about it.' He opened the wood-burner to check on the flames within, then tossed in a couple more pieces of firewood. 'This should still be warm in the morning, so we won't freeze. Mind you, I'm not planning on lying in.'

'I'm not sure I'll be able to sleep at all,' said Nina glumly. The quiet and solitude of the evening had only made the day's terrifying whirlwind echo more stridently in her mind. Carlson slashing at her with the knife, Novak killing Amy, then aiming his gun at her head . . .

Eddie sat beside her, wrapping an arm comfortingly – and protectively – around her. 'I'm knackered, and you must be too. You'll be asleep two minutes after we turn the lights out.'

'I'm not sure about that. What if someone comes looking for us in the night?'

'The security systems are on; we'll know if anyone comes. Don't worry, love.' He squeezed her. 'Nobody except Charlie knows we're here. And we're armed.' He indicated the two police Glocks, which he had put on a small table beside the couch. 'We'll be fine. You'll be fine. I promise.'

She smiled at him. 'Thanks. I needed some reassurance.'

'Any time you need it.' They kissed, then he held up the toothbrushes. 'Which one do you want? Red, or . . . red?'

'It's a tough decision,' she said with a grin, taking one and heading for the bathroom.

They got ready for bed, Eddie switching off the lights before burying himself under the blankets beside his wife. Both had stripped down to a single layer of undergarments, but it was more than warm enough. 'Night, love,' said Eddie, giving her another kiss.

'Night,' she replied. She made herself comfortable beside him, then closed her eyes.

It took rather longer than the promised two minutes, but she finally descended into a troubled, fitful sleep.

8

'Somebody's coming.'

The overnight snowfall had stopped after depositing a couple of inches of fresh white powder, but the clouds over the Adirondacks were still heavy and dark. The weather matched Nina's mood. She had not slept well, and the breakfast Eddie made from the cabin's dry supplies and the items he'd bought at the gas station did not especially revitalise her. To pass the time, she tried to work further on her deductions about the Shroud of Hades from the previous day. With no reference books or internet access, however, she had to rely on her own memory and experience – which wasn't enough to provide any new answers. Even something as simple as a map of Greece could have helped, but the cabin's supplies did not stretch to an atlas.

It was after ten o'clock when Eddie's warning snapped her attention away from her notes. A faint bleeping sound was coming from somewhere. 'What is it?'

Eddie opened a cupboard. The electronic trill became louder; the space contained a rack of electronic equipment and a small laptop. He opened the latter. 'That's the sensor covering the road,' he said as the screen lit up. 'Let's see who it is.'

Nina joined him. The laptop displayed the snowy track to the cabin, looking downhill. A black Range Rover was approaching the camera, which she guessed was mounted on a tree. 'Is that Charlie's car?'

'Could be – he likes his Range Rovers. Let's see if we can get a look at him.'

That turned out to be straightforward enough. The SUV stopped beside the camera, the driver's window lowing to reveal a crop-haired, square-jawed man wearing sunglasses. He looked directly into the lens and grinned, then drove on. 'It's him,' Eddie said with relief. 'I'll go and open the gate.'

Nina went with him. It felt colder than the previous day, the laden clouds threatening to drop more snow. It took only a few minutes for the Range Rover, equipped with snow chains around its tyres, to arrive, by which time Eddie had opened the gate. A cheerful toot came from its horn as it pulled into the compound. The window wound down again. 'Eddie Chase, you bald twat!' Charlie called out. 'Good to see you.'

'You too,' Eddie replied. 'Thanks for coming.'

'No problem. I always help out my mates. Let me park up.'

The couple followed the Range Rover back to the cabin. Charlie stopped beside the Kia. 'Didn't know you had a car,' he remarked as he got out. He was cut from the same former-military cloth as Eddie, fit and powerful even at fifty.

'It's not ours,' Eddie said grimly. 'You remember Amy Martin?'

'Cop, yeah?'

'Yeah. She's dead. Her partner killed her to try to get the bounty on Nina.'

Charlie's jovial air instantly evaporated. 'Shit, mate, I'm sorry.' He turned to Nina. 'Nina, hi. It's been a while. Sorry about the circumstances.'

'Hi,' she replied. She had only met the Londoner a few times before. 'Yeah, they're . . . less than ideal.'

'I've had some ideas on how to sort things out. Come inside and I'll tell you.'

They went into the cabin. The living room was warm, the woodburner radiating heat from a fresh supply of chopped logs. Nina had earlier washed using the water in the pan on top of it, which had been hot enough to need a little cold water from the faucet to reach the ideal temperature. Charlie hung up his coat and went to the satellite link. 'I tried phoning you on the way up but couldn't get through, then I remembered you hadn't asked for the code. You bloody dolt, Eddie.' He tapped at a keypad. A couple of amber lights on the device turned green. 'There. We've got comms. We'll need them for what I've got in mind.'

They all took seats on the couches. 'And what *have* you got in mind?' Nina asked.

Charlie smirked. 'Simple. I'm going to kill you.'

Eddie's eyes narrowed, and he put a hand on one of the Glocks beside him. 'Not something I'd joke about, mate. Two people have already tried. It didn't go well for them.'

The other man laughed, raising his hands in apology. 'Not for real, Christ. No, I checked Loost's message about how to claim the bounty. It's all done by phone, right? Kill Nina, then show the proof to someone – his adjudicator. Whoever that is, they're not going to have direct physical access to a body unless they show themselves in person. So – we fake your death.'

Nina blinked in surprise. 'Would that work?'

'I've done it before, for clients. I've even pretended to kill someone right in front of a witness, and they were fooled. I've got ways to make it look totally convincing. Had the idea on the way back up from DC, so I stopped in at home and picked up what I need.'

Eddie relaxed, slightly, but Nina noticed his hand didn't retreat too far from the gun. 'So what do you need me to do?' she asked.

'Play dead,' was the simple answer, delivered with a small smile. 'I'll handle the rest.' The smile disappeared, Charlie's air becoming fully businesslike. 'You said two people tried to kill you. Did either of them tag you like Loost asked in his message?'

'Yes.'

'And then what happened?'

'Loost came on to gloat. It wasn't him, it was a CGI copy programmed to respond to me. Then it described what the person had to do to claim the bounty.'

'Which was?'

'Simple enough. Kill me on camera, then let his adjudicator confirm it.'

Charlie nodded. 'We can work with that. The adjudicator isn't here, so that limits the checks they can do. How long can you hold your breath?'

'Uh – I don't know? A minute, maybe?'

'I'll make sure there are times when the camera isn't pointed at you so you can get some air.' He stood, extending a hand to her. 'So, you ready to die?'

'You're definitely sure that's safe?' Eddie asked, watching as Charlie loaded a round into the top of his own automatic's magazine. 'This is my wife you're going to be shooting that thing at.'

'She'll be fine,' the Londoner assured him. 'Nina, you comfy?'

'I've been better,' she said. She was wearing her sweater, which in the cabin's wood-fired heat made her uncomfortably warm, and the various items taped to her upper back under it felt awkward, tugging at her skin as she moved.

'Just roll with it, and everything'll be okay. Just think of what you're going to spend Loost's money on afterwards.' Charlie had offered to share the bounty with the couple after the fake killing: fifty–fifty to start with, then after a mock protest from Eddie a three-way split. 'So, Nina, you tell me what's going to happen, and what you're going to do.'

'Okay.' She took a breath, running through the plan in her mind. 'You tie my hands behind my back, then tag me with your phone. That should activate Loost's program. He gloats again, then tells you to kill me. So you turn me around and shoot me in the back.'

Charlie nodded. 'And then what happens?'

'The blood pack explodes, I fall down and pretend to be dead for as long as Loost's adjudicator needs to confirm it. Then, hopefully, all this is over.' Another breath, this with a deep exhalation. 'God, I hope this works.'

'It will. You just have to sell it. No screams, no flailing around – just drop flat on your face as hard as you dare and go limp.' He had already positioned a rug to give her a place for a relatively soft landing. 'Everything's rigged to make it look like I shot right into your heart at point-blank range. That's as near to an instant death as you can get.'

Eddie's misgivings had not been dispelled. 'You're still shooting her *with* something, though. That's not a normal blank.' Charlie's round had been modified by removing most of the gunpowder charge and the bullet itself, replacing it with a wax wad. Automatic handguns needed to be specially modified to fire blank rounds, which lacked the power to cycle the mechanism and eject the spent cartridge. In this case, an actual projectile, however soft, was essential for the illusion.

'The Kevlar'll stop it,' the other man assured him. A padded plate of the bulletproof material, about the size of a phone, had been stuck to Nina's back. On top of it was a plastic pouch containing fake blood – along with little gobbets of raw meat. 'Trust me, I've done this before. It gets the best of all worlds. You get a powder burn, a hole through the clothes, a splat of blood, and a real impact. That's what sells it. You can *see* that something hit. And if the adjudicator wants me to pull up your jumper to check the results, we've got that covered.' Charlie had used mortician's wax, various colours of make-up and more fake blood to simulate an entry wound, then covered it with the Kevlar and blood pack. 'I'll pull off the plate when I move your clothes. If they were here, it would only fool them for a few seconds. But they'll be looking at it on a screen. As long as you stay totally still, it'll look real.'

'Okay.' Nina had concerns of her own, but there seemed no alternative, other than remaining in a self-imposed prison sentence. 'Well . . . let's do it, then.'

'You need me to do anything?' Eddie asked.

'Just stay out of sight,' Charlie replied. 'If Loost asks, I'll say I killed you already.'

'Right.' The Yorkshireman retreated to a corner.

Charlie took a length of rope from a bag. 'Let's tie you up. Hands behind your back, please.'

Nina obeyed. Even knowing she was safe, the feeling of restriction, of helplessness, as her wrists were pulled together and bound was deeply uncomfortable. Once they were secured, Charlie gestured for her to kneel on the rug. 'Okay. Let's tag you, and see what happens.'

He took out his phone and held it up to Nina's face. A pause . . .

Then the Uzz fanfare sounded.

She readied herself for her second confrontation with a dead man. 'Congratulations, Charlie,' came the trillionaire's voice. 'It looks like you've found Nina Wilde! I just need to confirm that it's really her.' It was the same spiel as before, but Charlie was holding the phone closer than Novak had done; that was apparently enough to satisfy her tormentor. 'That's a full biometric match; it really is her. Well done. Now, Charlie, before we move on to what you need to do, I want to talk to Professor Wilde. Can you turn the phone so she can see me?'

Charlie did so. Nina scowled at Loost's simulated features on the screen. 'Whoever's really running this, you didn't expect me to survive last time, did you? You didn't change your digital dummy's speech. Is it going to start bragging about its quantum matrix next?'

As before, there was a subtle change to Loost's expression as he 'recognised' her. This time, though, the gloating smile only half-formed before disappearing again. It took a couple of seconds before he reacted. Was someone hastily giving the replica new instructions?

She didn't have time to think about it more. Whether it was a human or an algorithm at the other end of the line, the decision had been made to move things swiftly along. 'Charlie, I need to speak to you again.'

Careful not to catch Eddie in frame as he turned the phone, Charlie addressed Loost. 'So what do you want?'

'This is what you need to do to claim the bounty. Keep Nina in view of the main camera – then kill her.' Back on script, then, but the command was still alarming, even knowing she was safe. 'My adjudicator will confirm her death. Then, you'll receive a message via Uzz with the details of the digital currency wallet and the passcode to access it. It's a self-deleting message that can't be traced, so make sure you can take notes before you read it. Use it, and one billion dollars is yours.'

'No, don't do it!' Nina protested, playing her part. 'Please! Don't do it!' But Charlie pushed her around to face away from him, then took a step back. She cringed, her fear genuine now as she waited for the gunshot—

The round might have had most of its charge removed, but at such close range it was shockingly, terrifyingly loud. It felt as if someone had kicked her hard in the back. The Kevlar plate did its job, but the impact was still brutal. It took all her effort not to cry out at the pain. *Don't scream, just fall*, she remembered, toppling onto her front. She hit the floor with a bang, the rug providing little padding. Again she had to ignore the blow to her skull. *Eyes closed, lie still, don't move, don't even breathe . . .*

All she could do was wait to see if Loost's accomplices believed she was dead.

Eddie watched from behind Charlie's left side. Even knowing that everything was fake and his friend had been fastidious about taking every precaution, he was still on edge – and the moment when the gun went off, a burst of blood erupting from Nina's back, was as if his worst nightmare had come true. His wife fell face-first onto the rug and went limp. Every instinct screamed for him to rush over and help her. But he couldn't, not if this was going to work . . .

He clenched his jaw as Charlie listened to more instructions from Loost. 'Well done. But my adjudicator needs to confirm that she's dead. Use your phone's main camera to let me see her.' Eddie willed Nina to hold her breath and not move a muscle as the other Englishman slowly swept the phone over her. 'Show me the entry wound.'

This was where the plan would either work – or fail. But Charlie had prepared for it. He put his gun on the floor, then with a glance back at Eddie moved so the phone's cameras were temporarily unsighted – and used his free hand to grip Nina's sweater and tug at the plate beneath it. Any noise the micropore tape securing it made as it was pulled from her skin was obscured by a conveniently timed grunt. By the time the camera saw Nina again, the materials used for the deception were hidden inside her bunched-up clothing.

Again, Eddie felt raw horror at the sight. Charlie knew precisely what a point-blank bullet wound looked like, and had replicated it perfectly. At least, from this distance. How well it would hold up under closer scrutiny remained to be seen. But Charlie was right – there was a limit to how much it could be checked on a screen.

The Londoner brought the phone closer. Eddie saw the camera's view on its screen. The mortician's wax formed a crater of ruptured skin, the surrounding area subtly built up high enough to make it appear it had penetrated the flesh. Any sign of what lay within was concealed by fake blood. 'There,' said Charlie. 'Now, what about my money?'

Loost was silent for a moment. Then: 'It seems like this isn't the first time you've killed someone.'

'I've got military experience.'

'Yes. I see that from your website.'

Eddie couldn't see Charlie's reaction, but he felt a sudden unease. His friend's company openly advertised itself as providing security services, wherever needed in the world. He didn't think he was listed online as one of its advisors, but wasn't certain. If his name was linked to Charlie's, Loost – or his helpers – would surely make the connection . . .

Charlie shifted position, moving the phone away from Nina to let her take a breath. 'Then you know I can do the job. And you also know I work for money. I did what you wanted. So pay me.'

Another pause before Loost replied. Was someone feeding lines to his computerised replica? 'I will. But first, I want to check something. Show me her face.'

Charlie hesitated, then brought the phone down to do so. Nina hurriedly froze. The Londoner slowly panned the phone over her to give Loost's adjudicator a clear view. 'Happy now?'

'Not quite. There's one more thing I need you to do. Touch her eye.'

Eddie swore under his breath. Resisting the involuntary urge to flinch at physical eye contact required almost superhuman discipline and control. Which he knew Nina didn't have; she had once considered getting contact lenses instead of reading glasses, but the ophthalmologist hadn't even been able to put a soft test lens onto her eye, so strong was her negative reaction.

But he couldn't warn Charlie without giving the game away. He willed Nina to keep still. *Come on, love, your life depends on this . . .*

Charlie carefully lifted one of Nina's eyelids with his middle finger. She had prepared herself for the touch, managing not to move. Eddie tensed. She held her eye still, staring straight ahead. Charlie brought his forefinger closer, closer. *You can do it, just keep still—*

He touched Nina's eye – and she blinked. Eddie's heart fell.

'I suspected you'd try something like this, Nina!' crowed Loost. 'You thought you could outsmart me. But you failed. You *failed*.' His voice hardened. 'I'm disappointed in you, Charlie. But I'll give you a chance to redeem yourself. Kill her for real, right now, and the bounty is doubled. Otherwise I'll put that extra billion on *you*. Two billion dollars, Charlie. Untraceable. All yours. You know what to do.'

Nina had struggled to sit up while Loost was speaking, her bound hands making it difficult. Still blinking, she looked around in alarm at the two men. Eddie took a step closer, uncertain. Surely Charlie wouldn't betray him—

'It didn't work,' said the Londoner, sounding deflated. 'Sorry.' His hand darted towards the gun on the floor. 'But—'

Eddie was already moving.

9

Charlie was only halfway out of his crouch as Eddie kicked his right hand. The gun spun across the room, landing with a clang in the kitchen area.

The Yorkshireman didn't see where. All his attention was on Charlie. The other man had been a Royal Marines commando – not trained to the lethal level of the SAS, but still a formidable opponent. And he had the advantage of height and over half a decade's fewer years on him.

Charlie grunted, shaking the pain from his hand as he rose – and whirled to deliver a strike with his left elbow. Eddie tried to dodge, but had to stop short as he almost stepped on Nina. The blow pounded into his shoulder. He gasped at the burst of pain.

The Londoner struck again, lashing out with a spinning kick. It hit Eddie in the side, sending him across the room. He crashed against the small table. The Glocks skittered across the floor. He didn't have time to go after them – Charlie was on him once more. A balled fist slammed into his cheek. He staggered. Another fist came at him—

Eddie whipped up his left arm to block it, taking the painful punch on his forearm. He retaliated with one of his own. His knuckles caught Charlie's chin, jarring him.

Eddie hurled himself at the taller man. They slammed against a set of shelves, sending their contents to the floor. Plates shattered, scattering shards. Eddie lowered his head and drove two fierce punches into Charlie's stomach. His reward was a breathless snarl, his friend-turned-opponent convulsing. He had to overpower him for long enough to reach one of the guns.

But Charlie had the same goal. He kicked at Eddie's shins. One boot cracked agonisingly against bone. Eddie hopped back to avoid a second attack. Charlie pushed forward and grabbed him, trying to throw him to the floor. Eddie clamped a hand over his face and clawed at his eyes. A fist thudded against his side in retaliation. Both men grappled, staggering across the room in their increasing desperation to take the other down—

Nina had just risen to her knees. They ploughed into her, knocking her back to the floor. Charlie trod hard on her stomach. Nina folded with an anguished moan.

The sound snapped Eddie's attention to her. Was she hurt, how bad—

Charlie took advantage of his distraction.

He swung around, spinning Eddie with him, then let go to send him reeling backwards – before following up with a high kick to his midsection. Eddie fell back against the wood-burner. The heavy metal oven brought him to an abrupt and painful stop. A deep *clong* echoed through the room as its chimney shook, the pan of water slopping.

He jerked away from the heat radiating from the wood-burner. Charlie was already rushing at him for another attack—

Eddie grabbed the pan and flung its contents.

Charlie instinctively threw up both hands to protect his face as water burst over him. But it was merely hot, not boiling. It still gave Eddie a new opportunity. He lunged, swinging the pan. It hit Charlie's head with a ringing clang – only for the handle to snap off with the impact. The hefty pan itself tumbled to the floor, hitting Nina.

Again, Eddie's eyes flicked involuntarily towards his wife—

Charlie fought back. Water streaming from his clothes, he charged at Eddie, pounding him back against the wood-burner. The Yorkshireman careened off it – and slipped on a piece of broken plate. He landed face-first on one of the couches.

The Londoner pressed home his attack. He slammed a series of savage punches into Eddie's kidneys. Eddie convulsed with each blow, roaring in pain—

Nina had managed to stand – and kicked as hard as she could at the back of Charlie's right knee, trying to chop his leg out from beneath him.

On most people it would have worked. But he had a split-second of forewarning – a sound, a shadow, movement in his peripheral vision – and just barely twisted away. Her foot only grazed the back of his leg. The failed strike left her unbalanced, bound arms waving helplessly behind her. Charlie's counter-attack didn't miss. He kicked her hard on the hip. She fell onto the bucket beside the wood-burner, spilling logs and fire-raising implements.

Charlie swung back around to Eddie – only for his adversary to collide with him. Raw fury had overcome pain. Eddie headbutted Charlie, splitting his lips, then shifted to knee him in the groin—

Charlie leapt at him. Eddie's attack only caught his thigh. Charlie grabbed him, squeezing hard in a crushing bear-hug. Eddie thrashed and kicked, trying to break free. But the other man was using his greater size to force him back towards the wood-burner. He clawed at Eddie's head, pushing his face down towards the hot metal.

Eddie felt the rising heat on his skin. Every muscle straining, he fought to lift himself away, but Charlie's full weight was upon him, relentlessly driving him onto the scalding iron surface—

A click, a hiss – and Charlie screamed as intense flames writhed around his leg.

Nina had found the gas torch and wriggled around to pick it up in her tied hands, then rolled behind Charlie's legs and ignited it. The searing blue jet instantly set his clothing on fire. He jumped away, releasing Eddie and swatting desperately at the burning material to extinguish it.

Eddie sprang upright. The floor by the wood-burner was littered with firewood. He snatched up a solid hunk of chopped log and smashed it against Charlie's head. Pieces of bark flew off with the impact. Charlie almost fell. Fuelled by rage, Eddie hit him with the log again before hammering him with punches and kicks. Charlie was now entirely on the defensive. Eddie pounded a fist into his face, sending him staggering backwards against the sink, then drew back a leg, about to slam a foot into his groin and take him down—

The younger man struck out with a fast, low kick – hitting Eddie's other foot. Unbalanced, he fell to the floor.

Charlie turned, about to turn on the tap for water to splash over his smouldering clothes – when he saw his gun in the sink. He grabbed it—

'Eddie!'

Nina kicked a poker across the floor to her fallen husband. He snatched it up and hurled it just as Charlie brought the gun around. Eighteen inches of wrought-iron rod hit him squarely in the face. Blood spouted from his nose. He fell against the counter and thumped to the floor. Before he could get up Eddie had rolled back to his feet and booted the gun from his grip with a crack of breaking fingers, then sent a final kick at his head. More blood sprayed from Charlie's mouth, accompanied by broken pieces of teeth. He slumped onto his side, almost unconscious.

Eddie was barely more awake. Swaying drunkenly, he tottered across the cabin to Nina and dropped onto his knees beside her. 'Are you okay?' he asked her, fumbling to untie her hands.

'Yeah, I – I think so,' she said, shaking from the ordeal. 'What about you?'

'My kidneys feel mashed enough to put in a fucking pie.' He released her, then took the rope and went to Charlie. Before the other man could recover, he had been hogtied, hands firmly secured behind his back and then bound to his ankles. Eddie picked up his gun, then stood. 'Right. He's not going anywhere for a while.' He spotted Charlie's phone, which had been dropped when he first went for his gun. The screen was blank. Loost had disconnected, doubtless guessing that Charlie had lost the fight. 'We need to go, though. Soon as Loost realises you're still okay, he'll tell everyone where you are again.'

They both looked around as Charlie spoke. 'Surprised you didn't kill me, Eddie,' he said, weakly spitting out blood and drool. 'Grateful, but surprised.'

'Jury's still out,' Eddie growled. 'Why'd you do it, Charlie? I trusted you, so why'd you fucking try to kill me?'

'Because I'd rather have two billion dollars in my pocket than one billion on my head. If it'd been the other way around, you'd have done the same.'

'Bollocks I would.'

'You're no hero, Eddie. None of us are. And even if you were, this isn't a world that rewards heroes. You only have to look at the people who make it to the top to see that.' He glanced at the phone. 'People like Loost.'

'Loost's dead,' Eddie pointed out. 'And so are the two other people who tried to kill Nina. You want to be the third, keep pissing me off.'

Charlie wisely decided to say nothing more for the moment. But the silence was only brief, as the Uzz fanfare trilled from his phone. It was followed by another update from Loost, giving the cabin's GPS coordinates. 'Aw, crap,' sighed Nina. 'Yeah, we'd better—'

Another sound, this from outside: a raucous, multifrequency buzz. Eddie rushed to the door and opened it. The chainsaw rasp grew louder. 'Shit,' he snapped. 'Sounds like snowmobiles.'

Before he had finished speaking, the laptop in the cupboard started bleeping. Nina darted to it. Her husband was right; several snowmobiles were bounding up the track to the cabin. 'It is! They're coming here.'

'How many?'

'Six or seven? Some have got two guys on, though. But how could they have gotten here so quickly?'

'They were already coming,' Eddie realised grimly. He joined Nina to check the new arrivals for himself.

Behind him, Charlie rolled onto his side to see the screen. 'Looks like Don Miller and his mates. Local dickhead, thinks he's a bigshot.

I've had to kick him off my property a couple of times while he's been out hunting.'

Eddie looked more closely at the lead snowmobile as it passed the camera. 'He's not hunting deer.' The driver, a big, bearded man wearing a red baseball cap, had some variant of an AR-15 rifle, a civilian version of the military M16, slung over his back. Most of his companions were also visibly armed.

'That's the guy from the gas station,' said Nina in alarm. 'He *was* following us!'

'He must have figured out we were coming here, 'cause there's not much else on this road. Grab your stuff, quick.'

'Where are we going?' she cried. 'We can't take the car – they're coming up the only road. And they'll catch us if we're on foot.'

'We'll take the snowbikes.' He donned his leather jacket as Nina found her coat. The couple hurriedly retrieved their belongings, then rushed out.

'Hey! You're going to leave me here tied up?' Charlie called after them.

'You only need to worry if they start playing banjos,' said Eddie as he reached the porch and shut the door behind him. He looked down towards the gate. The snarl of multiple engines rose – and he caught his first glimpse of the approaching hunters through the trees. They would be in sight of the cabin in seconds. 'The shed's unlocked – take one of the bikes and head that way to the fence,' he told Nina, gesturing towards the compound's edge behind the cabin. 'I'll be right there.'

She ran around the little house. 'What are you going to do?'

'Show 'em what happens if you ignore the "no trespassing" sign.' He backed to the cabin's corner, peering around it as the convoy of snowmobiles came into view. They roared up the last stretch of track to the gate, then stopped. The man in the red cap – Miller, Eddie assumed – didn't get off to open it himself, but gestured to someone else. Even at a distance Eddie could tell the man riding pillion on the second sled, who clambered off and went to the gate, was annoyed at being ordered around.

The Yorkshireman checked Charlie's gun, a Sig-Sauer P365 automatic. He had only modified one bullet for the ill-fated mock execution; the others were standard nine-millimetre rounds. He estimated the distance to the gate. Roughly a hundred metres. Beyond the accepted effective range of a handgun, though a good shooter still had a reasonable chance of hitting a target at that distance – and Eddie was a very good shooter.

But he wasn't planning to kill anyone . . . yet. Even though the situation didn't look good, the snowmobilers hadn't done anything openly hostile. He would either scare them off – or spur them into doing what they had come to do anyway.

The man on foot reached the gate and started to open it. Eddie took aim – and fired three shots.

One bullet made a lucky impact and struck the gate with a piercing *thwack*, while the others smacked into the white-covered ground beyond, kicking up snow. All produced the desired effect. Some of the men dived from their sleds and flattened themselves behind them, while the others frantically gunned their engines and sped back the way they had come. That told him something about the group's composition. Civilians were likely to panic and flee under fire, even if that meant potentially exposing themselves to more danger. The men who had dropped flat, on the other hand, were probably ex-military, trained to deal with such a situation. Half the hunters – four out of eight – fitted that description, including Miller. The threat the group posed had risen.

But he now had a chance to get away while they were startled – or scared. He ran to the garage. Nina was awkwardly pushing out one of the snowbikes. 'How do I ride this thing?' she asked.

'It helps if you sit on it!' he shot back as he went to get the other bike. A row of blue LEDs on the handlebars told him it was fully charged. He yanked out the charging cable and brought it to the open door. The controls were almost comically simple: an on–off switch, a twist throttle like a motorbike's, and a single brake lever. Nina had by now straddled her vehicle. 'Push the on button, turn the right handgrip, and you're off.'

She tried it – and yipped in surprise as it leapt forward. She hurriedly squeezed the brake. The bike whined to a rapid stop as its regenerative braking system arrested it. 'It's twitchier than I was expecting!'

'Just be smooth and you'll be fine. It's like riding a bike – just one without wheels.' To demonstrate, he set off himself. The front ski cut easily through the snow, the narrow rear tread showering a frosty wake behind him. 'Come on!'

Nina nervously followed. This time, her touch on the controls was lighter. Eddie looked back to make sure she was with him, then accelerated, heading for the side of the broad clearing—

Gunfire erupted behind them.

10

Don Miller cursed as the people who had shot at him rode away, blocked from sight behind the cabin. Sons of bitches! He unleashed a final angry burst from his AR-15, which had been illegally modified to fire in full-auto mode, then lowered it.

He had rounded up some hunting buddies to help catch a prey that was worth a hell of a lot more than his usual targets like deer and bears, expecting sheer numbers to make it an easy job. There were only three properties on this track where the woman could have gone, and he knew the owners of two of them – which left the Limey bastard who'd had the brass balls to tell him to get off 'his' property. Miller had been hunting in these woods since he was old enough to use a gun, which had been long before he was legally allowed to do so. He didn't let the law tell him what to do, and he wasn't going to let some foreign fuck do so either.

Said foreign fuck was here; Miller recognised his Range Rover outside the cabin. The SUV this Nina Wilde woman had gotten into at the gas station was here too. The hunt should have been simple: surround the cabin, move in, make anyone else there surrender her, by force if necessary. One billion dollars; not bad for a morning's work! But things had already gone wrong, and now his prize was running like a scared hare.

'The fuck was that?' demanded another man, Newbold. Like Miller he had been in the military, hitting the snow-covered dirt the moment he heard the first shot. He retrieved his thick-framed glasses and brushed them clean before putting them back on. 'Thought this wasn't gonna be any trouble?'

'Guess you thought wrong,' Miller replied sarcastically. He looked around at his companions. The overweight Sullivan was the only other ex-forces hunter, and had also dived for cover, though his fat ass was probably visible from half a mile away. The remaining person who hadn't fled was Bobarty, now cowering behind Miller's sled. 'Yo, Jughead! Get up from there.'

Bobarty, a man in his thirties with protruding ears and winter clothing that was long past its best, scowled. 'Don't call me that,' he complained, getting up.

'I'll call you whatever the fuck I want. Hey!' Miller shouted down the track. 'Get back here, you assholes! We need to get after them!'

The snarl of engines signalled the return of the other snowmobiles. 'Where'd they go?' asked Felling, a man with a moustache and a blue cap.

Miller pointed. 'Towards the Spires. They're probably heading for the ski resort. Don't matter. They're on those little electric snowbikes – we can catch up, easy. Come on!'

Bobarty climbed onto the pillion seat of Felling's sled. Felling started to ride through the partly open gate. 'Where the fuck you going?' said Miller. Another gesture, this time taking in the whole of the compound. 'The Limey fenced this off; you ain't gonna get a sled through. We gotta go around.' Stung, Felling halted and clumsily reversed. 'Okay, let's go. We've got a bitch to catch!'

The six snowmobiles roared away, following the line of the fence into the surrounding forest.

The fence at the far side of Charlie's compound came into sight as Eddie and Nina rode over a small rise. 'How do we get through?' Nina called out.

Eddie rode up to the barrier, then hopped off his bike. 'We don't. We go over!' He tossed his vehicle bodily over the fence into the snow beyond. 'Climb over – I'll chuck yours too.'

Nina scaled the snow-covered slats as her bike thumped into a drift beside Eddie's. 'So where are we going?'

'I know the area, sort of,' he told her as he followed. 'Been out here with Charlie. There's a ski resort about five miles away.' He looked around, then pointed. 'It's . . . that way.'

Nina eyed him. 'You don't seem sure.'

'We just aim for the mountain. Big pointy thing, can't miss it.'

She regarded the forest ahead. Tall trees, heavy with snow, completely blocked all view of the landscape. 'I'm not seeing it!'

'We just need some clear ground.' He pulled her bike upright and waited for her to climb on, then recovered his own. From somewhere behind, he heard the buzz of the snowmobiles. Were they following their tracks across Charlie's property – or did they know it was fenced in, and were going around?

He had to assume the latter. 'They're coming. Let's go!' The couple both turned their throttles and zipped off into the forest.

The terrain immediately beyond Charlie's compound was relatively flat, but still rippled with numerous hillocks and humps. Boulders poked out from the snow amongst the trees, adding to the tension of navigating between the conifers. However, it didn't take them long to reach a hiking track, a clear white line that snaked through the trunks and around rises. The snowbikes bounded through the snow, kicking up a pure crystalline spray. Under other circumstances Nina might have found the ride exhilarating, but lacking proper winter clothing her legs were getting cold and damp – and her being hunted was another factor eliminating any sense of fun.

There was still no sign of any landmarks through the trees. 'Is this the right way?' she shouted. The bikes only made a fraction of the noise of a gasoline-powered snowmobile, but at their top speed of about forty miles per hour, the wind noise in her ears was becoming obtrusive.

'I think so,' Eddie called back to her. 'Should take us to a valley, and then we follow that to the ski resort.'

Even over the wind's hiss and ruffle, Nina still heard engines growing louder behind her. She risked a glance back. Headlights flickered between the trees. The hunters were also following the path. 'Eddie, how fast can a snowmobile go?'

'Depends on the snowmobile, but I know what you're really asking, and yeah – faster than these!' He looked to each side. 'These bikes are a lot narrower, though. If we go off the track where there's more trees, it'll slow them down.'

'And we might crash!'

'Aim for the bits where there's air rather than wood and you'll be fine. Follow me!' He peeled off the track, the front ski jolting harshly as he rode over a stone or root hidden under the snow.

Nina reluctantly went after him. The ride became harder in moments, the snowbike's suspension pounding. The more densely packed trees forced them to weave between them. She couldn't follow directly in Eddie's tracks without getting snow kicked up into her face, so had to pick out her own route. Trunks whipped past, small branches clutching at her. Even though she could hear her vehicle's motor straining with the increased effort, she had lost speed.

Their pursuers had not.

Some of the sleds were sticking to the track, their engines' monotonous, flat rasps underpinning the over-revving shrills of the others as they jumped over bumps. Nina glanced back again. At least two snowmobiles were coming after her, the riders expertly swinging the powerful machines around obstacles. Their headlights were brighter than before, closer. The snowbikes couldn't outrun them.

Eddie had realised the same thing. 'Through there!' he shouted, changing course towards a thicket of young pines. The smaller trees were packed closely together, none yet large enough to have established dominance over the space.

'We won't fit!' Nina protested.

'We should – but they won't. Pull yourself in as far as you can!'

He brought in his elbows against his sides, knees squeezing the bike's boxy frame, and rode into the thicket. Snow exploded around him as he clipped low-hanging foliage. He ducked lower, jerking the handlebars to swerve between the slender trunks.

'Shit,' Nina muttered, bracing herself and following.

The ride became a nightmarish videogame – one with a very real chance of injury or death at the slightest mistake. She didn't know how fast she was going, but it felt like two hundred miles per hour. Tree after tree rushed at her. Suddenly breathless, she tugged the handlebars back and forth, the snowbike jinking and swaying between the young conifers. Branches slapped her, stinging her exposed skin. She cringed, eyes squeezed almost shut to protect them.

Ahead, Eddie had angled right. She veered after him – only to see a stone poking through the snow in the gap she was about to take. Sudden fear jolting her heart, she released the throttle and swerved hard to the left. The end of her right handgrip clipped a narrow trunk. The impact jarred the front ski rightwards. She shrieked as the unexpected sharp turn almost threw her from the snowbike. Somehow she kept her balance, forcing the ski back into line. More freezing snow hit her face as she brushed another tree. The bike kept slowing, almost coming to a halt before Nina recovered from her shock and thumbed the throttle again. 'Shit!' she gasped again.

More cautiously, she threaded her way after Eddie. He looked back and saw that she had lost ground, cutting speed so she could catch up – then reacted in alarm to something behind her. 'Nina, *gun*!' he yelled—

The sharp crack of a gunshot and the thud of a bullet striking a tree right beside her were practically simultaneous.

Miller looked back at the other sled in angry disbelief. Bobarty, riding pillion, had taken a snapshot with his rifle – and almost hit his target. 'What the fuck? Don't shoot, don't shoot!' he shouted over the roaring engines. 'We need her alive! You fucking dipshit moron!' The jug-eared man lowered his gun, looking offended.

Miller didn't care. The woman and the guy with her – only wearing a leather jacket in this weather? Must be some clown from downstate who knew jack-shit about survival – had ridden their snowbikes into a stand of young trees. They probably thought the larger sleds couldn't fit through, and they were right. But they didn't know these woods. A track led around the thicket only a hundred yards away. A small detour, and he would be back on his quarry's tail in thirty seconds.

'Keep up with me!' he ordered, changing direction. 'Knock her off her bike!'

A zigzagging sweep between more small trees – and Eddie burst out from the thicket's far side. The conifers beyond were taller, spaced sufficiently widely for the pursuing sleds to fit through . . . but still close enough to make manoeuvring between them at speed risky.

At least the shooting had stopped, but he knew why: to claim the bounty, Nina had to be captured alive. Once *he* was in the hunters' sights, they wouldn't be so reluctant to fire. He slowed to look back. Where was Nina?

Off to his left, about thirty metres behind. She was just coming to the edge of the stand. He signalled for her to head towards him. The growl of engines now came from two directions. One group of snowmobiles still ploughing along the hiking path – and another beyond Nina. He spotted headlights tracking behind the younger trees. There must be a way around the stand. He swore. Of course the local yokels would know that!

And he hadn't yet got his bearings. The snowy trees still blocked any view of the surrounding mountains. He was sure they were going in roughly the right direction, but the further they went, the more chance of ending up on the wrong side of some terrain feature. The ground was already getting steeper.

But they had to keep going. 'Nina, come on!' he cried as she approached. 'They're trying to flank us.'

'They're gonna succeed,' she replied unhappily. 'We can't outrun them on these things!'

'We've got to try.' They both accelerated, carving through the snow between the towering pines.

But Nina's statement was quickly confirmed. The snowmobiles on the trail had now peeled off into the forest, vaulting over humps and smashing down small bushes as they homed in on the two bikes, and the ones that had rounded the thicket were rapidly closing from the other side.

Eddie fumbled with his left hand for the gun; his right was needed for the throttle. 'You go in front,' he told his wife. 'I'll try to discourage 'em.'

'No – we can't split up,' she protested. 'For a start, I have no idea where I'm going!'

'You know as much as I bloody do at the moment! Just keep going until you come out into a valley. The ski runs are further down it.' He checked behind. One especially fearless – or insane – rider from the larger group was closing the fastest, his sled flying through the air from the crest of a small rise before pounding down with an explosion of powder. 'All right, go!'

'Eddie—' Nina started to say, but her husband had already braked hard, dropping behind her. He waited a moment to make sure she kept going, then looked for their pursuers.

The stunt rider, a lanky man in his twenties, was closing fast, drifting his sled between the trees. A rifle was slung over his back – and Eddie glimpsed a large combat knife in a sheath attached to his belt. More snowmobiles weaved through the forest behind him, engines snarling and headlights flaring.

There was no way Eddie could aim accurately without slowing right down. All he could do was point the gun over his shoulder and hope the other man would be scared off. He fired twice, the shots painfully loud so close to his ear. *That'll do wonders for my hearing loss*, he thought with bleak sarcasm. The sled's engine roar changed in pitch as its rider hurriedly swerved away. But he hadn't fallen back far – and his much more powerful machine could make up the gap in moments.

And now a second sled was closing in. An overweight man with piggy eyes and a determined expression drew level with his younger companion. The two sleds jockeyed for position, one to each side of the Yorkshireman as they drew ever nearer. Eddie took another shot. This time, the snowmobile veered as soon as its rider saw the gun come up, the round going wide.

The other machine responded by revving hard and surging towards the snowbike. It was to Eddie's left, forcing him to blind-fire awkwardly back at it. The engine note didn't change. The rider hadn't flinched. Eddie looked ahead for anything he could use to his advantage – dense trees, clusters of rocks, something the narrow bike could pass through but sleds would have to avoid. There was nothing. If anything, the trees were starting to thin out.

Both snowmobiles accelerated, coming up on either side. The fat guy on his left was the one who hadn't been startled by his shot. He was probably ex-military – the greater threat. Eddie pointed the gun back towards him, this time turning his head to see exactly where he was. The man realised the danger and hurriedly swung away. Eddie fired. The bullet clipped the snowmobile's whirling tread. No damage. He looked ahead again—

A clump of bushes rushed at him.

He swerved, hard – too late. The front ski crashed through the lower branches, wood shattering with a cacophony of sharp cracks. Higher branches caught his extended left hand as he swept against the obstacle. The gun was almost snatched away. He just barely managed to curl his forefinger around the trigger guard to save it.

More trees directly ahead. He needed both hands to steer. Gun dangling from his finger, he seized the left handgrip and leaned sideways, curving the little snowbike in a slithering skid past the trunks.

But now Piggy had sped up again, also sweeping around to stay on his left side – and cutting him off from Nina. She disappeared amongst the distant trees. To Eddie's horror, he saw the two snowmobiles that had rounded the thicket pursuing her. 'Nina!' he yelled. 'Keep going, get to the ski resort!'

He couldn't tell if she had heard. Piggy was still closing in on him, reaching for a holstered handgun. Eddie sharpened his own turn and headed at full speed through the trees, briefly leaving the ground as he hit a hidden bump. Snow spat into his face as the front ski slammed back down. He blinked the freezing spicules from his eyes and powered on.

The electric snowbike wasn't up to the chase, though. Its speed had again topped out – while the snowmobiles kept coming. One, two, three, *four* sleds, five men in all upon them. He was outnumbered, outgunned and rapidly being outrun. And he still had no idea where he was heading.

The hunters did, though. They also knew that he would soon have nowhere left to go.

11

Nina fought back panic as her snowbike raced through the forest. The ground was getting steeper and more bumpy. Even when she found a comparatively level path, roots and rocks under the snow hammered the bike's suspension.

Her pursuers' two sleds closed relentlessly. She didn't have the horsepower to outpace them. One had two hunters on it, the other the man in the red cap she'd seen at the gas station – Miller, Charlie had called him. The latter was now only yards behind her, sweeping his snowmobile between the trees with effortless skill. She made a desperate swerve between two pines in the hope the gap would be too narrow for him. He instantly saw through the ruse and with a flick of his handlebars drifted around the trunks, dropping back in behind her with barely a second lost.

She burst through a snowdrift, frozen clods spraying over her already cold body. The woods were thinning – for the first time, she glimpsed mountains between the heavy white trees. But it wasn't enough to tell her where she needed to go. She was effectively riding blind, with faster opponents on her tail—

Literally on it. The snowmobile's engine note rose sharply, a triumphant roar – and she was almost flung over her handlebars as the pursuing vehicle rammed her from behind. The bike's rear track slithered sideways beneath her. Only an instinctive jerk on her controls kept her from flipping over.

But Miller was still right behind her. He swung his sled at her again. This time, it bashed the bike's boxy frame just behind her seat.

Another breathless gasp as she almost fell off, sawing at her handlebars to stay upright. One more collision and she would go over—

Sudden hope as she saw a fallen log breaking through the snow at the top of a small rise. There was a narrow gap between it and a neighbouring tree. It was too small for a snowmobile. But she could fit through. The hunter would *have* to break off and go around it. Even if it only gave her a few seconds' respite, that might be all she needed to find a true escape route.

Nina aimed for it. The hunter realised what she was doing and accelerated for another ramming attack, but she was already charging up the rise. The sled's snarl abruptly dropped as Miller braked and turned sharply away. Then she was through—

There was nothing beyond the log.

The tree had ended its life on the edge of a ridge. The drop into a snow-filled hollow on the far side was not far, six feet at most – but it was well beyond what Nina had expected, or could handle. Her machine fell away from under her as she plunged downwards—

The bike landed first in an explosion of snow, front ski collapsing – then somersaulted end over end. Nina came down on top of it. She managed to pull her arms up to shield her face, but the rubber rear track slammed against her chest. Then she too hit the ground.

A foot-plus of snow wasn't enough to cushion the impact. Agony surged through her shoulder as she hit something hard under the white covering. Then she tumbled helplessly across the ground, more unseen protrusions catching her back and hips and legs. She finally stopped face-down, freezing snow inside her coat's collar.

Sensation gradually returned. She blew snow from her nostrils and tried to push herself up. The attempt brought only pain from a collection of brand-new bruises. Trees swam woozily before her narrowed eyes.

Noise, harsh, getting louder. A snowmobile. Terrified adrenalin shot through her. She struggled upright, fear overcoming pain. Where was—

'Hold it! Hold it right fuckin' there, missy.'

Nina whirled – to see Miller standing at the edge of the bowl, rifle aimed down at her. His sled idled behind him. The second snowmobile pulled up, the two men aboard scrambling off and hurriedly covering her with their own guns.

She turned to run – but Miller fired his rifle. The bullet struck her downed snowbike with a shrill clank. She froze in terror.

'I said, don't fuckin' move!' he barked. 'Rule number one with me is, you do what the fuck I tell you to. Break that rule, we gonna have problems. And I am the last person on this earth you want problems with. My buddies here'll tell you that.' He jerked his head to indicate his companions.

'S'right,' said the older of the pair, an overweight man with a moustache and blue baseball cap. The other, with prominent ears and eyes that to Nina seemed far too close together, nodded. Something in his expression told her he'd had problems of his own with Miller. 'So, what we doing with her?'

Miller looked into the woods. Over the burble of the two stationary machines, Nina heard more engines in the distance. *Eddie!* They were still chasing him – and she knew that if there was any chance of his coming back to rescue her, he would do so.

But for now, she was trapped. With a billion dollars waiting for the hunter who killed her . . .

'We gotta get rid of the guy who was with her,' Miller said firmly. 'He tells the cops, we all go to fuck-you-in-the-ass prison, however much money we got. This stays one hundred per cent secret, okay?' He stepped closer to the youngest man with a definite air of threat. 'You got that, Jughead? You don't say shit to your mom, you don't say shit to that freckled bitch you think is your girlfriend. Not one fuckin' word to anyone. Okay? *Okay?*'

'Okay,' was the resentful reply.

Miller stayed in his face for a moment, then withdrew. 'You two, stay with her and guard her till the rest of us get back. She's worth a billion bucks, okay? But we gotta follow Loost's rules to get it. So she stays alive, and you keep your hands off of her, Felling,' that last was specifically directed at the man with the moustache, 'until we get her to somewhere with a cell signal. Then?' He grinned without humour. 'We're all rich.' He gestured for the others to descend into the depression. 'I'll be back soon as we deal with the guy. Don't let her go anywhere.'

'We got her, Don,' Felling assured him.

Miller slung his rifle, then boarded his sled and rode off in a spray of snow. The other hunters advanced on Nina, guns at the ready. 'So,' said Felling, with a grin as humourless as his leader's but far more sleazy and unpleasant, 'what we gonna do with you?'

Eddie rode at full pelt through the forest, the sleds powering along in a wide row about fifty metres behind him. That they hadn't caught up made him realise they were herding him. They clearly knew the area. But were they trying to force him somewhere he couldn't escape, like a box canyon or river – or harry him over a cliff?

For now, all he could do was make the most of the gap he was maintaining. From what he'd seen of the mountainscape through the thinning trees, he was heading in roughly the right direction. One of the peaks above the valley with the ski resort had a distinctive profile, and he had spotted it roughly ahead. But when he'd once trekked this way with Charlie, it had been off to the left. When he reached the valley, how much higher up it would he be?

A gunshot warned of more urgent concerns. A look back. One sled had two people aboard, the pillion rider firing his rifle over the other man's shoulder. The rough ride was throwing off his aim, but he might still get lucky. Eddie swerved to put tree trunks between himself and his pursuer, focusing on weaving between the obstacles . . .

Wait – he had *only* seen one snowmobile. Where were the others? And now he realised he could hear just a single engine behind.

The three others had peeled away to his right. He glanced in that direction. The downward slope steepened, his view quickly blocked by trees. Where were they going? Could he take advantage of only having a single sled on his tail?

A new chill, nothing to do with the winter air. He knew the answer: *no*. They had pushed him this way for a reason. The other hunters wouldn't have left him unless they were sure he was about to be driven to them.

Another shot echoed through the forest, reminding him that even the lone sled was still a threat. He rounded a humped mound, seeing more daylight between the trees ahead – then the awful truth was revealed.

The landscape opened out before him. He had reached a cliff-edge, a natural vantage point jutting out into the valley beyond like a battleship's prow. Eroded rock pillars stood beyond its end like gnarled fingers clawing for the sky. The drop was at least sixty feet. Eddie braked, searching for a way down. There was one, a snowy switchback path down a steep slope to the right – which would deliver him to the larger group of hunters. They would either surround him at the bottom, or pick him off before he even reached the ground.

'Bollocks to that,' he growled.

He flicked the snowbike into a sharp half-turn back the way he had come. Better to face two enemies than three. The sled's roar came from the far side of the hump he had just rounded, approaching fast. He judged its direction and speed – then jammed his throttle to full.

The snowbike's motor whined as power surged through it. Eddie raised himself on the footrests, ready to jump off. The bike reached the mound and hurtled up it in a burst of snow, still accelerating – and vaulted into the air from its top. The oncoming sled was exactly where he had predicted, coming right at him. He flung himself sideways from the bike as it arced back down to earth—

The sled's driver had just enough time to begin a shocked scream before the snowbike hit him, its front ski punching through his ribcage with a crack of shattering bone. Even though it was comparatively light compared to a snowmobile, the weight of the bike's batteries knocked him backwards off the saddle, taking the pillion rider with him. Both men hit the ground hard, the snowbike cartwheeling off them and crashing down into the snow. The sled veered crazily to one side, almost tipping over as it continued across the mound – then slammed into a tree, fibreglass bodywork disintegrating.

Eddie was prepared for his landing, immediately rolling as he thumped down on the slope. The moment he stopped, he sprang up. He had dropped the gun during his fall, but it took only a second to spot the angular hole it had made in the snow. He snatched it out and spun to find his targets. One man was dead, the snowbike's severed ski and part of its suspension jutting from his chest. The other, with a red beard, lay groggily beside him. His rifle poked out of the snow like a flagpole a few feet away. He raised his head, saw it, started to crawl towards it—

A hole exploded in his temple, spraying the pristine white around him with vivid red blood and glistening grey brain matter. He flopped face-first into the snow.

Eddie jogged to the corpses. Did they have anything he could use? Not their snowmobile; that was well and truly wrecked, its cargo and equipment including a tow rope and fuel can scattered around it. The impaled rider only had a short-barrelled revolver, inferior to Charlie's weapon. He investigated the rifle. An AR-15, but single-shot only, unlike the one with a full-auto mod that had been fired at him earlier. It might be useful, but he was facing men with equivalent or superior firepower, some of whom had military training. A straight gunfight would not favour him.

But they would soon be coming.

He had to be ready.

Miller caught up with the other hunters at the bottom of the cliff. Smart move to drive their prey to its top, he thought; must have been

Sullivan's idea, as he was the only one apart from himself with enough brains to come up with a plan like that. He regarded the snaking path down the steep slope. It was traversable by a sled if you knew what you were doing, so the smaller electric snowbike shouldn't have any trouble. Which would bring the bald guy right into their sights . . .

He heard Hostetter and Reffitt's snowmobile above. Any second, their target should appear and start down his only escape route. He readied his rifle. Any second—

The engine note suddenly changed, oscillating wildly – then was cut off by an echoing crunch. Sullivan looked at him. 'The fuck was that?'

'They crashed!' Miller said in realisation. 'Something's gone—'

He was interrupted by another sharp sound from higher up: a gunshot. Not a rifle, but a handgun. It could have been Hostetter's pistol, but somehow he knew it wasn't. Nothing but silence followed. 'Shit,' he growled. 'We gotta get back up there. That bastard's killed our guys!'

Nina looked up at the distant sound of a shot. Fear filled her – had Eddie been killed?

Her captors also reacted to the noise. The man with protruding ears – Bobarty, she had heard Felling call him – frowned. 'That weren't no rifle shot.'

'No,' agreed Felling. He turned to Nina. 'The guy with you – who is he?'

'My husband,' she told him. That it had probably been Eddie's gunshot was instantly reassuring. If he only fired once, it generally meant he had no need to do so again.

'He ever in the army?'

'You could say that. The SAS.'

The reputation of the British special forces regiment had reached even to rural upstate New York. Felling's eyes narrowed in momentary concern, before he covered it. 'I supposed to be scared?'

She kept her gaze fixed upon him. 'You tell me.' He was the first to look away.

'Shit, you think her husband killed one of us?' Bobarty asked him. A brief thought, then in a lower voice, 'Hope it was Miller, that son of a bitch.'

'Better not let him hear you say that,' Felling replied. Bobarty glanced around as if afraid that Miller might have materialised behind him. 'Hey, you know, though – if somebody *has* been killed, then . . .' He hesitated, briefly not daring to voice his thought. 'That means more money for the rest of us.'

The younger man's eyes widened. 'Damn, yeah! One billion dollars between seven people is, uh . . .'

Nina instantly had the answer. 'One hundred forty-two million, eight hundred fifty-seven thousand, one hundred forty-two dollars and eighty-five cents. Each.'

They both gawped at her. 'How d'you know that?' asked Felling.

She decided not to tell him the true reason; that one of the quirks of her Atlantean ancestry was an innate skill at mental arithmetic. 'I'm good at math,' she summarised instead.

'So how much would we have gotten between all eight of us?' said Bobarty.

'One hundred twenty-five million dollars each.'

'That's a lot of money,' Felling said, with a small whistle of admiration. 'But we'd get an extra, what, nearly twenty million dollars each if there was only seven of us?' Nina nodded. He scratched his moustache, then almost cautiously enquired, 'So . . . how much more if there was only *six* of us?'

'You'd each get an extra twenty-three million, eight hundred and nine thousand, five hundred twenty-three dollars and eighty-one cents. That's with you all getting a total of one hundred sixty-six million, six hundred sixty-six thousand, six hundred sixty-six dollars and sixty-six cents.'

Bobarty sucked in his lips. 'That's a lot of sixes. Kinda satanic. I don't like that.'

'Maybe, huh-huh,' Felling let out a hesitant little laugh, 'it'd be better if there was only *five* of us left, hey?'

'Then you'd each get two hundred million dollars,' Nina told them. 'And if four of you were gone, then that's two hundred and fifty million each. A quarter of a *billion* dollars.'

She didn't need to explain how they could increase that sum still further. The light of greed in their eyes revealed they had figured it out for themselves.

Four snowmobiles pulled up where the clifftop projected out into the valley. That their quarry had gained the upper hand was instantly obvious to the hunters. Hostetter lay sprawled on his back with a ski sticking almost comically out of his chest. Reffitt was close by, face-down in the snow with a bloody hole in the side of his head. Hostetter's sled was smashed against a tree near a snowy mound.

'Holy shit,' muttered Sullivan. 'He killed 'em *both*?'

'Sure the fuck looks that way,' said Miller darkly. 'Didn't take their guns, though.' Hostetter's pistol and Reffitt's AR-15 had been discarded by their bodies. 'Why not?'

'Maybe he don't need them.'

Miller gave him a sharp look, then unslung his rifle and surveyed his surroundings. Apart from the sled's tracks and the disturbed snow around the bodies, the only trail he could see was a single set of footprints that went to the wrecked vehicle before disappearing into the trees. 'There – that's where he went.' He consulted his mental map of the forest. 'He can't get down the cliff till he reaches the Cones' – a rock formation about half a mile away – 'and if he tries to double back, we'll see his tracks. We can cut him off – then kill the fucker!' Vigorous agreement from his companions. 'Newbold, you come with me. We'll go to the Cones, then if we don't see him, come back. Sully, Webster, go after him on foot so he don't hear you coming. We'll drive him back to you.'

Sullivan and Webster dismounted, the latter putting a hand on the grip of his oversized combat knife. 'If he comes to me,' he said, 'I ain't gonna shoot him. I'm gonna gut the motherfucker!'

'You do that,' said Miller, barely concealing his contempt for the lanky young try-hard. 'Get moving.' He nodded to Newbold. 'Let's round him up.'

The two sleds roared away through the forest. The remaining pair of hunters started to follow the tracks. Sullivan paused as they reached the smashed sled. Hostetter always kept his vehicle equipped for any emergency, something for which his hunting buddies had been grateful if they ran low on gas or needed a tow. The crash had thrown his panniers' contents into the snow – but it looked as if the man they were chasing had picked some of the items up, his footprints darting back and forth before heading away into the woods . . .

'What's up?' Webster asked impatiently.

'Nothing,' Sullivan decided. Their target hadn't taken the dead men's guns, and there wasn't anything on the sled that could be used against them. Besides, with his Browning BPS pump-action shotgun in hand and a dozen extra shells in the webbing on his chest, he felt safe, and certain he could handle any threat. 'Let's find this bastard.'

The two men set off again, ready for action.

12

After a few minutes of yomping through the snow, Sullivan was getting tired and sweaty. 'Hey, hey, hold up,' the overweight man called to Webster.

Webster looked back in annoyance. 'We can't slow down, man. He's getting away!' The snaking trail of footprints continued ahead.

'The others'll drive him back to us.' The two sleds were now some way off, their buzzsaw rasp muted by distance. 'Or they'll catch him. What's your rush?'

'What, you scared?'

'Fuck you, I'm not scared.' Sullivan hefted his shotgun. 'This thing'll rip him apart better than your goddamn Rambo knife.'

'Sure, sure,' was the dismissive reply.

The older man prickled. 'And bringing a knife to a gunfight, you dumbass? He'll shoot you before you're in fifty feet of him.'

'That's why I brought this.' As he waited for Sullivan to catch up, Webster unshouldered his gun, a Sig Sauer Cross Magnum hunting rifle of the latest high-tech design – a far cry from the traditional wooden-stocked firearms of some of the other hunters, and considerably more pricey. 'I'm gonna aim for his legs. Take him down, then . . . *schhhhhhppp.*' He mimed slicing a knife through a downed quarry's torso.

'Yeah, right,' Sullivan muttered, unimpressed. He plodded on for a few more yards – then halted. 'Hey, what the hell?' The running man's tracks divided, one set continuing ahead and the other angling away to their left, away from the cliff.

'He doubled back, trying to trick us,' said Webster, crouching for a closer look. 'See, he's left two lots of prints here. He walked back over his own tracks.'

'Here too,' Sullivan reported. The other set of footprints also had double impressions. 'So which way'd he really go?'

Both men looked. Each line of prints weaved into the trees, quickly disappearing from sight. '*This* is why we needed to move our asses,' said Webster accusingly. 'He already had a couple minutes' head start on us. We gave him time to set this up.'

'Shut the fuck up,' groused Sullivan. 'Okay, you follow those.' He gestured ahead. 'I'll go this way. You see him, shout out.'

'If I see him, you'll hear him scream,' Webster replied, with an unpleasantly wide grin. He jogged away.

'Dickhead,' Sullivan said under his breath. He sometimes wondered how the hunting group stayed together, since everyone in it seemed to despise at least one other member. Love of the sport, he guessed.

He kept walking. The doubled-up footprints couldn't go on for much further, surely; the guy simply hadn't had enough time to get far. The trail deliberately weaved, using trees to obscure where it went. But there was no movement ahead, and now that the sleds had gone, no noise nearby either. Was the guy lying in wait for him?

Sullivan slowed, raising his shotgun. The track curved tightly behind a large tree and a clump of snow-covered bushes. He carefully followed the trail. It would be a good place for an ambush—

He registered an out-of-place scent – sharp, familiar, biting at his nostrils – a split-second before something splashed around his feet. What the hell? He looked down in surprise. The footprints were filled with liquid, a pool of something spreading out across the surrounding virgin snow. He instinctively stepped back before his mind told him what he could smell.

Gasoline.

He looked up again in shock—

A figure in a black leather jacket darted out from behind the tree, swinging a plastic fuel canister with the top crudely sawn off. Its contents dashed against Sullivan in a stinging, choking spray.

The hunter staggered, blinded as the gas bit his eyes. He instinctively pulled his shotgun's trigger. The weapon boomed, fragmented bark spitting back at him as the blast hit the tree. He didn't know if he'd caught his attacker. Desperately wiping his face, he tried to open his eyes—

Another sense gave him a warning as he heard a sound. A popping crack, then a rasp like a giant match being struck – followed by the sizzling ignition of a road flare—

Flames erupted around him as Eddie tossed the flare into the pool of fuel. Sullivan screamed as searing heat surged up his gasoline-drenched outer clothing, his hair catching light and skin crisping. He reeled, a flailing human torch – then the shotgun shells on his chest detonated, a storm of red-hot lead pellets ripping open his torso as if a landmine had exploded inside it.

Eddie had ducked back behind the tree to throw the flare, protected from the inferno and the shell shrapnel. A small branch-cutting hacksaw from the snowmobile had carved open the fuel can. He leaned out to see the results of his handiwork. Satisfied, he hurried on, ready for his next target.

The shotgun blast told Webster he had followed the wrong set of tracks. The scream that followed revealed Sullivan had not taken down his prey. The younger man turned and raced through the forest towards the sound – which was cut off abruptly by another, louder detonation.

He soon saw where Sullivan was. Fire danced across the snowy ground. Suddenly scared, Webster slowed and snapped up his rifle, quickly scanning the trees ahead. Only flames were moving. Still wary, he reached the blaze. Sullivan's body was a crumpled, blackened mass inside a swirling column of orange and yellow, dark smoke gushing up into the snowy foliage above. 'Shit,' he hissed, on full, nervous alert. The bald guy had now killed three of the group. He had no intention of letting that number rise to four.

The tree closest to the burning corpse had a chunk blown out of its trunk. A shotgun, at very close range. Was the bald guy hiding behind it?

Trying to control his fear, Webster sidestepped to look around it, rifle raised. There was nobody there. But the tracks continued deeper into the woods. He checked them. Only one set of footprints. No doubling-back here, no attempt at deception. His target was running.

And he'd been hurt.

Webster felt a sudden thrill. Red spots were clear on the snow along the trail. Sullivan must have hit him!

He hurried along the tracks, seeing more dots of blood as he went. That meant an open wound, bleeding heavily. Webster had shot and wounded deer before; if there was this much blood, they wouldn't get far. The same would be true for the man they were hunting. He would get the kill. And then . . . a split of one billion dollars would be his.

He slowed, seeing the trail go behind a tree. A bigger patch of red came into view. There was something on the ground in the middle of it. He cautiously approached. A plastic bottle, its cap missing. More red liquid stained the snow around it.

Not stained. It was *melting* the snow. He realised what was in the bottle.

Antifreeze—

A noose dropped over his head from above, flopping onto his shoulders – then was savagely yanked tight around his neck.

Eddie dropped through the tree's branches in a shower of dislodged snow, his body's weight pulling down the nylon tow rope he had looped over a higher limb. The skinny Webster shot upwards with a choked gasp of pain, limbs thrashing. He hurtled up through the foliage – then his head struck the branch with a dull crack, the noose digging deep into the soft tissues of his throat and crushing his larynx. The Yorkshireman landed and gave the rope a final hard yank, then let go. Webster crashed back to earth, legs buckling beneath him. Eddie was ready to finish him off, but he was already dead, neck broken, skull fractured, eyes and tongue bulging sickeningly from his lifeless face.

Eddie picked up Webster's rifle. The long bolt-action Sig Sauer was a good choice for hunting, if more showy and expensive than some equally capable alternatives, but too awkward and slow-firing for his situation. That said, if, or more likely when, the other hunters came back on their sleds to investigate the gunfire, he might have a chance to use it. On an impulse he pulled Webster's combat knife from its sheath. Another fancy, expensive weapon. Like the Sig, it was oversized for its purpose, more about show – or compensation – than practicality—

A rising roar caught his attention. The other hunters were indeed returning. Would he have time to set up an ambush with the rifle?

No. The two snowmobiles had separated, approaching on parallel courses. The trees here were dense enough that by the time he'd locked onto one hunter, the other would be almost upon him. He needed to find cover—

The threat was closer than he'd thought. One of the snowmobiles exploded into view, vaulting over a hump in a shower of snow. The rider, a man wearing thick-framed glasses, spotted Eddie and swerved towards him.

Eddie was about to drop the idiotic Rambo knife and take a shot with the rifle when gunfire echoed through the forest. The branches above him jolted, showering him with snow and fragmented pine needles. He ducked behind the trunk. The other hunter, the man with the modified AR-15, had spotted him through the trees and slowed enough to take a full-auto snapshot.

If he stayed where he was, the guy with glasses would have a clear firing angle in seconds. He had to find a better position, fast.

THE SHROUD OF HADES

He raised the Cross Magnum and leaned out to take a snapshot of his own at the leader. Even shooting one-handed, the bullet passed close enough to make the oncoming man react in alarm and steer sharply behind the protection of a tree. That gave him a few moments of safety – from one opponent, at least.

The other, he still had to deal with.

Eddie broke from cover and ran, snow kicking up around his feet as he raced between the conifers. The second hunter, Newbold, angled to follow, but his rifle was still on his shoulder. He skidded the sled to a stop and jumped off, bringing his weapon to bear as he lumbered after the Englishman. 'C'mere, you fucker!' he shouted, unleashing a shot. It cracked against a tree trunk as Eddie disappeared behind it. A rapid tug at his rifle's bolt, and a new round was chambered. 'Get your ass back here!'

Newbold stomped after his quarry. The bald man's footprints curved around a large tree – but something was leaning against it. Newbold saw as he approached that it was Webster's fancy rifle. Part of his mind told him to ignore it and keep pursuing his prey – but it *was* worth something like fifteen hundred dollars, and Webster didn't need it any more. If he knocked it into the snow so Miller didn't see and lay claim to it, he could collect it later . . .

He slowed, bending slightly to swat the rifle's barrel and tip it over—

Eddie whirled out from behind the tree and stabbed the razor-sharp combat knife into the side of his throat with such force that it went fully through, its point slamming an inch deep into the wood. Newbold slumped, but didn't fall, held up by the blade transfixing his neck. Blood bubbled from his mouth as he tried to scream, the snow around his limp feet turning red. His rifle dropped to the ground.

The wooden-bodied weapon was shorter and more practical than the Sig Sauer. Eddie crouched to pick it up—

More bullets spat from Miller's AR-15, cracking against the tree trunk above Eddie's head and smacking wetly into Newbold's body.

The leader of the hunters was riding towards him at full speed, bracing his rifle on the sled's windscreen as he fired. That he was shooting left-handed while bounding over the bumpy ground didn't make him any less dangerous; he was spraying rounds on full-auto, hoping the sheer volume of lead in the air would hit his target.

Eddie dived back behind the tree. The gunfire stopped. But it would resume the moment Miller saw him again. Both rifles were still in the snow at Newbold's feet. If Eddie reached for them, he would be exposed. He needed better cover. There was a large rock between a couple of younger trees about ten feet away. He drew Charlie's pistol from inside his leather jacket, fired a single round in the sled's general direction – then ran.

His suppressing shot did its job. The rifle fire didn't restart – at least until he was almost at the snow-covered stone. He threw himself headlong over it as another burst of bullets seared after him—

A scrubby, snow-covered bush lay behind the rock.

Eddie threw up both arms to shield his eyes as he landed on it, branches cracking explosively beneath him. The bush's gnarled bole struck below his heart like a punch. Gasping, he hit the ground and rolled, smashed wood and snow scattering over him.

He clutched at his chest, trying to overcome the pain. The sled was still closing. He sat up to target it—

The gun wasn't in his hand.

Eddie hurriedly looked around. Where was it? Somewhere inside the bush. He pulled its branches apart, searching for a telltale glint of metal. Nothing.

The snowmobile howled into view, rounding a clutch of trees. Eddie ran as the AR-15 swung towards him—

Two rapid shots, the bullets tearing through the bush – then the firing stopped. The hunter's magazine was empty. He couldn't reload while riding.

Instead he revved his engine and powered towards the Yorkshireman.

Eddie heard the sled racing up behind him. A split-second glance to judge its distance – then he hurled himself sidelong as the powerful little vehicle roared past. Miller yanked hard at the handlebars, bringing the snowmobile around a tree in a tight, slithering loop. The engine revved to full power again. Glaring headlights pinned Eddie as he sprang back up—

His foot caught something hidden under the snow.

It wasn't much, a stone that shifted with the contact – but it was enough to affect his balance. By the time he caught himself, the sled was upon him—

The snowmobile's streamlined prow struck his leg. He spun and fell. It rushed past again, its spiked tread spraying him with snow.

Miller made another skidding turn. He grinned as he saw the downed man. A hard squeeze of the throttle lever, and he surged forward to mow down his target—

Eddie snatched up the stone he had tripped on – and hurled it at the oncoming rider.

One hand on the handlebars, the other still holding his rifle, Miller had no way to deflect it. The brick-sized rock smashed into his face. He fell backwards from the sled, landing hard. The snowmobile veered, missing Eddie by inches and crashing into a tree behind him, one of its front skis buckling underneath the bodywork.

Breathing heavily, Eddie got up. Pain surged through his leg where the sled had hit him. It wasn't broken; he could still walk, though running might be harder. Where was the hunter?

The bearded man was sprawled on his back. His face was smeared with blood from a broken nose. But while he was down, he was far from out. He still had his rifle – and was fumbling for a new magazine.

Eddie knew he couldn't reach him before he reloaded – not on foot. But the sled was only a couple of metres away—

One ski was broken. But that didn't matter. He wasn't going forwards.

He vaulted onto the snowmobile's seat and mashed his thumb onto the engine reverse button on the left handlebar. The idling motor all but stopped for a moment, then resumed – a jolt confirming that the crankshaft's rotation had reversed. He looked back. Miller had found a magazine, pulling the empty one from the rifle's receiver.

Eddie jammed the throttle to full.

The sudden rearwards acceleration almost threw him over the windscreen. A grinding rattle came from the sled's prow as the broken ski was dragged along beneath it, but with the track now pulling the vehicle it barely affected the steering. All Eddie had to do was use the handlebars to hold the speeding sled on course . . .

Miller slammed the replacement magazine into place and yanked on the charging handle. He twisted onto his side, rifle rising—

His snowmobile's spiked tread rolled right over his head.

Eddie braked as hard as he could. The sudden stop threw his full weight down onto the saddle, and Miller. A choked shriek came from beneath the sled. The Englishman reversed the engine again, then revved to full power – and released the brakes. The track whirled madly before finding grip, throwing the snowmobile forwards again – and kicking up a spray of red-mottled snow behind it. The gory shower splattered down in a fan on the virgin white behind the thrashing man, who was now trying to scream without a face, or even a lower jaw.

'Think you shaved a bit close there, mate,' said Eddie as he dismounted. The dying man had dropped the rifle as impossible agony consumed his senses. Eddie picked it up and quickly checked it. A full load of thirty rounds in the mag. Just as illegal in New York State as the full-auto modification. 'I won't tell the cops if you don't,' he said to Miller, then started back along the sled's tracks as quickly as he could on his aching leg.

He had to find Nina before the remaining hunters realised their companions were dead.

13

Bobarty peered nervously into the forest, weapon readied. A few minutes had passed since the last cracks of gunfire echoed through the snowy trees, followed only by a heavy silence. 'What do you think happened?' he finally asked Felling.

'Dunno. But I don't like it,' the older man replied. He also had his gun raised, though he kept it pointed at Nina. 'Can't hear any sleds.'

'He can't have killed them *all*!' protested Bobarty, before giving the redhead a worried look and adding: 'Can he?'

Nina gave him a shrug that appeared a lot more insouciant than she felt. 'Maybe. I mean, he's killed a lot of people.'

'How many?'

'How should I know? I don't keep count. And he's probably *lost* count.'

Bobarty's mood was not improved by learning that. He paced anxiously up to the rim of the depression, staring into the woods for any sign of movement. Felling watched him, almost calculatingly, then turned back to Nina. 'So what's your deal, anyhow?' he asked. 'Why *are* you worth a billion dollars?'

'You don't know?'

'Don phoned, said he was rounding up a hunting party and that we needed to get up to the Limey's cabin. Said you had a bounty on you, and if we caught you we could collect. He didn't mention how *big* the bounty was at first, the sumbitch.' A sarcastic sneer. 'I don't have Uzz on my phone, so I didn't know what all this was about until someone told me on the way up here.'

'You don't use Uzz?' said Nina, sensing an opportunity – if she could play it correctly.

'Nah. That crap's for kids. Whenever I have mine, they just spend the whole time staring at their phones. Ungrateful little . . .' His words trailed off into an unintelligible mutter.

'But your pal there,' she indicated Bobarty, 'I bet he uses Uzz, doesn't he?'

A dismissive nod as Felling lowered his voice. 'He ain't really my pal. He only hangs out with us 'cause he's a buddy of Reffitt's brother. Reason he's riding my sled with me is 'cause he's *too poor* to afford his own.' That last was louder, intended for Bobarty to hear.

Bobarty shot him an irate look. 'Yeah, well, when we collect the bounty, I'll be able to buy any goddamn thing I want, won't I?'

That was Nina's opening. 'You say, "when *we* collect the bounty" – but only one of you will be able to, won't you? You have to do it through Uzz. Which means only you,' she indicated the younger man, 'can claim it. The billion dollars goes to your Uzz account.'

Felling stared at her, mouth half-open as he took the revelation on board, then he stepped towards Bobarty. 'Hey! That true?'

'I guess,' Bobarty replied. He turned away from the forest – subtly bringing his gun towards Felling.

'So how do I get my share?' The man in the blue cap saw the movement and shifted so his own weapon was pointed roughly in his companion's direction.

'I transfer it to you, of course. Why, don't you trust me?' There was now growing hostility in both men's eyes as they locked gazes.

'Transferring half a billion dollars to a regular bank account will draw a lot of attention,' Nina pointed out. She surreptitiously looked for a spot where she could dive flat if – or *when* – anything kicked off. 'The cops and FBI will want to know where it came from. It's only untraceable as long as it stays in Uzz.'

Felling's voice became a low rumble. 'But I don't have Uzz.'

'That ain't my problem,' said Bobarty.

'It's a problem to me.' Nina saw Felling's fingers tighten around his gun's grip. She tensed, ready to drop. 'I ain't letting you run off with the full billion dollars and leave me in the shit!'

Bobarty's eyes narrowed. Nina guessed he was trying to devise a response, but the sudden rush of his fight-or-flight instinct kicking in had disrupted his thoughts. 'Yeah, well, I—'

He snapped his gun towards Felling and fired.

Felling did the same to him – a millisecond later. Bobarty's bullet hit him just as he pulled the trigger. Nina flung herself to the ground as a hole was punched through Felling's coat over his ample midsection, a pencil-thin jet of rich blood spouting out. He staggered backwards, letting out an awful keening shriek before collapsing heavily onto his back.

But Bobarty did not come out unscathed. The bullet impact had thrown Felling off-target – but not by much. The round clipped the younger man's waist, tearing through his flesh. He howled in pain, clutching at the raw wound.

Nina raised her head. Both her captors were incapacitated. She rose and pounded up the slope. She could take one of the sleds and escape—

A gunshot boomed behind her. Snow spat into her face as a bullet hit the rise ahead. 'H-hold it!' cried Bobarty, in more of a hoarse squawk than a shout. 'Get back here! Get fucking back!'

She stopped and turned. Bobarty's left elbow was pressed against his wounded side, forcing him to hold his rifle awkwardly – but it was still aimed at her. 'That's right,' he said, voice strained. 'You stay right there. God fucking damn!' He gave Felling an angry look. The other man was still alive, but from his feeble convulsions as blood pooled in the snow around him was not far from death. 'You shot me, you bastard! I can't believe you fucking shot me!'

'He probably thought the same about you,' said Nina.

'You shut the fuck up!' He painfully waddled towards her. 'Okay. I want my billion dollars, and then I'm gonna get to a hospital, and then I'm gonna disappear. You're gonna drive the sled, and I'll be right behind you with my gun in your back. You drive to somewhere with a cell signal. Okay?'

She gave him a mocking look. 'Not okay, actually. You're going to kill me once you do that, so why should I help you?'

''Cause if you don't, I'm gonna shoot you in both feet, then truss you up like a ten-point buck and sling you over the back of the sled.' He waved his gun at her lower legs for emphasis. 'I can drive one-handed if I got to.'

'I'm sure you do a lot of things one-handed,' she muttered.

'I – I ain't joking around!' he snapped, spittle flying from his mouth. 'You get your ass on the sled or there's gonna be shooting—'

One side of his head blew out in a slurry of shredded brain matter and shattered bone.

Bobarty toppled sidelong to the ground, slithering a few feet down the slope before coming to rest. Nina flinched in shock, but overcame her horror almost at once. She turned, seeing Eddie through the trees about a hundred yards away, a rifle raised to his shoulder. 'Eddie!' she called, waving.

'Are there any more of them?' he shouted back.

'No.' Felling had by now stopped moving.

Her husband quickly came through the forest to meet her. 'Are you all right?'

'Yeah. Shaken, but I'm okay. Jesus!' She felt suddenly tired, drained. 'Can we get out of here?'

Eddie nodded towards the sleds. 'Looks like it.'

They trudged to the waiting vehicles. Nina noticed he was walking stiffly. 'Are *you* okay?'

'I'll survive. Important thing is that you're in one piece.'

He took the driver's seat on one of the sleds, Nina taking the pillion position behind. 'Eddie, it's just as important to me that *you're* in one piece. I can't do this without you. I . . . wouldn't *want* to do this without you. I couldn't.'

He didn't immediately look back at her. 'So long as you stay alive, then I've done my job. You matter more than me, love.'

'No, I don't.' She jabbed him in the back. 'Where did *that* come from?'

Now he turned his head. 'Nothing. Doesn't matter. Besides, we're both still alive, and I mean that to carry on for a while yet.'

'A few decades, I would hope.'

'Yeah.' Something was on his mind, she could tell. But before she could ask more about it, he started the snowmobile, revving the engine loudly and powering away into the forest.

By following the hunters' tracks, Eddie found his way to the edge of the valley without trouble, this time emerging below the cliff on which he had been trapped earlier. He stopped to get his bearings. 'There it is,' he told Nina, pointing down the valley. The ski resort was visible in the distance, the white lines of its numerous runs cutting through the surrounding forest.

'Great,' said Nina, but she was distracted by a feature not far above their position. A line of rock pillars extended out into the valley beyond the jutting cliff. 'Fingers . . .'

'What?'

'They look like fingers, reaching out of the ground.'

Eddie looked for himself. 'Suppose they do, a bit.'

He was about to ride on, but she continued, still gazing up at the eroded spires. 'They reminded me of my notes about the Shroud of Hades. The part about his fingers reaching up into the sky. Maybe that's one of the clues to the location – it has rock formations which look like those.'

Eddie shrugged. 'They just make me think of that Bond film.'

'Which Bond film?'

'*For Your Eyes Only*. There's a monastery or something on top of a big rock pillar like one of those. Roger Moore has to climb up to it, and almost gets kicked off the top.'

'A monastery – wait, which country was this in?'

He thought for a moment. 'Greece.'

'You're sure?'

She couldn't keep the sudden excitement from her voice. Eddie eyed her. 'Ay up. Now what've you figured out?'

'A Greek monastery on top of a rock pillar? It has to be Meteora! I've never been there, but my mom and dad once did; they had photos. And, and . . .' Her mind was already working faster than her ability to speak. 'It fits with some of the other information from the records as well. It was at the western edge of ancient Thessaly, and hermits lived in the caves before the monasteries were built. The Underworld could be there! And if it is, then the Shroud of Hades could be too!'

Eddie was silent for a moment – then his expression creased into one of gentle mockery. 'So do you want to book a flight to Greece?'

She almost said yes, before realising he was not serious. 'Well, it's not a priority right now,' she admitted. 'But it's something! It narrows down the search, by a lot. And if I can find one of these things before anyone else, I could find others. So . . .' His smile slowly widened, which experience told her presaged a sarcastic comment. 'But, yeah, *okay*, it can wait.'

'Good,' he replied, smirking. 'All right, let's get to this ski resort and work out what to do next. For starters, we need to get you some kind of disguise. We don't need anyone else recognising you and kicking this whole bloody thing off again.'

'I'll just pop into the resort's disguise shop, then.'

He chuckled. 'You're feeling a bit better if you can get snarky with me.'

Nina grinned. 'You're either saving my life or driving me nuts. Those seem to be my two states of existence with you.'

'Happy to do both, love.' He leaned back to kiss her, which she gratefully returned, then took the controls again. 'Let's go and buy you some really giant sunglasses.'

***

In his cabin, Charlie Brooks struggled to break free from his bonds. The hunters had all ridden away after Eddie and his wife, leaving him alone – which in some ways was a relief, as they clearly hadn't come to borrow a cup of sugar. But he could have persuaded them to untie him. Eddie might be a blunt instrument and not as smart as he liked to think, but in particular areas he was an expert, and one of those areas was securing prisoners in ways that even Harry Houdini would have trouble escaping.

The rope was gradually loosening, though. Even in his barely conscious state, he had thought to clench his fists while Eddie was tying his arms, expanding his wrists by a couple of millimetres as his tendons bulged – just enough to give him literal wiggle room. He twisted his hands back and forth, gradually slipping the bindings over his skin. Another few minutes, and they should be slack enough for him to get loose . . .

A sound. The motion sensors. He froze. Were the hunters coming back?

But it wasn't the harsh buzz of snowmobiles he soon heard. Instead it was the low rumble of large V8s. At least two, perhaps even three. Suddenly worried, he doubled his efforts. One set of unexpected visitors was bad enough, but a second set so soon after could only mean serious trouble.

He felt the rope shift ever so slightly with each twist. The vehicles stopped outside the cabin. Come on, get loose, come *on*—

The door opened.

He blinked at the sudden flare of light. Men stood silhouetted in the doorway. Charlie knew instantly he was in grave danger. The mere way the new arrivals held themselves warned him they were prepared both to encounter violence and to deliver it. As a professional himself, he knew others in his line of business when he saw them. Mercenaries. He guessed they were after Nina – but who had hired them? And how had they got here so fast?

Two of the dark-clad men advanced, revealing they held guns.

They swept into the room to check for other occupants. Satisfied that the man tied on the floor was alone, they quickly went to search the rest of the cabin. Behind them, a third man entered. Charlie sensed a different air to him. He was as dangerous as his companions, a hulking and powerful gorilla compared to the lean panthers with him. But he didn't seem to be the group's leader – none of his companions deferred to him. Not the client, then. So who?

The man halted in front of Charlie, looking down at him. Light from a window caught something on his throat – no, *in* it, Charlie realised. He'd had surgery, and very recently from the skin's residual redness, to implant an object. A mechanical larynx? He'd met a couple of men who needed them after receiving combat injuries. But this looked smaller, more high-tech—

The man spoke. 'You must be Charlie.' Not a mechanical larynx; there was none of their robotic buzz. But there was still a definite artificial quality to his voice. The accent was English, either upper-class or affected as such. 'I assume Eddie Chase got the better of you. It's an annoying habit of his, isn't it?'

'How do you know who I am?' Charlie demanded. He did not trust his unwanted houseguest one inch. 'And how do you know Eddie?'

'When you tagged Nina Wilde on Uzz, it provided us with all your personal information. A surprising amount, actually. People just don't appreciate the risks of using social media. As for Chase . . .' The man pointed to the device implanted in his neck. 'I've had a prior run-in with him. It got me this. Well, it got me a much older and cheaper version of this, since the British government wasn't willing to spend any more on me than absolutely necessary. But my new benefactor has money to spare on the very latest speech-synthesis technology. Actually, all his money is technically now to spare, since he's dead.'

Charlie frowned. 'You're working for Loost?'

A nod. 'My associates here are a kind of cleanup crew. Their job is to make sure Nina Wilde really is dead and assist her killer with anything they need. Although things haven't quite worked out on that front, have they? She and Chase have killed one would-be executioner and subdued another already.'

'Two executioners,' Charlie corrected. 'Someone attacked them at their flat. He's dead.'

The man tutted. 'That's what happens when amateurs play against professionals. But the question is, Charlie . . . why aren't *you* dead? Chase is not a man known for mercy – especially to anyone who threatens his family.'

The men who had gone to search the cabin returned. 'It's empty,' one reported to another of the group who had been holding back at the door. He was older than the others, hair greying. Charlie took him to be the leader.

The man nodded, then addressed his team. 'We need to move on. Be ready for the next time Wilde is tagged.'

'I suspect Charlie here might have an inkling where they've gone,' said the British man. 'This is his cabin; he must know the area.' He crouched lower. 'Any suggestions before we leave?'

Charlie hesitated before answering. He had destroyed their friendship, but Eddie hadn't killed him, an act of generosity he wasn't sure he would have returned if the situations had been reversed. It was a debt that deserved to be repaid. 'No idea,' he said. 'Plenty of places they could go from here.'

The man with the artificial voice box regarded him emotionlessly, then stood. 'I'm sure we'll find them soon enough. They left a trail, after all.' He turned as if to leave, then paused. 'By the way, you didn't answer my question. Why didn't Chase kill you?'

'We were friends,' Charlie told him. 'Although I doubt he'll be inviting me to his birthday party after today.'

'Oh, I'm certain of that.' Even though his voice was synthetic, a malevolent coldness became clear within it. The Londoner realised to his horror that he was about to die. 'Any friend of Eddie Chase's, present or former, is no friend of mine. And people who are not my friends *don't live very long!*'

A sudden mad fury surged through him – and he snatched out a gun and fired five shots into Charlie's chest.

Steinitz hurriedly gestured for the other mercenaries to stand down as they reacted to the unexpected gunfire. He moved to stand beside John Brice, looking down at the bound corpse. 'Was that necessary?'

'Oh, absolutely,' Brice replied, breathing heavily as he recovered control. 'I'm here to drive Chase along, yes? Be the scary bogeyman from his past who's always right behind him so he doesn't have time to think? Well, learning that the friend he spared is now very much dead – and you should use the satellite phone to inform the authorities of that as soon as you can, by the way – will horrify him. As soon as he realises I was responsible, he'll become angry. And angry men make mistakes.'

The German gave him a sidelong look. 'Indeed they do.'

Brice smiled mockingly. 'Don't worry, I keep my anger on a tight leash. I only use it when I need it.' The smile tightened, becoming more cruel. 'And I'll need it for my reunion with Eddie Chase.'

Steinitz said nothing, instead leaving the cabin and signalling for the others to follow. Brice remained still, surveying the room with a professional eye. Had the fugitives left some clue to their next move?

His gaze fell on a couple of sheets of notepaper on the floor. He picked them up. A woman's writing; neat, rounded. Nina Wilde's. The subject matter confirmed it. Archaeology and mythology, an apparent attempt to recall and summarise more detailed notes to which she no longer had access. She really was obsessive; even with her life in danger, she couldn't stop working . . .

Brice skimmed through the pages. They concerned some ancient artefact potentially located in Greece. Nothing relevant to the current situation. They did, however, give him a strange feeling of *connection* to his prey, as if he might follow their trail like a bloodhound. Almost without thinking, he sniffed the papers, then folded and pocketed them and followed Steinitz and the others outside. Three Cadillac Escalade SUVs equipped with snow chains were parked by the other two vehicles. The group broke up, four men getting into the two rear Cadillacs, three in the first. Brice sat with Steinitz in the back of the leading luxury off-roader. 'So, let's see where Chase and Wilde might have gone,' he said.

Steinitz brought up a map on the screen mounted in the back of the driver's headrest. 'There is a ski resort here,' the German said thoughtfully, indicating an icon not far from their current position. 'Could they reach it?'

'Easily,' was Brice's opinion. 'I doubt it would take more than thirty minutes on a snowmobile.'

'If they haven't been caught first. There were tracks at the gate from at least five sleds. Some of them were deeper; they were carrying two people.'

Brice smiled humourlessly. 'I'd put decent odds on Chase against a bunch of yokel hunters.'

'You think he is that good?'

'I know how good *I* am. And he still got the better of me. Never underestimate him – or Wilde, for that matter. They haven't survived a ridiculous number of life-threatening incidents simply by luck.'

'Luck does not last for ever,' was the mercenary leader's pointed reply. 'But I will take your . . . *caution* under advisement.' He looked back at the map. 'There is no direct route. We will have to go back down to the road in the valley, then along it to here.' He pointed out the foot of another winding road, this one leading to the ski resort. A few taps on the screen, and the GPS provided more information. 'Twelve miles – nineteen kilometres. Much longer for us than them.'

'Once we get back on paved roads, we'll be fine,' Brice assured him. 'We'll be half an hour behind them, if that.' He leaned back in his seat, addressing the driver. 'Let's go.'

The driver glanced at Steinitz in the mirror, who nodded. The Escalade made a wide loop in front of the cabin to head back to the gate, its sister vehicles following.

Brice watched the snow-laden trees roll past on each side of the trail. After two weeks of waiting, two weeks of intensive training to bring himself back to peak fitness . . . the hunt had begun in earnest.

And he would have revenge most delicious against Eddie Chase.

14

The Elise Creek ski resort was a relatively new destination for winter sports enthusiasts, its slopes radiating outwards from a central cluster of buildings like the dust-coated arms of a spider's web. Along with the cars, pickups and SUVs in the parking lot, there were also several snowmobiles; trail riding was one of the activities on offer. Eddie halted his and Nina's sled beside them. 'Well, we're here,' said the redhead, with relief. Even in her coat, the cold was biting, and though he hadn't admitted to it she had felt him shivering. 'What now?'

'First thing we do is get inside and warm up,' her husband replied, dismounting. 'I'm freezing my fucking nuts off!'

'Delicately put, as always.'

He grinned. 'Then we get something to disguise you. After that, we need some hot food, and somewhere quiet where we can check the news. I want to see if the cops are after us.'

Nina surveyed the nearby buildings. Several appeared dedicated to accommodation, but one long wooden structure looked to be a commercial hub, with outdoor terraces where she could see people eating and drinking. This early in the season, the place was not especially busy, most visitors taking opportunistic advantage of the early snowfall. That was reassuring; the fewer people here, the less chance of her being recognised and tagged on Uzz. 'And after that?'

An unhappy shrug. 'Buggered if I know. But we can't trust *anyone*.' Eddie shook his head. 'Charlie. I can't believe it . . .'

Nina squeezed his hand in reassurance. 'Hey. We're still alive, and nobody knows we're here. We just need to keep moving until we can find somewhere safe to hide out.'

'Yeah, but where?' He surveyed the resort as if hoping an answer would present itself, then exhaled heavily. 'All right. Let's buy you a nice hat.'

The hat, when Eddie returned to her, was not one Nina would have chosen herself. 'What the hell's this?' she protested. It was big and brightly coloured, with a pointed top and large ear flaps. 'Did you get me a clown suit as well?'

'People'll be looking at the hat and not your face,' Eddie pointed out. 'Got you some sunglasses too.' He reached into a shopping bag and handed her a large aviator-style pair with reflective, blue-tinted lenses. 'Hopefully they'll cover you enough so nobody can tag you with their phone, but if you keep your hair tucked up inside the hat no one should look at you in the first place.'

She rolled up her ponytail and pushed it up against the back of her head before donning the hat over it. 'Are you saying that now I'm in my fifties, I won't catch anyone's eye any more?'

'Any bloke looks at you like that, I'll deck 'em.' They both smiled. 'All right. Try the bins.'

She put on the sunglasses. Eddie regarded her approvingly. 'I don't think anyone'll look at you and go, "Hey, that mouth looks like Nina Wilde's!" You look like a proper ski babe.'

'Why, thank you,' she said, peering coquettishly at him over the top of her new glasses. 'What else did you buy?'

He held up the bag. 'Warmer stuff for both of us – jumpers, gloves, stuff like that. It'll stop us from freezing when we have to move again.'

Nina sighed, the moment of levity past. 'To where?'

'Let's see if we can work that out. You hungry?' She had waited for him in a quiet corner of the long building's lobby, pretending to read a tourist brochure. He gestured towards a flight of stairs. 'My treat.' Another small smile, then they set off together.

The upper floor was home to a restaurant and a couple of bars. Nina and Eddie found a table by a window in one of the latter, Nina sitting with her back to the rest of the room. She looked out at the valley below while waiting for him to order food at the bar, watching skiers and snowboarders start their descents of the lower slopes and more visitors driving up the winding access road. It was not currently snowing, though heavy clouds uphill suggested more would come.

'Ay up,' said Eddie, returning and sitting facing her. 'Don't look now, but you're on TV.' He glanced towards a muted television mounted on a wall. Nina followed his gaze, to her alarm seeing a photograph of herself. The chyron read ATLANTIS DISCOVERER HUNTED.

She hastily looked away. 'Oh, great. Just what I need, people being reminded what I look like.'

'I checked my phone while I was at the bar. The cops *are* looking for us; turns out even if you leave a note saying exactly what happened, they still want to have words with you after two of their own get killed.'

'They'll want to question you about all those dead hunters, too,' said Nina gloomily. 'Anything else?'

He shook his head. 'Nowt useful. Main thing is that nobody knows we're here. Though seeing how close this is to Charlie's, probably won't be long before someone thinks to check it.' He looked over his shoulder at the vista outside. 'If the cops come up the road we'll have a bit of warning, but we should still think about moving as soon as we can.'

'Same question as before: to where? Do you know anyone else we could go to?'

'No. And even if I did, I can't risk 'em selling us out. Friendship's worth a lot less than a billion dollars, it looks like.' His shoulders sagged, deflated, then he looked up as a waitress bearing a tray arrived. Nina averted her face as their large plates were put down. 'Thanks.'

Like the hat, the food was not what Nina would have picked for herself, but right now a hot, high-calorie meal of burger and fries was probably what her body needed, both to recover from what she had been through and to prepare for whatever else might lie ahead. They ate quickly, not talking much. It was only when Eddie noticed something on the television that conversation resumed. 'It's her again. Loost's nurse.'

Nina looked around, recognising the woman from news broadcasts on previous days. 'They're repeating her interview? You'd think they had enough new material to fill an hour, what with, y'know, the world's top archaeologist having a billion-dollar bounty put on her head by a dead trillionaire whose private space station just burned up.'

'No, this one must be new. Every other time I've seen her, she was inside.' Natalie Bachand was on a snowy street, a microphone held in front of her as she spoke to an off-camera interviewer.

'Maybe they're asking if she knows anything else about what Loost was planning,' said Nina between mouthfuls. 'I mean, she must have been with him when he was setting everything up. She—' She froze, her fork halfway to her mouth.

Eddie also paused. 'What?'

'She might not have known what Loost was planning – but she could know who he was planning it *with*,' she said, speaking more quickly as her mind whirled into analytical action. 'She was up there in orbit with him the whole time, and he *must* have spoken directly to his inside man at Uzz to have set everything up. You don't arrange something this complicated by text message. She might know who it is!'

He nodded. 'And she's pissed off at Loost for not leaving her anything after he knocked her up. She could be willing to tell you.'

'Maybe. But where is she? Can we get to her?'

'She's in Canada, I think. Hold on.' Eddie checked his phone. As ever, personal information about people who had featured in the media was not hard to find. 'Yeah, she lives in Montreal.'

'That's right over the border!' The Canadian city was only around twenty-five miles beyond the northern edge of New York State. 'We could drive there in a couple of hours.'

'If we had a car,' he reminded her.

'It's worth trying. Uzz can end this whole thing if they know who hacked them.'

'As long as whoever did it's still working for them. What if they took Loost's money and buggered off to Bali?'

'Then a flight to somewhere sunny beginning with B might be in order. But Montreal will be a lot easier to start with.'

'Just one problem with that, love – we'll have to sneak across the border. If we go through a customs post, they'll arrest us, or at least hold us for questioning.'

'So we sneak across. It's the world's longest unfenced border – how hard can it be?'

Eddie laughed – with enough sarcasm to make Nina's face fall. 'It's unfenced, yeah, but it's not unguarded. I did some research about it for a job a few years back – with Charlie, ironically. It's five and a half thousand miles long, but every inch of it's monitored one way or another. Sensors, drones, planes, patrols . . . If a kid on the Canadian side accidentally kicks a football over the line, someone'll turn up to pop it. Probably with a bullet.'

'Oh. So it's impossible?'

He grinned. 'I didn't say that. I told you, I researched it. There are ways. They're risky, but we can probably do it.'

'Only "probably"?'

'Better than "maybe". Or "nnrgh, I'unno?"' He mimed an exaggerated shrug, then raised his phone again. 'I'll check the map. There were some places upstate that might be good options.'

'Just give me time to finish my food, okay?' She resumed eating as Eddie assessed possible crossing points, her gaze drifting to the slopes again. People in brightly coloured coats glided down them on skis and boards. From here their journeys looked serene, but she knew from experience it was a bumpy and energetic experience. The thought brought Macy back to her mind; the family had taken a vacation at a ski resort a couple of years prior. Should she call her again? The idea of asking for her help was one she had resisted earlier, but after Charlie's betrayal, her daughter was now the only person other than Eddie she could completely trust . . .

Something brought her attention back to the vista beyond the windows. 'Eddie,' she said uncertainly, her tone instantly snapping his eyes to her, 'if you saw three identical black SUVs driving in a line, what would you think?'

He swung around to see. A trio of Cadillac Escalades were nearing the top of the access road. 'I'd think either the president's making an unannounced visit – or some people are coming who we don't want to meet.'

Nina shovelled a final forkful into her mouth. 'Dammit, I was quite liking this.'

'Don't get up just yet. Let's see who we're dealing with.' They both watched as the three SUVs reached the parking lot. The lead vehicle continued towards the resort's buildings, while its companions stopped at the entrance, blocking any other vehicles from coming in – or going out. 'Okay, that's a bad sign.'

Nina stood. 'Eddie, come on . . .'

'Hold on, hold on.' He rose as well, but didn't move, tracking the Escalade. It pulled up in a disabled space. 'Who've we got here? Cops, feds, private security – who?'

The Cadillac's doors opened, about to provide an answer. The man who emerged from one of the rear seats was about fifty, with greying hair. The first thing he did was quickly survey his surroundings. Looking for threats; he was a professional. Bounty hunter? Mercenary? The driver, younger, got out of the front. Again, he had the air of someone who had been in either the military or security services – though of which country, the Yorkshireman couldn't tell. The older man appeared to be in charge, giving an order.

The other rear door opened. A third man climbed out, back to Eddie. He was broad-shouldered, upper body bulging with muscle. He looked up the valley towards the higher peaks, then turned.

Eddie froze. 'Shit . . .'

It was a face from his past, one he had thought – hoped, *expected* – he would never see again. The last time had been over a decade before, on a small Scottish island housing a secret prison run by MI6. He had gone there to see John Brice, the traitor who used an ancient weapon to destroy the Houses of Parliament in an attempted coup d'état, and to deliver a final well-justified beating before leaving him there to rot.

Someone had let him out.

Nina recognised him too. 'Holy crap! That – that's *Brice*!'

'Yeah.' The rogue MI6 officer had not only been one of their most devious and dangerous adversaries, but had kidnapped the then five-year-old Macy to try to force them into a lethal trap. 'When did he turn into the fucking Hulk?'

'And he's brought some friends.' By now the two other Escalades had disgorged their passengers, another eight men marching across the parking lot.

'Bollocks. We won't be able to get to the snowmobile without them seeing us.' The purloined sled sat with others not far from Brice's vehicle. 'We need to get out of here – but we'll be too slow on foot. We need skis.'

Nina looked at him. 'Are you kidding me?'

'Wish I was, love.' He tossed a banknote onto the table as a tip, then hurried with her out of the bar.

Brice gazed up the valley at the mountain peaks overlooking the ski resort. After thirteen years confined to a single windowless room, being out in the open wilds was almost intoxicating. He drew in a deep breath, relishing the cold, clean air, then regarded a natural feature in the distance: a group of rock pillars standing beyond the jutting cliff to which they had been attached aeons ago. 'Good climbing spot,' he remarked, almost to himself. While he could ski, it was not high on his list of recreational activities, but the precision and skill of free climbing was a long-standing source of challenge.

Steinitz looked at him over the SUV. 'What?'

'Those pillars up there. They'd be good for climbing. I conquered something similar in Greece when I was younger.' A brief frown. Nina Wilde's notes had also mentioned Greece . . .

Coincidence, he decided, dismissing the thought.

The German had already lost interest, turning towards the buildings. 'So, are they here? And if they are, where?'

'They're here,' Brice said. His total assurance brought Steinitz's gaze back to him. 'That snowmobile.' He pointed at one in a line of sleds beyond the car park. 'It's kitted out – panniers, bungee cords. None of the others are. I imagine Chase killed its owner, and probably all the other rednecks with him.'

'One man against so many?'

'Chase is one of those irritating people for whom the odds rarely seem to apply. The same with his wife. The question is: have they already moved on, or are they still here?' He stood completely still, as if scanning the nearby structures with x-ray vision. 'Still here, I'd say. They went from one life-or-death struggle straight into another. They need to rest, recover, probably buy proper winter clothing – maybe even some kind of disguise for Wilde. I'm sure we'll find them.'

'Then we know what to do.' Steinitz issued orders to his men. The mercenaries split into smaller groups, spreading out to check each building. Brice gave the scenery one last admiring look, then, as if a mask had dropped over his face, became all business.

His target was here. And he *would* find him.

15

One of the resort's businesses was a ski rental store. After quickly donning their new clothing, Nina and Eddie entered to find a group of a dozen chatty people returning their gear after a morning on the slopes. Only one assistant was at the counter, another sounding harried on the phone in a back room. The young man handling the returns was apparently new to the job, struggling to deal with everything by himself.

'This could work,' said Eddie, spying used skis and snowboards on a countertop to one side. 'When this lot are about to go, I'll distract him and you grab us a set of skis each.'

'We don't have ski boots,' Nina objected.

'You can use bindings with normal boots if you do 'em up tight enough. It'll hurt, but we won't be using them for long. We just need to get to the bottom of the valley and hitch a lift before Brice and his mates realise we're not here.'

Nina was not convinced, but moved to lurk near the side counter, pretending to be looking at her phone. Eddie waited for the last of the group to hand over their snowboard, then before the assistant could start to put away all the equipment, bustled up. 'Hello, excuse me, hello,' he said ebulliently, in an overblown imitation of an upper-class English accent. 'I was wondering if you could help me? I quite *faaarncy*,' the accent went off the rails for a moment, before recovering, 'a spot of skiing – not snowboards!' he added loudly, startling the young man. The comment was actually aimed at Nina, who had already surreptitiously picked up a board. 'I need *skis*, for *skiing*.'

'Well, we've got plenty of those,' said the assistant. His expression suggested he thought he was dealing with a lunatic. He glanced worriedly towards the back room, but the woman was still on the phone.

'Good, good. Never tried it before, but I thought, how hard can it be? And I certainly *don't want a snowboard*!' he said with considerable emphasis as Nina picked up another.

'Okay, I get it, skis, you want skis,' gabbled the assistant, flinching. 'Although if you've never skied before, you should probably book a lesson first? And there's, uh, there's a waiver about personal injury – I don't know, I need to check with my boss, this is only my second day?'

'You're doing a *maaarvellous* job, I have to say. There's a lot going on, it must be easy to lose track.' Nina was now clutching both snowboards close to her and sidling to the exit. 'Is that your boss in there?' Eddie pointed at the back room. The young man turned to look. Nina hurriedly scuttled through the doorway. 'Oh, she's busy, sorry. That's all right. I can come back later. Keep up the good work. Very nice meeting you.' He backed towards the door himself. 'Jolly good show!'

'Yeah, jolly good,' said the bewildered assistant through a fixed smile.

Eddie made a showy exit, then once he was clear hurried to catch up with Nina. 'Why'd you get bloody snowboards? I told you not to!'

'I wasn't going to get out of there unseen holding four bits of wood and metal that are taller than I am and clack together when I move!' she shot back. 'These were a lot easier to grab.'

'That's all very well, but I can't bloody snowboard!'

'Yes, you can.'

'No, I can't!'

She regarded him in bewilderment. 'But you did, that time we went on vacation with Macy. We all learned – *ohh*.' The true memory finally surfaced. '*Macy and I* learned, but you decided you didn't want to start from scratch like a baby and went off on your own to ski the black runs. While your wife and daughter had fun doing something together,' she pointedly added.

'I didn't say "like a baby",' he insisted. Nina gave him a heavy-eyed *oh, really?* look. 'Anyway, it doesn't matter. You need to go back in and get some skis.'

'You go back in! It's bad enough that we're stealing this stuff without increasing the chances that we'll get caught. And speaking of getting caught, *Brice* is here? Remember? We need to go before he finds us!'

She rounded the corner of a cabin overlooking the lower slopes. Annoyed, Eddie followed. The structure shielded them from the view of anyone in the resort's centre. The moment they started downhill, though, they would be visible.

Nina put one board on the ground, then handed him the other. 'You did one lesson, at least,' she reminded him. 'So you know the basics. Hopefully that's all you'll need.'

He stepped into the bindings and started to fasten them as firmly as he could around his boots. 'Yeah, it's not like I'll need to steer or anything.'

'Oh, come on, you managed that much, didn't you?' He said nothing. 'God damn it, Eddie!' She pulled her own bindings tight. They were extremely uncomfortable, the upper ratchet straps cutting into the tops of her feet even through her boots. They were also too large, producing an unpleasant sliding sensation with every movement. But she was able to waddle-hop her way the few metres to the beginning of the downhill slope without too much difficulty.

Eddie's journey was considerably more awkward. 'Fuck – fucking – fuckity – *fuck*!' he gasped in time with each clumsy shuffle of his feet. His arms were almost fully outstretched for balance, making him move like a drunken penguin. 'This is why I hate snowboarding.'

'And it's not because your wife and teenage daughter are better at it than you?' Nina said, looking back at him with a mocking smile. It vanished when she saw one of Brice's men about fifty metres away. Her hat and sunglasses suddenly felt a woefully inadequate disguise.

Eddie saw the cause of her alarm. 'Oh, well. Never too old to learn a new skill . . .'

They looked down the hillside. It was a nursery slope, a short run with gentle dips and rises and a dragline to bring beginners back to the top. Only a handful of people were using it. Below it, a more advanced and busy slope dropped away to cut through the snowy forest. A ski lift on the opposite side from the access road returned skiers and snowboarders to the heart of the resort.

But the couple had no plans to come back any time soon. 'Ready?' Nina asked.

Eddie grimaced. 'Cowabunga.'

'Do snowboarders say that?'

'How the bloody hell would I know?' With that, he wobbled his board around to face downhill and began his descent.

Nina did the same, more fluidly. 'Okay, nice and easy,' she told her husband. 'Stay balanced, you don't need to steer yet.' She watched with rising dismay as he started to peel away from her. 'I said, you don't need to steer yet . . .'

'I'm not! It's this bloody board, it won't go in a straight line.'

'Look in the direction you want to go. Turn your head and shoulders—'

'I know, I know, I *know*!' Eddie snapped, in the tone of someone used to giving such instructions rather than receiving them. Still with his arms extended wide, he turned his upper body to face straight down the slope. As his weight shifted, the board began to angle back in the right direction. 'All right, think I got it.' He glanced across at Nina – then back at her as he picked up speed and drew ahead. 'Okay, going faster, don't want to do that.'

'Ah – do a heelside turn,' called Nina, dredging up memories of her own lessons.

'A *what*?'

'Lean back on your heels, try to turn across the slope and slow down. If you fall, land on your ass so you don't break your wrists.'

'I *have* been on snow before,' he complained, but he was still gaining speed. 'Okay, lean back, lean back – oh, shit!'

He realised too late that he was heading straight for a couple shepherding two young children. A frantic twist of his shoulders and waist as he leaned back on his heels, and he turned – too quickly. The board skittered out from beneath him, dropping him on his backside. But he didn't stop, instead ploughing into the father's calves from behind. The man fell backwards on top of him. The sudden flurry of flailing limbs and ski poles brought the wife down too, and within moments the panicking kids were also sprawled in the snow.

Eddie groaned. The father was no lightweight, knocking the wind from him. Nina came to a hurried stop behind the tangled group. 'Oh, my God!' she said. 'Is everyone okay?'

'Yeah, yeah,' replied the mother, more concerned with her crying children. 'We're all fine.'

The father, however, responded with anger. He rolled off Eddie and jumped upright. 'What the fuck?' he screeched. 'What the fuck were you doing? You could have hit my kids!'

'Honey, honey, the kids are right here and they have ears,' said his wife, expression apologetic. 'I'm sure it was an accident.'

'Yeah, an accident caused by fucking retardedness!'

'Hey, hey!' said Nina. 'It *was* an accident, and we're really sorry. There's no need to let this ruin the day for your kids, okay? Nobody got hurt.'

'Speak for yourself,' Eddie wheezed from the ground.

She reached down to help him stand, glancing up the slope as she did so. The commotion had drawn attention, people at the top of the nursery run observing with interest—

A man wearing dark clothing joined them.

She didn't know for sure if he was one of Brice's companions, but he was certainly dressed like them, standing out amongst the brighter outfits. 'Eddie, come on, we gotta go.'

She strained to haul him off the ground. The man in the dark coat was paying them entirely too much attention. Her hair was covered by the hat, face partially masked behind the sunglasses – but she couldn't change her build, and it was possible her coat had been visible when Lou used Uzz to tag her. That there was a stocky man in a leather jacket with her might also be a giveaway . . .

The irate father hadn't finished. 'Hey! Where d'you think you're going?' he demanded, positioning himself downslope of Eddie to prevent him from leaving. 'If you don't know what you're doing, you should get the hell off the snow. You could have killed someone!'

'Wouldn't be the first time today,' the Yorkshireman told him coldly, staring unblinking into his eyes.

The younger man belatedly noticed the various facial injuries Eddie had accrued. Uncertainty replaced anger. 'Yeah, well – just stay out of my way, all right?' he said.

'If you could get out of ours, we'll be leaving,' Nina said impatiently. The father frowned, but shuffled back to clear their path. 'Eddie, I think we've been seen,' she said under her breath.

Eddie looked uphill. The man in black had been joined by a couple of others in identical clothing. One turned and called out to someone by the resort buildings. 'Maybe hold me upright,' he suggested.

'Ooh, I bet that stung to say.' But she gripped his arm to provide support as she turned her board. Leaving the family behind, they slid away down the slope.

Brice and Steinitz hurried to join the mercenaries at the top of the nursery slope. 'Is that them?' one man asked. He pointed at two figures heading downhill on snowboards.

Steinitz narrowed his eyes for a better look against the white background – but Brice was already drawing his gun. 'It's them,' he barked as he took aim.

The German reacted in alarm. 'No, wait—'

Brice fired, multiple gunshots cracking across the valley. People screamed. The family hurriedly dropped to the ground, both parents shielding their children, but another man whom Nina and Eddie had just passed tumbled to the ground as a ragged red hole burst open in his back. Other bullets kicked up little geysers of frost as they hit the snow.

His targets crested a small rise, starting to drop from sight on the other side. Brice cursed himself – the marksmanship retraining he'd done since being freed hadn't been enough to overcome thirteen years without practice – and focused before firing again. The shot still missed . . . but not by much. Chase flinched, flailing his arms as his wife tried to hold him upright before falling. They both disappeared beyond the snowy hump.

'What the hell are you *doing*?' shouted Steinitz, grabbing Brice's gun hand and forcing the weapon down. 'You idiot! Now people will call the police. You are here to scare him, not kill him!'

Brice fixed him with an unhinged stare, using his raw strength to raise the gun despite the German's efforts to hold it. 'Don't tell me what to do,' he warned, looking back downhill. Wilde and Chase were on the move again, the latter clearly struggling to stay upright. 'He can't snowboard,' Brice said in realisation. 'Chase can't snowboard!' A sharp laugh, then he pulled free of Steinitz and started towards the parking lot.

'Where are you going?' the mercenary leader demanded.

Brice's face broke into a terrifying grin. 'I'm going to scare him.'

'Jesus, that was close,' Nina gasped as she and Eddie gained speed. She was supporting him as he tried to maintain his balance. 'Brice is insane. There were *kids* on the slope, but he shot at us anyway! And bend your knees more.'

Eddie shifted his posture, his full attention on staying upright. 'I think he was shooting at me. I'm the one who put him in prison. How the fuck did he get out?'

'He must be working for Loost, or at least whoever's carrying out his orders. I guess a trillionaire can afford to pay mercenaries to break him out.'

'Great, now there's a psycho who hates me chasing us. I love the personal touch.'

They reached the bottom of the nursery slope. The dragline back to the top was to their left, but Nina steered past it, going through a line of marker poles with fluttering flags to bring them onto the much longer intermediate-level run beyond. 'Are you managing okay?' she asked him.

'Just about.' He looked ahead. The new run was broad, gently weaving as it cut through the surrounding forest. 'If I was on skis I could do this with my eyes shut.'

'Well, you're not, so keep them open.' They were now far enough from the main resort that the skiers and snowboarders had either registered the gunshots but not realised their significance, a few people having stopped to look curiously back up the hill, or simply not heard them at all. 'How far down into the valley do you think this goes?'

'I dunno. It's a big resort, so we might be able to—'

Surprise, then alarm, spread through the stationary skiers. Some hurriedly set off again, angling towards the run's sides. Nina looked uphill to see what they had seen – and her eyes popped wide in shock. 'Oh, crap!'

Eddie didn't dare look back in case he lost his balance. 'What is it?'

'It's *got* to be Brice – and he's coming after us.'

'On skis?'

'I wish!'

One of the mercenary team's Escalade SUVs was powering down the slope, the chains on its whirling wheels kicking up a huge spray of snow. It slalomed to follow the quickest path, drifting through each turn at the head of a frozen wave. A group of people were swallowed by the choking cloud as the Cadillac slithered past them – then a skier was hit by its fishtailing rear end and sent tumbling.

'Oh my God!' gasped Nina, horrified. She changed direction, turning towards one side of the run. 'If we get into the trees, he won't be able to follow us.'

'He won't need to, 'cause we'll be splattered against them!' he objected. 'I can hardly steer this bloody thing in the open, never mind weaving through woods.'

'Then we need to speed up, because he's gaining on us.'

'Let go of me,' Eddie told her.

'But you need my help to—'

'I'm slowing you down. You keep going – I'll get to the trees and go on foot. He'll have to get out to chase me.'

'He has a gun – he could just shoot you.'

'I've taken that twat down before, I can do it again. Go on, go!' He forcibly lifted her hands from him, then leaned backwards to angle away.

'Eddie! God *damn* it,' Nina cried, but he was already widening the gap between them even as he swayed with the effort of staying upright. Exasperated, but knowing he probably would fare better on foot, she dropped into a lower stance. The sensation of speed rose almost immediately, her board slicing effortlessly through the snow. Sense memories from the winter vacation returned. By the end of the trip she had become quite confident on a snowboard, if nowhere near as much as Macy.

She looked over her shoulder. Brice's Escalade had changed direction to pursue Eddie. He'd been right about the ex-agent's revenge priorities. That gave her better odds of escaping, but massively increased the danger to her husband. Could he even reach the trees before the SUV caught him?

The board's nose tipped upwards. She'd taken her focus off the run for too long. She hurriedly turned her head—

A humped ridge ran across the slope right in front of her. The board kicked up sharply – then suddenly she was airborne.

The ground was a couple of feet below. The biggest jump she'd managed during the vacation had been perhaps six inches. She yelled, flinging out her arms for balance as she dropped. She'd always erred on the side of caution and worn wrist protectors while learning to snowboard. If she fell forward at this speed, she could break both arms—

The board smacked into the snow. Nina bent her knees to absorb the impact, but the landing still jarred her spine. She lurched, toppling forwards – but threw both arms back just in time to counter the fall. She gasped, wavering before recovering from the unexpected stunt.

Eddie was also heading for the ridge, though – and he was looking back at the SUV. She tried to shout in warning, but he was already at the hump—

He was going more slowly than her, angling as much across the ski run as down it, but was still moving fast enough for his board to leave the ground.

Only for a moment – but that was enough.

He spun around, the toe of his board digging into the snow, then fell and bowled sidelong over the slope before ending up face-down.

Brice had seen him drop. The Escalade's engine roared, snow chains ripping into the mountainside's white covering as he powerdrifted around – aiming the hulking vehicle at the stricken Yorkshireman.

16

Nina turned hard, slicing across the run towards Eddie. He was higher up it. She followed a snaking path, swinging uphill whenever the dips and bumps of the snow gave her the opportunity. But the climb was costing her momentum, and the SUV was still bearing down on her husband.

Eddie struggled to get up. The board, its edge flat on the ground, kept him from moving his feet. Cursing, he looked around – to see Nina rushing towards him. He waved her back, about to shout for her to turn away when he heard an engine's roar growing louder, and louder—

The Cadillac hit the hump and launched into the air. Its blunt front end arced down at Eddie, a juggernaut about to crush him—

Nina sliced across its path – and grabbed Eddie's raised hand to yank him clear.

The Escalade slammed down like a piledriver where Eddie had been a split-second before, its front fender tearing away and the hood buckling. Nina fell on her side as her husband's dragging board acted like an anchor. She caught the briefest glimpse of the disbelieving, furious Brice inside the vehicle before it careered onwards down the hill.

'Shit!' Eddie managed to gasp. 'Bloody hell, love, this is one of those times I'm really glad I married you.'

Panting, Nina got back up. 'If you hadn't married me, you wouldn't be in this mess.' The Escalade slewed around as Brice stamped on the brake. 'Come on, gotta go!'

She hauled Eddie upright again. They resumed their descent,

heading for the trees at the run's edge. Eddie glanced back. The SUV halted, having spun almost through a full half-turn. It was pointing away from them. Even with snow chains, bringing it back around would take several seconds.

Brice had realised this. The driver's door opened – only to wedge against a mound of snow. He kicked angrily at the door to force it wider. 'He's coming,' Eddie warned.

'We're almost there!' Nina guided them towards the pines.

The door finally opened enough for Brice to squeeze out. He clambered from the Escalade and searched for his targets. It took a mere moment to find them—

'Gun!' Eddie warned. He ducked, pulling Nina down with him as gunfire cracked across the slope. But now they were just metres from the first saplings along the forest's edge. Snow puffed from their foliage as rounds hit them. Brice's shots were getting closer each time, zeroing in.

And the young trees were packed together, almost no gaps between them—

'Split up!' shouted Eddie, pushing the surprised Nina away from him. They passed on either side of a prospective Christmas tree, brushing through its branches and showering themselves in frost. Then they were in the forest, older, taller trees rising ahead.

Brice fired a few last shots. Nina flinched as bark exploded from a trunk and stung her face. The conifers were spaced widely enough for her to snowboard between them – if she was careful. 'Eddie, stay with me! Try and follow my tracks.'

But one look told her that he was in trouble. The ground was covered in snow even under the trees, and off-piste the glittering coating concealed stones and dead branches. Both boards jolted and jittered as they ran over hidden obstacles. She could just about handle the rough ride, but even with all his experience of skiing, Eddie hadn't yet adapted to the snowboard. He battled to maintain balance as he steered between the conifers.

One goal overrode the other. He threw both arms out to counter a near-fall – which jerked his board into a sharp turn. Too sharp. A tree loomed in front of him. He twisted back the other way—

Too late. His board's nose hit knobbly roots. Eddie came to an abrupt stop, cartwheeling over the obstruction and hitting the ground hard. One foot broke loose from the board's bindings. He yelled a barely comprehensible obscenity.

Nina skidded to a halt, bracing herself against a tree. 'Are you okay?' she called, worried.

'Shit, ow, fuck! Yeah, yeah. Bollocks to this, though.' He kicked angrily at the snowboard until the other binding came loose. 'I'll run.'

The surging roar of a powerful V8 engine grew louder. 'Run fast!' Nina told him, shoving herself off. She weaved downhill through the trees.

Eddie grabbed the board and raced after her. There was a relatively clear path behind the saplings along the ski run's edge. He followed it, choosing speed over cover. As long as Brice was in the SUV, he wouldn't be able to take an accurate shot—

Brice's weapon wasn't a gun.

The Escalade smashed down the small trees like a bulldozer. Its windscreen had been cracked by the nose-heavy landing. Behind the crazed spiderweb, Brice was hunched over the wheel with a demonic snarl twisting his face. He aimed the vehicle straight at Eddie, foot to the floor to crush him against the trunk of a pine—

Eddie hurled the snowboard at him.

It lanced over the Cadillac's bonnet – and punched through the damaged windscreen directly in front of Brice. He jerked back into the leather seat. The slab of hardened wood stopped mere centimetres from his throat.

Eddie dived sideways, the SUV's battered front almost striking his legs. He hit the ground at the same moment the Escalade hit the tree. Its nose crumpled around the unyielding bole. The windscreen burst apart, only the airbag keeping Brice from flying through it.

The Yorkshireman shook off the snow shaken loose from the branches above and rose. He regarded the wreck. Was Brice dead? If he wasn't, it might be a good time to correct that . . .

The swollen airbag collapsed, its job done. Brice sat up behind it. His face was bloodied, but other than that he appeared unharmed. If anything, the crash had only made him more angry. He glared at Eddie – then raised his gun.

'For fuck's sake!' Eddie cried. He fled downhill, weaving between the trees. More gunshots rang through the forest, Brice's bullets striking wood in his wake. Then the firing stopped. Was the ex-agent out of ammo – or pursuing on foot?

He risked a look back. The Escalade was almost obscured behind the trees, but he could see that the driver's door was blocked by a trunk. Brice would either have to slide across to the passenger side or clamber through the broken windscreen to get out. That would cost him time, but he would still be able to run as fast as the man he was hunting—

'Eddie!' Nina had stopped to wait for him. 'Come on!'

'I told you to get out of here!' he said as he approached.

'I tell you to do all sorts of things, but you never actually do them,' she fired back. 'Stand on the board and hold on to me.'

'Will you be able to stay upright?'

'As long as you don't wobble about like Jell-o, yes!'

'Someone's found the time to take her sarcasm pills,' he grumbled, but he did as he was told, taking hold of her waist and planting one foot on the board between hers. He used the other to push off, starting them downhill once more.

Nina brought them back onto the ski slope. It was clear of other people; those below had by now reached the bottom, and anyone above had stopped to get clear of the chaos. As they descended, Eddie looked uphill and saw a couple of men running towards the crashed Escalade. Brice's companions, he guessed. He doubted they would be happy with him.

'Okay,' he said, relieved, 'we're clear, for now. They shouldn't be able to get down to the main road before we do.'

'So what do we do when we get to it?' Nina asked.

'Pretend our car broke down and try to hitch a ride north. Then we've got to cross the border – and hope the Mounties don't always get their man.'

'Or woman,' she added.

The couple glided away down the empty ski slope.

Steinitz and the blond-haired Duger saw the wrecked Escalade beyond a swathe of flattened young trees as they yomped down the snowy hillside. Brice emerged from the woods to meet them. 'What the *fuck* was that?' the German demanded. 'If I tell you to stop, you stop! I am in charge of this operation!'

Brice's eyes narrowed to malevolent slits. 'You wanted Chase scared,' he replied. 'Now he's scared. He knows I'm after him. So he will run, and run, and run, until he has nowhere to go except where you want him.'

'You could have killed him!'

'I *tried* to. But I told you: he has a knack for staying alive. That will make it all the more rewarding when I finally get him.' He wiped blood from his face. 'Besides, it's Wilde you really care about, isn't it? She's fine. She's still caught up in your little game.'

Duger stared down the ski slope at the two tiny figures descending in the distance. 'They're getting away. We have to move. The police will be here soon.'

'The nearest town large enough to have a police station is over twenty minutes away,' Brice said, unconcerned. 'And if there should happen to be a patrolman closer than that, so what? We just kill them.'

The two mercenaries exchanged dubious looks, then Steinitz gestured for them to start back to the resort. 'We will leave before we have to do anything that drastic. And Brice?' He fixed the muscular Brit with a stony stare. 'Disobey my orders again and you will regret it.'

Brice's own gaze seethed with hatred. 'I was hired to kill Eddie Chase. I *will* do that.'

'Yes – but at the right time and place. Understand?' The former MI6 officer clearly had his own ideas about when those were, but gave him a reluctant nod. 'Good. Now, I have to call the Adjudicator about what has happened here. What a *fuck-up* has happened here, I mean.' He took out his phone and made a call as the three men traipsed uphill.

17

'Cheers, mate,' Eddie said to the taxi driver as he and Nina got out.

The man gave him a questioning look. 'You absolutely sure this is where you want to be?'

'Yeah. We're good.'

'Uh-huh.' The driver's expression became one of knowing suspicion. They had stopped less than two miles from the border between the United States and Canada, roughly equidistant from the two nearest official crossing points in a sparsely populated, largely forested area. It did not take the mind of a detective to guess why they might have come here.

The Yorkshireman handed him a fifty-dollar bill. 'Thanks for the ride.'

'Appreciate it.' The driver briskly pocketed the note, then pulled away.

Eddie watched the cab's tail lights recede down the isolated country road. 'We'd better get a shift on. Just in case he's got straight on the phone to the border patrol.' He surveyed their surroundings. The landscape was flat, the fields near the roadside giving way to trees beyond. The snow that had been omnipresent in the mountains was much thinner and more sparsely settled at this lower altitude, but it was still cold.

They set out, angling across the fields towards the woodlands. As much as they could, they avoided the patches of snow so as not to leave footprints. Nina huddled up in her coat. 'Why don't we just keep going up the road? I looked at the border crossing on Street View in the cab.

It's literally a gate with some concrete blocks. We could walk right around it.'

'There might be a patrol watching it. Same on the Canadian side. The further we are from anyone who can respond quickly, the better.'

'But they *will* respond, yes?'

'Oh, yeah. It's kind of funny, actually. The Mexican border's only half the length of this one, and it's the one the politicians are always ranting on about. But this is the one they've gone to town with guarding. Maybe they hope anyone crossing from Mexico will die in the desert, I dunno.'

Nina sighed. 'That sounds depressingly plausible.'

They kept walking. Her mind soon drifted with the tedium, a memory returning. 'Eddie . . . is something wrong?'

'No, I used some Preparation H the other night,' was his immediate wisecrack.

'Very funny. No, it's just – well, you didn't seem happy about what happened at the ski resort. Not the "Brice trying to kill us" part, I mean. The whole thing about you not being able to snowboard, rather.'

'If you'd got me skis like I asked, that wouldn't have been a problem.'

His defensive tone told her plenty. 'But there's *some* problem, isn't there?' He said nothing. 'Is it because *I* got *you* out of there, not the other way around?'

Eddie didn't reply at once, and when he did, it was without looking at her. 'Not the first time you've pulled my arse out of the fire. Nothing different this time.' He was, to Nina's mind, a little too firm in his assertion. He seemed to realise, continuing: 'And, you know, I'm grateful! Just not used to you doing it so many times in a row. I need to pull my finger out. Anyway, hold on, I need to get my torch.' He was clearly glad to change the subject.

The cause was their arrival at the forest, a mix of evergreens and deciduous trees that had shed most of their foliage for winter. It was now dusk, their hitch-hiking journey northwards from the mountains aided by three different drivers before they reached a town close to the border for their final cab ride. Darkness swallowed them as they went under the trees. Eddie was prepared, though, having a small but powerful torch in his emergency gear. He swept the ground ahead as they made their way through the woods. Nina spotted something in the beam. 'What are those tracks? Deer?'

He assessed them with a brief glance. 'Yeah. Quite a lot of them up here. If you stay still you can get them to come quite close.'

'You've been here before?'

'Not far away. Went hiking with Macy in the Gulf Unique Area – weird name, I know – a couple of years back, when you were at a lecture or something in Canada.'

'Oh, right.' An unwelcome thought came to her. 'So if there are lots of deer, what about other animals? Are there . . . bears?'

His reply was unsettlingly casual. 'Yeah, some.'

'What, actual can-kill-a-human bears? And we're strolling through their territory?'

'Only black bears – they're the smallest kind. They usually leave people alone if people leave them alone.'

'The word "usually" is doing a lot of heavy lifting there,' she muttered, moving closer to her husband as he led the way.

But if there were any ursine predators lurking in the dark, they stayed well clear. After a while, Eddie slowed. 'Shut your eyes while I turn off the torch,' he said.

Nina did so. The light clicked off; she kept her eyes closed for several seconds to let them adapt. 'Are we at the border?'

'There's a gap in the trees up ahead – I think that's it. We'll wait a minute and make sure nobody's around.'

They stood in silence. Nina opened her eyes. The surrounding woodland was nothing more than vague grey shapes in the night. What little she could see of the sky looked mostly overcast. There were certainly no artificial light sources nearby.

'All right, let's give it a shot,' Eddie said at last. They set off again. Nina's eyes had adjusted enough to let her pick out any obstacles in their path – and also a band of empty ground ahead, extending to the left and right as far as she could see.

'That's the border?'

'Yeah. They clear-cut it along the entire distance. Gives their surveillance gear a good view of anyone crossing.'

'They surveil *all* of it? Over five thousand miles? Jeez, so that's where all my tax dollars are going.'

'Surveillance is one thing, but they need people to catch us,' he pointed out. 'Hopefully the nearest patrol's a couple of miles away.'

'So you've got a plan to avoid the border patrol?'

'Yeah – run like buggery! Are you ready?'

'To do what?'

'What I just said. Come on, leg it!'

He broke into a run for the clear-cut line. Nina held in a protest and followed. They reached the gap in seconds – and raced across it. She glanced to each side as she crossed. Nothing but trees rising in perfect lines on either side of the empty snow-dusted space to her left – but on the right, she saw something standing against the sky, a dark line with a bulbous top. A small red light gave away that it was not a natural part of the forest.

Then they were back under the trees – in Canada. It was far from the first time the couple had made an illegal border crossing, but Nina found this one especially concerning. 'I saw something,' she said as they kept running. 'On the border, to the right. Like a telephone pole.'

'Surveillance mast,' Eddie told her. 'They have 'em every mile or so. The border's a straight line here, so they can see anyone crossing.'

'So they know about us already?'

'Yeah. Question is how long they'll take to react, and how long it takes anyone to get to us. Or anything.'

'What do you mean, any*thing*?'

Her question was answered almost immediately.

A shrill buzzing hum rose behind them. Nina looked back – and saw lights flitting between the trees with inhuman precision. '*Those* anythings!' Eddie said in alarm. '*Drones!*'

Two miniature quadcopters were making a beeline towards them, a thermal camera on one easily picking out their trail on the cold ground and sharing that information with its companion. They were BATs: Border Autonomous Trackers, a high-tech collaboration between the American and Canadian governments that were automatically released from their 'nests' atop the surveillance masts whenever an illegal border crossing was detected and sent to hunt down the intruders, using their onboard artificial intelligence to navigate the forest. 'Stay where you are!' a tinny recorded voice called from the leading drone. 'You have illegally crossed the Canadian border. Officers are on the way to arrest you. Attempting to run will add further charges against you. Do not move!' The warning was repeated in French.

'*Connards* to that,' said Eddie, surprising Nina with his grasp of multilingual obscenities. '*Do* move!' He snapped the torch back on and they both ran deeper into the woods.

The drones pursued, quickly closing. Nina glanced back at them – and almost slipped on a patch of snow. She gasped, catching herself and continuing.

Eddie, however, bent to scoop up and squeeze a large handful of the snow in one hand – and collect a stone in the other. He packed the latter into the heart of his snowball, then spun, spotting the nearest BAT as it swooped towards him. He lined up, threw—

The snowball struck the leading BAT square-on with a satisfying crack of breaking plastic. The high-pitched buzz of its rotors became a wavering screech, and the little machine spiralled crazily to the ground.

'Only meant to slow it down, but that works too,' Eddie said, before running again. 'Nina! Split up!'

He peeled off to the left. Nina angled right. The remaining drone zipped past its fallen fellow and went after Eddie. 'It's following me!' he shouted to her.

Nina, who had already slowed out of caution now that she was in darkness, turned to find him. His torch beam skittered through the trees. Behind, the second BAT rapidly closed the gap. She followed the lights, rejoining the chase as a pursuer.

Eddie heard the drone's mosquito whine grow louder. He knew from his research that BATs were programmed to stay close to their targets, constantly broadcasting their position so border patrol officers, from either country, could home in and make an arrest. He needed to take down the second mechanical pest before that could happen.

A cluster of intertwined trees ahead. He rounded them, grabbing another handful of snow. He'd expected the first drone to try to dodge, but it hadn't detected the danger until it was too late. Maybe its manufacturers had exaggerated the abilities of its AI. He might be able to take down both . . .

He pressed against a trunk, finding another stone and thumbing it into the snowball before clicking off his torch. The BAT's buzz was audible behind the trees. It would 'know' he had gone around them. Would it follow him, or go the other way to intercept?

The noise shifted – to his right. It *was* following him. Eddie moved again, circling the little group of conifers so as to catch up with it from behind. Never mind throwing something, he might be able just to grab the machine and smash it against a tree.

The buzz got louder, the drone's lights appearing in front of him. Too far away to reach, but it was an easy target, slowly turning as it drifted around the trunks. He threw—

The BAT suddenly dodged the snowball. Eddie swore. How had it known he was there? It hadn't been looking at him . . .

Because it doesn't see the world like a human, he realised. Its main camera probably had an extreme fisheye lens so it could watch for obstacles all around as it flew. The computer controlling it could observe every angle simultaneously. But now it had turned to face him directly, seemingly for intimidating effect. 'Stay where you are!' its recorded voice said again. 'You have illegally crossed the—'

A low branch swept down from a tree like a great fan. The only direction the drone apparently couldn't look was straight above. A *szzzzt!* sound came from its rotors as the plastic blades chewed into the twigs and needles. It fell to the ground, bouncing a couple of times as if in low gravity before spitting out the clogging vegetation and rising again.

It didn't stay airborne for long. Nina let go of the branch she'd pulled downwards and ran to deliver a kick that sent the BAT spinning past Eddie to smash into a tree. A strangled electronic gurgle came from its loudspeaker, then it fell silent.

'Nice,' he said, impressed.

'I got bored with it *droning* on,' she replied. Even in the dark, her grin was visible.

'Oi! You might keep saving me, but there's no way I'm giving up the shit puns.' He switched the torch back on. 'We need to get clear of here before anyone catches up—'

A new sound rose behind them. Another drone was coming.

But this was not a third BAT. Even before they saw it, Nina and Eddie knew it was larger. The whirr of its rotors was louder, lower-pitched, more powerful. It appeared a few seconds later, blinking red and green LEDs revealing its size – almost three feet across. It moved swiftly towards them with menacing purpose.

Eddie brought up the torch. The drone was revealed as a hexacopter, a six-rotor machine with a pair of landing skids and a pod packed with cameras and other devices beneath its central fuselage. In seeming retaliation, it snapped on a dazzling light of its own to illuminate them. 'This is the Canada Border Services Agency,' a voice barked. 'You have crossed the border illegally. Surrender and remain where you are until officers arrive. If you try to escape, we will use non-lethal force to stop you.'

'You know what this is?' Nina asked Eddie under her breath, half-raising her hands.

'Nope – must be new.'

'What's it armed with?'

'No idea, and I don't think we should hang around to find out. Split up and keep running north until we lose it.' He lifted his own hands in mock surrender – then whirled and ran.

He only managed three steps. A green laser dot flicked into existence on his back – and a split-second later it flared brighter as a fierce electrical arc lit up the forest, lancing from the drone to the running Yorkshireman. It was a stun laser, the intense beam ionising the air to create a perfect conductor for the fifty thousand volts following it. A localised thunderclap shattered the silence of the forest. Eddie fell as if his legs had liquefied, flopping nervelessly to the ground.

18

'Eddie!' Nina cried. The hovering drone pivoted towards her. She turned to flee. The green dot reappeared, finding her—

It didn't fire.

She didn't know if the stun laser needed to recharge after firing. All she knew was that she might only have a moment to escape – and she took it, bursting into a sprint through the forest.

The rotor buzz grew louder and more angry as the machine pursued. 'You can't get away!' the operator said over the speaker. 'This part of the border is patrolled by Predator drones with infra-red cameras.' She was no expert on military technology, but knew from media osmosis that a Predator was an aircraft, not a small 'copter. 'Wherever you go, you'll be tracked. We *will* catch you. Give up now!'

Nina had no intention of obeying. She weaved between trees, the drone's spotlight showing her the forest ahead. But even at her best speed, it was gaining. The light grew brighter.

A green dot danced over a trunk ahead—

She threw herself sidelong – and another lightning bolt flashed past, missing by inches. Fragments of bark blew from the tree where it struck. She gasped in fright. But now she had another grace period before the drone could fire again; she had to find a way to use it.

The stark light picked out something ahead; an old log lying across a small hollow, its branches long stripped by insects and animals. There was a space under it. A hiding place? The pursuing machine was surely too big to get into it—

Nina was already vaulting the log before the thought had fully coalesced. Snow had accumulated in the hollow, her feet kicking up white clods as she landed. But there was enough room underneath the log for her to fit – and it looked as if she might even be able to slip out from the other side. If the drone lost sight of her, she could double back and help Eddie before the operator realised what she'd done.

She squeezed beneath the old tree. The drone's hum grew louder. Light washed into the hollow as it flew above the log. She started to pull herself through the narrower gap on the other side . . .

The drone halted, hovering. Its light swept over the surrounding forest as it turned in place, searching for her. Nina wriggled out from under the log, looking back the way she'd come. How long would it take the operator to deduce where she had gone?

Only a moment. The machine dropped into the hollow for a look beneath the log just as Nina pulled her legs up. 'I see you!' said the operator, almost triumphant. 'You can't get away!' The drone rose again, flying rapidly to intercept her on the far side of the fallen tree—

She shoved herself back into her hiding place just as it passed overhead and spun to find her. The targeting laser came back on, green dot jittering over the frost-coated log – but the drone couldn't get low enough to pin her with it. Its motors powered up with an almost aggrieved whine and it flew back over the log, this time descending lower. Nina scrabbled back up through the gap as the spotlight found her again.

'Stay where you are!' said the operator, with clear exasperation. The drone repeated its earlier movement. Nina did the same, sliding back under the log. Another round of catch-me-if-you-can followed. She realised that the longer she could delay the drone, the more chance that Eddie would recover.

The drone operator had come to the same conclusion. 'Officers are on the way,' he said, annoyed. 'You're making things worse by resisting. Come out, now, and surrender!' Nina instead slid back down through the gap again – grabbing a broken branch as she went. The drone made another trip over the log, dropping still further into the hollow to bring the stun laser to bear. 'This is your last warning—'

Nina swung the branch – and hit one of its landing skids.

The blow sent the drone spinning. She rolled out before the pilot could regain control and grabbed the stricken machine. The downdraught from the rotors was surprisingly fierce. It felt like an animal squirming to break free. It took a surprising amount of effort to flip it upside-down – but the moment she did, it slammed heavily to the ground, some of the rotors breaking on impact.

A yelp of affronted outrage came from the speaker. 'That – that's criminal damage to Canadian government property! You'll be fined for that, maybe even get jail time!'

'I'll see you in court,' Nina quipped, before stamping hard on the drone's body. It fell silent, the spotlight going out.

She closed her eyes for several seconds to adjust to the darkness, then climbed out of the hollow. How was she going to retrace her route without light? Fortunately, she had a landmark. Eddie had dropped his flashlight, a glowing spot visible through the trees. She made her way back to it.

Her husband was already stirring as she arrived. 'Eddie, are you okay?' she said, crouching to help him sit up.

'Christ, what was that?' he growled blearily.

'I don't know. There was a laser, and then it looked like you were struck by lightning.'

'A staser. Stun laser,' he added in explanation. 'Never been hit by one before, and hope to fuck I never do again, because that really bloody hurt.' He looked around in sudden concern. 'Where's the drone?'

'Drone heaven.'

He managed a faint laugh. 'You're getting good at this.'

'Not good enough. The drone operator said there were cops on the way. Can you move?'

'I'll have to, won't I?' With her support, he stood. 'Jesus. Can't believe they zapped me.'

'I know,' Nina agreed as they set off again. 'I thought Canadians were supposed to be friendly.'

'Good job we weren't crossing the border the other way. I'd probably have been shot.'

Nina caught something in her peripheral vision to their right. 'That might still happen. Look!'

Some distance away, flashlights moved through the forest. Farther still were the pulsing red and blue strobes of a law enforcement vehicle. The drone operator hadn't been lying.

Eddie switched off his own light and angled away from them. 'Stay off any snow,' he warned. Paler patches were visible on the ground even without the torch. 'We don't want to leave tracks.'

Nina kept her eyes on the will-o'-wisp points amongst the trees. 'I think they already saw us. They're coming this way.'

'It's a big forest. If we're quick enough, we might lose 'em.' He increased his pace, marching determinedly through the dark.

Nina hurried along with him. 'The operator also said they had Predator drones with infra-red cameras watching the area. Will they see us?'

'Not under the trees. But – shit!' he exclaimed in sudden realisation.

'What?'

'I just remembered. I looked at a map on my phone while we were in the taxi. There's a road running parallel to the border, about a mile on the Canadian side. When we cross that, *then* they'll see us – the cameras on a Predator can spot people from miles away. And the cops'll be able to drive to where we crossed pretty quickly. If they bring in a big search party, or send dogs after us, we're fucked.'

'That's a reassuring assessment,' Nina said, fear mixing with sarcasm.

'Just telling it like it is, love. We need to camouflage ourselves, but how we'll . . .'

He trailed off, slowing. Nina almost bumped into him. 'What is it?' she whispered. The lights of the border patrol were still following, but there was nothing visible in the woods ahead.

'I don't know. I . . .' He sniffed. When he spoke again, it was with even more unease. 'I can smell something.'

'What?'

'*Blood.*'

As he said that, they both heard a sound. It was deep, ominous . . . and close by.

Something in the dark was breathing.

Something large.

'Okay,' Eddie said in a quiet, restrained voice, 'let's walk backwards, *really* slowly and carefully.'

Nina gripped his arm. 'It's a bear, isn't it?'

'Yeah. On the bright side, only a black bear.'

'Wow, that makes me feel so much safer!'

They retreated, step by nervous step. The source of the low, slow huffing did not seem to move. Eddie began to sidestep, drawing Nina with him. 'We can go around it,' he murmured. 'It's probably busy eating whatever it just killed. If we don't bother it, it won't bother—'

A growl came from the darkness.

They froze. 'Now what do we do?' Nina asked, fear surging through her body. 'Can we outrun it?'

'Nope.'

'Climb a tree?'

'They can climb too.'

'Oh. Great.' She warily turned her head. The flashlights were continuing their relentless advance. 'And the cops are still coming!'

'Stay with me.' Eddie resumed his sidelong retreat, Nina holding him. The menacing breathing continued – then a faint crackle of twigs warned of movement.

Nina held in a terrified gasp as she made out a shape in the darkness, a form that was humanoid but not human slowly rising higher, and higher. It was close to seven feet tall, a shadowy behemoth looming over them. It was a male, a big one, finding prey before entering hibernation for the winter. Another growl came as warning that if the intruders tried to steal its catch, they would join the deer it had killed as its final meal.

'No worries, we're going,' Eddie hissed to the beast. He and Nina kept moving, giving it an ever-wider berth. 'You just get back to your dinner, don't mind us . . .'

Beams of intense torchlight flicked through the trees – and caught the bear.

It flinched, blinking as it was momentarily dazzled . . .

Then it dropped back onto all four paws with a thump and roared, charging at the nearest threat.

Nina shrieked – but Eddie let out a furious roar of his own, rising to his full height and throwing his arms wide. *'Fuck off, Yogi!'*

To their shock, the desperate attempt at intimidation worked. The bear, already reacting as much out of fear as anger at the unexpected encounter, made a scrambling turn and fled.

Towards the border patrol officers.

Panicked shouts came from the forest, along with another roar from the bear. The pursuing lights suddenly retreated at speed.

'Huh,' Eddie said, relieved but surprised. 'It actually worked this time.'

'*This* time?' Nina asked, confused. 'Did you have a run-in with a bear that you didn't tell me about?'

'Not a bear, a tiger. That time in India,' he reminded her.

'Oh, yeah.' She shook her head. 'We've been through so much crazy stuff I've forgotten half of it. At least until my husband brings it up and restarts my PTSD,' she added, mock-critical.

He gave her a tired laugh. 'It'll get the cops off our back for a bit, anyway.' They turned northwards again and continued through the woods.

The trees gradually thinned, more snow on the ground making it easier to pick their way through the darkness. They stayed under the cover of the conifers, aware that any Predator drones cruising high overhead might pick them out by their heat. Eventually, though, remaining beneath the snowy foliage became impossible. 'There's the road,' said Eddie, halting. About fifty metres ahead, a ghostly grey line cut across their path.

Nina looked back. So far, there had been no sign that the border patrol had resumed their pursuit, but she doubted the search had been abandoned. 'So how do we get across without being seen?'

'I don't know.' He looked to either side. 'There's something over there,' he said at last, gesturing to their left. A blocky shape was visible through the trees. 'Let's have a look.'

It was a small shack, long derelict, the snow-covered roof partly collapsed. It had no door, the entrance an ominous rectangle of shadow. Not that they could investigate the interior; it was several metres clear of the protective covering of pines. However, something closer by caught Eddie's interest. 'That might be useful,' he said.

A pile of logs at the edge of the woods was covered by a crumpled tarpaulin. 'What, firewood?' said Nina.

'Being warm'd be nice, but I meant the tarp.' He pulled the covering under the trees. Loose logs clattered to the ground.

Nina cringed at the noise, but luckily there was nobody nearby to hear. 'What are you going to do with it?'

'People are hotter than the ground on infra-red cameras,' he said, flapping the tarpaulin to open it out. It was roughly eight feet by ten, tattered at the edges but otherwise intact. 'So the moment we go out into the open, boom – we're white spots on a black background and they know exactly where we are. But the cameras can't see *through* things, like trees,' he gestured at the overhanging branches, 'or tarps. Especially if you cover 'em in snow. Get down on all fours.'

Nina kept her voice deadpan. 'This isn't the time for that, Eddie.'

He laughed. 'You're getting dirty in your old age. Must be picking it up from me. No, I'll put it over you and stick snow on it, then we'll crawl across the road.'

She regarded the stretch of asphalt dubiously. 'And what if someone comes along it while we're crossing?'

'*Bump-bump*, twenty points.' It was Nina's turn to make an amused sound. 'Nobody's driven past since we've been here. It's night, we're in the middle of nowhere – hopefully it'll stay quiet.'

'Yeah. I mean, no reason why the Canadian border patrol should swing by after two illegal border-crossers smashed up their drones and set a bear on their officers.' But she got down onto the ground anyway.

He draped the canvas over her. 'Okay, hold still. I'll get as much snow on it as I can. Some of it's bound to fall off when we move.' He scooped up handful after handful of snow and dropped it onto the tarpaulin. After a few minutes, he was satisfied. 'All right, I'm coming under.'

He carefully raised the tarp's tail end and wormed his way underneath it until he was alongside his wife. 'Grab the front on your side and pull it along with us. I'll take my side. The road's not that wide; it shouldn't take us long to get under the trees across it. You ready?'

'To play real-life *Frogger*? Can't wait.' She started crawling forward, Eddie doing the same. Weighted down with snow, the tarpaulin was reluctant to move, dragging behind. But their combined efforts forced it to come with them.

It was not long before they had pushed through the undergrowth along the verge to reach the road itself. Eddie risked raising the tarpaulin's side to check that it was deserted. 'Clear this way,' he announced.

Nina followed suit. 'Same here – although the road curves,' she warned. 'I can't see all that far.' The highway disappeared from sight into the forest less than a hundred metres away. No lights were visible through the trees, though.

'Keep an ear out for anything coming. Okay, let's do it.'

They set off again. Nina winced as earth and grass gave way to hard asphalt, digging into her knees. 'God damn it,' she muttered. 'I stopped being able to crawl around without hurting myself when Macy was about four.'

'I'm five years older than you,' Eddie retorted. 'I had to grin and bear it since before she was born!'

Nina smiled, then peeked ahead. They were almost halfway across. The traversal seemed to be getting easier the further they went. 'Crap,' she said in realisation. 'The snow's falling off the tarp.'

'It should stay cold long enough for us to get into cover,' said her husband, unconcerned.

'Yeah, but what if a patrol drives along and sees the trail we've left? They might stop and take a—'

'Dump?' Eddie suggested, when her sentence remained unfinished.

If he was expecting a laugh in response, he didn't get one. 'I think I can hear something!' she whispered.

They both halted. The hiss and scrape of the tarpaulin over the road surface ceased – and the sound of an engine became clear. Nina hurriedly raised her side of their snowy cloak again. 'Someone's coming!' Headlights flickered between the trees.

'Shit,' Eddie growled, setting off again – more quickly. Nina hurriedly did the same. 'Come on, faster, we're almost there.'

The engine became loud enough to hear even over their frantic scrabbling. Nina risked another quick glance. The headlights were about to clear the last of the obscuring trees. 'They're almost here!'

Eddie increased his pace still further. 'Arse, arse, ars*arse*!'

Knees rasping on the road surface, Nina also moved faster – then felt cold soil and grass through her gloves. They had reached the far verge. But they still had to get into cover, and the vehicle was approaching fast, headlamp beams sweeping towards them—

'*Down!*'

Eddie dropped flat, pushing Nina down beside him. Prickly grass jabbed at her face. She grimaced but held still. The oncoming car was almost upon them. Its engine was a big V8, thrumming powerfully. The kind found in a law enforcement patrol vehicle.

They both froze. They would have left a trail of dropped snow across the road – and disturbed any on the verges. If the vehicle's occupants were actively searching for them, surely they would notice . . .

The car reached them—

And passed.

Neither Eddie nor Nina moved for several seconds. The vehicle rumbled on, the sound fading. Eddie lifted his side of the tarp again. 'They missed us.'

'Were they cops?' Nina asked, still afraid to move.

'I think so.' He raised himself back to his knees. 'We're about ten feet from the trees. Once we reach them, we can get out from under this bloody thing.'

'Great,' she said, relieved. 'I can't wait.'

It did not take long to cover the remaining distance. As soon as they were concealed from aerial observation, Eddie flipped away the tarpaulin and stood. 'We made it,' he said, exhaling. His breath steamed in the cold air. 'So now we head north and stay in cover as much as we can until we find some transport.'

'By find, you mean . . .'

'Steal. Sorry. This isn't doing much for your reputation as a law-abiding citizen.'

'At least I can tell the jury there were mitigating circumstances,' Nina said with a sigh. 'As long as they don't try to kill me, anyway . . .'

They headed onwards. The woodland eventually gave way to fields, but by that time they were over another mile from the border. The search would – they both fervently hoped – still be concentrated on the road's southern side. All the same, they stayed beneath the trees as long as they could until reaching an isolated farmhouse. The building was dark, it now being after midnight, but had a couple of vehicles parked outside. One was a relatively new pickup truck, but the other was much older: a Buick Roadmaster station wagon, a land barge with the smoothed-off soap bar lines of a vehicle from the 1990s, panelled in fake wood.

'We'll take the car,' Eddie whispered, producing a multitool from his backpack. 'It'll be a lot easier to hotwire.'

'That's if it runs,' said Nina dubiously. 'It must be nearly forty years old.'

'Yeah, but it's been well looked after. Probably had one owner from new.' They went to the Buick, Nina watching the house as Eddie worked on the lock. It took him only seconds to open.

'I feel kinda guilty about this,' the redhead said as they got in. 'Like you say, we're taking somebody's pride and joy.'

'It's not like we're going to wreck the thing. We only need it to get us to Montreal.' Eddie used his torch to illuminate the underside of the steering column as he prised off a panel and examined the wiring. 'I miss when cars were straightforward, like this. Not full of electronic crap that makes them harder to work on.'

'Maybe you should buy it from them,' Nina said with a smile. Her husband grinned, then fiddled with the wires. A couple of bright sparks lit up the footwell, then the old engine, another big V8, grumbled to life.

Eddie glanced at the house's upper floor. No lights came on. 'Think we're okay,' he said, putting the column-mounted shifter into reverse and carefully backing out of the farmhouse's broad dirt driveway. The Roadmaster wallowed on its soft suspension at every bump. He reversed onto the road and turned to face east. The shifter, though, was reluctant to move. 'What's wrong with this bloody thing?' he griped, jiggling the recalcitrant lever until it finally released. He put it into drive. 'Okay. Montreal, here we come.'

Nina looked at the dark road ahead. 'Let's hope this Natalie can help us.'

19

Montreal, Canada

The exhausted couple spent the night in a cheap motel in Brossard, a Montreal suburb on the eastern bank of the St Lawrence river. It was a calculated risk – Nina might have been recognised, and there was a chance the Buick had been reported stolen – but the night passed without incident. They left soon after dawn, everything shrouded in grey beneath the overcast sky. A light snow was falling with the promise of heavier to come.

The unseasonal cold had draped itself over Quebec as well as New York State, but the Canadian response was more efficient, snowploughs and gritters out in force to keep the streets clear. 'They're much better at dealing with snow than at home,' Nina observed as they drove to find breakfast.

Eddie gave her a half-smile. 'Did I just hear you say something critical about New York?'

'Hey, I'm a born-and-bred New Yorker, I'm allowed to. It's when other people do it that we get offended.' They both grinned. 'But they know how to deal with winter up here. Too cold to go out on the streets? No problem, everything downtown is connected underground. They have a whole extra city centre beneath the regular one. Twenty miles of tunnels, something like that.'

'Did you see much of the normal city? I've never been here before. Don't know what to expect.'

She shrugged. 'It's just a regular big North American city. Except with a lot more signs in French.'

'And more poutine on the menu,' Eddie added, slowing to turn into a diner's parking lot. 'This should do. We'll grab some nosh, then see if we can find Loost's nurse.'

Nina made sure her red hair was hidden beneath her hat, then donned her sunglasses. They got out of the car and went into the building. She kept a low profile as Eddie ordered breakfast, but nobody was interested in either of them.

'No one knows we're in Canada,' he pointed out after the waitress departed. 'Last person who tagged you was Charlie, and we were fifty miles away on the other side of the border. As long as we don't draw any attention, nobody's got any reason to look at you.'

'I'm not planning to cause a scene,' she said, taking out her phone. 'Okay, so: Natalie Bachand. How are we going to find her? It's a big city.'

'Maybe she's in the phone book,' Eddie suggested.

'Who the hell's in the phone book any more? For that matter, does anywhere still even *have* phone books?' But she did a search anyway – and was surprised by the result. 'Huh. Turns out Montreal *does* have a phone book, or a digital one, at least. And there are a couple of *Nathalie* Bachands, with an "h" . . . but only one Natalie.'

'Think it's her?'

'Let's find out.' She tapped the number on the page and put the phone to her ear.

'Course, she might not answer,' said Eddie as a dialling tone warbled. 'I mean, who picks up a call from an unknown number these days?'

Two rings, three . . . then the call was answered. A woman spoke. '*Bonjour?*'

'Uh – *bonjour*, hi,' Nina replied, a little taken aback; she had subconsciously agreed with Eddie, almost not expecting an answer. 'Is that Natalie?'

'Yes, it is.' The woman instantly switched to perfect English. 'Who is this?'

Nina glanced around to make sure nobody was eavesdropping, lowering her voice for good measure. 'My name is Nina Wilde. If you're the person I think you are, you probably know who I am.'

There was a pause before a reply came. 'Yes. I do.'

'So you did work for Rafael Loost?'

'I did.' There was deeply felt emotion behind the two words, quickly covered. 'What do you want?'

'I need to talk to you. About what he's arranged for me, and how I can stop it – before I get killed.'

Another silence, Natalie apparently considering her words carefully. 'I don't know how I can help you. I would *like* to, but . . . I don't know,' she repeated.

'Please,' implored Nina. 'Anything you can tell us might help, anything at all. You were on Loost's space station when he was setting this up, yes?'

'I was there until the end,' was the reply. 'When Rafael died. But I had nothing to do with what he was planning. I was one of his nurses, nothing more.'

'You were *something* more,' Nina said carefully. If she pushed too hard she might drive the other woman away, but she was her only hope of identifying Loost's inside man. 'You're pregnant with his child. And he left you both with nothing. I can help you with money, if you need it. But only if I stay alive. And the longer this goes on, the harder that'll be. Will you help me? Please?'

Seconds ticked by. Nina and Eddie exchanged concerned looks – until finally, Natalie spoke again. 'All right. What do you want to do?'

'I need to talk to you in person. If there's anything at all you can remember about what Loost did before he died – people he spoke to, anything he was working on specifically about Uzz – it could be a huge help in stopping this. We're in Montreal now; we can probably get to you within the hour.'

There was still reluctance in the Canadian's voice, but she said, 'Okay. Okay. I'll see you.'

'Thank you,' Nina replied, with genuine gratitude. 'Where are you?'

'I have an apartment on the Rue Saint-Urbain.' She gave the address. 'It's not far from Downtown.'

'We'll find it,' Nina assured her. 'We'll be there as soon as we can. Thank you.'

'I hope I can help,' Natalie said, before ending the call.

'Sounded promising,' Eddie said as Nina lowered her phone.

'Yeah, hopefully. Let me find her address.' She put it into her map app. 'It reckons it'll take us about twenty minutes to get there.'

The waitress returned, bearing plates. 'Let's eat first, though,' Eddie said hungrily. 'It was a long-arse night, and the day's probably going to be the same.'

Nina avoided the waitress's eyes, looking down at the table as her continental breakfast was placed before her. Eddie, meanwhile, received a plate of hot food. 'Wait, you really did order poutine, for breakfast?' she said once the woman had departed. 'I thought you were joking about that!'

'It's chips, cheese and gravy,' said Eddie, already taking his first forkful. 'Proper brown gravy, not that weird white stuff you Yanks make. What's not to like?'

'Travel the world, experience new cultures,' she said with a mocking smile, before starting on her own food. '*Bon appetit*. Then let's hope Natalie Bachand can tell us something useful.'

It took longer than the app's promised twenty minutes to reach Natalie's apartment building, the Buick slowed by snow-clearance work. Eddie parked behind a car across the street from it, surveying the neighbourhood. It seemed unremarkably middle-income, a mixture of terraced brownstone houses, low-rise apartment blocks and taller, newer high-rises. Snow was still falling, the few pedestrians wrapped up in heavy coats and hats and scarves.

'Looks safe,' he finally reported. 'Nobody's waiting for us.'

'Good,' said Nina. She looked up at Natalie's building. From the apartment number, the Canadian was on the twelfth floor, near the top. 'We should try to make this quick, though. Once we go up there, there's only one way out.'

Eddie nodded. 'Maybe you should ring her again and get her to meet us somewhere else.'

'It's too late now, we're here.' She made her own scan of the street. As Eddie had said earlier, nobody knew they were in Canada, and their purloined car hadn't drawn any attention. She tugged her hat fully down and adjusted her tinted glasses, concealing as much of her face as she could behind her coat's upturned collar. How good Uzz's facial recognition was she didn't know, but surely it couldn't identify someone from barely a quarter of their features? 'Let's see what she can tell us.'

The cold hit her as she exited the car. New York had its share of biting winters, but this felt different, a deeper chill to the breeze. She turned her face away from the wind, seeing a man in an overcoat and baseball cap standing on the sidewalk fifty feet away, having just got out of his own car. His phone was raised as if taking a photo – then he quickly lowered it and walked briskly away.

'Oh, shit,' she said as she rounded the Roadmaster to join Eddie. 'I think that guy just tagged me.'

Eddie whirled to challenge him, but the man had already turned the corner at an intersection, disappearing from sight. 'He doesn't know which building we're going to. You sure he tagged you?'

'I don't know, but I'd rather not take any chances. Like I said, let's make this quick.'

They crossed the street to the apartment building. Feeling suddenly nervous and exposed, Nina went to the Entryphone and keyed in Natalie's apartment number. A response soon came. 'Yes?' said the Canadian.

'It's me, Nina.'

'Okay. Come in. The elevator is on the left.' The door buzzed, the lock releasing. Eddie opened it, quickly checking beyond to make sure there were no unwelcome surprises, then ushered Nina in.

They took the lift up to the twelfth floor, finding Natalie's apartment. Nina knocked on the door. It opened almost immediately. She recognised the woman who answered from the TV news: in her early thirties, brown hair in a short ponytail. She was only just visibly pregnant. 'Hello,' she said. 'Come in.'

Nina and Eddie entered, being shown to a living room with an impressive view across downtown Montreal. 'I'm glad you agreed to see us,' Nina told her. 'We'll get out of your hair as soon as we can. This is my husband Eddie, by the way.'

Natalie nodded. 'Hello.' She sat in an armchair, gesturing for them to take places facing her on a couch. 'How can I help you?'

'Like I said on the phone,' Nina replied as she took her seat, 'anything you can tell me about who Rafael Loost was dealing with before he died could help us. Especially if it was anyone working at Uzz.'

'He spoke to his people at Uzz a lot,' said the Canadian. Though her tone was neutral, she seemed on the verge of frowning. At her visitors, or at the thought of her former lover? 'It was his main business. He usually did it in private, though.'

'Only usually?' Eddie asked.

'He never really stopped working, even when we were treating him. Sometimes he would be on calls while he was having his chelation therapy. Cleaning his blood,' she added in explanation. 'Filtering out accumulated toxins. That was what killed him.' The hint of a frown deepened slightly. 'The therapy could only slow the process, not stop it. He needed regular blood transfusions to stay alive. When his supply rocket blew up, it had his latest supply aboard. Because you made public the video of Rafael threatening to have you killed, none of his competitors were willing to deliver another. It might have exposed them to lawsuits. And, well, none of them had any love for him.'

Nina assessed the other woman carefully. 'Are you angry about his death? At us, specifically?'

Natalie drew in a slow breath before answering. 'I'm angry about everything to do with Rafael. I used to admire him – idolise him, even. He was the tech genius who was going to save the world! It was an incredible honour to be one of his personal nursing staff on the space station.'

'Going to guess all his nurses were women,' Eddie said. She nodded. 'Funny, that.'

'Whatever Rafael wanted, he got. And we were happy to be there! The pay was, ha, astronomical.' The laugh was brief, little humour behind it. 'But being there with him, the whole time . . . you see who he really is. Yes, he's incredibly intelligent, driven, charismatic – he has to be, to become the world's richest man, to inspire people to work hard enough to keep him there. But he has – had – a dark side. He was . . .' She paused, as if reluctant to say the words out loud. 'Ruthless. Selfish. He was a self-made man who overcame so much in life to reach where he did, but that meant the only person he cared about was . . . himself.'

'I think that's the same of any rich person,' Nina told her. 'We've dealt with plenty of billionaires over the years, and it's something they all seemed to have in common.'

'That, and most of 'em are dead after we were done,' muttered Eddie. His wife gave him a sharp look.

Natalie also shot him a disapproving glance, before turning back to Nina. 'And he could also be petty, vindictive – childish, even. If someone wronged him in business, he would go out of his way to make them suffer for it. When you have presidents and prime ministers on speed-dial, it's easy to make somebody's government contracts just suddenly disappear, you know? Or get a journalist fired, or end a patent lawsuit.'

'Or turn everyone on the planet into a potential assassin for a billion-dollar bounty,' Nina pointed out.

'Yes. Or that.' Natalie leaned back in her chair, thinking. 'I knew he had a vendetta against you. But I never realised how far he had gone to make it happen! If I had, I would have tried to stop it. It's – insane. And to think that he would do that, that the father of my *child* would do that . . . it's horrifying. I'm sorry.'

'I'm sorry too. For you, I mean – and your baby. Did he really leave you with nothing?'

The Canadian nodded. 'He knew I was pregnant before he died. And that he was the father – I mean, he was the only man there! He told me he would take care of everything. But after he died, I found out he had done *nothing*! There was not one penny for me, or our baby. All he left me was a child I will have to bring up on my own.' The frown finally broke through clearly, anger crunching her face.

Eddie shifted slightly. It was only a small movement, but one Nina knew well: he was readying himself for action, if necessary. 'You know,' he said cautiously, 'a billion dollars would take care of you and your baby for the rest of your lives.'

'I'm not like Rafael,' was the firm reply.

'I'm delighted to hear it,' Nina told her.

'I always wanted to be a nurse – to help people, to make them well, keep them alive. In the end, there was nothing I could do for Rafael. But there might be something I can do for you. So yes, I want to help you. If I can.'

Nina leaned forward. 'Thank you. So, if you can think of anyone involved with Uzz that he spoke to a lot, please try to remember. It might be my only chance to stop this.'

Natalie closed her eyes. 'He often spoke to Peter Hallister, but he was in charge of Uzz on a day-to-day basis, so that was not unusual. He left after the company was taken over. I think he works for Apple now. Who else?' Her frown returned. 'There were several people from Uzz, but they were all executives. There was no reason why he wouldn't speak to them.'

'Anyone in programming?' Eddie asked. 'Whoever helped Loost

set this up was good enough to hack into Uzz so that the people who run it now couldn't stop it.'

The Canadian opened her eyes again. 'The CTO, I suppose – Chief Technical Officer,' she clarified. 'I don't remember his name; he was American, I think. Although—' She stopped mid-sentence with a thoughtful expression.

'What is it?' Nina asked.

'There *was* someone else. He was the CTO at Qbial, Rafael's quantum computing company, in charge of his AI development. He was Indian, although I think he became an American citizen. What was his name?' She nibbled on her lower lip for a moment. 'Vishal,' she announced. 'Vishal Varna. Rafael spoke to him several times that I know of – and I remember that once, they were definitely talking about Uzz.'

'Weren't the two companies connected, though? Loost told me that Uzz used AI powered by quantum computers to scan everything people did on it.'

'Rafael owned them both, but they were separate companies. Uzz had to pay for quantum computer time the same as anyone else. Maybe they got a discount, I don't know. Rafael once called Vishal his "secret weapon", though. I think he was his top AI programmer. Nobody knew how it worked better than he did.'

'Do you know where he is now?'

'He left the company when it was taken over after Rafael died. He got a big payout, millions of dollars.' Another pause for thought. 'Actually, he bought one of Rafael's houses. In Malta. I heard that from someone.'

'Does he live there?'

'I think so.'

Nina considered the new information. Could Varna have set up the backdoor into Uzz via Qbial? He had the ability, and also a financial incentive . . . 'Is there anyone else you can think of who might have been able to hack into Uzz?'

Natalie shook her head. 'No. But I only overheard his calls when he was making them during treatment sessions. He could have spoken to anyone in private.'

'Okay.' Would Loost have been trusting enough, or blasé enough, to hold confidential discussions in front of his nursing staff? It was possible, Nina mused. Especially towards the end, when every minute of plotting his revenge became precious . . . 'Thank you, Natalie,' she said, standing. 'Thank you for helping me.'

'I hope it's enough,' the younger woman replied. 'If I think, I might be able to remember more.'

'If you do, then you've got my phone number. But we need to get moving. The less time we stay in one place, the safer we are.' She glanced at the window. The snowfall outside was now heavier, the clouds darkening.

Eddie also rose. 'Thanks for seeing us,' he said to their hostess.

Natalie got up to show them out. 'I hope you get through all this. I really do. It would be good to see you again.'

'Thanks,' said Nina, with a grateful smile. 'If I do, then if you need anything, any help for your baby . . . get in touch. Okay?'

The Canadian gave her a nod in return. 'Thank you.'

The couple left, returning to the elevator. 'So, what do you think?' Eddie asked as they descended. 'This programmer bloke – could he be the one who hacked Uzz?'

'I don't know,' Nina replied. 'But he's the only lead we've got so far.'

'So what now? I'm thinking we should get out of the city, in case that guy outside really did tag you.'

'I agree. But where do we go? Malta?'

'It'd be warmer than here.' The lift reached the bottom floor. Eddie held Nina back, checking the lobby. 'It's clear.'

'What about outside?'

He went to the main doors as Nina emerged from the elevator. 'Can't see anyone hanging about. Nobody by the car, either.'

'Maybe we got lucky,' she said, relieved. Eddie opened the door, and they hurried out into the falling snow.

The man in the baseball cap had made a circuit of the block, coming back onto the Rue Saint-Urbain and stopping beside a large panel van parked fifty metres from Natalie Bachand's building. The window lowered to reveal three men in the cab's seats: Steinitz, Duger . . . and John Brice. 'I tagged the woman,' the new arrival said.

Steinitz held up his phone. 'We saw. The alert went out on Uzz. Thank you for keeping watch; we didn't know how long it would take her to get here.'

The man nodded. 'Gratitude is fine, but it won't pay the rent. My money?'

The German took a well-stuffed envelope from inside his coat. 'Fifty thousand dollars Canadian, as agreed.'

The other man took it, opened it and quickly counted the bills inside. 'Thanks. But maybe I should have gone for the billion. She resisted arrest, oops, she's dead.'

'I'm glad you didn't. It would have interfered with our plans.' There was a hint of a threat behind the bland words.

Brice made a noise of irritation. 'We're here, they're here, so why don't we just kill them now instead of playing games?'

'You know why,' was Steiner's impatient reply.

'If we lose them again, we might not find them. You're putting a lot of faith in them following your late boss's oh-so-clever trail of breadcrumbs—'

Two things happened at once.

The first was that two people emerged from the apartment building's door. Brice recognised them instantly: Eddie Chase and Nina Wilde.

The second was the street's relative quiet being suddenly shattered by the thunderous roar of large motorcycle engines. Several

Harley-Davidsons sped around a corner and rode past the van, pulling up by the Buick Roadmaster parked across from the apartment block – the car that Brice's targets had just reached. The riders all wore heavy black leather jackets with *Devils Defenders* written on the back in red gothic letters. 'Shit!' said the crooked cop. 'That's not good.'

'What?' Steinitz asked.

'Those bikers – they're one of Montreal's gangs. Part of the Consortium.'

'Which is what?' asked Brice.

'The city's biggest organised crime alliance. It controls most of the drugs trade. The Defenders are guys you don't want to deal with if you can avoid it. Frank Knox, the leader, is a fucking psycho. And he's right there.' One biker, a large man with a long moustache, had dismounted and removed his helmet.

'They want the bounty!' Brice snapped. He turned to the cop. 'Are they killers?'

'Shit, yeah,' came the reply.

Brice glared back at the new arrivals as the rest of the group got off their bikes and surrounded the Buick – and his prey. 'No. Chase is *mine*,' he snarled.

Nina and Eddie had just left the building when the echoing snarl of multiple motorcycle engines reached them. They looked around as the line of bikes rounded a corner – and raced towards them. 'Get in the car,' Eddie snapped.

But it was too late. By the time they reached the Buick, the leading bikes had swept past, frighteningly close, before pulling up alongside the Roadmaster's front. Others blocked it in behind. The tail-enders formed a rough semicircle in the street around the parked car. Unfriendly eyes glared at the couple from inside matte-black crash helmets. 'Uh, hi,' said Nina nervously. 'If we're in your space, we'll move!'

A tall, wide-shouldered man got off his bike, turning as he did so to show the words *Devils Defenders* in red on the back of his well-worn leather jacket. It took all Nina's effort not to remark on the ungrammatical lack of an apostrophe. He removed his helmet, revealing a deeply weathered face with a long, drooping moustache. 'It ain't the space we want, darlin',' he drawled, sounding as if he gargled a cupful of gravel each morning. 'It's one billion US dollars. Or about one-point-four billion Canadian, if you wanna do the conversion.' Some of his fellow riders laughed. 'Specifically,' he went on, drawing a gun, 'we want *you*, Nina Wilde.'

20

Eddie positioned himself protectively between Nina and the leader of the bikers. 'Not happening, mate.'

The act of resistance brought nothing but sarcastic laughter. 'That ain't a request, *mate*,' came the reply, a thin grin exposing nicotine-yellowed teeth. 'You got two choices. Walk away, or get shot.'

'You're going to shoot someone on the street in broad daylight?' Nina protested.

'These are *our* streets, darlin'. We own them, we're connected. You think I ain't shot people in broad daylight before? There could be a cop down the street and he wouldn't see nothin'.' His narrowed eyes turned back to Eddie. 'You got five seconds to decide. Walk, or die. Four.'

Nina saw Eddie tense. He wouldn't walk away, she knew that – but doing anything else would surely get him killed.

'Three.'

She was about to try to bargain with the bikers when loud, manic music reached her. Two cars were approaching at well over the speed limit, deep bass thudding from them. Whoever was inside, the Defenders considered them a greater concern than their captives. 'Frank!' one biker shouted, hurriedly pulling a gun of his own. 'It's the Batras!'

'Shit!' the leader snarled. Both cars, heavily customised and colourful Honda Civic Type R hatchbacks with large spoilers, glowing neon underlighting and sound systems to rival a nightclub, pulled up sharply across the street. Young men with guns were already leaning from the windows, weapons pointed at the biker gang.

Eddie, hands half-raised more in readiness to fight than a show of surrender, looked between the Defenders and the new arrivals. 'What the bloody hell is this?'

'What the bloody hell is this?' exclaimed Brice. All the Defenders had now drawn weapons, but the amount of firepower on both sides had brought an immediate stand-off.

'Shit,' said the cop, dismayed. 'That's the Batra Group – one of the Punjabi mafia gangs.'

The Englishman gave him a disbelieving look. 'You have a *Punjabi* mafia?'

'You don't wanna know how many different mafias there are in Montreal. And these guys aren't in the Consortium. Pash Batra hates Frank Knox, and the feeling's mutual. They'd be happy to kill each other.'

'This might be their chance,' said Steinitz, watching as the new arrivals left their cars, keeping their guns on the bikers.

'The fuck you doing here, Batra?' demanded Knox, now pointing his gun towards the seven Indian men as they approached. The loud Bhangra music continued to pound from their vehicles behind them.

The newcomers halted, their own weapons raised in gangster-style sideways holds. The leader, a bestubbled man in his late twenties wearing a casual but expensive designer coat with a hoodie beneath, regarded the bikers with sneering contempt. 'I'm here for her, Knox.' Batra nodded at Nina. 'So you and your batty-boy leather buddies should just ride off before you get hurt.'

The Defenders responded to the insult with predictable anger. But nobody was yet prepared to risk pulling the trigger. Nina realised she and Eddie were no longer the centre of attention. 'Eddie,' she whispered. 'If we can get to the car . . .' They were only a few feet short of the Buick.

Eddie nodded. 'Slowly,' he replied under his breath. They both edged towards the Roadmaster—

Then froze as Knox snapped his gun at them. But it wasn't because he had noticed their movement. 'She's worth a billion dollars to someone,' he growled to Batra. 'But I'd gladly shoot her to make sure it ain't *you*. I'd rather get nothing than you get a cup of hot piss, never mind a billion bucks.'

Batra's sneer deepened. 'Oh, you won't get nothing. I've got plenty of bullets for you.' His gun was a Glock with an extended magazine protruding from the grip, suggesting it had been modified to turn it into an auto-firing machine pistol. Some of his men had similar weapons. Only one of the Defenders had anything of comparable firepower, a compact Mac-10 sub-machine gun.

Knox kept his own gun aimed at Nina. 'You ain't got the balls to shoot me, kid. Not when you'd die too. So get back in your little Jap shitboxes and drive away while you still have the—'

A van skidded to a stop, blocking the street.

'Is this a *joke*?' Brice snapped. A dented and dirty long-wheelbase GMC van had just passed the mercenaries' vehicle at speed before slithering to a halt, blocking both lanes of the road. Its rear doors and sliding side panel flew open, another group of gunmen jumping out.

'It's the Dockside Boys,' said the cop unhappily. 'They're Irish, part of the Consortium, but they don't especially like the Defenders. You know, it's been great doing business with you, but I'm gonna go now. I'd recommend you do the same, 'cause there's about to be trouble.' He stuffed his money into his coat, then rapidly headed away from the three-gang confrontation.

'I'm not going anywhere,' said Brice firmly. He turned to address the other mercenaries in the windowless rear. 'I need a suppressed weapon. Now!'

Nina and Eddie watched in disbelief as more armed men got out of the newly arrived van. This group were all Caucasian, wearing drab and functional workmen's coats or heavy winter jackets. 'And what the fuck is all this?' said the apparent leader, a heavy-set man in his forties with thinning hair and intense grey eyes. His accent was strongly Irish, and he had a gun in each hand. 'You got yourself into some trouble here, Frank?'

'Nothing we can't handle, Jim,' Knox replied coldly. His own gun had left Nina to cover the new threat. 'No need for you to be here.'

'Oh, but there is. The lady in the hat and sunglasses there. Professor Nina Wilde, is her name. World-famous archaeologist – even I'd heard of her, and that was *before* Rafael Loost put a billion dollars on her head!'

Nina, again edging towards the Buick, shook her head. 'So are more and more people going to keep turning up to fight over me?' she said quietly.

'Bring 'em on,' Eddie replied. 'If they're fighting each other, they won't be looking at us.'

That seemed to be true, the Defenders' attention now divided between the other gangs. The Irishman waved a gun towards the Batra Group. 'And how about turning down that fucking noise, Pash? Sounds like someone torturing a pig in a disco.'

Like the other groups, the Indians had been forced to split their aim. They were now considerably outnumbered, but unwilling to back down. 'Jim Kelly,' said Batra with disdain. 'You're a long way outside your territory, aren't you?'

'This whole city's the Consortium's territory, kiddo. Now, fuck off home for a curry – and Frank, you better go too. We'll handle it from here.'

'The fuck you will,' Knox growled. 'We were here first. The money's ours.'

'I don't think so.' The Dockside Boys stopped, the three factions now arranged in a rough triangle. Of them, the Irish contingent had the heaviest weapons, handguns accompanied by a couple of MP5 sub-machine guns and even a Kalashnikov assault rifle. 'Now I know we're supposed to be in an alliance, but for that much money? I'm willing to break it. You can't win here, Frank. Or you, Pash. Gold's no good to you if you've got lead in the brain. Do the right thing, and save your arses.' Kelly grinned. 'I'll send you both postcards from Bermuda.'

Knox's scowl deepened – then he realised his prisoners were now at their car. 'Hey!' he yelled, whirling to face them again. 'Stand the fuck still!'

Nina and Eddie froze – but Knox's sudden movement triggered responses from the rival gangs, guns whipping back and forth as fingers curled more tightly around triggers. 'Hold it, hold it!' shouted Batra. 'Nobody shoot!' Kelly gave much the same order to his own men. The Indian retreated slightly towards his car – muttering a command to his smartwatch. Its little screen lit up as it made a call.

'Shit,' Eddie hissed to Nina. The bikers around them were as tense as drawn bowstrings, adrenalin surging in expectation of violence. 'This is going to go bad any second. Get ready to drop – and get into the car if you can.'

'Last chance!' the Irishman called. 'Turn her over. Now!'

One of the mercenaries gave Brice a suppressed handgun. He would have preferred a more powerful weapon, but at the range involved, he was confident it would do an adequate job.

'What are you doing?' Steinitz demanded as the Englishman lowered his window.

'Your boss wants Wilde to play his game? I'm making sure she gets the chance.' He leaned out, looking down the gun's sights. Most of the Dockside Boys were blocked from view by their stationary van, but he had a clear bead on one man near the roadside.

He exhaled to steady himself, lined up his shot . . . and squeezed the trigger.

Frank Knox's gun was still aimed at Eddie. 'You can go fuck yourself, Kell—'

One of the Dockside Boys fell as the back of his skull exploded.

His hand spasmed as he collapsed, finger snatching at his submachine gun's trigger – and unleashing an echoing burst of fire.

For a fraction of a second, nobody moved, shocked—

Eddie grabbed Nina and dropped to the ground. *'Down!'*

Then the street turned into a war zone.

All three gangs started shooting at once, nobody knowing who had fired first, or caring. Bullets struck cars, bikes, walls – and people. A Defender near Nina and Eddie toppled backwards from his Harley, the red lettering on his jacket despoiled by a ragged exit wound of a deeper, wetter shade. One of the Batras spun with a scream and fell onto a Honda's hood, sliding down it and streaking the paintwork with blood. The Dockside Boys, slightly further away, ran for cover as they opened up with their automatic weapons. Another Defender was caught by the spray of gunfire, the Roadmaster's rear windscreen shattering behind him. He fell from his bike and landed hard on the asphalt beside his machine.

Eddie stayed down, sheltering Nina beneath himself until the initial panicked wildfire eased. Those who had dived for cover had now reached it; it would take a few seconds for them to recover from their shock. 'Get in!' he said, reaching up to open the Buick's door.

They both scrambled inside, Eddie taking the driver's seat. The gang members were already shooting at their enemies from cover. Cracks of gunfire echoed from the surrounding buildings. But the shots were cautious; nobody wanted to move to aim at one of the rival gangs only to expose themselves to the other.

Hunched low in the seat, Eddie fiddled with the ignition wires. The station wagon might have been almost forty years old, but it started first time, the big V8 rumbling to life. He raised his head just enough to see over the dash. The car parked in front was too close for him to peel out that way. Instead he jammed the selector into reverse. 'Stay down,' he warned Nina. She squeezed into the footwell as he stamped on the accelerator.

The Buick leapt backwards – and slammed into the Harley-Davidson behind it.

The bike toppled, landing on the wounded man, then both the Harley and its screaming owner were scraped along the road surface like a bulldozer blade amidst a shower of sparks and blood. Eddie flicked the wheel to swing the car out from the roadside. The bike spun away, the man trapped under it hitting the kerb head-first with a crack of breaking bone.

Knox, hunched down behind his bike, was focused on the Batra Group – until he realised his prize was escaping. 'Hey!' he yelled to the other bikers. 'She's getting away!' He rose to mount his Harley, but had to duck again as one of the Punjabis fired at him.

Across the street, Batra had also heard Knox's warning. He peeked over his car, seeing the old Buick powering away in reverse. 'Come on, into the cars!' he cried. 'Forget these assholes – get that bitch!'

Eddie whipped up a hand, adjusting the rear-view mirror to see where he was going. The Dockside Boys' van blocked most of the street. He swerved to aim for the gap in front of it, which looked barely wide enough to fit through. Some of the gang were crouching beside the van or the nearby parked cars, hurriedly moving when they realised the oncoming Roadmaster wasn't going to stop. 'Hang on!' he warned Nina, bracing himself—

He had misjudged the gap. The Buick jolted as it clipped the van's corner.

Jim Kelly had taken cover behind the GMC, the impact knocking him down. He swore, then looked under the van to see both the Defenders and the Batra Group scrambling to their vehicles. A rapid glance the other way, and he saw the old station wagon retreating backwards, seemingly with nobody driving except a disembodied hand clutching the steering wheel. 'Ah, shite!' he barked, jumping up. 'Lads, come on – there's a billion bucks in that car!'

***

Brice twisted in his seat to track the Buick as it passed the parked panel van. He had lost sight of his targets in the chaos, but now glimpsed Eddie Chase hunched low in the driver's seat. 'There they go!' he snapped. 'Get after them – we can't risk losing them!'

Steinitz started the engine, but with a noticeable lack of urgency. 'We know where they're going to go.'

'Only if they do exactly what Loost expected, and if he'd been able to do that, he wouldn't be dead. Come on, go!'

The German put the van into gear and started to move – only to brake abruptly as more vehicles tore past. The Defenders had been the first to set off, their Harleys racing thunderously down the street. Close behind were the two customised hatchbacks of the Batra Group, music still thudding. The Dockside Boys' van was the last to get going as the surviving gang members piled into its open doors and it skidded around, rear wheels spinning before finding grip on the wet road. To Brice's frustration, Steinitz remained stationary until it passed, then looped around to join the chase.

21

Nina looked up at her husband from the passenger footwell. 'Uh, Eddie, we're still going backwards. Wouldn't forwards be faster?'

'I need room to do a J-turn,' Eddie replied, eyes fixed on the mirror. He spotted a gap amongst parked cars where an alley ran between two buildings. 'Okay, hold on!'

He spun the wheel to bring the Buick around in a slithering quarter-turn, gripping the gear selector to move it from reverse to neutral, and then into drive—

The shifter didn't shift.

'What—shit!' Eddie yelped. He tried harder, but it still refused to move. The car was now committed to its backwards turn. He sprang up to look back through the broken rear windscreen as the Roadmaster bounded over the gutter and into the alley. Its left flank rasped ear-splittingly along a brick wall before he twitched the car into the centre of the passage.

Another loud noise replaced the shrill of scraping metal – the hammering roar of a big motorcycle engine. One of the Defenders had turned into the alley, and was rapidly closing. He groped awkwardly inside his jacket with his left hand for a gun.

'Nina!' Eddie barked. 'I need to see where we're going, but there's a guy with a gun catching up. Tell me where he is.'

'You want me to put my head *nearer* the bullets?' But she pulled herself up to peer nervously over the dash. The biker was trying to aim at their car, but the combination of using his off-hand and the bumpy ride down the snow-spattered alley was throwing him off.

'Okay, he's having trouble aiming, but – *whoa!*' More pursuers had entered the alley – and she gasped as another of the Defenders was crushed against a wall by one of the Batra Group's cars. The hatchback swerved clear as the Harley tumbled over its rider. 'Scratch one biker, but not the one closest to us.'

'Tell me when he's going to fire,' said Eddie, focused on holding the Buick on course.

'He's going to fire!' Nina instantly replied.

She ducked, Eddie dropping as low as he could as gunshots rang through the alley. But the Defender was aiming at the car, not its occupants, the bounty foremost on his mind. Bullets struck the hood with shrill clanks. The biker briefly held fire to recover as the bike hit a bump, then found a new target – one of the front tyres.

He took aim and pulled the trigger—

The Honda rammed him from behind.

The Defender got off one shot, hitting the Buick's radiator grille, as he was thrown from his Harley. He managed a short scream before he smashed face-first against the ground – then the hatchback bounced twice as it ran him over.

Eddie raised his head. One threat had gone, but the situation was no better. The Type R accelerated. A man leaned from the passenger window, bringing a gun to bear. The Yorkshireman ducked again as a bullet punched through the windscreen and blew a hole in the seat just above his head.

Nina could partially see her wing mirror from her position – and glimpsed something coming up fast. 'Eddie, brace!' she shouted as she reached across—

And tugged at the steering wheel.

The Roadmaster veered to the right – and clipped the corner of a wheeled dumpster at the alley's side.

The collision sent the bin spinning into the wall behind it – and rebounding back out into the alley. It caught the speeding Buick's front wing, whirling around into the hatchback's path.

The Honda's driver stamped on the brake, but the car slithered on the wet surface and ploughed into the hefty metal obstacle. The man leaning from the window was flung against the windscreen pillar with sternum-cracking force. Its front end mangled and hood bent upwards, the Civic skidded to a standstill in a twisted embrace with the dumpster, almost blocking the alley.

The second of the Batra Group's cars, with the gang's namesake inside, stopped and was forced to reverse as the Defenders roared past and slipped through the narrow gap. The Dockside Boys' van was about to turn into the alley, but on seeing the obstruction swung back into the road to continue around the block.

The Buick, meanwhile, had reached the alley's far end. Eddie tried again to free the jammed shifter, but it remained locked in place. He had no choice but to keep going in reverse, flicking the station wagon into a skidding turn onto the new street.

The leading Defender followed him around the corner. 'Oh, shit!' Nina gasped as she raised her head. 'This guy's got an Uzi or something!'

Eddie guided the Buick past a snowplough, then quickly looked back. 'Mac-10,' he corrected, 'but duck anyway!' This biker also held his weapon in his left hand so he could work the throttle with his right – but he was a natural southpaw, wielding the compact sub-machine gun with total confidence.

The Mac-10 locked on to their car. They both dropped behind the dashboard again—

The damaged windscreen exploded as bullets sprayed across it, chunks of safety glass cascading over Nina and Eddie. A second burst of fire tore into their seat backs and headrests, shredding the leather.

Then the shooting stopped – but the Harley's flat thunder grew louder, the biker moving to fire through a side window—

Another shot – but from a different gun.

The single retort was followed by a loud crash and shrill of metal spinning over asphalt. Someone shouted over the cacophony. Nina risked a peek – to see that Knox was the second shooter, having gunned down the trigger-happy Defender. The warning he was giving to his gang was obvious: *She's worth a billion dollars – but only if we kill her on Uzz!*

She had no time to dwell on the insanity of the situation. Two more vehicles rounded a corner almost simultaneously: Kelly's van and Batra's car. They jockeyed for position as they came through the turn, the men inside exchanging a couple of shots, before the heavily customised hatchback took advantage of its lighter weight and greater power, surging after the Buick.

It would not take long to catch up. The Roadmaster's maximum speed in reverse had topped out with the speedometer showing fifty-five kilometres per hour, the transmission shrieking in protest. A car coming the other way hooted its horn – then swerved into a bank of newly ploughed snow when its driver realised there was more coming towards her than the old station wagon. Eddie dodged the car's protruding back end, then immediately jinked back to avoid another vehicle. But the street beyond it was clear—

He saw why.

A van blocked the road at an intersection ahead. Unlike the Dockside Boys' ratty workhorse, this had been treated to an expensive custom paint-job: another Batra Group vehicle. Pash Batra had called in reinforcements. Two more armed gang members jumped out from it. One toted an MG3 machine gun with a chunky hundred-round ammo box at his hip.

The other shouldered an RPG-7 rocket launcher.

'Where are the fucking Mounties when you need 'em?' Eddie yelled, jerking the wheel as the machine gunner opened fire—

A fusillade of bullets tore into the Buick's tail, the remaining windows shattering. Nina squashed herself down into the footwell as her seat jolted with multiple impacts.

Eddie also dropped as far as he could. He was driving blind, relying on his last glimpse of the street to guide them. He was sure he'd seen another alleyway off to the right. If he could reach it, they would be shielded from the heavy weapons—

The alley was there – but there was a thick bank of ploughed snow in front of it.

The Roadmaster hit it at an angle, kicking up into the air as if it had hit a ramp. Nina and Eddie were both thrown sideways as the car tipped over. The Yorkshireman was still gripping the steering wheel, inadvertently pulling at it – and swinging the Buick back out into the street, balanced precariously on two wheels.

The surprised machine gunner paused his fire – but the man with the RPG-7 had already pulled his trigger. The rocket-propelled grenade burst from the launcher with a sizzling *whoosh* and streaked down the street on a trail of smoke.

Batra's Honda sideswiped a Defender into a parked car as it powered after the Buick. The other bikers hurriedly cleared its path. Batra leaned from his window, aiming at the driver's side of the canted, wavering Buick. Take out the bald guy, and Wilde would be his, shortly followed by a billion dollars . . .

The rocket shot *underneath* the Roadmaster, almost clipping one of its raised wheels. Then the station wagon slammed heavily back down, spraying broken glass from what remained of its windows.

But the rocket flew on. Batra had a split-second of realisation as he saw it coming straight at him, but that wasn't even enough time for him to open his mouth to scream—

The Civic exploded, somersaulting to smash down on its roof in the middle of the street. The remaining Defenders braked to avoid flying debris, then swarmed past the blazing wreck.

The landing had jarred everything in the Buick. On an impulse Eddie gripped the shifter – and felt it move. 'Hold on!' he warned Nina. 'I'm going to spin us around!'

The roar of motorcycle engines grew louder. The Defenders flanked the car as Knox rode up alongside it. The gang leader aimed his gun at Eddie. At almost point-blank range, he couldn't miss—

Eddie spun the wheel.

The reversing station wagon slithered sharply about on the wet road. The front end hit Knox's bike, bowling him onto its bonnet. The Yorkshireman threw the car into neutral as it continued around – then slammed it into drive and stamped on the accelerator as it completed its half-turn. It surged forward.

Behind it, Knox's Harley fell to the road, scything the front wheel of another Defender's bike out from under him. The man was thrown screaming into the air, his brief flight coming to an abrupt end as he smashed face-first through a parked car's windscreen.

Knox slid across the Buick's hood, one flailing hand catching the broken windshield's lower frame. He pulled himself higher and looked into the car – just as Nina raised her head again. Their eyes met. His prize was within his grasp – once he removed one last obstacle.

He rolled onto his side, again pointing his gun at Eddie—

Nina sprang up and punched him hard in the face. '*Devil's* has an apostrophe, asshole!'

The gang leader lost his grip, rolling off the hood's side. He landed on his arm, wrist breaking with a gruesome crack. Knox howled, his tumble along the road finally stopping as the Buick sped away. Rage dulling the pain, he staggered to his feet as the remaining bikers stopped to help him—

Bullets ripped through their bodies as the machine gunner opened fire again. The Defenders fell, dying with their leader.

The gun swung back towards the station wagon. Eddie and Nina ducked. More bullets clanged against the Buick, this time punching into the engine—

The Dockside Boys' van, the last of the gang vehicles in the chase, had been forgotten. But now it had caught up – and the men inside were well armed. Automatic fire blazed down the street. The machine gunner fell back against his van, blood splattering its custom paintwork. The man with the rocket launcher had retreated into the vehicle to find more ammo; he dived flat as bullets stabbed through its side.

Eddie swerved past the van and turned onto the street crossing the intersection. That provided a few moments' respite, but the Dockside Boys would follow in seconds. The new road had a tree-lined central divider – and he was on the wrong side of it, having to veer around an oncoming car. Luckily, the two lanes ahead were empty. 'How long had you been waiting to correct his punctuation?' he asked Nina.

'From the moment I saw his stupid jacket – hey!' She looked ahead. 'I know where we are, I've been here!'

A couple of blocks down the street, a giant ring some thirty metres in diameter was supported between two buildings. A plaza with snow-covered trees stood beyond it at the top of a broad flight of steps. 'What is it?' Eddie asked.

'The Ring.'

'Yeah, I can see that. But what *is* it?'

'Art, I guess! But I came to a restaurant here last time I was in Montreal. There's an entrance to the Underground City. If we can reach it, we can lose them!'

Eddie's gaze flicked to the mirror. The Dockside Boys' van screeched around the corner. He heard the wail of sirens in the distance. 'Cops are coming. If they arrest us, we're fucked. How do we get into this place?'

'From that plaza.' She pointed at the space past the Ring. 'Think we can drive up those stairs?'

'We'll be lucky if we can drive on the *road* for much longer!' The temperature gauge had shot into the red, steam swirling from the ruptured radiator and alarming clunking noises coming from the engine. But he pushed down the accelerator, squeezing all the remaining power from the elderly Buick. They flashed through an intersection, gaining speed as they raced towards the steps—

A snowplough came around the corner directly ahead of them.

The approaching vehicle was a long-wheelbase grader with wing ploughs extending from each side so it could clear two lanes in a single pass. The driver had raised one plough to take the corner; it was now lowering and tilting back into position—

Braking would have skidded the Buick straight into the grader's front snowplough. Instead Eddie jammed his right foot to the floor and aimed at the descending wing plough.

'Not a good *ideeeeaaaa*!' Nina screamed – as the car rode up over the angled steel blade.

The station wagon was launched skywards, barely clearing the bottom of the giant metal ring. Part of the plaza beyond it was occupied by a great glass rectangle: a canopy roof shielding the restaurants and businesses below from the elements. The car arced down towards it. 'Shit!' yelled Eddie, bracing himself not just for the landing but the shattering plunge that would surely follow—

The Buick hit the canopy – but the thick reinforced glass held.

Eddie's foot was already mashing the brake down as hard as he could. With a wail of overstressed rubber, the Roadmaster screeched to a stop.

Shaken, Nina cautiously raised her head and exhaled in disbelieving relief. 'We made it!'

Eddie half-laughed in response. 'Yeah. That was bloody close, but—'

The canopy gave way.

It was supported by beams of more reinforced glass to provide the maximum natural light to the Underground City. They were designed to withstand the weight of the worst snows that Quebec could throw at it, but two tonnes of catapulted automobile was beyond that limit. Nina and Eddie both screamed as their car dropped twelve feet into a subterranean atrium. Its landing was cushioned by the tables and chairs of one of the restaurants. The few diners there at this morning hour had already fled, food and furniture crushed behind them. The Buick rocked on its broken wheels, then its punishing journey finally came to an end.

***

On the street above, the Dockside Boys had been forced to stop by the snowplough. Their van reversed back to the intersection, switching to the other side of the road to reach the steps. The driver had no desire to recreate the station wagon's crazy flight, and halted at their foot. 'All right, lads,' said Jim Kelly, readying his gun. 'Cops are coming, so we need to be fast. Get up there, grab the woman, and—'

'Jim!' interrupted the driver. 'Someone behind us!' Another van, larger, almost hit their vehicle as it made an abrupt stop.

Kelly turned to the men in the back. 'Open the doors and shoot 'em!' he ordered. 'Nobody's getting our billion dollars, not after all this!'

The Dockside Boys raised their guns as one man threw open the rear doors—

The other van was already backing away. A hulking man leaned out of its passenger window. Almost casually, he lobbed something into the GMC. It clanged down on the metal floor between the men. 'Aw, shite,' whispered Kelly in stunned horror as he saw a hand grenade rolling towards him.

The Buick's passenger door opened, Nina flopping out with her sunglasses askew. Even with the mangled furniture absorbing some of the impact, it still felt as though someone had whacked the base of her spine with a mallet. She crawled clear of the debris. 'Eddie? Eddie! Are you oka—'

A sharp bang came from somewhere beyond the smashed ceiling, followed by screams. Eddie had been sprawled dizzily in the driver's seat, but the chillingly familiar sound jolted him upright. 'That was a grenade,' he said, forcing his door open. 'These people have gone fucking mental!'

'Seems like the whole world has,' said Nina wearily. She straightened her sunglasses and looked around. 'We can get out through there,' she told Eddie, pointing at a corridor between two of the restaurants.

He joined her. 'Where does it go?'

'Pretty much everywhere in Downtown! We just need to keep going until people stop looking at us, then get out. Speaking of which . . .' She tugged down her hat and buried the lower part of her face in her coat's collar as a wide-eyed woman took out her phone to photograph the scene of destruction.

Eddie positioned himself in front of his wife to block any amateur paparazzi – or people using Uzz. 'Yeah, this isn't the kind of Canadian hospitality I was hoping for.' The couple made their exit as quickly as they could.

It was only just quick enough. Barely had they rounded a corner than men ran down the stairs at one end of the atrium. Brice led the way, Steinitz and Duger behind. Their guns were hidden inside their coats, but instantly accessible if needed. 'There's the car,' Brice barked, seeing the wrecked Buick amongst smashed glass and wood. He rushed to it, but found it empty. 'Where are they?' He faced the growing body of onlookers and gawpers who had come to investigate the commotion. 'The man and the woman – which way did they go?'

'Er, that way, I think,' said a man in glasses, gesturing vaguely towards one of the exits.

Brice sprinted down the corridor, halting when it opened out at an intersection. More passages led off in multiple directions. He looked around, seeing stores, shoppers, stalls – but no fugitives. He clenched his fists in frustrated rage. '*No!*' he roared, forcefully enough to distort his electronically synthesised voice. People nearby changed direction to give him a wider berth.

The two mercenaries caught up. 'The police are here,' Steinitz warned. 'We have to go. *Now.*'

Brice glared at him, anger burning in his eyes, then reluctantly followed his companions through the underground maze.

22

Nina and Eddie left the Underground City not long after making their escape, knowing that remaining in an enclosed space, however large, would increase the chances of eventually being caught in the police dragnet. They bought cheap weatherproof cagoules to wear as disguises over their clothing, then headed briskly out of Downtown. At one point a police car sped towards them, siren howling, but it passed without their being spotted.

They eventually stopped to rest and shelter in a coffee shop. 'When I think of Canada, I think of mooses, Mounties, and maple syrup,' said Eddie, bringing hot drinks to their table. 'Not biker gangs and the Indian version of *The Fast and the Furious* and whoever the hell those Irish guys were, all of them armed to the fucking teeth!'

'The plural of moose is moose,' Nina corrected, taking a welcome sip of coffee.

'Moose, meese, mice, whatever. But I think we should get out of Montreal pronto.'

'Agreed. Where to, though?'

'Well, this programmer bloke who might have hacked into Uzz is the best lead we've got. We should be able to find out where Loost's house in Malta is. We'll get a flight over there and have words with him.'

'I'm not sure hopping on a commercial flight is a good idea,' she said. 'It only takes one person to recognise me and this whole thing starts all over again. Maybe we should see if Macy and the Knights of Atlantis can help out. She told me they've used private flights.'

The idea unsettled Eddie. 'I thought we weren't going to get her involved in this.'

'If she can help us without putting herself at any risk, I don't see it as a problem.' She regarded him quizzically. 'You don't agree?'

'I'm just not keen on doing it,' he replied. 'We shouldn't be asking our daughter to sort out our problems for us.'

'You've called on friends to help us out ever since I've known you.'

'That's different. They're not family. It doesn't feel right.'

Nina felt there was something else bothering him about the idea. But she knew he wasn't yet willing to talk about it – and besides, a more urgent concern had come to mind. 'There's something else that doesn't feel right.'

'What?'

'All of this. I don't mean the situation as a whole, that's obviously completely screwed up. But our being here, in Montreal.'

Eddie frowned. 'I don't get you. We came here because it's where Loost's nurse lives.'

'Exactly. Loost's nurse, who was with him on his space station and intimate enough to let him get her pregnant. Then he leaves her nothing, so she's all over the media saying how much she hates him right before he sets everyone on Uzz after me. And she lives here in Montreal, which is handily close to New York, and she's even right there in the phone directory, even though anyone who disses Loost publicly gets harassed by his cult of sycophants. Then she agrees to see us at the drop of a hat, and tells us exactly what we need to know and where we should go next. It's all been too convenient!'

'Us almost getting killed by three different gangs felt pretty inconvenient to me,' Eddie countered.

'Yeah, but that guy who tagged me when we arrived? How could he have known who I was? I was in a car, wearing a hat and sunglasses, but he was *right there* when I got out, with his phone ready. Like he was waiting for me.'

'How could he have been, though? Nobody knew where we were going. Except for – *oh.*' Realisation lit his face. 'Natalie.'

Nina nodded. 'She was hand-picked by Loost, someone he literally trusted with his life. She was willing to spend months in space attending to him. On a very personal level, it seems. That's more than just a job, however much she was paid. She was there with him while he was setting all of this up, planning his revenge. If she was that close to him, and knew he was going to die before he could get a new blood transfusion, she probably had equally strong feelings about me.'

'So you think she's part of Loost's plan? She's setting you up?'

'I'm sure of it. We're being *led*, Eddie. Everything was arranged so we'd think to go to Natalie, and she was in relatively easy reach of us. Then she tells us how to find the one person who could have hacked Uzz – the only person who can call off the hunt. It *has* to be a trap, something special Loost planned that's more personal than some random Uzz user killing me. He doesn't just want me dead. He wants me *defeated* first, humiliated, to prove he was smarter all along.'

Eddie laughed sarcastically. 'Like Homer Simpson once said: "If he's so smart, how come he's dead?"'

Nina gave him a brief smile before continuing, serious again. 'And we're not just being led – I think we're also being *driven*. That's why Brice is involved. Loost had him broken out of prison because he's someone we both consider a genuine threat – and who we'd want to stay well ahead of. Natalie was the carrot, and he's the stick.'

He considered her words. 'When we were outside Natalie's flat and all three of those gangs were pointing guns at each other ... someone shot one of the Irish guys, and everything kicked off. But I didn't hear anyone fire – not until *after* he was killed.'

'Could it have been Brice?'

'Maybe. But why would he help us? He wants me dead.'

'Maybe that's what he's been promised,' Nina suggested grimly. 'Loost gets me, Brice gets you. We both die, they both win. Even if Loost has to settle for a posthumous victory.' Another moment of deep thought. 'The victory conditions for the hunt have been made as difficult as possible to fulfil for anyone who wants to try their luck. They can't just shoot me and claim the bounty; they have to capture me and let Loost's so-called AI deliver its little speech first. Which gives me more opportunities to escape. Like I already have – thanks to you.'

'All part of the service, love,' said Eddie, pleased to receive the compliment.

'But the fact that so many people are hunting me gives me a very big incentive to keep moving, to follow the trail. And the trail leads right to Malta. Which I'm now thinking is the absolute last place we should go.'

'So where should we go instead? We can't stay here. Really, you should stay as far away from people as possible until this is over.'

'But how long will that take?' she asked rhetorically. 'I can't hide in a cave for the rest of my life. If nothing else, I'd miss the *New York Times* crossword.'

He took a long swig of coffee. 'Somewhere nobody'd expect you to go, and out of the way,' he suggested. 'Where you're less likely to be recognised. Although since you're the world's most famous non-fictional archaeologist, that's a bit harder than you'd think.'

'For once, I'd probably be less noticeable if I looked like Lara Croft,' Nina sighed. 'Although if I was working, I could cope with being in a cave . . .'

Eddie gave her a long stare over his cup as she fell silent. 'All right,' he said, finally lowering it. 'What bloody batshit idea that's going to get us both into trouble have you had now?'

She fixed her eyes upon his, unable to keep excitement from her face. 'The Shroud of Hades.'

'The invisibility thing? What about it?'

'I think I know where it is, remember? Meteora, in Greece. The underworld of Greek mythology is inside one of the rock pillars, and its entrance is at the top. At least, that's what the information I've collated suggests. But Meteora is rural, out of the way, and at this time of year it won't exactly be swarming with tourists. Nobody will expect us to be there, so nobody will be looking for me. We can keep a low profile *and* try to find the Shroud.'

THE SHROUD OF HADES

He put down his coffee and sighed. 'So, hold on. You're being hunted, potentially anyone in the world might try to kill you . . . and you think *now's* the perfect time to go on a relic hunt?'

'Why not? The alternatives are either go into hiding for months or even years, or walk into an obvious trap. I don't want to do either! Going to Meteora wouldn't be any more dangerous than anywhere else – and there's a chance of making an amazing archaeological discovery. Besides,' she added, seeing that her husband was about to roll his eyes, 'a cloak – or helmet, or cap, or whatever – that can turn me invisible might be pretty useful right now, don't you think?'

When Eddie spoke again, it was with long-suffering resignation. 'You've already made your mind up, haven't you?'

'Is it that obvious?' Nina said innocently.

'Yes.' They both smiled. 'You actually think this thing's real – that it makes people invisible?'

'Would that be any weirder than armour that lets you fly, or a staff that can control the weather? A dagger that causes earthquakes? And it's better I find it than someone who might abuse its power. That's what I've been doing for the past twenty-five years: keeping these things out of the wrong hands. I intend to keep on doing that, preferably for a long time to come.'

He nodded. 'All right, you've convinced me.'

She was a little surprised at the speed at which he had reached agreement. 'Really?'

'No, but once you start on about something like this it never ends until I let you do it.'

Nina cocked an eyebrow. '*Let* me do it?'

'You know what I mean. So how are we going to get there?'

'I still think we should ask Macy for help. A private flight might not be very ecologically sound, but we wouldn't have to worry about other people on the plane recognising me.'

'The security and customs people at either end might do, though, whatever kind of flight we take. And you were the one who didn't want to bring her into this,' he reminded her. 'I think you were right. We need to keep her safe.'

'Maybe we should ask her what she thinks,' Nina said pointedly.

Eddie ignored her, taking out his phone. 'If we go business or first class, that'll mean less people in the cabin with us. What was the place called again? Meteora?'

'Yes.'

'Okay, let's see what the nearest big airport is . . .' A search quickly provided the answer. 'Thessaloniki,' he said. 'So how do we get there?' Another search, and he reacted in mild surprise. 'There's a direct flight from Montreal, this evening. Handy.' He looked up at Nina. '*Too* handy?'

She considered it, then shook her head. 'I don't think the airlines specifically arranged their flights because Loost thought we might go looking for a mythological artefact.'

'Probably not. All right, our EU visas should still be fine 'cause we were over there a few months ago, so I'll see if we can get seats.' He was about to tap the screen to start the booking process, but hesitated. 'You absolutely sure about doing this?'

She gave him an apologetic shrug. 'Unless you've got a better alternative?'

'Wish I did, but, well . . .' A shrug of his own, then his finger went to the screen. 'Let's Greece ourselves up.'

After exiting the Underground City, the mercenaries had regrouped in a safehouse, an expensive apartment overlooking the Saint Lawrence river, waiting for Nina Wilde to be tagged again on Uzz so the hunt could resume. As the day went on, though, it seemed their prey had managed to escape unseen, to Brice's rising frustration and impatience. It wasn't until night had fallen that Steinitz received a call. 'Well?' Brice demanded as it was concluded.

Steinitz put down his phone on the marble countertop dividing the kitchen from the luxurious living room. 'That was the Adjudicator,' he announced. 'Wilde and her husband just left Montreal by plane.'

Brice frowned. 'They weren't detained at customs? Everyone knows they're in Canada now, and it should be obvious they entered illegally.'

'Canadian immigration uses Mr Loost's AI company to process data. It made sure they weren't flagged so they could fly out.'

'Loost's plan worked after all.' He sounded slightly surprised. 'Well, if they're on their way to Malta, we'd better prepare for the end of the game.' A small smile of anticipation twisted the corners of his mouth.

'There's a problem. They're not going to Malta.'

The smile vanished. 'What do you mean? Where *are* they going?'

'Greece. Thessaloniki, specifically.'

The Englishman stalked towards Steinitz, fists slowly clenching tight. 'And *why* are they going to Greece?'

'We don't know. The Adjudicator used Loost's AI – it can break into government systems, which is how we located you – to go through everything on record about Wilde and Chase. As far as we know, they don't have any friends or contacts there they might go to for help. Wilde went to Greece a few times as a child, but she and Chase have only been there twice since; in 2011 and 2018. They didn't fly in to Thessaloniki on either occasion.'

Brice stopped directly in front of Steinitz. His overmuscled body was taut with barely contained anger. The other mercenaries realised a confrontation was looming and shifted uncomfortably. 'So what you're saying,' he hissed, 'is that . . . you've *lost* them?'

'We'll find them again,' Steinitz said. 'It is only a matter of time. Someone will tag her, and we will know exactly where she is.'

'Greece is rather larger than Montreal. And you don't have the benefit of knowing where they're going to go. It could take us hours, even a full day to catch up. And by then, they will already have moved on.'

'We *will* find them,' the German repeated.

'We would have had them already, if not for Loost's ridiculous revenge scheme!' Brice's fists were now clenched so tightly that the tendons on his forearms stood out like steel cables. 'I could have killed Chase the moment he stepped out of that woman's apartment. But no, we have to string them along – and why? So a dead man can play a gloating video?'

'You will get to kill Chase just as was agreed,' Steinitz said impatiently. 'Until then, your job is to drive them along Mr Loost's chosen path.'

'They have *left* the path!' Brice's sudden electronically distorted roar made Steinitz flinch. 'They've seen the trap, and are making sure they avoid it. Nina Wilde is not an idiot, and whatever I may think of Chase's intellect, he's cunning enough to have stayed alive through everything that's been thrown at him. Underestimating these two is a mistake a lot of people have made over the years, to their cost!'

The mercenary leader regarded him with sneering disdain. 'As you know very well,' he said, indicating the device implanted in Brice's scarred throat. 'Will taking Chase's life make up for his taking thirteen years of yours?'

Brice glared back at him, motionless for a long moment – then struck with terrifying speed.

The knuckles of his right fist slammed into the unprepared German's throat. Steinitz lurched back, eyes bulging and mouth gaping breathlessly – only for Brice to grab him by the hair and smash his forehead down on the corner of the marble counter. Bone cracked with a sickening snap. Brice yanked the other man back upright, blood streaming from the angular wound. The attack had been so rapid and shocking that the other mercenaries had only just started to react.

But Brice was not finished. Still gripping Steinitz's hair with his left hand, he drove his right thumb deep into the other man's eye socket. Blood and fluid gushed out as he hooked his thumb inside the cavity. Steinitz screamed. Brice smiled – then repeated the horrific mutilation with his other hand. For a moment he paused, fingers digging with brutal force into the howling man's scalp . . .

Then with another roar he pulled his hands apart with all the strength his powerful frame could muster.

Bone cracked again, this time with an awful splintering crunch as Steinitz's fractured skull split apart. The skin of his face stretched in different directions, the ragged edges of the break pushing outwards beneath. The stream of blood from his forehead wound became a crimson waterfall.

He fell silent and limp. Brice pulled out his gore-covered thumbs and released his hold. Steinitz's twitching body crumpled to the floor.

The mercenaries had disarmed after reaching the apartment, not expecting further trouble. The only weapons they had ready were their bare hands, and none were capable of what the ex-MI6 man had just done. Those men who had reacted quickly enough to jump upright now froze as Brice turned to face them. A manic grin cut across his blood-speckled face. 'Does anyone else have something foolish to say?' he asked.

'Not me,' was the hurried reply from the nearest man: Flagg, the bearded American. He slowly sat back down. 'Holy *shit*.'

Eyes turned to Duger, who as Steinitz's number two was next in the chain of command. He glanced nervously towards the various weapons on a table near the door, then back at Brice. 'Mr Duger,' Brice said to the Austrian, taking a couple of steps towards him. Duger recoiled as if being approached by a predatory lion. 'I'm not going to have any similar problems with you, am I?'

'Not at all,' said Duger, eyeing his former leader's sightless corpse.

'Good.' Brice flicked his hands to shake off some of the bloody ooze. 'The carpet will need a good shampoo; better leave a large tip for the maid.' He grinned again. A couple of the mercenaries responded in kind, but with rictus dismay rather than amusement. 'Now, back to business. I'll be assuming command of the operation from now on. If that's all right with you?' he added to Duger. The Austrian could only manage a nod in return. 'Good. Now, we need to find out where Chase and his wife are going.'

Palancio, the Italian, took off his tinted glasses with shaking hands. 'How will we do that?'

'Logical deduction. I'm sure with more information, Loost's AI can help narrow down the reasons why they might have gone to Greece . . .' He trailed off, eyes widening. 'No,' he almost whispered. 'It *can't* be that, surely?'

'Can't be what?' asked Duger.

'At the log cabin – Wilde had made notes about an archaeological relic. She thought it was in Greece. I don't believe that's a coincidence. Wait.' He went through his pockets, finding Nina's notes. He unfolded and speed-read them. An unpleasant smile slowly formed. 'I know where they're going. I know where they're going!'

He picked up Steinitz's phone and tried to unlock it, with no success, then pointed its screen down at Steinitz's ruined face. Unsurprisingly, the facial recognition system failed to work. Annoyed, he raised the dead man's right hand and pushed its thumb against the screen. The phone finally unlocked. A few taps and swipes, and he called the last number dialled.

'Yes?' The voice that answered was as synthetic as Brice's own, neutral and male and stripped of identifiable tones.

'This is John Brice,' said the Englishman.

'Where is Steinitz?'

'Dead. Don't worry, I gave him a cracking send-off.'

'What – what do you mean, dead?' Even through the anonymising filter, the Adjudicator's alarm was clear.

'His incompetence lost our targets. They were meant to go to Malta; instead, they've gone to Greece. They've obviously realised the whole thing is a trap. Now, I know where they're going. But I'll need resources to catch them.'

'Where *are* they going?'

'Wilde had made notes about a lost archaeological site, the description of which fits Meteora in Greece to a T. I've been there, I'm familiar with it. She's going to Meteora to look for a relic. I'm certain of it.'

'While her life is in danger? That seems . . . unlikely,' was the carefully considered reply.

'If I'm wrong, you can fire me,' said Brice, faintly mocking. 'But I know Wilde, better than your AI. She wouldn't have flown to Thessaloniki on a whim – and it's the closest major airport to Meteora. Now, I need a private flight there arranged for us as quickly as possible.'

'You work for me, Mr Brice. Not the other way around. I don't take orders from you.' Despite the blankness of the modified voice, the person behind it was deeply disquieted by the turn of events.

'Very well,' said Brice with an exaggerated sigh, 'may I *humbly suggest* that if you want to make Nina Wilde suffer before she dies, you provide me with whatever resources I may request so I can find her for you? After all, I'm sure the late Mr Loost wouldn't have wanted all the time and effort and expense needed to set up his little hunt to go to waste. Hmm?'

'I do not appreciate your sarcasm, Mr Brice. But . . . I will make the arrangements.'

'Thank you,' Brice almost purred. 'Much appreciated. Let me know when the flight is ready.' Before the Adjudicator could say anything else, he ended the call, then regarded the other men in the room. Steinitz's abrupt and gruesome death had genuinely shaken some of them; even hardened soldiers of fortune could be stunned by a sufficiently psychopathic act of violence. 'Now, I assume your payment for this operation is contingent upon its completion, yes?' A couple of the men who were not native English-speakers gave him confused looks. 'You get money when job done, yes?' he restated, speaking slowly and more loudly.

Understanding, then agreement, followed. 'And I assume you would all like to receive your full payment?' Confirmation came more quickly this time. 'Then let's get ready to go.'

23

Meteora, Greece

Eddie looked up at the giant rock pillars dominating the scenery. 'So, you reckon the Underworld is below one of these things?'

'Yeah,' said Nina. 'Or even inside one. But to get to it, we have to climb up to the top first.'

'I do love a nice relaxing holiday,' was his sardonic reply. Meteora was probably a beautiful place to visit in the summer, but at the edge of winter with an overcast sky and a persistent drizzle dampening everything, it was less appealing.

'At least it's not busy.' The miserable weather had deterred tourists; so far they had only seen a handful of people near the great rocks, and none had paid any attention to Nina.

In fact, they had not drawn any particular notice since arriving in Greece. The customs officials at Thessaloniki airport asked only mundane questions about the purpose of their visit, accepting the equally mundane falsehoods they received in answer, and did not make the connection between the name on Nina's passport and the woman with a bounty on Uzz. As Eddie had observed afterwards: 'Why would they? They think you're on the other side of the Atlantic.'

After renting a car, they had travelled from Thessaloniki to the town of Trikala, twenty-five kilometres from Meteora, where an online search had told them a shop specialised in climbing equipment. Once kitted out, they headed to the outskirts of the village of Kastraki, nestled amongst the feet of the rock columns.

Even in the rain, they were a spectacular, if bizarre, sight. Millions of years ago, a mass of sedimentary rock had been pushed upwards by geological forces, then the weather had carved great vertical clefts down through fault lines to leave giant pillars standing tall above the surrounding landscape.

They were not merely imposing natural features, though. Some were inhabited. 'So which is the one where they filmed the Bond film?' Eddie asked, looking around.

Nina had done more research while Eddie drove. 'The Monastery of the Holy Trinity,' she replied. 'We can't see it from here, though. It's on the other side of these rocks.' One group of towering sandstone pillars stood before – and above – them, rising hundreds of metres into the grey sky. They did indeed somewhat resemble outstretched fingers as the records of the Brotherhood of Selasphoros had described, grasping for the clouds. 'You might be able to see it once we climb up, though.'

'So you definitely think one of these is where we'll find this Shroud?'

'I wouldn't say "definitely". But . . . probably. Maybe.'

Eddie shrugged. 'Trip to Greece on a hunch; we've done madder stuff that's paid off. Okay, so how do we get up there?'

Nina brought up a map on her phone; she'd had the foresight to save it to the device earlier in case the local cellular coverage was poor, which had turned out to be the case. 'Okay . . . that way,' she said, after getting her bearings. She pointed uphill from the track where they had parked. Above, woodland rose up a slope that became progressively steeper until it met the wall of one of the great rocks. 'At the top, there's a fairly short climb – I hope! – to a ledge that goes around to the other side of this big pillar here. The reason I think it's the right one is that the Brotherhood said the entrance is at the knuckle of the longest of Hades's fingers. If you look at this one in 3D – I saved a screenshot, here,' she switched apps to show him, 'then the ledge on the other side is proportionately where the second knuckle is on a real finger.' She held up one of her own to demonstrate.

'Glad you didn't use your middle finger,' Eddie said with a grin.

She laughed. 'There's another reason as well – one which neither the Knights' nor the Brotherhood's old records covered. There are the ruins of a small monastery on the same ledge, dating from probably the fourteenth century. Now, I think that's important because this place has been a tourist attraction for decades, and people have climbed over every square inch. If the entrance to the Underworld, supposedly marked by a dark narcissus, was obvious, it would have been found already. But if it's hidden by ruins, maybe even in plain sight . . .'

He nodded. 'Got you. So we climb up and see if we can see a dark narcissus, whatever that is?'

'It's a flower – well, a genus of flowers, actually. Daffodils.'

Eddie regarded the cliffs above. 'Don't think we'll find any growing up there at this time of year, dark or not.'

'It might not be an actual plant. But I guess we'll see once we get there.'

'Suppose you'll want me to grab all the climbing gear, then?'

'Don't worry, I'll carry half of it. The lighter half.' They shared a smile, then Eddie opened the hire car's hatchback and began to take out the equipment.

Nina's hope that the climb would be relatively easy was, to her relief, true. The cliff they needed to find their way up was practically vertical, but plenty of others had made the ascent before, enough climbing spikes already in place that Eddie only had to add a few of his own. He picked his way upwards with little difficulty, letting down a rope behind him. Even the far less experienced redhead climbed a decent percentage of the way under her own steam without needing her husband's assistance.

Eventually, they reached the ledge. It started off narrow, just a few precarious feet across, but widened as it curved around the great rock. The couple followed the ledge to the other side of the pillar, revealing a new vista. 'There's your James Bond monastery,' said Nina, pointing at another pillar roughly half a mile away. A huddle of red-roofed buildings was visible on its humped summit, higher than their position. 'There are five others still in use, and something like twenty abandoned ones.'

Eddie surveyed the landscape below. 'Not a bad view. Shame the weather's so crap.' The drizzle had not eased during the climb, distant scenery fading into a damp grey haze. He turned to regard the ledge. 'So where are the ruins on here?'

'I don't know,' Nina had to admit. All she could see from their position were rocks, tough grass and the occasional hardy shrub. She had assumed the lack of online photographs of the monastery was because of its small size and lack of importance, but it was entirely possible so little remained standing that the typical tourist didn't notice it. 'But the ledge isn't that big. If we search, we should find it.'

'Just be careful,' Eddie warned. 'There's a fair bit of loose rock near the edge. And a lot of cracks too.' He looked up at the rest of the pillar above them. It was heavily weathered, deep clefts lancing through the rock at steep angles where water had worked its relentless way into the weaker layers of ancient sediment. 'One decent-sized earthquake and this whole thing'll come down.'

'At least nobody can use Earthbreaker to start one,' Nina replied. Said earthquake-generating dagger was currently in the possession of the Knights of Atlantis, though even with her own daughter in charge she was far from happy about its being in the hands of the secretive organisation. 'Okay, let's start looking.'

They set off along the ledge, keeping clear of its treacherous edge. Even moving cautiously, it did not take long to check. 'Hey, is this something?' Eddie called out, crouching. 'Looks like a bit of a wall.'

Nina joined him. 'Yeah, it is,' she said. Though largely covered by an accumulation of thin soil and the grass that had taken root in it, a line of carved stones was visible. She examined the surrounding area with an expert eye. 'There's a corner there, but nothing beyond it, so this was probably an outer wall . . . Let's see.'

She slowly advanced, her gaze sweeping the ledge. Little remained of the structure that had once been here, at their very tallest the ruins barely eighteen inches high, but she could clearly pick out the ghostly traces of several walls. Parts of stone floor slabs were visible through the sparse topsoil between them. '*Really* not a big place. I can't imagine there could have been more than about a dozen monks, even if they were stacked in bunk beds.' She went to the face of the cliff above; the remains of the building butted up against it. 'They had water, though. Look, this was probably a spring.' A nook had been eroded from the cliff face, a dark line running down its rear where a thin trickle of water emerged from the rock.

'No drains, though,' Eddie noted. 'They must have just peed over the edge. Bad news if you were walking underneath.' He moved on several metres further, then stopped. 'I don't see anything else past here.'

Nina nodded. 'I think that's the whole building.'

'So if the entrance to the Underworld is here, where is it?'

She knelt to look more closely at one of the half-hidden slabs, scraping away the soil to expose a surface worn smooth by countless feet. 'It depends if the monks knew about the Underworld or not. If they were trying to protect it and keep anyone else from reaching it, they would have made it very hard to find. Even all the way up on the tops of these rocks, the monasteries were often raided by the Turks. But if they used whatever originally marked the entrance as a convenient foundation, they might not even have realised what was under it.'

'Was there anything marking it?'

'The dark narcissus is the only thing specifically mentioned in any of the records. But there had to be *something*, because, well, Hades was revered as a god! Their worshippers like to build things in their honour. Here, give me one of your climbing spikes.'

'Please,' said Eddie with a sarcastic smile as he handed her one of the metal pegs. She smirked, then used it to sweep away more soil – before pausing to give him a meaningful look. 'Work's never done,' he sighed. He took a spike for himself and joined her. Other slabs were gradually exposed.

'Huh,' Nina eventually said, rubbing her hand over two adjacent pieces of flat stone. 'That's interesting.'

'What is?'

'This stone,' she tapped the one she had most recently uncovered, 'is a lot smoother than the others. It's a different material, too. Different colour.' Most of the ruin's remains were the same yellow-brown shade as the towering rock itself, but the new slab was a pale grey.

'You think it's a leftover from whatever was originally here?'

'Possibly. Give me a hand.'

They both worked to remove the soil from the stone. It was revealed as rectangular, some two feet by three – and damaged, a corner missing and replaced by a piece of sandstone that had been chiselled into shape to fit the gap. Eddie gave Nina a look, then when she raised no objections to his unspoken suggestion, inserted his spike to lever the sandstone chunk upwards. More soil and grit was revealed beneath. A couple of taps with the spike's tip showed that the layer was just millimetres thick, solid rock below. 'Well, nothing under there,' said Eddie.

'Let's see if we can find more slabs like this one.'

Their search pattern changed, small holes being dug to determine the colour of the slabs underneath the soil. If they were brown the couple moved on, but more of the paler pieces of stonework were soon discovered. Nina became increasingly excited as the new slabs were unearthed. 'They're concentrated over here,' she announced, realising that a rough circle was being formed. 'I don't know if there was an ancient building here or not – anything that was left probably ended up three hundred feet below us.' She nodded towards the ledge's side. 'But there could have been some kind of platform, built up enough to make a flat surface. The rest of the ledge has a slope, but the monastery's floor is pretty much level. The monks might have decided it was the perfect base on which to build their new home – without realising what was hidden under it.'

'Wouldn't they have looked?' Eddie asked, dubious. 'If I was going to build something on the edge of a cliff, I'd want to make sure it wasn't going to slide off it the next Tuesday.'

'They maybe thought it was a gift from God. Which it kind of was, just not the god they were thinking of.' She stood, a finger extended to point out each of the grey slabs they had found. 'The perimeter goes there, there, there . . . so the centre is somewhere *there*.' She stepped over the broken remains of a wall and past a bush to stand on the place she had indicated. 'And the middle's the most logical place for the entrance to be, don't you think?'

Eddie shrugged. 'Don't ask me, I'm just the digger.'

'You're a lot more than that, Eddie! Now come here and dig.'

He laughed, then went to her. They both began to clear away more soil.

Before long, they had exposed more slabs to the light for the first time in centuries. As Nina had suspected, all were made from the apparently older, harder grey stone. But any musings about their geological origin vanished in an instant when Eddie's sweeping piton rattled over something beneath the thin layer of dirt. 'Ay up,' he said, using a hand to brush it clear. 'Got something here.'

Nina hurried over to look. A symbol, about the size of a hand, had been carved into the face of the flat slab. She quickly used a fingertip to shift residual soil from the grooves forming it. 'Now, what does that look like to you?' she asked, almost breathless with the thrill of discovery.

Eddie regarded it. 'It's a flower.'

'Not just any flower. It's a daffodil – a narcissus!' The image was a stylised outline, but still perfectly recognisable. 'And look, there's a different stone inset into it – a *darker* stone. It's the dark narcissus the Brotherhood mentioned, it has to be!'

Eddie sat back on his haunches. 'So this is the way in?'

'Let's see!' She used her climbing spike to dig out the soil filling the surrounding gaps. Her husband joined in. Once enough had been cleared, Eddie used more pitons to lever the slab open. A narrow crack of darkness appeared beneath as he forced it upwards. He dug his fingers into the gap and with a grunt of effort pushed it clear.

Nina peered into the hole that was revealed. The top was man-made, carefully carved stones placed to act as a cap, but she could see raw rock not far below. 'Have you got the flashlights?'

Eddie took one from his pack and shone it into the opening. A shaft dropped vertically for around fifteen feet to the floor of a steep tunnel descending into the great rock's heart. He scanned the beam over the walls. 'Looks natural, but someone's knocked out bits of it to make it easier to get through.'

'My assessment exactly,' said Nina with a smile. 'I'll make an archaeologist of you yet.'

'Eh, I've seen things like this before. I mean, we found the Iron Palace a few months ago and the way down into it was just the same. You go underground as often as we do, it all blurs together.'

'Well, we'll get to go underground again in a minute. This is obviously the entrance to the Underworld; it perfectly matches what the Knights and the Brotherhood said in their records.'

'You know, there's still time to hide out in a beach hut in Bali.' But he was resigned to the inevitable, already taking out a coil of rope.

It did not take long to secure it and drop a length down to the bottom of the hole. Eddie put down the rest of the coil, then gathered his gear and quickly descended, Nina following. The air below was damp and musty. They both shone their torches around the small chamber at the bottom. Part of the sandstone wall had been ground smooth to form a kind of plaque, into which was inscribed text in ancient Greek.

Nina translated it. '"Only those who know Hades, lord of the Underworld, shall reach him in the Elysian Fields. For all others, eternal torment in Tartarus awaits."' She used her phone to take a photograph of the inscription.

'Tartar sauce?' said Eddie.

'Tartar*us*. Like the Underworld's underworld – basically Hell. The Greek Underworld itself isn't necessarily a bad place, it's just where the dead go to face judgement. Pass, and you go to paradise. Fail, and, well . . .' She pointed a finger downwards and made a spiral motion.

'Great. I'm sure we've never done anything that'd get us sent to hell.'

'*I* haven't,' Nina said primly. 'But if the judges see your internet history . . .'

He laughed, then aimed his torch into the descending tunnel. It was steep, but not dangerously so, curving downwards out of sight. He aimed the beam at some loose stones on the sloping floor, then up at the ceiling above them. A ragged crack ran across it. 'Not keen on that. We should have bought helmets.'

Nina took a closer look. A discoloured streak ran down the wall from one end of the crack. 'Probably water erosion. This whole thing is sandstone – it weathers easily.'

Her husband looked back up the shaft at the grey sky above the opening. 'I love being inside something really heavy that'll dissolve like a sugar cube under a bit of rain.'

'It's not *that* delicate. I hope.' She brought her light back to the tunnel. 'Shall we?'

'If we must . . .' Eddie said, letting out a comically exaggerated sigh before leading the way downwards.

The tunnel ran in a rough spiral, jinking as it followed faults in the rock. Further signs of damage, more cracks and broken stones, appeared worryingly often during the descent. Nina paused to examine a particularly fragile-looking cleft in one wall – then sniffed the air.

'Somebody dropped one?' Eddie asked mischievously. 'Wasn't me.'

The joke barely warranted a sigh. 'I can feel a draught,' she said, sensing a faint breeze on her face. 'Coming up from below.'

'The tunnel can't be blocked lower down, then.'

'Yeah, but where's the air coming in? There aren't any entrances further down the pillar – they would have been found by now.'

'Might be coming through holes that aren't big enough for anyone to fit through,' Eddie said. 'But if there's fresh air, at least we don't have to worry about suffocating.'

They continued down the darkened path. After a while, it was Eddie's turn to pause and sniff. 'What's wrong?' Nina asked.

'Something whiffs,' he replied, wrinkling his nose. 'And not me, for a change. Smells a bit like bleach.'

Nina took in a couple of sniffs of her own. A sharp, yet not entirely unpleasant, scent scraped the back of her nose. 'Ooh, yes. What is it?'

'We'll probably find out soon. I first thought I smelled something a minute ago. It's getting stronger as we go down.'

They resumed the descent. The tunnel became steeper in places, forcing them to find handholds to avoid slipping. The walls also showed more signs of erosion. 'We must be close to ground level by now,' said Nina, cautiously rubbing a finger down a crack and feeling dampness. 'Water's starting to collect.'

'Be a bit of a pisser if we've come all this way down here and it turns out the Underworld's totally flooded,' Eddie replied.

'Just finding that it really exists would be a good enough start for me.' She navigated another steep section of the slope, then pointed her flashlight ahead. 'Although . . . oh.' Disappointment filled her. 'I can see water. It really might be flooded.'

Eddie aimed his own torch downwards. The beams found a smooth, almost oily surface a short way beyond where the floor finally flattened out. He sniffed again. 'That smell's even stronger. You sure that's water?'

'Not so much, now.' They made their way down. The tunnel opened out into a large chamber, their footsteps echoing. Nina approached the water – or whatever it was – and shone her light along its bank. It seemed to be a man-made channel, nearly straight, the darkly shimmering surface over a foot lower than the sandstone floor. To their left, it ran for some forty feet before ending at a sheer wall. She turned to see what lay to their right—

A man grasped at her with an outstretched hand.

24

'Shit!' Nina shrieked, jumping back. Even Eddie flinched. 'God damn!'

Their shock quickly subsided as they realised the figure was actually a statue, of a bearded man wearing robes, on a small stone plinth. His extended right hand was held palm upwards, as if waiting to receive something. Eddie exhaled, surprise giving way to relieved amusement. 'Ay up. Who's this, the greeter?'

'He might well be.' Nina brought her flashlight beam down, seeing something attached to the back of the plinth. She swept the light over the dark water, revealing a boat, large enough to take perhaps eight people at a squeeze. Beside the statue, a short slipway had been carved out of the bank. 'I think it's meant to be Charon, the ferryman.'

'As in, don't pay the?'

'Yes. And if he's Charon, this must be the river Styx.' She aimed the beam at the surface in front of her. It remained almost impenetrable even up close, a deep purple in colour with a faint, soapy sheen. 'According to legend, Achilles was dipped in it as a baby and became invincible, except for—'

'His heel, yeah. Even I know that story. Bit of an oversight on his mum's part.' He frowned. 'I wouldn't put anyone's baby in that, though. It's where the smell's coming from. Feels like it's sandpapering my sinuses.'

Nina checked the rest of the chamber. The 'river' was more of a small, roughly rectangular lake filling the bottom of the chamber. On the far side, a smaller ledge rose about a hundred feet away, what appeared to be a tunnel mouth beyond it blocked by a metal gate. A post stood at the water's distant edge, a rope tied to it running across the water not far above its surface. She looked back at the boat. The rope went through a small hole at its bow, passing the length of the craft and out of a second hole at the stern – which was docked to the statue's plinth. 'It looks like you're supposed to use the rope to pull the boat across.'

Eddie nudged the boat with a foot. It barely moved, firmly affixed to the stone base. 'Is there some way to unlock it?'

'I expect so. But . . .' Faint ripples moved across the water's surface, showing Nina something that didn't feel right: there was no floating detritus, no algae or plant remnants. 'Whatever it is, I think we need to find it, because I don't fancy swimming across.'

'Yeah.' He went through his gear to find a climbing spike. 'Let's try this . . .'

He dipped the pointed end in the Styx. Nothing happened for a moment—

Then bubbles frothed around the metal.

The couple exchanged concerned glances. Eddie held the piton in place as the hissing bubbles grew larger. He lifted the spike, and grimaced. It was pitted and discoloured, corroded by only a short exposure to the dark water. 'Nope, definitely not swimming.'

'So why hasn't the boat been affected?' Nina wondered out loud. A closer inspection revealed the craft was not made of wood or metal, but instead a dark, slightly shiny material, looking like woven strands of something that had been compressed into a solid. She touched it. It had a slightly rough texture, yet also somehow felt a little oily.

'What's it made of?' Eddie asked.

'I'm not sure, but . . .' Her mind was already retrieving an answer from the stacks of its vast library. She let out a small laugh. 'Of course! It matches the descriptions of Charon's boat given by Pliny, Plutarch and Pausanias.'

'The Three Ps? They were never as funny as the Three Stooges.'

'Greek philosophers and writers, which I'm pretty sure you

guessed. They all said the boat was made of a horse's hoof. Or in this case,' she rasped a fingernail's tip over the gunwale, 'keratin. It's what hooves are made of – and nails, and hair.'

'I wouldn't know about that last one,' said Eddie, rubbing a hand over his bald head. 'So, you're telling me this is a boat made of *toenails*?'

'Maybe. I'm not going to get a microscope and check the ingredients. But keratin is highly resistant to alkalis. And bleach is an alkali – which explains the smell.' She gestured at the Styx.

'All right, so to get across we have to ride the toenail boat. But how do we get it loose? We don't want to risk breaking it.'

Nina turned her attention to the statue. 'There must be a lock mechanism – which means there has to be a way to release it.' She carefully touched its upturned hand to see if it would move. It didn't. 'In mythology, Charon demands payment to take people across the Styx. That's why the ancient Greeks had the custom of putting obols in the mouths of the deceased.'

'Obols?'

'Coins.'

'So they come down here and spit coins into his hand like they're a fruit machine in Vegas?'

She laughed at the ridiculous image. 'One was probably enough. Have you got any coins?'

Eddie rooted through a pocket and took out a quarter. 'Here.'

'Thanks.' She put it in Charon's hand. Nothing happened, though she had not expected any different. 'Had to check.' She moved her light over the rest of the statue, searching for anything that might indicate a moving part. Finally, she spotted something. 'Look, here. Inside his mouth. There's a little hole.'

The Yorkshireman retrieved his quarter, then peered into the small opening. 'You're not going to fit a coin in there.' The hole was only millimetres across. 'Might get a spike in, though.'

'Or a nail,' Nina said thoughtfully. Eddie looked at her, awaiting the inevitable explanation. 'The word "obol" in ancient Greek comes from *obelos* – which means nail, or spike. They used copper and bronze spits as currency in trade, about so big.' She held her hands roughly a metre apart. 'They'd flatten them down into coins to make them easier to handle. So if we give Charon an obol in its original form . . .'

Eddie produced another spike. 'Shove this down his throat and see what happens.' He made a retching sound.

Nina smiled and took it. She used her phone's camera to capture the statue and boat as they had been through the centuries, then she delicately inserted the piton into the hole in Charon's mouth. She felt it scrape against the stone, worrying that it might be too wide to fit all the way in – but then it hit something at the back, which moved as she applied pressure. A faint, metallic clunk came from inside the statue, followed by a deeper, louder one as a small mechanism tripped a larger one – and the boat rocked slightly as whatever held it in place was released.

'It's loose,' Eddie confirmed, taking hold of the boat's stern and gently pushing it away from the statue. A metal hoop emerged from a slot cut into the plinth. 'That wasn't too hard.'

'If you know your mythology,' Nina pointed out.

'Are you clued up on the rest of it? Hades and the Underworld and all that?'

She nodded. 'It's one of the centrepieces of Greek myth. The question is, which version of it is right? There are as many variations as there are writings about it.'

'Pluto, Pob and Pastrami all agreed about the toenail boat, though.'

'One of the rare occasions when multiple sources actually said the same thing. Let's hope it's easy to figure out who's right on the other side.'

Eddie climbed into the boat, straddling the rope at its centreline for balance before gingerly taking a seat at one side of the stern. 'Okay, you get in. I'll pull us across.'

Nina carefully joined him, sitting at the bow. The stinging scent of the corrosive Styx was almost unbearable. But she knew they both had to endure it for as long as it took to make the crossing. Eddie pulled on the rope to start them across. The strange little craft silently glided out over the dark waters.

The journey took only a couple of minutes, Eddie going slowly and carefully to avoid any risk of splashes. At last they reached the other side. Nina took hold of the post to keep the boat in place as her husband clambered out, then he returned the favour so she could disembark without rocking it. The rope's friction stopped the craft from drifting away from the bank. 'Right,' he said, 'what have we got?'

Nina had already surveyed their landing spot. 'Not much, except this gate.' It was made of metal bars with plates between them to block any view of what lay beyond. A large ring acted as a handle.

'Is it locked?'

'That's not what worries me. In mythology, the gate to the Underworld is guarded by Cerberus.'

Eddie frowned. 'Hang on – haven't we met him before? Dog with three heads, drips acid?'

'Yes, in the Tomb of Hercules.' Entrance to the legendary hero's long-lost tomb in the Algerian desert had only been possible through a series of traps and challenges based upon his twelve labours. Cerberus had been one of them. 'But the original would be here. So . . . where is he?'

'Maybe we'll get lucky and Cerberus'll turn out to have been just a nice, friendly puppy. Who died thousands of years ago.'

'You think there's any chance of that?'

'Course bloody not,' he scoffed. 'But there's nowhere else we can go, so I suppose we're opening this.'

'We can't really turn back now, can we?'

'Our lives would have been so much easier if you'd listened to me saying yes whenever you said something like that . . .' He took hold of the handle – and pulled.

The gate was heavy, but moved smoothly, if slowly, on its hinges. Eddie maintained his effort – until a rattling sound from inside made him pause and cautiously aim his torch through the opening to find its source. 'Buggeration and fuckery. There's a chain attached to the inside – and we just pulled it.'

Nina looked for herself. A taut length of bronze links ran from the back of the gate near its hinged edge into a hole in the floor. 'Great. We probably just activated a booby trap.'

'You know, we *can* turn back. Just saying.' Nina eyed him. He sighed. 'Yeah, I thought so. Arse.' He sighed again, then fully opened the entrance to the Underworld.

The narrow passage beyond, barely more than a metre wide, was immediately unsettling. 'Okay, I don't like this,' said Eddie, holding out an arm to make sure Nina didn't hurry through in her excitement. 'This *has* to be a trap.'

'Or lots of traps,' she said. Their flashlight beams revealed that both walls were covered in carvings of creatures. There were two kinds: dogs and snakes. All were threatening, angry mouths gaping wide.

Eddie brought his torch to the closest stone heads. 'The dogs I get. They're Cerberus, right? Only he's got a lot more than three heads. But what about the snakes?'

'It's another different version of the mythology,' Nina explained. 'Or rather, this is the original, and different versions emerged from it over time. Cerberus having three heads became the accepted image, probably because it's easier to grasp, but there are earlier interpretations where he had fifty heads, or a hundred. The snakes were part of that too. Sometimes he had a snake for a tail, or his back was covered in snakes.'

The Yorkshireman cautiously shone his light into one dog's snarling mouth. 'There's a slot in here, a few inches tall. Looks like something might come out of it. A blade or a spike, maybe.'

'Well, he's the guardian of the Underworld, so I guess he has a nasty bite,' she said, aiming her own torch at the floor. It was tiled, slabs about a foot square running its length. Each bore an embossed design. She crouched to examine them. A trio of images: a dog head, a snake head, and a twin-pronged spearhead: a bident. She looked further along the passage. There did not seem to be any pattern to their placement, the three different designs seemingly scattered randomly.

But she doubted that was the case. 'It's a puzzle,' she told Eddie. 'We're supposed to step on the tiles in a particular order. Get it wrong, and we get bitten. Or worse.'

'Like them.' He directed his light to the confined tunnel's far end. The beam found two huddled shapes. Corpses, long dead and desiccated.

Nina took in the sight with professional intrigue rather than shock or distaste. 'Someone else has been down here before us? That means the place must have been maintained, up to some point in the past. Somebody put the boat back where it belonged and replaced the slab covering the entrance. I wonder how long ago?'

'If the dead guys got across, how did the maintenance crew get to the boat without going in the Styx?' Eddie asked.

'They could have brought down a boat of their own.'

'*Two* toenail boats? Pedicurists must have done great business in ancient Greece.'

'Enough with the toenail boats, let's worry about booby-trapped tunnels.' She squatted for a close look at the first row of tiles. The only apparent differences between them were the designs. Their function, experience told her, was familiar. 'I think they move if anyone steps on them. Pressure plates.'

Eddie made a grumbling sound. 'Bloody marvellous. So how do we work out which tiles we're meant to tread on?'

'I . . . don't know.' She surveyed the walls again, even the ceiling, looking for some kind of clue. Nothing presented itself. She turned to check the back of the gate. There was nothing of help on the metal barrier. 'There *has* to be something. If people came down here to maintain things, they'd need to know how to get through this without setting off the trap! Considering how distorted the mythology of this place has become, they couldn't rely on oral tradition – don't even,' she added, as Eddie began to smirk. 'But bringing a physical record with them would run the risk of its falling into the wrong hands. So how did they get past Cerberus safely?'

Eddie considered the matter for a moment, then ushered his wife back to the gate. 'If we know what we're dealing with, we might be able to get through without needing to work out the right path. Hold back, and I'll see what happens.'

'You sure that's wise?' she asked as he returned to the first row of tiles.

'What could go wrong?' he replied, showing the gap between his front teeth as he grinned broadly at her. 'If anything kicks off, run outside, fast.'

He positioned himself ready to spring backwards, then, with a wary eye on the carved animal heads, extended a leg and cautiously placed a boot heel on the nearest tile, a dog. The square moved fractionally, making a faint grinding sound that in the tense silence of the tunnel felt as loud as an air horn . . .

But nothing happened.

'All right, at least we know that one's safe,' said Eddie. He repeated the motion on the neighbouring snake tile. Another little rasp, but still with no effect. 'This must be the trick one, then.' He went to the final tile in the row, which bore the symbol of the twin spearhead. 'Ready, set . . .'

He brought his heel down on the tile – then dived for the gate.

Again, nothing happened.

'Huh,' he said, surprised. 'Maybe only a few of 'em are rigged, then. Hold on.' He took off his rucksack and tossed it to land on the second row of tiles. Still there was no reaction from the menacing carvings. 'Cerberus isn't much of a guard dog, letting us come right in without waking up.'

He went to retrieve the pack, but paused when Nina made a sound of excited realisation. 'Oh! Eddie, that's it! You're a genius.'

'I am?'

She grinned. 'In your own way. But Cerberus,' she gestured at one of the carved dog heads, 'isn't here to guard against people coming *into* the Underworld. He's there to stop the dead from getting *out*! I guess Hesiod got it right, not Virgil. More Greek philosophers,' she explained, noticing her husband's expression of incomprehension.

'I didn't think the second one was the bloke who flew *Thunderbird 2*,' he replied.

It was her turn to adopt the expression. '*Anyway*,' she went on, 'once you come down here, that's it – you get judged and sent to either the Elysian Fields or Tartarus, and stay there for ever. Only a few people ever came down here and got out again. Heracles – Hercules – for one. Remember the challenge in his tomb? He was tasked with bringing Cerberus out of the Underworld, which he did, even though Cerberus was fighting him every step of the way.'

Eddie frowned in confusion. 'But *this* is Cerberus – he's a load of statues, not a real animal. How did Herc manage that?'

'That's something for the historians who specialise in ancient Greece to figure out,' she said, with a half-smile. 'It's not my problem right now. But I don't think the trap is activated on the way in. When you try to come back out, though . . . that's when the trouble starts. Those two guys down there,' she indicated the corpses, 'barely made it three paces before they got killed.'

'We're not really any better off, though, are we? We still have to get through the traps, just later rather than sooner.'

'But if we find the Underworld, the information we need to get back out safely might be there. If you know you can get in without trouble, you don't need to pass down the method or risk writing it down. It can be kept in the Underworld itself – though it's probably hidden somehow, so robbers can't just waltz back out again with anything they've stolen. We'll have to find it. But we did it, Eddie,' she insisted, suddenly determined. 'We found the Underworld! The Knights of Atlantis and the Brotherhood had all the clues; they were just never able to put them together. So now I can make sure that if the Shroud of Hades really is here, it won't fall into the wrong hands. And it kept us away from Brice and anyone else Loost sent after me. We have to go on.'

'Famous last words,' Eddie grumbled. But he picked up his rucksack and threw it further along the passage. It landed where four tiles met, all shifting under its weight. But there was no reaction from the trap. 'It *does* look safe, I'll give you that. But still be careful, okay?'

'I always am.'

Eddie's mocking laugh echoed through the tunnel. She huffed, then followed him along it.

25

'So,' said Brice, staring down at the ground below, 'they're here somewhere. But where?'

The helicopter approached the great rock pillars of Meteora, the cheerful red roofs of the two villages at their feet standing out even under the grey sky. But the ex-MI6 officer's attention was on the towering features themselves. Wilde would not have wasted any time searching for her prize, he was sure. 'Binoculars,' he ordered, holding a hand back between the chopper's front seats.

Duger, in the row behind, handed him a pair. 'I still don't know why you are so sure she's here. What if she's just hiding somewhere in Greece?'

'I mean, yeah,' added Flagg, 'she'd be crazy to carry on with her job while everyone in the world is trying to kill her.'

'You don't know her,' Brice replied patronisingly. 'I do. She came to this part of Greece for a specific reason, and that reason was in her notes. She thinks this relic is here. I can't comment on whether or not she's crazy, but I *can* say that she's obsessional, at least about archaeological matters. She's more than willing to put herself and others in danger to find these things.'

'Like I said, crazy,' said the American. 'And not the only fucking one,' he added, not quite under his breath.

Brice ignored the remark. There were more important concerns. He took out Nina Wilde's notes and re-read her words. They were scattershot, stream-of-consciousness. But the clues that had led him – and, he was certain, her – to Meteora were clear.

As were more specific hints to the location of her prize. 'Fingers reaching to the sky . . .' he recited quietly, before looking out of the cockpit again. Which group of pillars matched that very specific description?

He discounted many with a mere glance as not finger-like. Too broad, too misshapen, not arranged with others. But one cluster fitted the bill with surprising accuracy: even from the air, it was hard *not* to think of them as the digits of a hand reaching up from beneath the earth. From the ground, it would have been an inevitable comparison. 'We'll check those first,' he ordered, pointing. 'Look out for climbers, or any ropes. They had enough of a head start over us to be up there already.'

The pilot hired by the Adjudicator, a Greek, brought his aircraft around the pillars. Brice and the mercenaries methodically scanned both the rocky heights and the forest around their bases with binoculars. They passed along one side of the first tower, the second—

'There are ropes there,' Lannard suddenly said of the third pillar. 'On that cliff, up to the ledge there.'

Brice had already trained his binoculars on the cliff the shabby Frenchman had indicated. There were indeed ropes running up it. The ascent would be relatively straightforward; easily within Chase's abilities, and he imagined Wilde could manage it with her husband leading the way.

He brought his gaze to the top. The ledge curved out of sight around the pillar. 'Go to the other side,' he ordered. The pilot complied, the landscape wheeling about below.

The rest of the ledge came into view. There was nobody on it, but there were suspiciously linear shapes amongst the grass and bushes clinging to the weathered rock. The remains of buildings? 'Take us closer,' he told the pilot.

The Greek was unhappy with the command. 'It is dangerous to do that,' he said, in stilted English. 'The backwash, it will hit us from the rock.' He briefly took one hand from the controls to mime whirling wind.

Brice stared unblinkingly at him with cold eyes. 'I believe at least four of us are able to fly a helicopter.' He put his other hand on the co-pilot's controls. 'Including me. Now, take us closer. *Please.*'

There was no mistaking the threat behind the seeming pleasantry. 'Okay, okay,' the pilot muttered. 'But if anything goes wrong – we all die. Okay?'

'*You* certainly will,' was Brice's icy reply. 'Now, if you don't mind?'

The pilot reluctantly brought the helicopter to a hover, then sideslipped towards the pillar. The cabin jolted as the aircraft was hit by its own rebounding rotor wash, prompting a muted gasp from one of the men in the rear seats. The Englishman ignored it. The situation was not dangerous – yet.

He surveyed the approaching ledge. Yes, there had definitely once been buildings there. The merest stubs of walls remained, but they were still distinct. They were not tall enough to hide anything, though, and nor were the bushes that had taken root in the shallow soil. If there was a way inside the rock here, it couldn't stay hidden for long . . .

There!

An empty space stood out beside an old stone slab within the ruins. Was it just a hollow where part of the old monastery's floor had slipped loose, or something more? 'Go higher!' he barked.

The pilot immediately obeyed. The helicopter rose. The perspective shift revealed the answer – and it was what Brice had hoped.

It was a hole in the ground, with a darkened shaft beneath. A rope dropped into it. 'That's it,' he said. 'We found them!'

The others peered down at the opening. 'Are you sure?' Flagg asked, dubious.

'Yes. They've gone down into that hole. Which means, their only way out is back through it again. We've got them trapped!' He turned in his seat to face his men. 'Duger, you stay in the chopper. Remain on station. If by some chance anyone but us comes out, eliminate them. Everyone else, rope down with me.' Knowing the nature of

Meteora's terrain, he had made sure the helicopter was equipped for such an action. 'We're going to get them.'

'I do not have fuel to fly for ever,' the pilot protested. 'Two hours, no more.'

Brice gave him a mirthless smile. 'Don't worry. I'm sure we'll be done by then.'

Nina and Eddie reached the first of the two corpses. It was long dead, a desiccated skeleton coated in cobwebs and dust. The cause of death was obvious. A metre-long metal blade had sprung from the mouth of one of the numerous dog heads – transfixing its luckless victim through the chest.

Nina brought her flashlight beam to the floor. The dead man's final step had been onto one of the tiles marked with a bident. 'Well, we know not to step on that one on the way out. But what about all the rest?'

Eddie carefully ducked beneath the age-rusted blade. The second body was not far behind the first. 'Christ. I don't know what happened to this one, but it looks painful.' The figure lay twisted and contorted on the floor, its last moments spent writhing in unbelievable agony. Unlike the first, which still had some remnants of dried flesh and clothing, the head and upper body of this had been stripped to the bone. More than that; the bones themselves were pitted as if attacked by a powerful corrosive.

'It could have been the same liquid from the Styx,' said Nina, joining him. 'I certainly wouldn't want it sprayed over me.' She shone her light into a snake head. 'The snakes have round holes rather than slots. I guess the dogs have fangs, and the snakes spray poison.'

'Look, here,' Eddie said, seeing something on the floor. Several metal discs had scattered from the second corpse's hand. 'Are they gold coins?'

'Obols. Only a lot more valuable than copper ones.' She looked ahead, seeing that the passage soon turned a corner, obscuring any sight of what lay beyond. 'They must have come down here to raid the Underworld. Cerberus made sure they never left.'

'So how do we stop him doing the same to us?'

'Like I said, I'm sure the answer will be somewhere inside the Underworld itself. We just have to find it.'

They traversed the last few metres of the Cerberus passage and reached the corner. Not far around it was another metal gate. This one, though, had been damaged. A large, deep crack bisected the ceiling above it, broken chunks of stone on the floor. Some had hit the gate as they fell, buckling its top inwards. Darkness lurked beyond the twisted gap.

They both stopped to examine the obstruction. 'Probably works the same as the first one,' said Eddie. 'I bet there's a chain attached to the other side. Open it and it sets the trap so it'll get us on the way out. Hi bloody ho.' He started to move the larger fallen stones.

'What are you doing?' Nina asked.

'We're going to have to shift them anyway to get the thing open. Might as well get it over with.'

'I don't know.' She inspected the top of the gate. 'Do you think we could fit through that gap? If we can, then we don't have to open the gate at all.'

'You might. Not sure about me.'

'I think you could. You might have to take off your jacket, and maybe your sweater too. But it looks big enough.' He still seemed dubious. 'At least boost me up so I can go through. You never know, there might be a way to release the gate without setting the trap.'

'Okay, okay,' was his reluctant reply. He moved to the gate and interlocked his fingers to provide Nina with a step. 'Go on, then. I'll chuck your rucksack through after you.'

She removed her pack, then stepped up onto his hand. He easily lifted her high enough to get her arms through the opening. A quick sweep of her flashlight revealed another tunnel angling downwards. She squirmed through, twisting around to take hold of the gate's top.

Straining to hold her weight, she pulled her lower body over the threshold and into the darkened space beyond, then dropped clumsily down, landing with a breathless gasp.

'You okay?' Eddie called.

'Hard touchdown. I'm not twenty-eight any more. But I've had worse.' She stood and reached up as her backpack came through the opening. 'Thanks. Now, what have we here?'

Her light revealed that there was indeed a chain connected to the gate; pulling it open would doubtless prime the traps in the Cerberus passage. 'You were right – opening the door is a really bad idea. Do you think you can fit through?'

'Going to have to, aren't I?' came the grumpy response. Rustling noises came through the gap, followed by Eddie's leather jacket and top layer of clothing. 'Bag on the way,' he warned. Nina moved to catch his pack as it was shoved through. 'All right. Breathe in and think thin . . .'

He jumped up, hands grabbing the gate's top as his body thumped against it, making it rattle. Nina shot a nervous glance at the chain, but it didn't move. More bangs followed as Eddie pulled himself up, feet scrabbling against the metal. His head appeared in the gap. 'Ay up, love,' he said. 'Fancy meeting you here.'

Nina smiled. 'Can you get through?'

'Maybe. Should have picked up a bottle of baby oil with the other gear so I could grease myself up.'

'I'm not sure whether to be aroused or appalled.'

He cackled. 'We can always wash the sheets after. Now, let's see . . .' He worked both arms through, then began to lever the rest of his body over the top of the gate. 'Bollocks, this is a tight fit. And it's a tight fit for my bollocks. God!' A strained grunt as he fought to bring his hips through the narrow opening. 'If I can get my shoulders in, I should be able to get my arse in too, I'm not *that* fucking fat.' He let out more sounds of effort as he inched forward.

'Ah . . . do you want me to catch you?' Nina asked cautiously.

'No, I'll be fine, just got to – *shite!*' The waistband and belt of his jeans had snagged, bunching up and holding him back – before suddenly popping free. He swung downwards, about to drop head-first to the floor when Nina threw her arms up to catch him by his shoulders. 'Okay, maybe a *bit* of help would be useful. Thanks.'

She supported him until he was able to get first one leg, then the other through the gap. He dropped down. 'Are you okay?' she asked.

'Yeah. *You* saved *me* again. Starting to feel like I'm not needed any more.'

Under other circumstances, she would have pushed him to find exactly what was troubling him; not for the first time lately, she could tell there was something deeper behind his words. But they were now close to finding whatever was hidden inside the great rock, and that took precedence. 'We're nearly there, I'm sure of it. Let's keep moving.'

Eddie donned his clothes again, then they retrieved their packs and continued down the new passage. The walls showed more signs of dampness, water trickling across the floor in places. He sniffed. 'You smell that? It's like flowers.'

'Down here?' Nina said dubiously. But then she detected it too: a faint but distinct floral scent. 'And that breeze is stronger as well.' It was still only gentle, but enough to disturb the fine hairs on her face.

Eddie stared down the passage, then switched off his torch. 'Turn yours off too. I think there's something down there.'

Nina obeyed, closing her eyes just before the tunnel plunged into darkness. But when she opened them again, she saw it was not absolute. There was a dim, washed-out light somewhere below, a grey rectangle marking the passage's end. 'That looks like daylight!'

Eddie flicked his light back on. 'If there's a hole big enough to let the breeze in, maybe there's another way out.'

'Let's go see.' She relit her own flashlight, and they continued downwards.

It did not take long to reach the bottom of the sloping tunnel. The air now felt moist, and the quiet echoes of dripping water reached them. 'Must be a pretty big cave,' Eddie said, listening to the sound. 'How big's this Underworld meant to be?'

'Enough to have multiple rivers,' Nina told him. 'Of course, every written version is different, as usual.'

They passed through the tunnel's mouth, the walls opening out around them. 'Now you get to find out which one was right.'

Nina's eyes widened in wonderment as she took in the astonishing sight awaiting her. 'Oh, wow . . .'

26

The couple had entered a large cave, roughly oval, with a towering, gradually narrowing conical ceiling that put Nina in mind of a cathedral. Numerous shafts of light stabbed down into it from holes high in the walls. Even the overcast gloom from outside seemed like searchlight beams in the darkness. The incoming daylight reflected off the pools and streams of water spread across much of the cave's floor, breaking it up almost into islands. Signs that the place had been shaped at least partially by humans were immediately apparent: some waterways were crossed by stepping stones, and even a couple of little bridges. Metal objects gleamed all around the cavern's perimeter.

Nina's light revealed the closest example as a pillar of distinctly Grecian design. Not even the passage of the ages had fully tarnished the surface. 'I think it's silver,' she said. 'Score another for Hesiod – he said the Underworld was supported by silver pillars! Although he also said they were in the dwelling of Styx, so he wasn't entirely accurate . . .'

Eddie was less impressed. 'Oh, God. It's the bloody Iron Palace all over again.' Their discovery in Turkmenistan likewise had metal pillars bracing its walls. 'Why does everywhere we find always have to be in some horrible underground cave?'

'We had to go up a mountain to find the Midas Cave,' Nina reminded him.

'Still a cave – it's right there in the name!'

'We found the lost city of Paititi in a jungle; is that better?' She turned back to the cave's interior, spying something where one of the beams of daylight touched down. 'Okay, now that's something I didn't expect to see down here.'

'I did say I smelled flowers,' Eddie remarked, following her to the spot.

Enough dirt had accumulated on the cave floor to form a thin layer of soil. Growing from it was a patch of what could have been taken for daffodils, if not for their colour. Instead of shades of white and yellow, these were purple and violet, their protruding central coronas speckled with iridescent spots. Other clutches of the same plants were scattered about the cavern. Nina knelt for a closer look. 'The dark narcissus,' she said.

Eddie joined her. 'Didn't think daffs could be purple. My mum once worked in a florist's when I was a kid, and I don't remember ever seeing anything but yellow ones.' He bent down to take a sniff – then recoiled. 'Jesus! Send those to someone, and you'll never hear from them again.'

Nina tested the flowers' scent more gingerly. Even then, it was enough to sting her nostrils. 'It smells like the Styx,' she realised. 'That same alkaline, bleachy stench. Only it was a lot more concentrated in the river.' She regarded the flowers thoughtfully. 'Maybe that's what the water of the Styx is – some highly concentrated distillate made from these? Narcissus flowers are naturally quite alkaline, so these might be some mutation that's even more so. One that's adapted to growing in these conditions.'

'Is this enough light for them to grow?' Eddie asked doubtfully. 'When Macy had to grow stuff for her science homework, the plants that didn't get a decent amount died off pretty quickly.'

'They're here, they're alive, so I guess it is. Although . . .' She looked across the cave, seeing something beyond the lancing shafts of light. 'That might have helped them survive.'

Eddie followed her gaze, then groaned. 'Might have bloody known that stuff'd be involved somehow. Can't seem to escape it any more.'

THE SHROUD OF HADES

At the cavern's far end was a large rock of a different colour from the sandstone in which it was set. It was a semi-reflective purple in colour, flecks of green catching the reflected light from the water below. Both Nina and Eddie had seen other examples of the material in the past, varying in colouration but always with the same properties. It was a conduit for earth energy, the still-mysterious flow of power through the planet itself that when properly channelled and controlled allowed its user to perform seemingly impossible acts. The Staff of Afrasiab, recovered from the Iron Palace, could control the weather; the armour of the Knights of Atlantis generated a field that not only protected them from physical harm, but gave them the power of flight.

If the Shroud of Hades was here . . . perhaps it too used earth energy to accomplish the impossible.

As to where the Shroud might be, the answer seemed obvious. A bronze band ran across the face of the tooth-shaped rock, halfway up, with a doorway carved from the purple stone at its centre. The opening was blocked by a large metal gate, similar to those at each end of the Cerberus passage. A flight of stone steps led up to a terrace that had been built in front of it.

Eddie used his torch to check the streams between them and the stairs. 'Looks like water, but I still wouldn't step in it, just in case. We can go that way, then over that bridge.' He traced a path with the flashlight's beam.

They picked their way across the chamber, using stepping stones to cross the wider bodies of water. Finally they traversed the small bridge and headed up the stairs. 'Ay up,' said Eddie warily as they neared the top. 'We're not the only ones here.'

Three larger-than-life statues of men stood in a curving line before the metal door. In front of each figure was a low circular bronze podium. Two of the statues held weapons, a knife and a spiked sceptre, while the third pointed down at its podium as if demanding that anyone facing it kneel. The thing that most immediately caught the couple's attention, however, was that all three bearded men were completely naked.

Eddie snorted in amusement. 'Wash day tomorrow. Nothing clean, right?' he added in a monotone Arnold Schwarzenegger voice. 'So which Greek philosophers are these three? Ballsac, Peonis and Scrotorius?'

'Minos, Aeacus and Rhadamanthus, actually,' Nina replied.

He looked at her. 'Yeah, of course you knew that. Don't know why I'm surprised. So, they are . . .?'

'The judges of the dead. They decide who's worthy to join Hades in the Elysian Fields, and who gets cast down into Tartarus for all eternity.'

'All right. And, obvious question: why are they stark bollock naked?'

She smiled. 'To show they have nothing to hide. The people being judged are the same, everything that they've done in their lives exposed.'

'You can always hide *something*. I once hid a homing beacon up my – well, you can guess.'

Nina decided that on this occasion, ignorance would definitely be bliss. '*Anyway*, the dead have to stand before the judges, who then make their decision. I think,' she said, taking a closer look at what appeared to be drainage holes around one of the podiums, 'this pointing guy here is Minos, who makes the final judgement.' She shone her flashlight into one of the holes. Far below, the beam glinted on murky water – or was it the same corrosive liquid as in the Styx? 'I suspect that if you're judged unworthy, this drops you into Tartarus – and you won't be coming back out.'

Eddie regarded the doorway beyond the statues. 'But if you pass, the door opens and you can go and meet Hades, right?'

'Probably. The question is: how can you be judged by inanimate statues?'

While Nina considered that, Eddie investigated the door. Probing with the various crude tools he had, as well as fists and feet, proved fruitless. 'Can't open that with anything we've got now. Sledgehammers and crowbars'd do it eventually, but it'd take a long time with just the two of us, and I'm assuming you don't want anyone else knowing about this place. Even Macy.'

'Yeah,' she replied with a nod. 'The fewer, the better.'

'Did that bloke who got things right about this place say anything about the judges?'

'Hesiod? No, not that I recall. Homer mentions them in *The Odyssey*, and Plato and Ovid wrote about them as well. Who else?' She closed her eyes, working through her mental library. 'Virgil, Pindar, Lucian . . . but did any of them say anything that might help us?' More intense thought. 'Damn it, if I had the books in my study I could figure this out in thirty seconds. I can almost see which book and what page it's on! There was something about, something about . . .' A quiet growl of frustration – which was abruptly supplanted by a little exclamation. 'Oh! Pindar, of course. He described what the dead had to do to survive judgement under earth.'

'We could save a load of shelf space if you just used e-books,' Eddie commented with a smirk.

'Quiet, you. I love having physical books. But he said something like, ah . . . "whoever has been of good courage and abided steadfast thrice on the side of death", if I remember the Myers translation, when they face the judges gets to follow the path of Zeus. Which is the good result. Here, it has to mean through there.' She pointed at the closed doorway.

He nodded. 'But what does that actually *mean*?'

'I'm gonna guess, something to do with standing on those podiums. Three judges; three times when you have to be steadfast and show courage while facing death.' She stepped back to regard the naked statues. 'Two of the judges have weapons, and one has a trapdoor over a pit. I think I can see where this is going.'

'Yeah, me too.' Eddie went to the figure holding a knife in one hand, which was outstretched almost to directly above its podium. He scrutinised the statue's arm, being careful not to step on the circular bronze platform. 'The arm doesn't move – there's no hinge or anything, it's all metal. But the *knife* looks like it springs out from the hand.' He moved his torch around to illuminate it from different angles. 'Yeah, the handle goes back into the arm. It's probably on a rod.'

Nina came to see for herself. 'How far do you think it comes out?'

'Far enough to stab anyone standing on the circle. And there's something here on the body, too.' He brought his light to the side of the statue's chest. A recess stood out amongst the sculpted muscle, a thumb-sized metal bar within it. 'Looks like a lever.'

'Or a trigger.' She stood beside the podium and reached out to hover her hand just above the lever. It was a stretch to reach. 'Clever. I bet your weight on the podium arms the challenge. You *have* to stand on it to trip the trigger.'

'You could just stick a load of rocks on it to weigh it down,' Eddie suggested.

'I'm sure the builders would have thought of that. The intent's obvious: you stand on the podium, move the lever, and face death from the statue – in this case, a knife coming at your chest. If Pindar was right, then if you stand your ground and show courage by not trying to jump clear, you pass.'

'And if he's wrong?'

'Then your day's not going to end well! But that must be what he meant. You get judged three times by facing death. Be brave, and you get your reward – entrance to the Elysium Fields.' She indicated the gate again.

'All right,' said Eddie, rolling his shoulders to psyche himself up, 'I'll do it.'

'What? No, no,' Nina insisted. 'Like you said, what if Pindar's wrong? Or what if *I'm* wrong? I can't let you take that risk for me.

Besides, you're the one who's had proper first-aid training. If anything goes wrong, I'll need you to stitch me up!'

She meant it as a joke, but Eddie was not laughing. 'And what if something goes wrong, and you *die*? You might as well have stayed in Central Park shouting, "Come and get me!"'

'I'm not going to let Rafael Loost decide how I die,' she said forcefully. '*I* control my life, not him. Yes, it's a risk, but it's my choice, my risk to take. If the worst happens, then at least it was on my terms, and I was doing what I do: discovering the truth about the past.'

'You're willing to die for that.' It was not a question. The cold anger behind Eddie's words told her that it was a fact he had long known, even if he did not want to accept it.

'I don't *want* to, trust me! I'll take every possible precaution. But I really do think I'm right about this. I mean, I usually am, aren't I? It's how we got here. And not just *here* here; I mean, in life. You, me. Us.'

'There was a lot of luck involved too,' he warned. 'And sooner or later, it runs out.'

'Then let's hope it's not right now.' Before Eddie could stop her, Nina stepped onto the podium – and reached out to push the little lever.

The bronze disc dropped slightly under her weight, something clunking beneath it – and another metallic clatter came from inside the statue itself. The dagger in Rhadamanthus's hand sprang forwards, darting at Nina's chest—

And stabbing through her clothes.

She gasped at the pain, teetering back. She'd been wrong, and was now paying the price—

A sharp *thunk* within the statue's hand – and the knife abruptly halted. Nina staggered backwards, clutching at her chest. The blade remained in place, a thin smear of red on its tip.

'Nina!' Eddie yelled, rushing to help her. He caught her before she could fall and lowered her carefully to the terrace. 'Jesus Christ!' He pulled up her clothing. Her bra was stained with blood – but not as much as he had feared. He tugged it down to assess the wound, training and experience quickly telling him the verdict. 'It's not too deep. Fucking *hell*, Nina! You scared the shit out of me! Never do that again!'

She panted for breath. 'I'm not planning to! Oh, my God! Can you fix it?'

'Yeah, I can. You might need some antibiotics, but you should be okay.'

'Thank God.' She let out a relieved breath, then looked up at the extended knife. As Eddie had thought, it was indeed on a rod, a length of bronze extending back into the statue's forearm. 'I was right, the knife stopped – but not quite soon enough. They must have expected someone with longer arms. I can't believe I got stabbed in the boob! Not sure I'll mention that in my next book.'

'You should. To warn people not to do anything so bloody stupid.' He stood. 'Right, now to do something bloody stupid.'

She looked up at him in alarm. 'What?'

'You were right – if you stand your ground, you don't get hurt. Well, you don't get *killed*, at least,' he added, eyeing her bloodied chest. 'So I'm not letting you do that again. I'll do it.' He went to the statue holding up the sceptre. 'What was this bloke's name again?'

'Aeacus, and don't be so goddamn crazy, Eddie! You can't—'

But he had already stepped on the podium and reached out to push the little lever set into the statue's chest.

This time, the figure's whole raised arm was hinged at the shoulder. Nina shrieked as the sceptre dropped. Eddie cringed, bending his knees and drawing down his head between his shoulders. Luckily, the sceptre stopped with a bang as an internal detent halted its descent, one spike only millimetres above the top of his bald skull. He carefully leaned backwards, eyes crossing as he focused on the perilously close point. 'For once, I'm glad I'm not six foot three,' said the stocky Yorkshireman, grimacing. 'All right, two down.'

'Eddie!' Nina snapped, hand back on her wound. 'You could at least have stopped my bleeding first!'

'If these have a time limit that you have to do 'em all in, I don't want to have to go through this again,' he said, going to the final statue: Minos. 'You reckon this drops you down a pit if you try to jump off, right?'

'Maybe, but I'd really rather you didn't – *aaah!*'

He had already mounted the podium and pushed the last trigger. The bronze disc beneath him lurched. Eddie stayed put upon it even as every instinct told him to leap clear – though he did throw his arms wide to catch himself, just in case.

It proved unnecessary. Metal rattled beneath the terrace's stone slabs, but the podium – or trapdoor – remained closed. Instead, the statue of Aeacus shifted, rotating slightly. A small nook was revealed in the floor beneath the figure's toes.

Nina rose to investigate. 'There's another lever here – a gold one. It looks a bit like a key.'

With a cautious look at the statue of Minos, Eddie hopped off the podium and went to her. 'You think it opens the gate?'

'After all that, I damn well hope so!' She pulled the golden lever.

A *clack* came from beneath it as some mechanism was tripped. A moment later, a muffled rattle sounded under the stone slabs, the vibration travelling towards the doorway – then an almost musical clanging tone echoed through the chamber. With a low creak of ancient hinges, the metal gate swung open.

Nina and Eddie stared at it. 'Well, there it is,' said Eddie after a moment. 'We found where Hades lives.'

'We did,' Nina agreed. 'But before we go in – can you put a frickin' Band-Aid on my tit?'

27

The dull clatter of the mercenaries' footsteps became an echo as they reached the bottom of the first winding tunnel. 'There's a cave here,' reported Hassani, an Iranian with dark circles beneath his eyes.

'So I see,' said Brice, sweeping his torch across the walls – then snapping it to one side at a stifled exclamation of surprise from one of the other men. 'Relax,' he said, seeing what stood in the beam. 'It's just a statue.'

'What's it doing down here?' asked Duger.

'Proving that Wilde is right, I suspect.' The Englishman shifted his attention to the dark lake beyond the figure. 'This doesn't smell right, figuratively or literally. I need a pen or something. Come on, come on,' he barked impatiently when there was no instant response. 'I don't have all day.'

Palancio hesitated, then dug into an inner pocket. 'Here,' he said, producing a slim and elegant metal fountain pen.

Brice took it, then crouched at the edge. He dipped the pen into the still waters below. In moments, it started to hiss and bubble as the corrosive took effect. 'Hmm. Wading may not be a good idea.' He stood and returned the smoking pen to the dismayed Palancio. 'Thank you.'

'*Mia madre mi ha comprato quella penna,*' the Italian muttered, but not too loudly.

Duger's flashlight swept the rest of the chamber. 'There's a boat on the other side,' he reported.

'Chase and Wilde must have used it to go over.' Brice examined the rope spanning the dark pool. 'Too risky to traverse using that; you'd melt your back off.' He thought for a moment. 'We have a grapnel gun, yes? Who has it?'

Craine, a tall Canadian with his hair in a topknot, shrugged off his backpack. 'Me.'

'Good. Now, do you think you can hook that boat without the cable falling into a river that will dissolve it like Mr Palancio's pen?'

'I'll . . . try,' said Craine uncertainly.

Brice gave him a wolf-like smile. 'Do your very best.' He went to the statue as the Canadian took out the grapnel gun. 'Of course. The river, the ferry – this must be Charon. Just as mythology said. Wilde does have rather a knack for this, I must admit.'

'Sounds like you admire her,' said Flagg, with a hint of mockery.

'She's very intelligent, and has managed to cheat death while finding these kinds of things for a quarter of a century. That makes her highly capable – or, as an enemy, dangerous. Appreciating the threat someone poses is not the same as admiring them.'

The American snorted. 'She's a fifty-year-old egghead. I'll believe she's a threat when I see it.'

Both men reacted to the sudden retort of Craine's gas-propelled grapnel gun. The glinting steel hook arced across the river. It hit the rock wall on the far side with a piercing clang and dropped to the small ledge behind the boat. Craine had already clapped his hand to the controls of the launcher's inbuilt electric winch, hastily reeling in the trailing cable. It slapped down on the dark water, kicking up ripples, but then pulled taut as the grapnel caught against the boat. The metal line rose again, dripping.

Brice frowned, but as the Canadian carefully drew in the cable, the boat gently drifted clear of the far bank, beginning a slow voyage back across the Styx. 'Whatever's in that river, it must take prolonged exposure to have full effect,' the Englishman mused. 'Everyone, do try not to fall in.'

He watched impatiently as the empty boat made its languid crossing.

'I can't believe you said "tit",' Eddie smirked as he and Nina approached the gate. He had treated and bandaged her wound. 'That's not like you, Mrs Prude.'

'What, I can't be as rude as my husband?' she replied. 'Although if anyone asks, I'll—'

She broke off, looking around in surprise at a sudden noise. 'What was that?'

Eddie listened as the distant *clang* faded. 'That was metal! Shit. Somebody's found the tunnel.'

'How?'

'They might have seen our ropes and climbed up to see where we'd gone. The big hole going down into the rock would be a bit of a giveaway.' He looked back at the gate. 'We need to get a shift on. As soon as whoever it is realises what's down here, they'll get the local authorities involved, your face'll be all over the news, and we'll be back where we started.'

'What if they make it all the way down here and find us?' Nina asked, worried.

'They won't be able to get across the river without the boat. Unless they've got a grappling hook with 'em, and what are the odds of that?'

'I hope they realise the Styx is dangerous.'

'I'm sure they'll figure it out, one way or another.' He grinned to show that he was joking. 'Come on, then. Make your big discovery.'

'Okay. You're right that we need to move fast, but – let's be careful, all right?'

'I always am.'

'Ha!' she exclaimed sarcastically as she went to the open gate and shone her flashlight inside. 'Well, I don't see any fields, Elysium or otherwise. But there's quite a lot in here.'

Eddie moved alongside her. 'Yeah. Is this meant to be a tomb, or a museum?'

They entered the chamber cut from the heart of the purple rock. Dominating the space was a large chariot decorated in gold and silver, four statues of horses posed as if pulling it at a gallop. Plinths around it held smaller artefacts: a two-headed spear, a primitive crossbow and several bolts also with two points on their heads, a drinking horn. 'They're relics of Hades,' Nina whispered reverently as she carefully advanced to examine the new discoveries. 'This is his bident.' She illuminated the sharp twin prongs of the bronze weapon. 'And this must be his gastraphetes.'

'Gastro-feet what?'

'It's a crossbow. The ancient Greeks had developed them by at least the fourth century BC. Although since Hades was a figure in Atlantean mythology as well as Greek, it must have been a lot earlier than that.'

Eddie took a closer look at the bow. 'Pretty nicely made. It almost looks modern.'

'They knew what they were doing. The knowledge just got lost for a while before being rediscovered. Like so much from the Atlantean era.'

Eddie shone his light to one side. 'Looks like those two dead blokes managed to get in here.' He illuminated an open stone chest filled with not only gold coins, but other precious metals and gems of all colours. 'Hades was loaded, then.'

'It's more that his domain was,' said Nina, less interested in the immense riches than the archaeological treasures. 'All these things come from beneath the ground. Hades is generous, if you're willing to devote your effort to him.' She turned her attention back to the other artefacts, then swept her flashlight at the area behind the chariot. 'Oh . . . I think we found him.'

A large sarcophagus of smoothly polished white marble stood on a broad plinth at the chamber's centre. Carved into its expansive side were scenes from Hades's life. Nina crouched to illuminate them. 'This must be the same chariot,' she said, finding an exquisitely sculpted relief showing a tall man with a long beard, presumably Hades himself, riding in a four-horse open carriage. One hand held the reins, his free arm wrapped tightly around a young woman.

'Who's she?' Eddie asked.

'Persephone, the goddess of spring – the daughter of Zeus and Demeter. Hades was her uncle. He was in love with her, so kidnapped her to become his wife and the queen of the Underworld.'

He snorted. 'Greek mythology is very incesty, innit? Why are so many gods complete arseholes?'

'The same reason regular people with too much power are. Rafael Loost was a case in point.' She checked the other marble images. 'And there's Hades with Zeus himself, and that must be Poseidon, dividing the world between them after defeating the Titans. Hades forcing Sisyphus to roll a boulder up a slope for all eternity... Hmm, if that was a real event, then this shows how it worked. It must have been a case of "if you can get the boulder to the top, you win your freedom" – except that the last section before the top is so steep nobody would be able to push it up there. I wonder if there's anything to say where the site was?'

'Focus, love,' said Eddie, knocking on the top of the stone coffin.

'Sorry, sorry. I'll have to come back to that one. But – ah.' She pointed at the next carving. 'We know who that's meant to be.'

'Cerberus.' The image was of a large and fearsome-looking dog, but with three heads where one would normally be. Its body was completely covered by more snarling faces, both canine and colubrine, dozens upon dozens of hounds and snakes expressing their anger towards anyone facing them. 'So that's what he looks like.'

'Obviously not in reality.' Nina frowned, running her finger along what appeared to be a decorative series of icons beneath the picture. 'Look at these. Dog heads, snake heads and bidents – just like the floor tiles in the Cerberus passage.'

'Is that the clue saying how to get out?'

'Maybe. They seem to be in a random order – dog, bident, snake, snake, bident, dog . . .' She took out her phone to photograph it. 'If it *is* telling us the sequence we need to get back through the trap, better to get a picture of it now, just in case.'

'I probably shouldn't ask, "In case what?", should I?' Eddie rumbled. 'Okay, you found Hades – you're not going to lever this thing open to take a photo of him, are you?'

'It's not my immediate plan, no. My priority is finding his shroud.'

'And then what? Nick it?'

'Secure it for safekeeping is more what I had in mind,' she said, a little spikily. She surveyed the area beyond the sarcophagus. 'There's something else back here.'

They went to it. It was another marble plinth, though much smaller than the one bearing the stone coffin. It too supported a container: an ornate carved chest, about two feet square. Rather than images, this had ancient Greek text scribed into its face.

Nina read it. '"The unseen one, the king of the Underworld, leaves this gift for those who succeed him."'

Eddie glanced back at the sarcophagus. 'Nice of him. You going to open it?'

'It certainly seems like an invitation. But . . . let me have a piton, will you?'

He produced one, then retreated as Nina held it at arm's length and gingerly positioned its tip beneath the chest's slightly overhanging lip. She slowly levered it upwards. Nothing deadly flew, sprayed or gushed from the interior. She raised the lid fully and looked inside . . .

She wasn't sure quite what she had expected to find, but it was not the item she saw. 'Huh,' she said, somewhat surprised.

Eddie voiced her feelings. 'That's not a shroud.'

'No, it's not.' It was instead a helmet, large enough to protect the top and back of the wearer's head down to around ear level, but no more. The design was plain and functional, but textured rather than being smoothly hammered or cast metal. 'That actually fits with a lot of the mythology of Hades: he's far more commonly described as wearing a helmet or a cap that lets him become unseen rather than a shroud. But if that's the case, why did both the Knights and the Brotherhood *call* it a shroud?'

She brought her light closer to inspect her discovery. The texture took on form – *familiar* form. 'I've seen this before,' she said, with concerned realisation. 'It's the same kind of pattern as the Knights' armour. If the person wearing it can channel earth energy, they can make it transform.'

'Into what?'

'Maybe a shroud, I dunno! But these,' she indicated the tiny scale-like markings, 'are just like what I saw on Rain's armour, when I wore it after she got hurt. I did what she told me to; I *willed* it to change. And it did. Into . . . well, you saw it.'

'An angel,' said Eddie, nodding. 'A kick-arse one with a New York accent, at that.' He tapped the helmet. 'So what does this turn you into?'

'Maybe nothing, if it works as advertised. Or at least the appearance of nothing. That's how Hades could turn invisible. The Knights' armour warps light to hide the wearer's face behind a kind of halo. This might warp light all the way around them.'

'Like the Predator?'

'I . . . suppose, yeah.' Sci-fi was not Nina's preferred movie genre, and she had to think for a moment to recall what he was describing. 'Although I was hoping for something a bit more mythic. But there's only one way to find out.' She reached for the helmet.

'You sure about this?' Eddie asked.

'We came all this way to find it. And if it's an artefact that uses earth energy, it has to be protected. I'm the only one of us who can channel it. So . . .' She readied herself – then placed her hands on the metal.

THE SHROUD OF HADES

The resulting sensation was all too familiar. She had unearthed several artefacts like it in the past, which reacted to the parts of her DNA that traced back to her distant ancestors from Atlantis. She felt the same surge of power through her body, the feeling that her senses had expanded beyond its confines. This time, though, her perception was not free to travel along the lines of energy, as it had with some of her other discoveries. She was somehow tied to the helmet itself, able only to feel what was around it.

But perhaps that was enough. Perhaps that was how Hades had become invisible – by using the flow of energy to affect light from his environment, bending it around him to make himself seem to vanish.

She picked up the helmet. It seemed almost to shiver in her hands, the scales eager to reshape themselves. The Knights' armour had done the same, turning from metal bands in the form of necklaces and bracelets to an all-covering layer as thin as gold leaf but given immense strength by the power running through it. Something similar was about to happen here, she knew. She could guide it, shape it. All she had to do was *will* it, and it would happen . . .

She carefully placed the helmet upon her head. It was too large, sized for a man's skull, but in a moment it had shifted to fit her more closely. *Okay,* she thought, focusing herself. *Make me disappear.*

The helmet changed shape again – this time completely.

It flowed over her, the ultra-thin scales sliding and skittering to find their new positions. Unlike the armour, which had become form-fitting as it transformed, this was indeed a shroud, dropping to cover her whole frame like a loose cloak. She could still see even as it covered her face, small gaps between the individual metal leaves giving her a view like looking through a fine gauze. It reached the floor – and she felt a new surge as the shroud came to life. It was working, she knew, extended senses telling her the empowered artefact was warping light itself. 'Oh, my God,' she gasped, amazed. 'Eddie, it works, it's real!' Her voice sounded oddly hollow, vibrations in the air affected by the field surrounding her. She turned to face her husband—

To find him regarding her with a less-than-impressed expression. 'I can still see you.'

'What?' He couldn't, she was sure. 'No, I can tell that it's—'

'I mean, I can't see *you*,' he clarified. 'That thing covered you, and then *ping*, you vanished. But I can see exactly where you are.' He pointed his torch at her. 'You're *sort of* casting a shadow on the wall – it's fuzzy, but definitely there.' Nina turned to see with dismay that he was correct. A dark patch was visible in his flashlight's beam; translucent, like smoke, but still enough to reveal *something* was partially obscuring the light. 'And I can see your shape where you're standing. It's hard to describe, like . . . I don't know, you really do look like the Predator. When he's cloaked, I mean,' he hastily added. 'Not when he's got his helmet off.'

'Thanks,' was her sardonic reply.

'Try moving, see if it changes when you do that.'

Nina stepped backwards, then paced sideways. Her sinking feeling deepened when she saw Eddie was tracking her movement perfectly. 'Sorry, love,' he said. 'If anything, moving makes you easier to see. Whatever's behind you distorts like you're looking at it through a magnifying glass.'

'Oh. Okay.' She couldn't keep disappointment from her voice. 'I mean, it's an amazing find, but . . .'

'It's a bit shit, innit?' He laughed. 'All the things you've discovered, all these artefacts which can threaten the entire world and have insane billionaires and warlords after them – then you finally find one that nobody else even knew about, and it's rubbish.'

'That makes me feel so much better, Eddie.'

'But at least you still found this place, right?' He swept a hand to encompass the tomb, and the Underworld beyond. 'Something for your next book. And you can add it to your big list of mythological stuff that was actually real.'

She willed the shroud to return to its original form. The thin cloak of metal leaves withdrew upwards, retracting with an almost unsettling sense of purpose until in moments she felt the weight and shape of the original helmet upon her head. 'I suppose, yeah. Speaking of which, I should get photos of everything in here.' She took out her phone.

Eddie indicated the helmet. 'What about that?'

'I'd better put it back where it belongs for now.' She returned to the stone chest and lifted the helmet from her head, then paused.

'What's wrong?'

'Nothing. It just feels like I can do more with it. The Staff of Afrasiab, when I held it, felt almost as if it *wanted* to be used, like there was some echo of Afrasiab himself coming through it. Maybe Hades left some impression on this as well. It feels like . . .' She frowned, holding the artefact in front of her – then focused upon it. Another effort of will, trying to understand what it was subconsciously telling her . . .

And the helmet changed shape.

Even though she was controlling it, Nina still felt surprise as she watched the seemingly impossible happen before her eyes. The countless individual flecks of fine metal making up the artefact shifted over each other, sliding into the new form that she envisioned in her mind. Almost before she could take in the miraculous transformation it was complete, leaving her holding a chunky torc necklace. Though smaller physically, it was the same weight as the helmet.

Eddie was startled. 'Bloody hell. So *that's* how it works. Christ, if I hadn't just watched it happen, I'd never believe it. Does it stay like that when you put it down?'

'Yes,' she replied, with total confidence – even though she didn't actually know for sure. But she lowered the torc into the chest and let go. It did indeed remain in its new form. 'Oh, damn,' she added, suddenly dismayed on a professional level. 'I should have kept it as the helmet so I could take a photo!' She picked it up again—

Another distant metallic noise rolled through the chamber. This time, though, it was louder, nearer – the rumbling scrape of a large object being moved.

They both looked around at the doorway in alarm. 'What the fuck was that?' Eddie asked.

Nina realised immediately. 'That was the gate at the end of the Cerberus passage. Whoever came down after us just opened it – and armed the trap!'

28

Brice watched as the mercenaries pulled the buckled metal gate open. Part of its lower edge ground against the rock floor, producing an unholy banshee shrill. Other moans came from the old barrier as it was freed from its stasis of – who knew how long? Centuries, millennia? The corpses in the tunnel behind were certainly ancient.

Neither had been Chase or his wife. So the Cerberus-themed traps that had killed the two robbers were no longer working. It was safe to continue the pursuit.

'We could have climbed through the hole,' said Duger. He gestured at the gate's top. 'Wilde and Chase managed it, so we could have too.'

Brice shot him a dismissive look. 'I couldn't have.' Squeezing his prison-hardened upper body through the confined space would have been impossible. 'Come on, hurry up.'

The gate was slowly forced open. As the gap widened, an ominous *thunk* came from beyond the gate, as if some mechanism had been tripped. Suspicious, Brice went to the opening and leaned around it to illuminate the gate's back. A taut chain was attached to it, disappearing into a hole in the floor. 'Damn it! I think that rearmed the traps behind us.'

The mercenaries reacted with alarm. 'You mean we're *stuck* down here?' said Flagg. 'Those bodies back there – they got stabbed, or fucking *melted*! How the hell are we supposed to get out now?'

'The same way whoever built this place did,' Brice replied. 'There's obviously some sequence to the tiles on the floor. We just have to find it.'

'And if we can't?' demanded the American, challenging.

Brice gave him a cold smile. 'Two ways. Either people go through one by one until we find the correct sequence by trial and error. Or, which I'm sure would be all our preference, we use the means at our disposal that didn't exist thousands of years ago to neutralise the traps. Which would be your choice?'

Flagg retreated slightly under his menacing stare. 'The second one.'

'Good. Although the first *is* still an option. Remember that.' He waved for the mercenaries to finish opening the gate. 'Let's keep moving. We're committed now.'

'*Someone* shoulda been,' Flagg muttered as the group pulled again.

It did not take long for the gate to be opened wide enough for them to fit through. Once it was wedged in place by a couple of rocks, the mercenaries continued their descent towards the Underworld.

Eddie went to the tomb's entrance and looked out across the shadowy chamber to the tunnel mouth. 'It won't take 'em long to get down here. We need to be ready, in case they're not friendly.'

'Why wouldn't they be friendly?' Nina asked as he returned to her. 'Nobody knows it's us down here.'

'Loost's people probably figured out we're in Greece by now.' He picked up the gastraphetes and checked that it was intact. 'Our passports were logged at both ends – and I had to use my credit card to pay for the flight and the hire car.'

'But how would anyone know we'd come to Meteora?'

'I don't know, but I'd rather be safe than dead.' The weapon appeared to have survived the ages in good order. Eddie tried to puzzle out how to cock it, then with an 'Ah!' of discovery, pointed it down at the floor and placed the end of the long slider protruding from its front on the stones. He then rested his stomach carefully on the carved concave bar at the rear of the stock. Holding each end like handlebars, he leaned forward, his weight pushing the crossbow's body downwards and drawing its string tighter. With a solid *clack* as the trigger's latch caught it, the slider locked into place. 'There we go!'

'Will it still work?' Nina asked uncertainly.

He took a twin-pronged bolt from the plinth and placed it in the groove running the slider's length. Then he raised it to his eye and took aim through the open doorway – and pulled the trigger. The bar-taut string and slider slammed back to their original positions, sending the bolt hurtling through the opening. A faint splash followed a couple of seconds later.

Eddie nodded. 'Yep. That must have gone easily fifty metres. If I angled it up to make a ballistic shot, it could probably do a hundred.' He took another bolt and began to reload. 'Turn the lights out.'

Nina did so. The tomb went dark, the only illumination the shafts of grey daylight beyond the doorway. Her husband was reduced to a silhouette in front of it. She moved past him to look out at the tunnel. Who was coming? Were they a threat? She didn't see how that could be possible, but Eddie was probably right to take precautions. Long and painful experience had taught her that unexpected arrivals were also often unwelcome . . .

No sign of anyone, yet, but over the creak of the gastraphetes she heard a faint sound: footfalls on stone. More than one set. Several people, moving almost at a march. 'Eddie,' she warned, turning to face him. 'I can—'

She broke off as she realised she could still see him – in silhouette. The illumination behind him was faint, but enough for her to make out his shape. Somewhere, at the back of the chamber, light was leaking in.

'What?' Eddie asked, completing his reload.

'It sounds like several people coming.'

'Shit. Not good,' he muttered, hoisting the crossbow and coming to the doorway to take up a watching brief. Nina, meanwhile, went deeper into the tomb. 'Where are you going?'

'There's light coming in back here. There might be another way out.' She relit her flashlight, picking her way past the relics to reach the rear wall. She belatedly realised she was still holding the Shroud of Hades, in its new form; unsure what to do with it, she put the torc around her neck.

She saw where the light was coming from. A crack lanced diagonally down one wall: a stress fracture, a split in the purple rock widened by past earthquakes. But where the walls met at the corner it had done more than merely split it – it had broken it open, a crooked gap leading through to the chamber outside. Beyond, she saw the quake had done similar damage to the sandstone, forming a narrow, ragged ledge where it had sheared apart.

'Eddie!' she called, turning off the flashlight. 'There *is* another way out! It's tight, but we might be able to fit through it. It could be how those robbers got in here without being judged.'

'Okay,' he acknowledged, 'but shush – they're coming.'

'Don't you "shush" me,' she griped as she went back to him. He positioned himself at the doorway's side to give himself cover while he aimed at the tunnel mouth. Nina looked over his shoulder, her nervousness rising as the tramping footsteps grew louder. Lights danced over the inside of the passage. Who had found them?

A man holding a flashlight was first to enter. Nina didn't recognise him, but guessed from his appearance that he was of Persian descent. He looked around in surprise at the underground wonder, lowering his torch – but kept his other hand raised.

It held a gun.

'Shit,' she whispered. The newcomers *were* hostile. But were they after the bounty because she had been tagged on Uzz without knowing it, or . . .

More men entered. All were armed.

Among them was John Brice.

Nina's heart sank. The rogue MI6 agent and his team had found them. But *how*?

'Move back,' Eddie whispered. She obeyed, retreating. The intruders shone their lights around, searching for their prey. She instinctively ducked back as one man's beam swept towards the entrance. A shout – but he had seen the statues guarding the gateway, not the two people lurking beyond it. More lights turned their way.

Brice's voice carried clearly across the cavern. 'They must be up there. Move in. Let's get them.'

Eddie lined up the crossbow on Brice as the mercenaries approached the stairs. The other Englishman dropped behind the terrace's edge, then gradually reappeared as he and his men ascended. Eddie exhaled, steadying himself as he prepared to fire. Brice rose higher, step by step, his chest coming into sight—

Eddie pulled the trigger.

The ancient crossbow unleashed its twin-pronged bolt with savage force – only for it to hit Bakst in the head as the Belarussian jogged up the steps, passing directly in front of Brice. The missile punched right through his skull, both barbs bursting out of the back of his head with a crack of splintering bone. Bakst fell backwards, a flailing arm catching Brice and knocking him off-balance. 'Down, get down, cover!' another mercenary yelled.

The intruders leapt from the stairs and flattened themselves against the terrace's wall. Eddie was already jamming himself down on the gastraphetes's stock to cock it again. But Brice recovered and jumped into cover before he could load a new bolt. 'Shit!' the Yorkshireman growled.

Muted calls came from below, the mercenaries quickly regrouping to face the threat. A man with long blond hair scurried backwards from the terrace and fired a sub-machine gun up at the gateway. Eddie hastily retreated as bullets cracked off the rock and spanged against the metal gate itself. Other men joined the attack. 'Shut the door, shut it!' the Yorkshireman shouted to Nina. She ran to join him, the couple forcing the barrier closed with a groan of old metal. More bullets struck like hurled hammers, dents erupting on the rear side. Brice yelled an order, the fusillade intensifying – but the gate reached its latch with a decisive clank.

Nina and Eddie jumped back and ducked as more bullets struck the barrier. Heavier impacts split the metal, thin spears of light stabbing through it. But then the gunfire tailed off as Brice commanded his men to cease fire.

Eddie waited a couple of seconds in case it was a bluff, then risked putting an eye to one of the holes. Their attackers were making their way up the stairs, guns raised. He withdrew. 'Get back,' he told Nina. 'They're coming.'

Nina retreated to behind Hades's sarcophagus. 'Now what do we do?' She looked back towards the faint wash of light at the tomb's rear. Could they get out that way?

Before Eddie could answer, a voice came from outside. 'Chase! Surprised to see me?' The words had a strange timbre, as if coming through a loudspeaker.

'A bit,' Eddie replied, finding cover behind a plinth. 'How'd you find us, Brice? Call in a favour from some old mate in MI6 and use their spy satellite?'

'Nothing so elaborate. Simple detective work, that's all. Your wife left some notes at your late friend Charlie's cabin,' Eddie reacted with dismay, knowing at once that Brice had been responsible for his friend's death, 'about an ancient artefact in Greece. Then Loost's AI told us you'd *gone* to Greece, so the connection was obvious. And I had the advantage of personal knowledge; I'd been to Meteora before. "The fingers of Hades stretching into the sky", that was the clue that brought you here, wasn't it, Nina?'

Nina was appalled at having led their pursuers to them, but covered it. 'What do you want, Brice?' she demanded.

'I would have thought that was obvious. The pair of you, dead. You took a lot from me: my freedom, my voice. I think it's only fair I pay you back, with interest.'

'Eddie,' Nina whispered, while Brice was still speaking. 'Let's try to get out through the back.'

He nodded. 'You go. I'll keep him talking.' He raised his voice as Nina hurried towards the damaged corner. 'Last time we spoke, you were wheezing away like Darth Vader. Sounds like you got an upgrade.'

'A gift from my employer, Rafael Loost – or his estate, rather. An electronic voice synthesiser, powered by a kinetic battery. Technology has advanced in the thirteen years you took from me.' The device was evidently capable of reproducing emotion, as Brice's voice became mocking. 'Time seems to have taken a lot from you too, Chase. Your hair, for one thing. You look *old*. I always thought that children grow by draining the life force of their parents. Judging from your appearance, Macy was quite a handful.'

Eddie glanced back. Nina was at the crack in the wall, starting to squeeze through it. 'Judging from *your* appearance, they only gave you spinach to eat in prison. Or steroids.'

'I took up bodybuilding as a hobby. There wasn't an awful lot else to do in that cell.'

'There was *one* other thing. I mean, your right arm's a lot bigger than your left. I always knew you were a wanker.'

Brice laughed, though it was more of an irate hiss. 'Joke all you like, Chase. You don't have long left to do it. I've waited a long time for this. Do you know what kept me going in that prison? The thought that one day, I would be able to kill you with my bare hands. And now, that day has come!'

Nina paused and leaned back out of the rift in the rock. It seemed she could fit through it – if she had time. Distracting Brice might give her that time. 'Your boss won't like it if you just kill me,' she shouted. 'Loost wanted to tell me he'd outsmarted me, so either he plays his video saying so before I get murdered by someone after his bounty, or I go looking for his guy in Malta who put the backdoor into Uzz – and walk into a trap.'

Another laugh from the former MI6 officer, this with genuine, if gloating, humour. 'Of *course* it's a trap! Anyone with half a brain would see that. This Loost was nowhere near as clever as he thought. A common failing amongst the rich, in my experience.' Now that he was in full flow, Nina slipped back into the crack, hauling her backpack through the confined space behind her. 'But it's a trap you're going to have to walk into, isn't it? Because the alternative is to stay on the run until, eventually, someone claims the bounty. How many times have you almost died in the past few days? Do you think you can survive indefinitely?'

Eddie took over the task of keeping Brice talking. 'We've done all right so far.'

'Perhaps. But only by luck. And your luck only has to run out once, Chase. However, Nina, I'm willing to make *you* an offer.'

Nina froze. She was now over halfway through the crevice. If she replied, her voice might carry out through the far end, revealing there was another exit from the tomb . . .

Fortunately, Eddie had also realised the danger, and spoke for her. 'What kind of offer, Brice?'

'I'll save your wife the hassle of making her own way to Malta, and take her myself. We all know she's going to end up there eventually, so it makes sense to cut to the chase – no pun intended.'

'And what about me?'

A malevolent relish filled the synthetic voice. 'Oh, I'm going to kill you. My desire to wish harm upon Nina is purely on a professional level. But with you, Chase, it's *personal*. I'm going to make you *suffer*. And you'll let me, because you love your wife, and you don't want *her* to suffer, do you?' Brice started to breathe more heavily. 'Everything you've done to me, Chase, every pain you've caused me, every indignity you've heaped upon me . . . you're going to feel them all fifty times over before you *die*.'

Eddie responded by imitating the sound of a cuckoo clock. 'I should have killed you in your cell, you fucking nutter – they would have let me get away with it. You're a shit salesman, Brice. Just like you were a shit spy. You fucking traitor. Take your offer and shove it up your arse.' Knowing that fireworks were about to follow, he ran after Nina – grabbing the bident from its stand on the way. Any weapon was better than none.

The heat of Brice's seething anger could almost be felt, even through the metal barrier. 'Blow this gate open,' he growled. The mercenaries backed down the stairs – taking out hand grenades.

Eddie reached the broken wall and shone his torch into the gap. 'Nina!' he said in a low voice. 'Are you through?'

'Not quite,' came her reply from within the rock.

'Then hurry up, 'cause Brice is about to bang on the door!' He shrugged off his pack and held it ahead of him as he squeezed into the ragged opening, pulling the spear along behind.

Nina was almost at the far end, struggling to bend and twist through the final few feet. The crack had narrowed, and was partially blocked by broken chunks of the purple stone. 'I can't! There's a rock in the way!'

Eddie forced his way through after her. His larger frame made it more difficult than his wife had found it, but he had to ignore the pain as the rough stone scraped and gouged him. 'I've got the spear, I'll try to—'

Metallic bangs came from behind him: grenades clanking against the gate's outer side. *'Fire in the hole!'* he barked, dropping everything to put his hands to his ears. Nina knew the warning and hurriedly did the same—

The grenades exploded. The mercenaries were professionals, timing their detonations to be practically simultaneous. Multiple blasts pounded the heavy gate, ripping away its lower hinge and splintering the surrounding rock. A shockwave roiled through the tomb, showering it with gritty debris and kicking up the dust of ages. Eddie closed his eyes, coughing as the stinging cloud surged past. He felt the rock walls pressing against him shudder. 'Nina, you okay?' he said.

'Yeah, yeah,' she replied. 'But I'm still stuck.'

'I'll pass you the spear. Hang on.' He leaned sideways, groping for the fallen bident. Straining, he managed to find the spear's bronze shaft with his fingertips and fumble it into his grip. 'Got it. Here.' He pulled in his stomach and passed the weapon through to his other hand. The trailing twin barbs snagged on his clothing, but he tore them free and worked the spear along the narrow space to Nina. 'See if you can lever the rock out of the way.'

'I'll try.' She retreated slightly to give herself room to manoeuvre.

With effort, she drove the end of the bident's shaft into a gap between the obstructing rock and the crevice's side. Metal ground against stone. She pushed the spear back and forth. The rock shifted, millimetre by millimetre. 'It's moving!' she whispered back to Eddie.

He heard voices echoing through the tomb. Brice's stood out amongst them. 'Can you push it open?' The question was followed by grunts of exertion and the dull moan of strained metal, but there was no almighty bang of the gate falling. 'More grenades. Bring it down!'

'Nina, hurry up,' Eddie implored. He dragged himself closer to her, taking hold of the spearhead to add some of his strength to hers. The broken rock crunched against the walls as it shifted. 'Come on, it's moving, we've got it—'

Another round of harsh clanks came from the gate.

'Oh, shit, *shit*!' Nina gasped. She twisted the bident, trying to work it deeper into the gap, and pushed against it as hard as she could. The rock jolted – then broke free.

She squirmed through the now-clear gap. Behind her, Eddie again clamped his hands to his ears—

More grenades exploded. This time, the blast ripped the gate from its remaining hinge. It toppled and hit the tomb floor with a thunderous *boom* as deafening as the detonations. Cracks lanced outwards through the purple rock from the damaged doorway, a deeper rumble rolling through the cavern. Hunks of rock fell from the tomb's ceiling and smashed down on the fallen barrier, a thicker wave of dust and flying grit filling the chamber.

The shockwave passed – though the echoing tremors through the ancient stone were stronger and more prolonged. Eddie recovered and squeezed through the crack after Nina, collecting his backpack and the bident along the way. He emerged on a narrow ledge in the outer wall of the Underworld. The couple were thirty feet above the cavern's floor; too far to drop down. 'Are you okay?' Nina asked, worried.

'Yeah,' he replied. 'But it won't take 'em long to realise where we went.' He got his bearings. The strange rock containing the tomb of Hades – which now had a jagged rent across its surface, bits of debris spilling from it – was to his right as he gazed out into the chamber. He could just see one end of the terrace. None of the mercenaries were in sight, but that wouldn't be the case for long.

He peered to his left. It took a moment for his eyes to adjust, the beams of light piercing the Underworld masking detail in the shadows around its edge. The ledge gradually rose before reaching a near-vertical gouge where rocks had broken away and fallen to the floor beyond one of the winding waterways. Could they descend there? The whole thing ran behind the silver pillars, some of which had buckled as the rockface to which they were fastened moved. The metal columns were just wide enough to hide behind. He looked across the chamber to its entrance – realising that if they could climb down, they would be on the far side of the pools and streams and could make a straight run for the way out.

He was about to tell Nina, but she had reached the same conclusion. 'We can get down over there,' she said. 'Come on!' She sidestepped quickly along the narrow path, ducking behind the pillars. Eddie hesitated, about to leave the long and awkward bident, but then decided to keep it. Back pressed against the cavern wall, he started after his wife.

***

The mercenaries waited for the swirling dust to thin, then cautiously advanced into the tomb, weapons at the ready. Some had laser sights, red and green lines stabbing through the hazy air. Bright dots of light and flashlight beams swept across the artefacts ahead; the chariot, the plinths displaying the various possessions of Hades. But none of the men cared about ancient history. Their minds were entirely on the here and now. Where was the man who had killed Bakst – and where was the woman worth a billion dollars?

Brice added his torch to the lights of the others. It found no signs of life. 'They *have* to be in here,' he growled. 'Spread out and search.'

His men obeyed as he went to the sarcophagus beyond the chariot. 'Hades, I presume,' he said to himself. He was about to examine the carvings on the coffin when he noticed a smaller stone container – this one open. He went to it, finding it empty. 'And this must have been the Shroud of Hades. Tomb raiding, Nina? Tut tut.'

'Brice! Over here!' Lannard shouted from the chamber's rear. 'There's a crack in the wall – they must have gone through it.'

'There's nowhere else they might be?' Brice asked. The response from the other men was negative. 'Back outside, quick! *Find them!*'

29

Nina squeezed behind a damaged pillar that had bent inwards over the ledge, then pressed on. The top of the slope was not far ahead. It looked as if they would be able to climb from there down to floor level relatively easily.

If they could reach it alive—

Shouts and footsteps warned that Brice and his men were returning. Nina froze, looking back. Eddie had just reached the buckled pillar. His face fell as he saw she had no concealment of her own. He hurriedly gestured for her to come back, but she shook her head. There was no way he could reach the previous pillar in time.

She scrambled up the incline, hoping to find a hiding place in the broken gouge. But there was nothing deep enough.

The first mercenary leapt from the terrace down to the cavern floor. She was trapped in the open, helpless, defenceless—

The necklace responded to her fear – and transformed.

It split apart, the scales racing into a new form as if knowing the urgency of the situation. Before Nina even consciously knew what was happening, the Shroud had covered her body, more of the foil-thin flakes clambering upwards over her head. Again, she could see through it to a degree – well enough to see more men appear. Guns came up, tactical lights and laser sights sweeping over the cavern wall to find the ledge. Eddie had ducked behind the pillar, but she could do nothing but stay statue-still as the beams came towards her . . .

And passed.

She held her breath. A flashlight had definitely caught her, its flare dazzling. But she hadn't been seen. More lights scoured the ledge – still finding nothing. She risked turning her head towards Eddie. The beam glinted off the bent pillar, but he was shielded behind it . . . looking back at her with an expression she could only think of as 'gobsmacked'.

'Where are they?' Brice's uncanny-valley voice stood out clearly. Nina looked back at the mercenaries. The ex-agent moved to the middle of the group, his own light darting over the wall, then to the ground beneath it. 'It's too high for them to have jumped down.'

'Maybe they went back in,' one man, a bearded American, offered.

Brice signalled to another. 'Hassani, go and check. Fire a few shots into the gap.' The Persian man nodded and jogged quickly back to the stairs.

Unable to find their quarry where they expected, the group spread out to check the wider cavern. Nina cautiously moved the final few feet to the summit. She leaned out a little over the edge. There was definitely a route that she could follow down to the ground—

'What—'

She froze at the sudden exclamation from a tall man with a top-knot. He was looking in her direction – and now his gun whipped up at her, green laser sight flicking on—

Nina cringed as the beam found her – but no bullets followed it. The man frowned, moving his sub-machine gun to sweep the laser dot back and forth over her position. Out of the corner of one eye she saw the intense green spot was being scattered across the sandstone wall by the effect of the Shroud, breaking up as if viewed through a kaleidoscope. If he noticed, and realised what that meant, she was dead.

She held her breath. The laser played over her again . . .

Then moved away.

'What was it?' Brice demanded.

'I thought I saw something,' said the mercenary. His accent was Canadian. 'But there's nothing there.'

Brice stared intently up at the top of the ledge. Nina could almost feel his eyes burning through her camouflage. The urge to move, to make a break for the exit, rose . . .

Gunfire echoed through the Underworld. Everyone looked around at the noise from the tomb as Hassani sent several rounds into the crack. The last made it cleanly through the narrow gap to impact against rock at the bottom of the ledge, spitting stone chips. 'They're not in there,' the Iranian shouted.

Brice made an irritated sound, which emerged from his artificial voice box almost as a buzz. Then he holstered his sidearm and clicked his fingers at a squat, muscular Indian man with a sub-machine gun. 'Vikram. Give me your gun.' When the mercenary hesitated, unwilling to surrender his weapon, Brice took an angry step towards him. 'Now!'

Vikram hurriedly did as ordered. Brice gave the gun a rapid, professional check – then snapped it up and stitched an evenly spaced line of bullet holes along the wall of the ledge at chest height.

Nina saw Eddie tense, scrunching himself against the pillar as the impacts came towards him. But she had nowhere to go, and moving would reveal her presence, invisibility or no—

A round slammed into the wall beside Eddie's position, showering him with grit. The next struck on the other side of the silver pillar. The bullets kept coming, smashing little craters into the rock, closer to Nina, closer—

She felt splinters hit her metallic cloak – then the firing stopped. A click came from Brice's weapon. He frowned. 'Reload!' he barked.

Vikram didn't hesitate this time, tossing him a replacement magazine. Brice caught it and ejected the empty mag, slotting the new one into place and tugging the charging handle. The entire process took barely three seconds. He brought the gun up again, aiming to resume where he had left off.

Nina's fear took control. She dropped flat, even knowing the movement would be seen—

A deep rumble shook the cavern.

She felt the ledge shake beneath her, gripping its edge to hold herself in place. The silver pillars creaked – and *swayed*, rock cracking as some were torn loose, others bending with screams of tormented metal. Bangs and cracks came from above as debris cascaded down the walls in a sandstone avalanche.

Brice looked up in alarm. The other mercenaries also reacted to the new danger, turning to hunt for escape routes. More fractures lanced through the great purple rock embedded in the cavern's side as the vast weight of stone above found a new weakness and bore down upon it. Fragments from pebble-sized to as big as a man's torso exploded from the tomb's wall and showered across the Underworld, kicking up splashes where they landed in water – and ricocheting off the hard floor. Ossovich had to dive aside to avoid being hit.

The chamber shook again, streams of dust falling from on high. One of the shafts of light piercing the Underworld winked out as its opening was blocked by falling rubble – but another widened as the outer wall crumbled around it.

Seeing that their opponents had greater concerns, Eddie sprang from his hiding place and scrambled up the trembling ledge to Nina. 'Go, go!' he said.

She needed no urging. Still cloaked, the redhead scrambled over the summit and hurriedly dropped down through the broken gouge in the cavern wall. Eddie followed, tossing his backpack and the bident behind some rocks below to free up his hands.

The clang as the ancient weapon landed drew attention. 'There, there!' cried Vikram. Without his weapon, all he could do was point at the Yorkshireman as he scrambled down.

Brice, beside him, was distracted by Hassani's shout as he ran from the tomb. 'It's collapsing!' yelled the Iranian. 'Get—'

He was abruptly silenced as a car-sized boulder slammed down on top of him, reducing him to a red spray. Even Brice was startled by the sudden violence of his demise. By the time he reacted to Vikram's alert and whirled to bring up his gun, Eddie had jumped down after Nina, diving into the cover of a clutch of rocks with dark narcissus flowers growing between them. '*Chase!*' Brice roared.

Nina willed the Shroud to return to its previous form, finding the all-enveloping cloak too restrictive to move in freely. It shrank back into the torc around her neck. 'Now what do we do?'

Eddie looked past her. The tunnel mouth was thirty metres away – much closer to them than to Brice or his men, even if they travelled in a direct line through the various water obstacles. 'We fucking leg it! Ready?'

She took a breath. 'Yeah.'

Eddie retrieved his pack and donned it, then picked up the bident. He looked up – seeing more large stones break from the cavern's ceiling and drop towards the area in front of the terrace. 'Get ready . . .' They hit the ground with earth-shaking impacts, scattering debris and prompting panicked shouts from the mercenaries. '*Now!*'

They burst from cover and sprinted towards the exit. As Eddie had hoped, the falling rocks had left their enemies distracted and reeling. But they were already recovering, a couple of the men splashing through a thigh-deep pool to head for the tunnel.

More warning yells as the couple were spotted—

Nina reached the tunnel mouth just as the nearest merc, Palancio, opened fire. She flung herself through it with a shriek as bullets savagely spattered the cavern wall behind her. The Italian switched targets, bringing his gun around to find Eddie – but the Yorkshireman had already hurled the bident. It arced through the air, slicing down at Palancio. He tried to dodge, but was slowed by the water. The twin spearheads stabbed into his stomach. He fell backwards with a choked screech, splashing down in the pool with the weapon jutting from his body like a flagpole. The water around him turned red.

Eddie followed Nina into the tunnel as more guns opened fire. The rockface behind him spalled under a storm of bullets. But they were both clear. 'You okay?' he said, helping Nina to her feet.

'Yeah,' she gasped. Eddie readied himself to run again, but she hesitated, glancing back into the Underworld. 'I just have a feeling this is the last time I'll see this place.'

'Suits me fine. Come on!'

'That's not what I – God *damn* it,' she growled as he set off up the tunnel. She reluctantly raced after him.

The return journey was all uphill, but adrenalin drove them on, both from the fear of Brice and his surviving men catching up and more immediately from the increasingly forceful tremors. The strange rock containing the tomb of Hades was apparently a keystone – and the explosive damage to it had triggered a domino effect within the huge sandstone monolith.

'Christ!' Eddie said as another jolt sent him staggering. 'The whole thing's going to come down! Dunno how we'll get all the way back to the surface in time.'

'Run really fast, I guess,' Nina replied, panting. Her flashlight beam flitted over damp rock and loose stones – then glinted off metal. 'Whoa, whoa. We're at the Cerberus trap.'

'And those bell-ends have armed the fucking thing,' Eddie said with dismay, seeing that the damaged gate was now open. 'How are we going to get through without being shish-kebabbed or melted?'

'That's a good question,' she answered as they hurried through the entrance, halting at the corner. 'Hope I can answer it in the next thirty seconds or so!'

They both aimed their lights down at the tiled floor. The seemingly random arrangement of dogs, snakes and bidents stretched out ahead, the ancient corpses a reminder of the penalty for a single mistake. Eddie illuminated the tile under the nearest body's foot. 'Well, he stepped on a snake, so we know not to do that.'

'But which of the others do we step on? There has to be a pattern . . .' She looked down at the first few rows of tiles, trying to determine if there was some logic behind their positioning. But even with her innate mathematical abilities, there was none she could see. Besides, she didn't know which, if any, of the early tiles were booby-trapped. The dead robbers might have got as far as they did because there were no triggers in the early rows, or survived on pure luck. Without enough information, she couldn't make a deduction—

She suddenly remembered she *had* the information. At least – she hoped.

A tremor faded, the rattle of dislodged stones dying away, only for a new sound to echo up the tunnel. It was distant – but getting closer. 'They're coming,' Eddie warned. 'We'll have to run across and hope we're quicker than the traps.'

'No, no, wait,' Nina pleaded, fumbling to take out her phone and open its photo library. 'The way through – it was on Hades's sarcophagus! Look.' She found the relevant picture and zoomed in on one of the carved panels on the stone coffin's side. 'Here! Under the picture of Cerberus – there are these little images of dogs, snakes and bidents. I think they tell us which tiles to step on.'

Eddie looked for himself. 'First one's a dog. Okay, we haven't got time to mess about, so—'

He stepped onto the tile bearing the image of a dog's head in the first row. Nina cringed, but no mechanisms tripped and unleashed blades. 'That's a start,' she said in relief.

'What's next?'

'Bident.'

The appropriate tile in the next row was directly in front of his position. He advanced. Again, there was no response. Nina moved onto the dog tile behind him. 'Next is a snake.'

That was ahead and to the right. Eddie stepped diagonally across to it, warily watching the snarling animal faces in the walls. They remained still and silent. 'Snake,' Nina told him.

This one required him to step all the way over to the passage's opposite side, navigating around the corpses. Careful not to clip any of the intervening tiles, he stretched across to reach it. Nina followed, one step behind. The rattle of running footsteps behind them grew louder. 'Bident,' she said. Eddie stepped forward. 'Oh, crap!'

He froze on the spearhead tile. 'What?'

'I didn't notice before – there's a gap in the pattern on the coffin. It goes bident, then a *space*, then a dog.'

'What does that mean? A bit of the carving fell off, you can step on any of the next row, you *can't* step on any of them, what?'

'I – I don't know!' She zoomed in further, hoping to see some clue, but there was nothing. 'In context, I'd say the most *likely* meaning is that all the tiles in the next row are booby-trapped and you have to step over them, but . . . I don't know,' she repeated helplessly.

Eddie took a deep breath. 'Well, you usually know what you're talking about with this stuff, and you haven't got me killed yet, so . . .'

He made another long step, his foot passing over the next row to land on a tile bearing the image of Cerberus—

The traps remained inert.

Relieved, he brought his other foot over the dangerous row. Nina moved up to his previous position. 'Still alive, always good,' he told her. 'What's next?'

'Dog, bident, snake,' she told him. He advanced in that pattern, the redhead doing the same. 'Space, snake, dog, snake.' They kept going. Only a few more rows remained – but the sound of the men running up the tunnel drew ever closer.

'Shit, they're almost here,' said Eddie, looking back. Dancing torch beams played over the walls just beyond the Cerberus passage. 'What are the last ones?'

'Dog, bident, snake,' Nina hurriedly replied.

Eddie hopped onto each symbol in turn, making a final spring-heeled leap through the gateway. He turned to watch Nina follow him – and beyond her saw not only the beam, but the lens of a torch appear at the other end of the passage. 'They're here! *Jump!*'

She threw herself forward, skipping the final row of tiles entirely to stumble through the gateway. Eddie pulled her sideways – as laser lines and taclight beams stabbed after her, followed a split-second later by a furious spray of automatic fire. Bullets clanged against the metal gate as the couple dived behind it.

'They're right here!' yelled Flagg, one of the two mercenaries who had fired. The rest of the group were racing up behind them. 'Get 'em!' He and Vikram ran into the tiled passage—

Flagg stepped on a slab marked with the image of Cerberus – and a long metal blade, still sharp and deadly even after millennia, burst from one of the dog heads. It punched into the side of the American's chest, his ribs cracking as he was flung sideways by the impact. He crashed against the opposite wall, shuddering and twitching as the ancient fang pierced his lungs and heart.

Vikram, slightly ahead of him, fared even worse. By fluke his first step had not activated a trap, but his second did – and with a crack of shattering earthenware from behind the carved wall, one of the snake mouths blasted an acrid gout of dark liquid at him. He screamed as the potent corrosive seared into his exposed skin, what protection his clothing provided quickly vanishing as it too was eaten away. His agonised shrieks echoed through the tunnel as he staggered blindly – only to step on a bident tile. A real version of one of the twin-pronged spears burst from a gap between two of the heads and stabbed into his skull. He instantly fell silent and limp, sizzling chunks of flesh dropping from his body as it hung from the weapon.

Brice and the three remaining mercenaries had all wisely halted at the corner. '*Yebena mat'!*' gasped Ossovich, gawping at the carnage.

Brice clicked his tongue. 'Well, at least now there are fewer traps to worry about.' He snapped up his torch at a sound from beyond the far gateway – two sets of feet retreating at speed. '*Chase!*' he bellowed, artificial voice distorted by his rage.

'See you later, fuckface!' the Yorkshireman shouted back. 'I'll save you some Strepsils!'

With a snarl, the ex-agent fired several shots through the gateway in the hope of catching his target, but they struck only stone. Lannard winced at the piercing noise of gunfire in the confined space. 'Duger will shoot them from the helicopter when they reach the surface,' said the Frenchman.

Brice gave him a mocking glare. 'There might not *be* a surface in a few minutes,' he growled, as another tremor rattled the passage. 'We need to get out before this whole thing collapses.' He regarded the floor ahead, then fired again, this time at one of the tiles beyond the bodies. The mechanism beneath clearly operated on a hair-trigger, as the impact of the bullet was enough to trip it. Another blade sprang from a dog head, reaching the limit of its reach with a *clank*.

'We don't have time to test each tile,' the Englishman decided. 'How many grenades do we have left?'

The other men quickly checked their gear. 'Three,' Craine reported.

'Use them,' Brice snapped. 'Destroy that floor!'

The mercenaries exchanged concerned glances, but did as ordered. The group retreated around the corner. 'Fire in the hole!' Craine warned, pulling the pin on the first grenade and tossing it to land just beyond Vikram's corpse. He jerked back into cover and turned to shield his face, hands to his ears. The others did the same—

The grenade exploded, the blast sending the men reeling even in cover. Debris showered around the corner.

Brice was first to recover as the detonation's echoes faded. He swept his torch through the drifting dust. Both ancient corpses had been blown into fragments, while Vikram and Flagg's bodies were shredded by shrapnel, now barely recognisable as human. But the explosive had done its job. Numerous tiles were shattered, exposing holes in the floor beneath them where the triggers had been attached. The gaps between what remained of the mechanisms were easily wide enough to step on without risk. 'Now the rest,' Brice barked. 'Clear the way!'

He withdrew into cover again as the remaining grenades were

thrown. More detonations shook the tunnels. Brice impatiently returned to the corner even before the last pieces of debris settled. Almost the entire floor was now destroyed. A few traps had been triggered, blades and spears jutting across the tunnel and a pool of steaming liquid slowly draining into the holes. 'It's clear!' he said. 'Move!'

The mercenaries picked their way along the passage. The blast-damaged heads of Cerberus snarled impotently at them. Brice led the way through the gate at the far end. As he'd expected, the man and woman he was pursuing were gone.

But they hadn't escaped yet. 'Come on,' he said, running up the next stretch of tunnel. 'They still have to get across that river. We can catch them there!'

30

'That's one way to get past a trap,' said Eddie grimly as the sound of the last explosion reached him. 'Blow it the fuck up!'

He and Nina were in the boat, Eddie pulling on the rope to bring them over the deadly alkali pool. Nina looked back at the small ledge they had just left. 'We should cut the rope when we get across,' she suggested.

'That'll make it a bit hard for archaeologists to get down to the Underworld.'

'I think we're way past the point of worrying about that.' Even here, the tremors running through the rock pillar were causing damage. Several chunks of the chamber's ceiling had plunged into the Styx, kicking up fierce ripples that rocked the boat. If another landed close by, they would be showered by the corrosive. 'It won't take them long to get up here.'

'I know, I know.' He kept hauling at the rope. The figure of Charon loomed on the far bank.

'If we can reach the statue, we can lock the boat in place,' said Nina. 'They won't be able to cross!'

They heard the echo of running footfalls. Not as many as before, so Cerberus had claimed more victims – but if the couple were still in the boat, one man with a gun could kill them both. Eddie made a mental calculation, and didn't like the result. 'We won't reach it in time. We'll have to jump as soon as we're close enough. Get to the front.' She clambered past him, the shift of weight rocking the little craft again.

Another rock fell, but luckily far enough away that the splash didn't reach them. How long that luck would last was another matter.

Nina looked anxiously between the statue ahead and the ledge behind. The thud of boots grew louder. How much further? Fifteen feet. Too far to jump. The distance shrank with each pull on the rope – but now she saw lights in the tunnel. 'Eddie—'

'I know!' A couple more frantic yanks on the woven line, then he rose to a crouch. 'Jump, now!'

It still seemed too far, but Nina had no choice. She stood, the boat pitching beneath her, and planted one foot on the bow – then leapt at the narrow slipway beside Charon.

She threw out one leg, aiming to land just beyond the lapping black waters—

And falling short.

Her heel hit the Styx's edge with a wet slap – followed by a hiss as the corrosive liquid ate into her boot's sole. She threw herself up the little incline. At the top she rolled, tugging desperately at her laces.

Eddie made a hard landing on his side behind her. 'Ah, fuck, my hip!' he gasped, following a moment later with a more annoyed, 'Ah, fuck, I'm definitely getting old – I just complained about my hip!'

Nina had her own concerns. She finally yanked off her boot and tossed it aside. Just in time, she saw as she brought up her flashlight. There was a hole in the leather, a chunk of the sole beneath it completely dissolved by the caustic chemical. 'Jeez!' she said, panting. 'Another second and I'd be missing half my foot!'

Eddie instantly became serious. 'Did you get splashed?'

'No, no, I'm okay.' She saw movement across the Styx. 'Crap, they're here!'

She jumped up and broke into a lopsided run, her remaining boot raising one heel higher than the other. Eddie followed, muttering, 'Fuck, fuck, *fuckeration*!' as pain spiked through his hip. They reached the tunnel just as Brice appeared on the ledge. He whipped up his gun with an angry shout and fired several shots. But the bullets struck only rock behind them.

Eddie clapped a hand to the back of his head as a stone fragment hit like a wasp's sting. 'That was a bit bloody close,' he said as they hurried up the passage. 'But at least it's a straight run to the top.'

As if in response, the floor shuddered beneath their feet, making them stagger. 'Or a wobbly run,' said Nina. Deep moans of tormented stone rose up through the walls like distant whalesong. 'God, how long before the entire pillar gives way?'

'Let's try to be on the ground before we find out,' her husband retorted.

'Yeah, a long way away.' They continued their mad dash towards the surface.

Brice glared angrily across the Styx as his prey disappeared. 'Chase's refusal to die is becoming *really irksome!*' he snarled, before controlling his rage and addressing the more immediate issue of survival. 'Where's the boat?'

Torch beams jabbed across the glistening waters, finding the craft bobbing just short of the opposite bank. Lannard retrieved the grapnel gun. 'We can hook it with this.'

'Give it to me,' Brice ordered. The mercenaries now knew better than to challenge him, the Frenchman handing it over without delay. Brice holstered his gun, then took careful aim and fired the grapnel. It landed neatly in the boat. He immediately raised the cable high to keep it out of the deadly river. The hook caught on a seat. He began to draw the craft back towards them.

An ominous crackle from somewhere deep below warned of an impending tremor. Brice braced himself as the cavern shook. Waves kicked up along the Styx's length, sending the little boat rolling madly. The Englishman gritted his teeth, dragging it closer even as the rope running through it threatened to snag.

'Careful!' warned Ossovich. 'If that breaks—'

'I'm well aware of the danger, *thank* you,' Brice snapped. The shuddering eased, the waves also dying down. The boat slid more easily along the line. Before long, it was at the ledge. Brice detached the grapnel, then climbed aboard. The others warily followed. 'Everyone pull,' the ex-agent ordered. 'We need to get across as fast as we can.'

The mercenaries all took hold of the keratin rope. They quickly synchronised their movements so two were pulling while the others brought their hands forward. The boat's return crossing was rapid enough to raise a bow wave in the inky river. Brice aimed his light at their destination. 'Halfway there. Keep—'

Another tremor, this more violent. The boat shook as waves struck it from both sides. Ossovich let go of the rope and clutched the gunwale for balance—

A falling stone hit the water just a metre from him – splashing his hand.

The Russian screamed as the corrosive seared through his skin. He jerked back in blind panic, flailing his wounded arm. 'Keep still, you imbecile!' Brice shouted. 'You'll tip us over!'

Ossovich either didn't hear or didn't care. The flesh melting from his bones, he tried to retreat from the boat's side, bashing forcefully against the other men in his terror and rocking the craft so far over that the churning waves almost sluiced into it—

Brice lunged and drove a jaw-breaking punch into his face – then pitched the stunned Russian bodily over the gunwale. Ossovich managed a final scream before disappearing into the Styx, the other mercenaries jerking back from the splash. A surge of frothing bubbles rose from beneath the surface, his dissolving face briefly reappearing with mouth agape in a silent shriek of agony before sinking again.

Brice sat back down and retook his hold on the rope. 'We'll go faster without the extra weight.' When Lannard and Craine responded only with horrified stares, he added with a growl: 'Come on, then! Move it!'

The two men hurriedly grabbed the rope and resumed the crossing, Brice sitting tall in the bow like a figurehead.

***

Nina and Eddie battled up the steep slope towards the surface. The redhead was panting, throat dry and muscles burning, and even her husband felt the strain of the merciless climb. But both knew they couldn't stop to catch their breath. The straining of the rock pillar was a tortured cry rising from the depths of Hell, the angled strata shearing apart.

Another jolt shook the floor, sending the couple stumbling. 'Dammit!' Nina gasped, catching herself against a wall. She had discarded her remaining boot to make it easier to run, though loose stones kept jabbing painfully through her socks. 'How much further?'

'Can't be far to the top,' said Eddie, regaining his own balance. 'But we've still got to get down to the ground – and then run before this whole thing collapses on top of us.'

'Oh, I love knowing that however bad things are, they can still get worse!' They resumed their increasingly torturous ascent.

But Eddie had been right; it wasn't long before light became visible beyond their torch beams. The sight invigorated them, the final stretch taken at a near-sprint. The vertical shaft to the surface appeared at the top of the tunnel. To their relief, the rope Eddie had secured when they entered was still there. 'I'll go first,' he said. 'Then I'll pull you up.'

'Thanks,' replied Nina, slumping against the wall. The Yorkshireman gripped the rope and made a rapid climb. As he dragged himself out through the opening, she jerked her head around at other noises from below. 'Eddie! They're still coming, I can hear them!'

Eddie looked down through the square of grey daylight. 'I'll pull the rope up after you, trap 'em inside.'

Her heart still pounding, she looped the line around her waist, then gripped it tightly. 'Okay, I'm ready.'

He braced himself and hauled on the rope. Nina used her feet to help propel herself upwards. She tipped her head back, feeling drizzle on her face. The sensation was oddly welcome after the overbearing sense of enclosure within the giant rock. She rose the last few feet – only to hear a new sound. A helicopter—

Loud. Close.

And getting closer.

'Uh, Eddie,' she warned as he bent forward to pull her out. 'I can hear a—'

She saw it – side-slipping quickly towards them behind Eddie. The cabin's rear hatch was open, a man inside it aiming a sub-machine gun.

Nina rolled out of the shaft, grabbing Eddie by his jacket and yanking him sideways – just as Duger opened fire. Bullets impacted on the old stone slabs around the opening. Eddie let go of the line and dived with Nina over the low remains of a wall, both pressing themselves flat against it. The length of rope dropped back into the hole as more rounds cracked against the crumbling barrier.

The gunfire ceased. 'Shit!' Eddie snapped. 'I really am going deaf – I didn't hear that coming!'

'You *were* concentrating on something else,' Nina pointed out. 'Although your selective deafness is usually aimed at me, not people trying to kill us!'

The helicopter's engine note rose as it climbed, trying to give the gunman a clear firing angle. 'We can't stay here,' Eddie said. He glanced out. The way back to where they had first climbed to the ledge was completely exposed. 'We'll never reach where we came up. Have to use another way down.'

'Ah – there isn't one,' Nina pointed out.

'Then we make one!' The rope into the shaft had only used a short length of the whole coil – which sat beside the spike where he had secured it. 'I've got a plan.'

'A good one?'

'No, it's fucking terrible, but it's all we've got! When I say go, jump over the wall and follow me to the side of the ledge.'

'And then what?'

'We go down to the ground – quick, but hopefully not *too* quick!'

He looked up. The chopper's rotors came into view over their cover as the aircraft slid closer. 'Okay – *go!*'

They jumped up and vaulted the wall. Eddie snatched the coil of rope as he and Nina ran across the ledge. Duger fired again, but the helicopter was now over his targets. His seat belt limited how far he could lean out to track them. 'Back off, back off!' he yelled at the pilot. The Greek did so rapidly and with relief.

Eddie fed out the rope as he ran, shrugging the cuffs of his leather jacket down as far as he could over his hands. He reached the edge, the damp Grecian landscape opening out vertiginously below. 'Grab onto me, and don't let go!' he shouted over the engine noise. Nina clung to his back. 'And maybe close your eyes!'

'Oh, that never means good things!' she wailed – as he leapt from the ledge.

A burst of bullets struck the rock where they had just been standing, but neither Eddie nor Nina even noticed as they plunged. The wind whistled past them, more forceful than the rotor wash. Nina screamed, eyes shut tight.

The coiled rope fell away beneath them. Eddie squeezed his hands around the line to slow their fall. A rasping hiss came from the leather protecting him as the whipping nylon scoured it. He instantly felt the heat of friction, even through his cuffs. Nina's weight pulled more heavily at him as they started to slow. They were spinning, the cliff and the forest below switching places in a dizzying whirl.

The trees rushed up at them – too fast.

He clenched his hands more tightly. The heat became searing, an acrid stench of smoke scouring his nostrils. They were still slowing – but not enough. Treetops thrust at them like spearheads. He somehow found extra strength and gripped even harder. Slowing, slowing—

Thin branches whipped at him, rapidly becoming thicker, stronger. Slowing—

Nina screamed again as branches snapped explosively beneath them . . . then they stopped.

Eddie hung in silence for a moment, then opened his eyes. The very end of the rope twitched just before them. He looked down. His feet were about ten feet above the sloping ground at the cliff's foot. 'Nina?' he said through clenched teeth.

'Yeah?' came the panting reply.

'Let go and drop down.'

Nina fearfully opened her own eyes, then released her death-grip on him and fell. She hit the earth with a thump and slithered downhill to land against a tree.

Eddie also let go. Smoke trailing from his cuffs, he dropped, rolling to absorb the impact. He bowled down the incline to thud against the tree beside Nina. 'Ow, arse!' he growled, blowing on his hands. The leather had protected him from the worst effects of friction, but he still had angry red marks across both palms and the flesh of his fingers. 'I need some water!'

'We need to move,' Nina countered. 'That chopper's coming down – and I think the rock's about to follow it!' Even as she spoke, the soil underfoot trembled, setting the branches above waving. Stones clattered down the cliff, bouncing off the rough surface and spinning into the woods around them.

'Then let's get the rock out of here.' They hurried downhill, weaving between the trunks to shield themselves from the falling debris.

The trees, foliage all but gone in anticipation of winter, would not protect them from bullets, however. The helicopter descended, Duger leaning out again to fire down at them—

Suddenly the aircraft's engines went to full power, dragging it back skywards with a turbine shriek. 'Where's he off to?' Eddie wondered.

'As long as it's nowhere near us, I don't care,' was Nina's heartfelt reply. Without boots, she had to pick her footfalls carefully to avoid jutting roots and sharp rocks, and the removal of one potentially deadly distraction was a huge help.

Another, though, remained all too active. A thunderclap came from high above as rock broke apart, an avalanche of broken stone tumbling down the pillar's side. 'Come on, gotta go, gotta go!'

'Hurry up!' Brice bellowed into his radio. He and the two surviving mercenaries had reached the ledge to find that not only had Chase and Wilde disappeared, so too had the helicopter. A run to the edge revealed it over the forest below. One furious order was enough to reverse its descent, but the rock pillar was now shaking so much, there was the genuine fear it would not arrive soon enough.

He hunched down and braced himself as the ledge shuddered again. A roar came from one side as a section of the cliff face above fell in a cloud of dust and flying rubble. The column was a rotting tooth, the cavern at its centre an abscess – and one hard bite had cracked it and broken it apart. That he was the one who had taken the bite escaped him. As far as he was concerned, there was only one cause – his countryman, his nemesis.

He shielded his eyes as the helicopter reached the ledge and slowed to a hover. Rotor wash blasted him, the furious vortex rebounding from the cliff. Brice saw the pilot working the controls to hold the aircraft steady against the buffeting wind. 'Get closer!' he shouted, gesturing. 'Open the door!'

Duger's silhouette was visible inside the cabin. He didn't move. For a moment, Brice thought he was going to tell the pilot to abandon the other mercenaries and fly to safety. His hand went to his gun; if that happened, the Greek would be dead before the helicopter travelled ten feet. But then the Austrian slid across the seats to open the hatch. 'Come on!' shouted the Englishman, waving it nearer.

The helicopter almost reluctantly side-slipped towards him, the rotor blades whirling dangerously close above Brice's head. He hunched lower, judging the distance – then leapt at the aircraft. He slammed against the seats beyond the open door. The chopper swung like a pendulum. Duger grabbed him and pulled him inside. He clambered over the Austrian. 'Get the others in.'

'*Danke*,' Duger muttered sarcastically, but he moved to help the two other mercenaries aboard. Lannard was first, the Austrian catching him and dragging him inside. He waited for the Frenchman to squeeze over him into the cabin, then turned towards Craine as he prepared to jump—

The Canadian suddenly fell away as a chunk of the ledge broke apart beneath him. Topknot flapping as he dropped, Craine screamed, plunging towards the ground amidst a cascade of disintegrating rubble.

Duger reacted with shock, but Brice was already issuing a command. 'Go, go!' he shouted. The pilot increased power again and pulled his aircraft sharply away from the ledge, gaining height as it turned.

Brice looked out of his window. Clouds of dust gushed from the pillar's flanks as faults widened and swathes of rock shattered and fell – then with a thunderous rumble that tore the air like a volcanic eruption, the entire monolith collapsed.

At first its upper parts dropped nearly vertically, smashing down into the cavern at its heart. Then the outer layers disintegrated, an almost liquid flow of stones and rocks and boulders rushing into the surrounding forest before being swallowed by the swelling dust cloud.

Duger swore. 'What the hell happened in there?'

'Chase and Wilde happened,' said Brice, catching his breath.

Lannard was also recovering from the frantic race to the surface. 'At least they are dead, yes? They have to be.'

Brice's eyes went to Duger. 'Well?'

The answer took a moment to come. 'I . . . don't think so. I saw them run into the trees. I was trying to shoot them when you ordered me to get you!' Duger added accusingly.

Lannard responded with angry disbelief, but Brice merely sat back, drumming his fingers on the armrest. 'I suppose I shouldn't be surprised,' he said at last. 'It often seems that the only things that will survive the apocalypse are cockroaches . . . and Nina Wilde and Eddie Chase. But I have to give Loost his due. He was right about them.' He donned a set of headphones to speak to the pilot. 'Does this helicopter have a loudspeaker?'

'Yes,' came the puzzled reply.

'Excellent. Patch me in. Then circle over the forest.'

Brice waited for the Greek to do so. The pillar, now nothing more than a jagged stump rising from the dust cloud, wheeled into view through the front windows. He regarded it expressionlessly, then spoke.

Coughing, Eddie and Nina stumbled downhill through the forest. They had got clear of the swirling dust, but still felt the choking cloud's effect. 'Stop, stop,' Nina gasped, leaning against a tree.

Eddie halted too. 'You okay?'

'*No*, not even remotely,' she replied, in a whirl of anger and dismay and frustration. 'I'm exhausted, my throat feels like it's been sandpapered, I lost count of how many stones have stabbed into my feet, and, and . . .' She trailed off, taking a deep breath – then jabbing a furious finger at the remains of the rock. 'And I discovered something incredible, something nobody else knew existed, something lost to the world for thousands of years . . . and those *fucking assholes* blew it up! I can't believe it's happened to me *again*!' She pushed herself off the tree and waved both clenched fists at the sky in an outpouring of pure fury. 'Fuck you, Brice! You prick, you fucking piece of shit!' Her accent became the most strongly New York Eddie had ever heard it. 'And you too, Loost! I almost wish you weren't dead so I could strangle you with my bare hands, you fucking, fucking . . . *fuck*!' That last was roared with such venom that she went momentarily hoarse.

Eddie decided to wait until her voice returned before speaking. 'Feeling better now?'

'No, I'm not! Those assholes! They . . . *aaargh*!'

'At least you saved the Shroud of Hades.' He nodded towards the necklace.

She touched it, as if having forgotten it was there. 'Yeah, but – oh, crap,' she gasped. 'I hardly even took any photos! I was so caught up in what I'd found that . . . son of a *bitch*,' she moaned, covering her face with both hands. 'Some archaeologist I am. I didn't even—'

The clatter of the circling helicopter had been a mere subconsciously registered background noise amongst the continuing rumble of rocks – but suddenly it became the focus of their attention. 'Chase!' Brice's voice boomed from on high. They both looked up, spotting the aircraft through the trees some distance away. 'Professor Wilde! Apparently you're still alive. Congratulations.' The word dripped sarcasm. 'But I wouldn't crack the champagne just yet. The hunt is still on. And we all know there's only one place you can go to end it, don't we?' The helicopter changed course, sweeping away to the east. The former spy's mocking words faded into the distance as it flew off. 'See you in Malta!'

Eddie stared after it. 'Oh, that *bastard*. I'll fucking kill him!'

'Join the line,' Nina said sourly. Her eruption of temper had subsided, but she was no less angry at the situation. 'And you know what the worst thing is? He's right.'

'We can still hide you out somewhere.' But the Yorkshireman's words were unconvincing, even to himself. They both knew it was a truth they could not escape.

Nina shook her head. 'No. I just . . .' She repeated the gesture with a more general air of resignation, then looked downhill. 'We have to go. People'll be coming to see what happened, and if anyone tags me, we're back at square one. Let's get to the car.'

'Assuming it's not underneath a ten-ton boulder,' Eddie said gloomily. With a final glare after the retreating helicopter, he held Nina's hand and they set off again through the wet woods.

31

To Nina and Eddie's relief, their rental car was still intact, far enough below the collapsed pillar for the debris to have been caught by the intervening forest. However, as the redhead had feared, the destruction had drawn numerous people from nearby villages. Even before they reached the car, a young man did a double-take on seeing her, and she knew it wasn't because she only had wet, dirty socks on her feet. He was already holding his phone to video the damage, and in seconds another kind of damage was done as other phones chimed with the Uzz fanfare.

'Bollocks,' Eddie growled. 'At least we're leaving rather than arriving.' They got into the car. 'So where are we going?'

'I guess Malta, eventually,' she sighed as Eddie started the car and began a quicker-than-safe descent of the track. 'Brice was right – which means *Loost* was right, God damn it. He's playing his game from beyond the grave, and at the moment he's winning. I can't survive on the run for ever. It's been what, four days? And I've almost been killed I don't know how many times.'

'You've survived every time,' Eddie pointed out as he swung the car around a tight bend.

'But I only have to fail once and it's game over. It's me versus three billion other players. Even if only one per cent of one per cent of Uzz users are actually willing and able to try to kill me, that's still three hundred thousand people worldwide. And I don't know who or where they are. Meanwhile, a lot of the rest of them seem perfectly happy to play along and tag me so the potential killers can find me, and for what? Fake money, points on Uzz. People are sick.' She let out a despairing huff.

'Welcome to the wonderful world of social media,' said Eddie grimly.

'Yeah. Macy always thought I was old-fashioned by not using Uzz, but maybe anything more advanced than a telegram was a mistake in hindsight . . .' She paused as the car reached the bottom of the track and turned bumpily onto a paved road. 'So, sooner or later, we have to go find this programmer in Malta. It's a trap: we know it, and Brice and everyone else working for Loost knows we know it – but it's still the only way to end the hunt.'

'That's if Natalie wasn't lying,' said Eddie. 'The bloke might not even be there. He might not even *exist*.'

'He probably does exist, and really did work for Loost,' she replied thoughtfully. 'That's something we could confirm online easily enough. But you're right: whether he's actually in Loost's former house in Malta is another matter. But for now, let's say that he is. How do we reach him and make him use his backdoor into Uzz to shut down the hunt, without being killed and Loost winning?'

Her husband pursed his lips, thinking. 'If you can't avoid a trap,' he said, 'the only way to deal with it is to go into it on *your* terms, not theirs. You find a way to mess it up that they hadn't expected – like in the Underworld. We got around the Cerberus trap by going over the door rather than through it. Granted, Brice and his arseholes fucked it up for us, but still . . .'

'How can we do that?' Nina asked.

'Don't know yet. We need intel – exactly where this place is, what the surroundings are like, that kind of stuff.'

'Once we get somewhere with decent cellular reception, we can find all that out on our phones.'

He nodded. 'We actually have to *get* there, an' all. Which means even if we can get through customs without being stopped, and even if nobody tags you along the way, Brice will still know exactly when we'll be arriving in Malta, same way he found out we came to Greece.'

Nina gave him a rueful look. 'Loost's AI.'

'Yeah. And knowing that gives him a massive advantage over us. If we want to turn it the other way, we have to get to the island without anyone knowing.'

'How do we do that?'

'There's only one person we can totally trust now – Macy.'

Her eyes narrowed. 'I thought *neither* of us wanted to get her involved in all this.'

'I don't, but she won't be – not directly, anyway. But the Knights of Atlantis have got connections all over the world from that charity they use as a cover organisation, right? The one for sailors. I bet she could arrange for someone to give us a ride from Greece to Malta by sea, off the books. Probably with any gear we need too.'

'I don't know,' she said, hesitant. 'Even then it's a risk. Can we trust MacDuff? Or Rain, even?'

'Rain, probably.' The young French-Vietnamese woman was Macy's best friend, a relationship strong enough to survive the revelation that their meeting had been set up by the Knights as a way to keep watch on the young New Yorker before asking her to join them. 'MacDuff? Well, he knows if he causes any trouble for Macy, I'll beat the crap out of him. Or she will. Dunno about anyone else there, though.'

She was far from happy at the prospect of bringing their daughter into the hunt. But Eddie was right: if anyone could help them it was her, with the Knights' resources backing her. 'Okay, I don't like it, but . . . like going to Malta, I don't really see that we have a choice.'

'Nor do I,' Eddie replied. 'When we get to the next town we'll call her. Hopefully she's somewhere with phone reception.'

Nina leaned back pensively in her seat. 'I can't help thinking it might be best for her if she isn't.'

***

The drive to the town of Trikala took a little over half an hour. Several emergency vehicles passed them en route, heading for Meteora. Nina looked away as they drove by, to avoid being caught by dashcams.

She stayed in the car when they stopped in a quiet side street, window wound down. Eddie leaned against the door to block her from the sight of passers-by, and also so she could join in the conversation over his phone's speaker.

'*What* happened?' Macy cried in disbelief from the other end of the line.

'You know, the usual,' said Eddie. 'Found the long-lost tomb of a Greek god, then it got destroyed, along with part of a major tourist attraction. Oh, and we found the—'

'It was the tomb of Hades,' Nina cut in forcefully, unconsciously touching the torc around her neck as she tried to prevent her husband from revealing its existence. 'I figured out where it was, so we came to Greece on the grounds that it was as safe as anywhere else.'

'In other words, not at all,' was Eddie's dry comment.

'Unfortunately,' she went on, giving him an annoyed look, 'Loost's people were able to track us. They decided that high explosives were the best way to get into the tomb, and that was the end of that.'

'Oh, my God!' Macy exclaimed. 'Are you both okay?'

'Still ticking,' her father assured her. 'Banged up and bruised, but we've had worse.'

'Well yeah, since you've both been shot, stabbed, and I don't even want to imagine what else. But – how did you find the tomb, Mom? The stuff I sent you was way too vague to give a specific location. I read it.'

'I did some deep research, and found connections to other sources,' was Nina's evasive answer.

'What other sources?'

'It doesn't matter right now. Your dad – well, both of us – need to ask you something.'

'Yeah,' said Eddie, taking the prompt. 'It's not something we want to do, love, but . . . we need a favour.'

'Of course, anything! What?'

'It's not just from you, it's from the Knights, and that charity of theirs.'

Macy sounded puzzled. 'The Order of Behdet? It's kind of on hold right now, since a lot of the people running it got killed by Loost's mercenaries. Including Rain's mom and dad.' That last was said in a lower voice, suggesting her friend was nearby.

'I know, honey,' said Nina. 'But we need to get from Greece to Malta, and we need to do it without anyone knowing.'

'So we're asking if you can sort out a boat ride for us,' Eddie went on. 'Someone who works for the Order, or owes them a favour. If they can also get us wetsuits and scuba gear, and even guns, that'd be grand.'

'You don't need much, do you?' was their daughter's slightly sarcastic reply. 'Anyway, I don't know about any of this stuff myself. I'd have to ask Rip.'

'Rip?'

'Euripides. Mr MacDuff.'

'Oh yeah, the guy whose parents must have hated him,' the Yorkshireman said with a grin. 'But do you think he'll be able to sort it?'

'Maybe. I'll have to call you back after I've spoken to him. But why do you need to go to Malta?'

'It's the only way to end the hunt,' said Nina. 'At least, in theory. There's a man who used to work for Loost, his head AI programmer; we think he's the person who put the backdoor into Uzz. He bought Loost's house in Malta.'

'So if you find him, you can make him use it again to stop this?'

'Like I said, in theory. But . . .' The redhead took a long breath. 'It's a trap. Loost planned it before he died. His nurse from the news, the programmer, John Brice – everything's been set up to force us there. Where he's no doubt got something especially unpleasant waiting for us.'

'Wait, what, go back,' Macy said hurriedly. 'John Brice? The – the guy who *kidnapped* me when I was a kid? I thought he was dead!'

It was Eddie's turn for an awkward inhalation. 'Er . . . no. He was actually in a secret MI6 prison. I didn't tell you because I didn't want you to worry.'

Macy's annoyance was clear even over the phone. 'Oh. Great. Thanks, Dad. And I thought *Mom* was the one who kept secrets from me!'

'That's not fair,' Eddie said sharply, seeing Nina's face fall, before becoming more conciliatory. 'But yes, I should have told you, I'm sorry. I just never thought it'd be an issue. Loost paid to have him broken out of prison so he could chase us – and keep pushing us towards the trap, I suppose.'

'I'm sorry too,' said Macy. 'I shouldn't have said that. Sorry, Mom. I know the whole secret-keeping thing is behind us.'

Nina was glad her daughter couldn't see her grimace. 'Yeah, honey, yeah. It is.' Eddie shot her an *oh really?* glance, which she tried her best to ignore. 'So do you think you can help us?'

'I'll try. Let me call Rip in Portugal and see what he says. I'll phone you back once I know anything. Hopefully it'll be good news.' Emotion entered her voice. 'You both stay safe, okay? And if you need me to come help you in person, I can be in Malta with Rain probably by tonight if we drop everything. We'll bring our armour and weapons – we've got them with us.'

'That's okay, love,' Eddie said quickly. 'We just need the boat ride. Don't want to risk you or the Knights getting found out.'

'Okay,' came the reluctant reply. 'I love you both. Please, come back alive.'

'We love you too,' said Nina, heartfelt. 'We'll see you soon, okay? I promise.'

'I'll hold you to that,' said Macy, trying hard to keep her voice from cracking. 'Talk soon. Bye.'

'Bye,' said Eddie, as the call ended. He lowered the phone. 'Christ. That was . . . surprisingly hard.'

'She's worried for us,' Nina told him. 'Which, y'know, so am I.'

'Didn't want to tell her about that thing around your neck, then?'

She was not pleased with the pointedness of his question. 'You know why. I already told you.'

'And are you sure it's the right thing to do?'

'If I didn't, I wouldn't be doing it. But that's not the issue right now,' she snapped. 'Let's get somewhere quiet and wait for her to call back.'

Eddie shrugged, knowing the current line of discussion was unwelcome, and rounded the car to get in. 'Do you think Macy will be able to arrange this?' Nina asked him.

He started the car. 'If I know her, we'll find out soon.'

32

The Ionian Sea

Eddie was indeed right about Macy. His daughter had called back in less than an hour, telling the couple that, with Euripides MacDuff's help, she had arranged for a boat to take them from the port of Preveza in western Greece across the Ionian to Malta. The voyage would be a long, overnight one, a distance of four hundred miles. Again, she offered to come to Malta to aid them in person. Again, Nina and Eddie insisted she did not.

'Feels weird to have to ask Macy for help rather than the other way around,' Eddie said. He and Nina were sitting on the aft deck of their vessel, a sixty-foot motor yacht called the *Stefani*. Its owner, a burly and bestubbled Greek named Vasilios Petrou, was content to leave them to their own business as he guided his craft across the sea. He had once been saved from financial ruin by the Order of Behdet, and was happy to repay the favour. 'That's always been what I do for her.'

'She's not a child any more,' Nina reminded him. 'She's eighteen, an adult – and she's left home to fend for herself.'

Her tone was a little maudlin, but Eddie's, when he spoke again, was more so. 'Job done as parents, then.' He sighed, slumping in his seat.

'I don't think a parent's job is *ever* done, really. Not a good parent's, anyway – and you are a good parent. And I used the present tense on purpose,' she added. 'We both got Macy through her childhood, but that doesn't mean we have to stop caring about her. Or' – her gaze fixed firmly onto his – 'the other people who matter to us.'

He sat up. 'Yeah, you're right. I mean, I still have to keep my pain-in-the-arse wife out of trouble!'

Nina laughed. 'And I'm glad you do. Thank you so much.'

'My pleasure. Although it does kind of feel like I should be saying that to you just as much these days.'

She raised an eyebrow. 'What do you mean?'

'I mean, you keep pulling my arse out of the fire. That dickhead at our flat who hit me with pepper spray; Charlie; when Brice was about to run me over on the ski slope – even that drone in Canada. You saved me from all of 'em. It seems like it's not just Macy who doesn't need me any more. Maybe Brice was right: I *am* getting old.' He sighed, long and deep. 'Job done. For everything.'

Nina was silent for a moment, regarding him thoughtfully. Then: 'Is *that* what this is about?'

'What do you mean, "this"?'

'I mean, you wandering mournfully around the apartment like the Grey Lady, complaining that you don't have anything to do now Macy's left.'

'Well, I miss her,' he said defensively.

'So do I! But just because she's moved out doesn't mean she's completely disappeared from our lives – or that *your* life suddenly doesn't have a purpose any more. I'm still with you, I still love you – I still *need* you. And not just for saving my life every so often. You're my love, my best friend – you're my *husband*, Eddie, and I hope you always will be.'

'Not planning on changing that,' he insisted.

'Good! But you were just as down when I helped you those times you mentioned, and you have no reason to be. I know that your thing is being the hero and rescuing people – usually me – but . . . we're a team, Eddie. You save me, occasionally I save you. I don't keep count. I'm just grateful that you're always there for me. And

I'll always be there for you when you need me. Whatever you need me for.'

Eddie didn't have an immediate answer, gazing out at the sea. 'Tell the truth,' he said at last, 'I *have* been feeling a bit down. A bit useless.'

'You're anything but useless,' Nina said firmly.

'Maybe it's because I hadn't realised just how big a part of my life Macy's been for the last eighteen years. And then all of a sudden . . . she's not there any more.'

'Empty nest syndrome.'

'I know what it's called. I just never imagined how hard it would hit me. You've still got your work, but apart from the odd bit of consulting for Charlie I haven't really done much for the past few years that hasn't involved Macy. So now I'm left . . . huh.' He shrugged. 'Wandering mournfully around the apartment like the Grey Lady.'

Nina regarded him sympathetically. 'You should have said something.'

'I didn't want to bother you. You were busy.'

'I'm never too busy for you.' She leaned towards him. 'Maybe I had the same problem, but I tried to ignore it by working even harder. Filling the silence. I might have overdone it,' she admitted. 'And look where it's got us.'

'It's not too bad right now,' said Eddie, gesturing out at the ocean. For the first time since leaving New York the weather could be described as 'pleasant': there was no rain, few clouds, and they were at a latitude far enough towards the equator for the temperature to be warm, even on the brink of winter.

'There's always somewhere where it isn't cold and wet, I suppose,' Nina mused. 'You just have to get off your ass and go there.'

'Would have been nicer to do that off our own bat than be forced into it, though.'

She laughed, with little humour. 'Yeah. Although,' she added, 'I probably wouldn't have found the Underworld without everything else that happened.'

The tone of Eddie's reply was subtly guarded. 'You're not saying it was all worth it, are you?'

'No, not at all! I mean, the Underworld and the tomb of Hades were destroyed – I would rather they hadn't been found than that. I'd probably have made the connection to Meteora eventually, though, even without seeing the rock pillars near the ski resort. It would have just taken time. I'm sure I'll eventually figure out the locations of the other artefacts I've been researching too.'

From his reaction – an almost imperceptible shake of the head – she realised her answer had disappointed him. He quickly covered it, speaking before she could respond. 'You know,' he said, 'there *are* other archaeologists in the world. You don't need to run around chasing after all these things yourself. You've already found all the big stuff – you've got to leave a bit for everyone else.'

'It's not about my being the first to find them,' Nina replied, a little hotly, and still unsure quite why her words had not met with his approval. 'I already told you – it's about making sure these potentially dangerous relics don't fall into the wrong hands. The IHA's lost sight of what it was created to do, I still don't fully trust the Brotherhood of Selasphoros, and as for the Knights of Atlantis . . . I trust Macy, of course, but I can't be totally sure of the people with her. And she's still young, and impressionable – she was completely taken in by Loost and that creep in the Knights who was working for him. What if someone else tries to sway her into finding other artefacts for their own purposes? Or even handing over the items the Knights already have?'

'You really think she would?'

'I'd hope not, but I don't know who else is there, or who she's meeting, so I can't be one hundred per cent sure that nobody is trying to manipulate her. So until I can, I'm not willing to let the Knights grab these artefacts either. They already had *Excalibur*, for God's sake – which we thought we'd made sure nobody would ever find! Who knows what else they have tucked away in their vault?'

She sat forward, any anger forgotten as she became more intense. 'I'm the person best suited in the world to the job, Eddie. So I *have* to do it.'

She half-expected him to argue with her. Instead, he gave her a crooked smile. 'We've got to stop everyone in the world trying to kill you first.'

'Yeah, that's a good point,' she said, disarmed. 'But hey, at least you've got something to occupy your time now. I'll keep you busy.'

His smile widened. 'Glad to hear it. And I'll do my best to keep you out of trouble. All right, *get* you out of trouble.'

'You always do.' They both grinned.

'Hey, all okay?' came a voice. Petrou had emerged from the flybridge on the deck above and was looking down at them over the railing.

'We're good, thanks,' Eddie told him.

The Greek nodded. 'I turn on the autopilot. Straight line to Malta from here. We get there tomorrow afternoon. You want food?'

'That would be great, thank you,' said Nina.

'Okay. You both look hungry, I make you something big.' He retreated.

Nina regarded the sea ahead. It was fairly calm, but the sun was dropping towards an ominous bank of cloud along the horizon. Things would probably get rough overnight – and, she suspected, over the following day as well. Her gaze shifted to an antenna on a mast above the flybridge. The yacht had a satellite internet connection. She'd already found out during the drive to Preveza that Loost had a few years prior bought an expensive Maltese villa, but more information was needed if they wanted a chance to survive. 'We need to plan what to do when we get there.'

Eddie nodded. 'Yep. Just blundering in there and making it up as we go won't work this time.' He rose, extending a hand to her. 'Shall we?'

Nina took it. 'Thank you,' she said with a smile as she stood, new sneakers squeaking slightly on the deck. Her husband returned it. 'Okay, let's get started.'

As Nina had predicted, the voyage turned rougher overnight. Though the conditions were far from stormy, there was enough wind to send the motor yacht pitching over the choppy waves, and her sleep was unsettled. It came as a huge relief when dawn arrived and the sea calmed.

She and Eddie had spent the previous evening studying their destination, and continued the work through the morning. Petrou finally called down to them not long before noon. 'Land ho!'

The couple joined him on the flybridge. Instead of clouds on the horizon, they now saw a line of low, gently undulating orange-grey hills. They were approaching from the north-east, the small island chain of Malta at its widest to them. Their captain greeted them, then said: 'To get to Valletta is about two hours. But you do not want to go to the port, no?'

'No,' Eddie confirmed. They had discussed the matter with him the night before. 'Do you know a good spot?'

'Yes. There is a beach north of Marsaskala.' He pointed to one end of the distant land ahead. 'This late in year, it will not be busy. I come in to about half a kilometre from shore, then turn. You two go over the side and swim. If you need me, I wait for you in Valletta.'

'We'll be fine, but thanks for offering.'

Petrou nodded. 'You got my phone number just in case, okay? All the gear you ask for is in the hold.'

'Thank you,' said Nina. 'We're very grateful.'

He smiled, then looked ahead again. 'I call you when we are thirty minutes out. Then you can get ready.'

'All right,' Eddie replied. 'I'll go and check the stuff.' He gave Nina a cheeky look. 'Shall we put on our rubber outfits?'

***

The rubber was of the neoprene variety, Petrou's supplies including a pair of wetsuits, scuba gear, fins and goggles. It had been a while since either had needed to wear such outfits, and Nina regarded her husband admiringly as he fastened his garment's zipper. 'Looking good there, Mr Chase,' she said.

He put on a mock-lecherous face as he gave her a similar once-over. 'And pretty bloody hot yourself, Professor Wilde. We're not too bad for a couple of old farts, are we?'

Nina laughed. 'Oh, I wish Macy were here to hear this. She'd probably cover her ears and run screaming.'

'Or throw up. Ah, I miss being able to embarrass her in public.'

'*I'm* the one she was always embarrassed by. You could get away with anything.' She examined a scuba tank. 'How long will these last?'

'We won't be going too deep, so about an hour. It won't take us that long to swim half a klick.' He started to load their few belongings into a waterproof bag. 'There's a gun in that box there,' he said, indicating a container he had brought from the hold with the rest of the equipment. 'Can you chuck it to me?'

'Not literally,' she replied, opening the box. She had no interest in or liking for weapons, but had enough experience with them to know the one she found was probably not what Eddie had hoped for. 'Will this do the job?'

She passed him a small, short-barrelled revolver, with enough of a patina of wear over its surface to suggest it was several decades old. 'Colt Detective Special,' he told her. 'Yeah, it will – as long as I'm not too far away from whatever I'm aiming at. Mind you, Brice is as wide as a fucking bus now, so it should be okay if *he's* what I'm aiming at.' The gun was placed carefully inside the bag, followed by their clothing and a couple of towels. Eddie had to squeeze its sides tightly to close the zip. 'Okay, that's everything. Let's go for a swim.'

They went to the aft deck, both donning their fins and scuba tanks. Eddie attached the bag by its tow rope to his weighted belt. By now, the coast had swelled to fill the western horizon. Above, Petrou saw they had appeared. 'We are almost there,' he called. 'The coast guard call on radio to ask who I am and what I am doing, but I am an EU citizen in an EU boat going from one EU country to another. There will be no problem.'

'Let's hope,' said Nina quietly. She scanned the surrounding waters. There were no other vessels close by. Nor did the beach appear to have anyone on it. Actually reaching the island seemed relatively straightforward.

It was what would happen once they were there that concerned her.

Eddie peered over the yacht's side. 'Bit of a swell, but it shouldn't be much trouble.' He looked back at Nina. 'You ready?'

'No, but that's never stopped me before.'

He gave her a reassuring smile. 'We'll get this sorted. We can't kill Loost again, but Brice is going down this time, I guarantee that. And this programmer *will* end the hunt, or he'll get a bullet in the brain – pushed up there via his arsehole.'

Nina made a sound halfway between amused and appalled. 'You always had a way with words, Eddie.'

'Most of 'em either "buggeration" or "fuckery". All right, Vasilios, are you ready?'

The Greek nodded. 'I will turn north-west. You dive from starboard side so nobody on land can see you. Good luck!' He returned to the controls. The yacht swung lazily about to head parallel to the coastline.

Eddie went to the starboard gunwale. 'Nina? Let's go.'

She took a deep breath, then put on her goggles and slipped the scuba regulator into her mouth. Eddie gave her a thumbs-up. She sat beside him on the edge of the boat, then they both rolled backwards into the sea.

The swim to shore took slightly over twenty minutes, Nina and Eddie staying a few metres down until the shallowing water forced them to surface amongst the breaking waves. On taking off her goggles as she waded onto the beach, Nina saw some people off to the south-east, but they were far enough away either not to have noticed or not to care about the two wetsuited figures emerging from the ocean.

The couple made their way up the rocky shoreline to the dirt track running along the foot of the low hillside beyond. A squat concrete building that appeared to be an old military bunker gave them an opportunity to change out of their swimming gear, quickly dry off as best they could and put on their clothes. Still damp, they emerged into the sun. The day was warm, but a gritty wind blew across the dusty landscape.

'Okay . . . that way,' said Eddie after getting his bearings. He pointed north-west along the coastal track. 'I checked the map after Vasilios said where he was going to drop us. There's a road further up the beach that'll take us inland. After that, we can walk to Loost's old gaff. The whole island's smaller than New York.'

'And you found a place where we can check out the villa?' Nina asked.

'Yeah, on a hill across from it. Should be able to see if anyone's keeping watch. Then I can work out the best way to get in.'

Nina readied herself for the trek. 'Okay. Then let's go and pull Loost's plug.'

33

The Maltese villa of the late Gabriel Loost was, as expected, a place made for a trillionaire. It was vastly bigger than a single person could need to live in, even with a full staff serving them. In contrast to the scrubby and dry terraced farmland around it, the grounds of the ultra-modernist hilltop mansion had been landscaped and watered, olive trees providing shade along winding pathways. The house itself was a cluster of interconnected buildings of between two and four storeys, with rooftops entirely covered by solar panels and countless rooms with mirrored floor-to-ceiling windows.

Petrou had provided a small pair of binoculars, which Eddie used to survey the sprawling structure from behind bushes along the top of a rise half a kilometre away. 'What do you see?' Nina asked.

'Nothing much,' he replied, 'which is worrying me.'

'How so?'

'No guards, but they're expecting us to turn up sooner or later, so the place is probably covered in electronic surveillance. And the windows look like one-way mirrored glass, so they can see out while we can't see in. No telling how many people are inside, or where they are. If this was a military operation, I'd either be asking for a lot more men, or getting air support to put a Brimstone through a window before we move.'

'Neither of which are really options now.'

'No.' He lowered the binoculars, frowning. 'Loost probably got his AI to work out all the possible ways we might get in there, so he could cover them. I mean, look at those trees.' He indicated one of the rows of olives. 'They've been *moved*, recently – I can see marks where they used to be. If you were heading for them on foot, it'd look like you could stay hidden under them. But whichever way you go, you *always* have to cross a bit of open ground – where you'll be spotted from the house.'

'I doubt an AI could have done that,' Nina countered. 'They can't *think* – they're not HAL 9000. They just regurgitate whatever's been fed into them in a slightly different way. Anybody who claims to have created a genuine artificial intelligence is juicing their company's stock price for gullible investors. It's more likely they got Brice or someone like him to handle security.'

'Fucking Brice,' Eddie spat, bringing the field glasses back up to scour the grounds again. 'I suppose if you wanted a sneaky twat to do that, he'd be your man. Shit,' he added as a thought struck him.

'What?'

'Brice knows we're coming, even if he doesn't know we're here right now. But he knows *me*. He knows how I was trained by the SAS, how they work. So he'd know I'd scope the place out before going in.'

'Which means?' she asked, becoming worried by his obvious concern.

'Which means, he would have worked out the best places I could do that from. Like – right here.' He hurriedly looked around as if searching for surveillance devices. 'This is the most obvious spot. Brice could be on the way already!' He dropped lower, ready to make a hasty retreat.

Though alarmed, Nina stayed put, checking the terrain behind them. A few houses were dotted amongst the rough farmland, but there was nobody in sight – no teams of armed men rushing to capture them. 'I don't see anyone. I think we're safe, for now.'

'Yeah, but how long before we're not?' He drew the revolver from his leather jacket. 'We need to move.'

She looked back at the villa. There was no visible activity within the grounds. Nor had anyone appeared on any of the approaches to their position. 'Eddie,' she said, making herself adopt a voice that was calmer than she felt, 'this is Brice's plan. He *wants* you to get paranoid and scared that he's right behind you, and rush into making a move. It's why he was hired to chase us in the first place! Don't let him set the rules. Do things *your* way, not his.'

It seemed that he was about to get angry at being challenged in his area of expertise. But then a thoughtful look flashed across his face – followed by a wry smile. 'Yeah,' he said. 'You're right. If we do anything he's planned for, he's already won. So what *can't* he have planned for?'

He rose again, casting his gaze out not at the villa but the surrounding landscape. More farms scattered amongst the terraces, a winding road serving them, a distant construction site where new luxury houses were being built – and closer, an older villa that was being demolished, presumably to be replaced by a bigger and more expensive one. An excavator with a bucket arm was parked amongst piles of rubble. Near it was a grubby and dented yellow dump truck. It was a Sunday; nobody was working at the site.

Eddie's smile widened into a grin. 'All right,' he said to Nina, 'he won't have planned for *that* . . .'

The only sound in the Maltese countryside was the chirp of birds and the rustle of the wind. That was, until it was shattered by the roar of a large diesel engine.

Eddie was at the wheel of the hotwired dump truck, foot to the floor and slamming it up through the gears as he charged around the last bend on the road to Loost's villa. He had taken Nina's advice that he should do things his way well and truly to heart. 'See what you think of *this*, you Cyberman-voiced bell-end,' he growled as he drove the vehicle at the villa's gates. Pillars to either side housed security cameras, but while anyone in the house might see him coming, short of there being a minefield hidden beneath the drive there was nothing they could do to stop him.

The gates were metal, designed to slide open on rails. They instead burst apart as the heavy truck ploughed through them, frames buckling and stanchions spinning through the air. Eddie had ducked just before impact – wisely, as an errant wrought-iron pole punched through the windscreen above the instrument binnacle like a spear. He grimaced, then popped his head back up to aim for the rapidly approaching building.

The drive led to a wide oval plaza with access to below-ground parking. The villa's main entrance was a set of mirrored glass doors set into a much larger expanse of reflective windows, the lobby within at least two floors high. Or so Eddie hoped – because if there was a girder or concrete floor halfway up, it would scythe straight across the cab. He brought the truck onto a direct course for the doors, bounding over a small floral lawn at the plaza's centre, and braced for impact—

The doors opened. A man ran out – the one who had shot at him from the helicopter. He held a sub-machine gun. His eyes popped wide in alarm as he saw the juggernaut barrelling towards him – then he snapped up his weapon and fired.

Eddie threw himself flat across the seats as the windscreen exploded above him. The engine note dropped sharply as his foot came off the accelerator, but the truck was doing over seventy kilometres per hour, momentum carrying it onwards. The vehicle mounted the patio step with a jolting slam that pitched him into the footwell.

Another swathe of bullets tore through the dashboard before Duger turned to flee – but it was too late—

The truck's blunt nose mowed the Austrian down, driving him face-first into the glass doors before they – and he – disintegrated in a storm of mirrored shards. The lobby beyond was indeed two floors high, a pair of elegant curving staircases leading up to a balcony at the rear. Out of control, the dumper ploughed through the room, riding up onto one of the staircases and smashing its banisters before lurching to a stop.

Eddie had been thrown against the front bulkhead. He grunted at the new bruises he had acquired, then crawled to the cab door and opened it, revolver in hand. Nobody was in sight in the lobby. He pulled himself upright and rapidly checked his wider surroundings. Again, the room seemed deserted. Had the assault taken everyone by surprise? He wasn't convinced. If the guy from the helicopter was here, Brice almost certainly was too. But where?

He scrambled out, darting to the undamaged staircase so he could see the rest of the lobby. Apart from the remains of Duger smeared over the polished marble, there were no enemies present. Doors stood on each side of the large room, as well as another beneath the balcony, and he imagined at least one upstairs. A lot of places to cover for threats.

'Eddie!' He looked back at the gaping hole in the windows to see Nina running onto the patio. She had crept into position close to the gates before he set off in the truck, ready to follow him. 'Is it safe?'

'Looks it, but I'm not sure.' He nodded towards the bloody trail between the entrance and the truck. 'That guy had a gun. See if you can find it.'

Nina's face wrinkled in disgust at the sight. 'Oh, gross.' She hurried into the lobby, spotting the sub-machine gun on the floor near the truck and collecting it. 'Got it.'

'Okay, let's find out where the fuck everyone is.' He waited as she ran to join him—

The door beneath the balcony opened.

Eddie whirled to face it, instantly aiming at the figure who came through. Nina also whipped up her newly acquired gun – but neither fired. The man who had just entered was a short, middle-aged Indian, overweight and with a greying moustache. He froze at the sight of the armed intruders, his own hands empty.

'Ah – Vishal Varna, I presume?' said Nina.

The man blinked, about to answer automatically in the affirmative, before fear took over. With a shrill yelp, he fled the way he had come. The couple exchanged glances, then pursued.

The long, softly lit room they entered was a museum of sorts, ranks of display cases and dummies wearing samurai and ninja outfits along its length. Varna ran down the central aisle towards another exit at the far end. Eddie easily caught up before he was two-thirds of the way there. He grabbed the smaller man and swung him around, pounding him backwards against a wall. The various bladed weapons mounted upon it rattled with the impact. 'Ay up! Where're you going, arsehole?' he growled. Varna gasped in terror.

Nina reached them. 'I think you know me, don't you?' she said, bringing her gun up at Varna's head. He cringed. 'We need to have a little chat.'

'Yes, yes, I know you,' Varna replied breathlessly. 'Nina Wilde, you're Nina Wilde. Please don't kill me! I – I only did what Rafael asked.'

'Yeah, and because of that you set three billion people trying to kill my wife,' Eddie growled. He thumped Varna against the wall again, making him cry out, then abruptly released him. The programmer almost fell. 'So what's all this?' the Yorkshireman demanded, jerking a thumb at the exhibition of ancient Japanese warriors. 'Think you're a fucking ninja? Maybe I should try one of these out on your balls.' He reached up as if to take a katana from the wall. Varna shrank away.

'It's probably Loost's,' said Nina, regarding the displays. 'People like him are often into performative warrior machismo. And also nerds tend to be weeaboos.'

'They're what?' Eddie asked.

'Westerners who are a bit too much into Japanese culture. I learned the term from Macy. I guess she encountered some online. I can certainly imagine Loost having a collection of manga catgirl figurines or whatever.' She looked back at Varna. 'So. You put a backdoor into Uzz before you left, yes?' He gave her a fearful nod. 'Then you can use it again. End the hunt, program your copy of Loost to announce it's over, and then tell the people at Uzz how to close the backdoor.'

'Otherwise,' her husband added menacingly, 'you won't live long enough to go to prison.'

'Okay, okay,' Varna whimpered. He struggled upright. 'I can do that. I'll do that.'

Eddie glowered at him, then looked suspiciously towards each exit. 'Where's Brice?'

'I don't know. I haven't seen him today.' He lowered his voice as if afraid of being overheard. 'He is mad!'

'I'm pretty pissed off too,' the Yorkshireman rumbled. 'Okay, you must have a computer that you run the hunt from. Take us to it.'

'Okay, yes. It is in the server room. This way.' Varna hesitantly started towards the door at the room's far end.

They went with him, guns still raised and ready for trouble. But the Indian was too cowed to cause any, and when he opened the door, the hallway beyond was empty. By now Nina was as suspicious as Eddie of the absence of any other guards, but the sprawling house was silent as Varna led them through it.

They finally stopped at a door in a part of the villa that seemed more like a workplace than a home. 'Open it,' Eddie ordered quietly. Varna did so – and was pushed sharply inside, almost stumbling. But nobody hiding within reacted to the sudden entrance. A rapid check on the hallway, which was still deserted, then Eddie whipped in after Varna, bringing his gun sharply around to cover the new room. There was nobody there. 'It's clear,' he told Nina.

She quickly followed him and closed the door before looking around. It was indeed a server room, long racks of computer hardware along the two side walls and a large air-conditioner whirring in the ceiling. But what immediately drew her attention was the chamber's centrepiece. It was a black glass cylinder, eight feet tall. LEDs blinked in patterns behind its tinted façade. A desk was positioned in front of it: a terminal with an ultra-widescreen monitor. 'Is this it?' she asked.

Varna nodded. 'One of Rafael's quantum computers. He had it

installed here for me. It has a direct connection to the others at Qbial – and to Uzz through them.'

She frowned. 'Is it running Loost's virtual copy?'

'Yes.' The 3D screen displayed a swirling screensaver, almost dizzying in its dimensionality. Varna tapped a wireless mouse and the abstract colours vanished, replaced by numerous information-packed windows. One, though, showed an image.

Rafael Loost.

The trillionaire – rather, his CGI copy – appeared to be aboard his space station. He was not doing anything in particular, merely sitting in front of his virtual camera, but was still animated, subtly moving as if alive. Nina noticed he was even apparently breathing. 'Does that run even when it's not talking to anyone through Uzz?'

'Yes,' Varna replied, taking his seat at the terminal. 'He is always active.'

Eddie eyed the screen suspiciously. 'Can he see us?'

'Only when the camera is on.' A high-end webcam was set into the bezel above the screen's centre. An LED was visible by the lens, but it was unlit. Varna reached towards the device.

Nina rapped him on the shoulder with her gun's barrel. 'Let's not do that. You've got one job right now – end the hunt.'

'Tell us how you're going to do it first,' Eddie added. 'Just in case you get any funny ideas about calling for help.' His own weapon's muzzle moved to the back of Varna's head.

The Indian took a nervous breath. 'Okay, okay. I will use the backdoor to get into Uzz. Then I will spoof the conditions needed to trigger the payment of the reward. Once they are met, Rafael will deliver a message to everyone on Uzz that you are dead, and the game is finished.'

'Can it be restarted?' Nina demanded.

'No. Once it is done, the program ends.'

'What about the reward?' asked Eddie. 'Who's getting the money?'

Varna let out a brief, worried giggle. 'Well, I thought, ah, me.'

'Nope, not happening,' Nina said firmly. 'You don't get to profit from this. Give it to . . .' She thought for a moment. 'A million random people in Africa. A thousand dollars each will do more good than one person getting the lot. Let's spread Loost's wealth around a bit.' She withdrew slightly, but kept the gun trained on Varna. 'Okay, get started. And remember, my husband is a computer expert. If you do anything he thinks is suspicious, he'll kill you. Understand?'

'Yes, yes, absolutely I understand,' Varna said, shaking. Behind his back, Eddie gave Nina a quizzical look, to which she replied with an amused shrug.

The programmer began to type, bringing up a command line window and entering instructions of increasing complexity at a frenzied pace. Nina quickly became unable to follow exactly what he was doing, but a new window appeared with Uzz's logo and a password entry request – which the computer itself completed without any prompting from the man at its keyboard. Then more windows followed as Varna drilled deeper into the social media network's private systems. He briefly detoured to one run by Loost's quantum computing company, Qbial. Even at his typing speed, she still picked out enough to see he was asking the AI to choose randomly selected African Uzz users. He was obeying that far, at least.

Soon Varna paused, as if physically exhausted. 'Okay, I am nearly ready,' he said, looking up at Nina. 'Do I have your word that if I do this, you will not hurt me?'

'If you do it, we won't need to,' she replied.

'And you will not turn me in to the police?'

'Let's not go that far. You willingly set this up. I don't see why I should let you off the hook for it.'

Varna's response was almost petulant. 'What if I say that is the price for doing this for you?'

Eddie shifted his gun to the Indian's lower back. 'What if I shoot you in the spine and put you in a wheelchair for the rest of your life?'

The seated man looked up at Nina as if hoping for support. Her green eyes were as cold as jade. 'Ah . . . okay,' he said, mouth audibly going dry. 'I will do it if you let me live. That sounds . . . a good deal. Yes.' He turned back to the terminal as Eddie withdrew, and typed a final command. 'All right. Everything is ready. I just—'

His face exploded in a bloody burst across the screen.

Nina and Eddie jerked back in shock. Then they spun – to find they were no longer alone.

John Brice and the French mercenary, Lannard, stood in the doorway, guns raised. Smoke curled from the muzzle of Brice's automatic – which had already switched targets from the back of Varna's head to the front of Eddie's. Lannard, meanwhile, was covering Nina with his own weapon.

'Hello, Chase,' said Brice, with a malevolent smile. 'I *told* you I'd see you in Malta.'

34

'Drop the guns,' barked Lannard. Nina's sub-machine gun was still pointed at Varna's slumped corpse. Caught, she reluctantly let the weapon clatter to the floor.

'And you, Chase,' Brice said, his handgun fixed unwaveringly on the Yorkshireman. His smile vanished, replaced by a chilling absence of expression. 'I'd prefer not to kill you where you stand. I have plans for something more satisfying. But I will if I have to.'

Eddie remained motionless for a moment, assessing his chances. Then, with even greater reluctance than Nina, he dropped the revolver.

'Kick them away,' Brice ordered. Husband and wife both kicked the fallen weapons across the server room. 'Good. Now, there's someone I'd like you to meet.' Gun still trained on Eddie, he called back through the open doorway, with a hint of sing-song sarcasm: 'Oh, Adjudicator? It's safe to come in.'

Footsteps approached the entrance. Nina and Eddie looked past Brice and Lannard to see who was coming. A figure appeared in the doorway.

Natalie Bachand.

'*You're* the Adjudicator?' exclaimed Nina as the pregnant Canadian halted between the two mercenaries. 'Let me guess – Loost didn't really leave you with nothing, did he?'

'No,' Natalie replied, fixing her with a look of not merely contempt, but loathing. 'He left me *everything*. His baby, most of his fortune – and a plan to deal with the person who killed him.' She took a step closer. 'You don't know how hard it was for me to lie to you in Montreal, about Rafael. I told you I hated him.' The mere thought seemed to hurt her. 'But the truth is, I loved him. I still do.' She waved a hand. 'Mr Brice, move them away from the terminal, please. Monsieur Lannard, move . . . *him*.' A disdainful gesture towards the twitching Varna.

'You heard the lady,' sneered Brice. 'Move.'

Nina and Eddie, hands raised to chest height, warily backed off. Lannard took Eddie's place and with a grunt hauled the Indian's body from the chair. He looked for somewhere to put it, but on seeing Natalie's impatient expression simply dropped it with a thud beside the desk.

Natalie sat at the terminal, using the edge of one hand like a wiper blade to clear the splattered blood and brain matter from the screen. 'Jesus,' said Nina, appalled.

'I'm a nurse, Professor Wilde. I've gotten my hands dirty in a lot worse. Now, let me see . . .' She examined the windows Varna had created, frowning. 'Huh. He was actually going to do what you wanted. And after Rafael made him rich. No loyalty.'

'Maybe Loost should have got *him* pregnant too,' Eddie snarked.

Natalie shot him a dirty look, then turned back to the monitor, reaching up to activate the webcam. 'Now, I think Rafael would like to speak to you.'

The image of Loost expanded to fill the screen, the background expanding horizontally so he was perfectly framed. Loost's eyes shifted as if scanning a display of his own, then – unsettlingly – his gaze locked on to Nina. 'Ah, there you are, Nina,' he said. 'I was wondering when you'd get here. But I knew you would.'

'*You* know nothing,' Nina shot back. 'You're just a chatbot with preprogrammed delusions of grandeur.'

Loost put on an expression of mocking affrontery. 'Oh, that cuts like paper, Nina. I'm hurt.' His face hardened. 'And you should be more polite, since I hold your life in my hands.'

'You don't *have* any hands,' Eddie pointed out.

Nina half-expected Loost to raise his simulated appendages to prove him wrong, but he only cast a disapproving glance towards her husband. 'I arranged this whole game so you would eventually have no choice but to come here,' he went on, addressing her again, 'or else die trying. You survived several attempts on your life, which is impressive. But whether you survive what I've prepared for you here, well . . .' He leaned closer to the virtual camera, eyes narrowing. Even at a closer range, his computer-generated visage appeared totally realistic. 'I guess we'll see which of us is *really* the smartest.'

'*That's* what this is all about, isn't it?' said Nina, with a disbelieving – and dismissive – huff. She faced Natalie, turning her back on the screen. 'The richest man in history, who literally rose above the bonds of Earth . . . and all he could think about as his last act was getting petty revenge on someone who outsmarted him? I'm not even going to talk to this digital mannequin. It's pathetic. And so was he.'

Natalie drew in an angry breath. 'Don't you *dare* talk about him like that.'

'It's okay, Natalie,' said Loost, in an almost soothing tone. 'I can take care of myself. It's Nina who needs to worry.' The Canadian smiled, mollified.

Nina's disbelief grew. 'You're acting like this is actually Rafael Loost! It isn't – it's a talking head with a copy of his voice, a fancy version of the Eliza program. It's nothing but a database plucking out replies to what people say to it. It can't think, it's not real – it's not *him*. You loved him when he was alive, okay, but if you love this *thing*, then you're delusional.'

Natalie flushed with fury, giving Nina a hateful glare. But before she could say anything, Loost spoke for her. 'You're underestimating my technology, Nina. I assure you, I really am Rafael Loost. Reborn in a new form, but still the same mind. Preserved for eternity – and able to learn and grow infinitely.'

'Bull. Shit,' was Nina's considered response. She still didn't deign to look directly at Loost's avatar, giving him a disdainful sidelong glance. 'What, while you were floating in space for the last couple weeks of your life, you magically came up with a way to record the exact state of all eighty-six billion neurons and the hundred trillion different connections between them in your brain?'

'I once read a spy thriller with a gadget that did that,' Eddie remarked. 'It was pretty good.'

Nina ignored him. 'It's pure science fiction. The human brain isn't a computer.'

'Not a *digital* computer,' said Loost. 'But a *quantum* computer? That's something else entirely. Did you think I built Qbial just to create a better social network? No, this was my goal all along – to grant myself immortality. And I achieved it.'

'Until someone pulls the plug,' she shot back. 'Which I'll enjoy doing.'

'You'll never get the chance,' Natalie said. 'Rafael, it's time to start the challenges.'

'What challenges?' Nina demanded.

'Oh, I'm sure you'll appreciate them.' The smug amusement in Loost's voice made her turn to look directly at him. The digital recreation of the trillionaire could certainly mimic emotion convincingly – explaining why Natalie, in her state of grief, would have latched onto it as a way to avoid facing the truth about Loost's death. 'You inspired them, actually. In your first book, *In Search of Atlantis* – a very turgid read, by the way; I'm not surprised Hollywood spiced it up when they made a movie from it.'

Nina made an affronted sound. 'Oh – kiss my ass.'

'No thanks. But you described what you went through in the Temple of Poseidon in the Amazon jungle. Three challenges: of strength, of skill and of mind. You're going to go through them again. But they're a little more modern now. I designed them myself, just for you. And this time, you won't have anyone else to help you.'

'Then we won't be needing Chase any more,' said Brice, giving the Yorkshireman an unpleasant smile. 'Good. I can finally do what I joined this little crusade to do.'

'Not yet,' Natalie said sharply. 'We use him to force her,' a sneering glance at Nina, 'to do what we tell her.'

Brice scowled. 'Hardly solid leverage. She knows I'm going to kill him anyway.'

'She doesn't know *how* you're going to kill him.' She turned back to Nina. 'Quickly, or slowly. It depends on you.'

'Thank you for giving me the choice,' the redhead replied with bitter sarcasm.

'So you can't kill me right now?' Eddie piped up to Brice. 'Cool, I'll make the most of it. You twat. You fucking bell-end. Give us a song, then, tin-throat. Thirteen years in solitary and all you thought about was me? I'm here now, so I'm surprised you can keep yourself from whipping your cock out and having a wank.'

It took all Brice's self-control to restrain himself from physical retaliation. 'Try to goad me all you like, Chase,' he snarled. 'You won't be laughing for long, I promise.'

'Enough,' cut in Natalie with impatience. 'Bring them to the control room.' She stepped closer to Nina, though remained a precautionary distance beyond her reach. 'It's time to start the challenges.'

Brice and Lannard held Nina and Eddie at gunpoint as the group made their way through the sprawling villa. Their destination resembled a television studio's control room, banks of screens on one wall. The largest was already active, Loost watching them enter. 'You made it,' he said, smirking. 'Good. Now the real game begins.'

Natalie sat at a console and gestured towards a door at the room's far end. 'Mr Brice. Put her in there, please.'

'Watch Chase,' the hulking man ordered Lannard, who took up position with his gun aimed at Eddie. Brice grabbed Nina roughly by one arm and pushed her towards the door. With his vastly greater strength, she was powerless to resist.

'I should explain the rules first,' said Loost. Brice halted, keeping a firm grip on his prisoner.

'Oh – of course. Sorry.' Natalie was genuinely apologetic.

Nina was unimpressed. 'You just said sorry to a computer program, for God's sake.'

The other woman's expression became venomous. 'Stop calling him that!'

'You're underestimating my technology, Nina,' said Loost. 'I assure you—'

'I'm the real Rafael Loost, quantum computer, blah blah blah,' Nina interrupted mockingly. 'Yeah, you said that already. In pretty much the exact same way. Almost as if you're just a bunch of regurgitated soundbites.'

The avatar sighed. 'I see I haven't convinced you yet. But it doesn't matter. There are three challenges beyond that door,' he went on, switching subjects and tone with conspicuously less smoothness than in previous conversations, further hardening Nina's belief that he was merely an overblown chatbot. 'The Challenge of Strength, the Challenge of Skill, and the Challenge of Mind. I designed them so you'll be able to get through all of them – *if* you perform to the absolute best of your ability. Anything less than perfection, and . . .' He shrugged. 'You can probably guess what happens.'

'She wins a *Blankety Blank* chequebook and pen?' Eddie suggested. 'No, I know – Dusty Bin.'

Everyone looked at him, mostly with incomprehension. Only Brice had a different reaction: a small, involuntary laugh at his sheer gall.

'Those are consolation prizes from old British game shows,' said Loost after a short pause. Nina suspected even the quantum computer had needed a moment to puzzle out her husband's references. 'Very amusing.' He sounded anything but amused. 'Each challenge has a time limit, Nina. You'll be tracked at all times by automated sentry guns. If you don't reach the exit before the timer reaches zero, they'll fire.'

'Yeah, I kinda figured that,' she said sourly. 'And what happens if

I *do* complete all three challenges? I go free and win your billion dollars?'

Loost did not seem to have an immediate answer to that, as if the possibility had never been envisaged. However, Brice spoke instead. 'I'll save you from the pain and anguish of watching your husband die horribly by killing you first, nice and quickly – how does that sound? And maybe I won't even go looking for your daughter. I know Macy's out there, somewhere. You wouldn't want me to find her, would you?'

Eddie visibly tensed, sudden anger rising. Lannard thrust his gun closer to deter him from moving. 'You shut the fuck up about Macy,' the Yorkshireman growled.

Brice merely smirked. 'Oh, yes, I remember. She's your berserk button, as Philippe Mukobo found out when you murdered him in cold blood. Unfortunately for you, unlike him I'm not tied to a chair – so bluster away, Chase.' He looked to Nina. 'And threatening your wife gets nothing? Nina, perhaps you should reconsider your marriage. While you still have time.'

'I feel the same way as Eddie, asshole,' she told him. 'Any parent would. Any non-insane parent, anyway.' She directed that last at Natalie.

The Canadian half-rose from her chair. 'Get her in there,' she snapped.

Brice shoved Nina to the door and opened it. 'See you on the other side,' he told her, pushing her through. 'Perhaps.'

Her reply of '*Fuck y—*' was cut off as he slammed the door behind her.

35

'Son of a *bitch*,' Nina hissed. The door's inner side was blank, no lock or handle. The only way out was through Loost's version of the Challenge of Strength.

She turned to see what it entailed – and froze at the sight of a compact sub-machine gun mounted on a tripod. The stand was topped by a motion base that could turn and tilt, camera lenses on either side of the weapon giving it stereoscopic vision. A mechanical linkage went from the base to the gun's trigger.

The SMG was pointed directly at her.

Another sentry was positioned across the room from its twin. Both were surrounded by arcing lines of black and yellow painted on the floor. She took a cautious step forward. Both guns turned slightly to keep her precisely in their sights. 'If you hadn't guessed,' Loost's voice said suddenly, making her flinch, 'if you cross the warning lines, you'll be shot.' A 3D screen was set into one wall, the trillionaire staring at her from it.

'Gee, thanks for telling me. I would never have worked that out.'

Beyond the two guns, at the room's far end, was a cylindrical steel tube about four feet in diameter, with an opening large enough for her to fit through at a crouch. A thick joint ran around the pipe's surface above the entrance. She looked up. The room was three storeys high, the tube going all the way to its ceiling. She advanced towards it. The sentry guns tracked her with soft, menacing whirrs. The top of the tube was connected to the far wall. The way out?

Probably – if she proved her strength first.

'By the way,' said Loost, 'you have five minutes. The timer starts now.' A digital countdown clock was superimposed over his image, showing 5:00.

4:59.

4:58 . . .

'Crap,' she gasped, hurrying to the tube and peering inside. The metal was quite thick, with recesses cast into it at regular intervals up each side. Handholds and footholds. White LEDs inside them provided illumination. She had to climb, that much was obvious – but what was the actual Challenge of Strength?

She crouched to enter . . . and got her answer.

The way up was blocked by a steel disc that filled the entire vertical shaft. It was supported by four protruding inch-long metal pegs. The challenge, it seemed, was to lift it above her to the top of the climb within the time limit. The gap between the disc and the wall was a couple of millimetres at most. She imagined the disc itself was thicker than that, to prevent her from pushing up one side to flip it out of her way.

Nina glanced back out at the screen. Four minutes and fifty seconds left. She quickly started to climb, her hands reaching the disc's underside in moments. She spread her fingers wide and pressed her palms against the cool metal surface, then pushed.

To her relief, the disc wasn't too heavy to lift. It took a degree of effort to do so, though; she estimated it to weigh eight or nine pounds, perhaps four kilograms. As much as two two-litre bottles of soda. It was more awkward than heavy, forcing her to spread her elbows wide to support herself against the walls while she brought up each foot in turn. But she could do it, she was sure—

The disc rose clear of the pegs – and with a mechanical *snap*, they retracted into the tube.

Before she could react, a louder metallic sound came from below, a rumble that reverberated through the pipe. What she had thought was a joint on the outside of the tube was actually a track – and a curved steel cover rolled around it and slammed to a stop, blocking the opening.

No backing out. She had to get to the top before the timer reached zero. But at least inside the thick metal cylinder, she couldn't be shot—

The floor at the bottom of the pipe retracted with a rattle. Below it was a metal grille – and under *that*, another sentry gun, pointing directly upwards.

'God *damn* it!' Nina gasped. She began a hurried ascent, pushing the disc above her. After a couple of steps up the rungs, something came into sight set into one of them. A digital countdown clock, telling her she had four minutes and thirty-two seconds remaining. She kept climbing, timing herself and performing some rapid mental arithmetic. If each step upwards was a set height and took a certain number of seconds, could she reach the top before the clock reached zero?

Yes, easily. If she maintained this pace, she would have over a minute to spare. Loost had underestimated her, not for the first time—

Something hit the disc from above with a sharp *clack*.

She caught her breath, freezing in surprise – before realising that whatever had just happened would not be to her benefit and resuming the climb. Another *clack*, echoing in the confined space, then another, the gap between each impact two seconds. A faint skirling, rattling sound reached her through the disc as she pushed it upwards. What was it?

Loost gave the answer as the strikes continued. 'If you're wondering what that noise is, Nina, it's my version of the original challenge. Ball bearings are being dropped onto the plate. Each one weighs fifty grams. I'm sure you can work out how much that will add to the total weight you have to lift each minute.'

She could. Fifteen hundred grams, or one and a half kilograms: over three pounds. By the time she reached the top, the weight above her would have more than doubled. It would gradually slow her as it increased. *Now* could she make it in time?

It was impossible to calculate. There were too many unknown variables: the exact height of the climb, how many ball bearings would drop, and the biggest of all – her own strength and endurance. All she could do was go as fast as she could, and hope her body was up to the test.

Nina pushed on, the sound of each new bearing hitting the disc joined by clattering as those already on it rolled and collided. The shift of weight above made her cargo tip, catching the tube's wall and making it harder to move. She adjusted her hold to bring it level and inched it higher. A task that had been an effort soon became a struggle. Even if the weight hadn't been increasing, holding it above herself for a prolonged period would have been a strain. She shifted position, twisting to add the support of one shoulder and her head.

It wasn't enough. Each step higher was a little harder than the last. The relentless tattoo of falling steel became like a chisel into her skull. She reached another timer. Three minutes and six seconds left. Was she even halfway up? She looked down to see how far she had climbed. At a guess, over twenty feet. She had to be close to the midpoint. The sentry gun's steel muzzle glinted malevolently beneath the grille.

One foot higher, then the other. Push the disc upwards. Repeat. But the faint burning in her arm muscles became hotter. The bang of each falling bearing was an awful metronome, counting down her remaining life.

Which would end soon, abruptly and painfully, if she didn't reach the top in time. She was certain Loost's version of the Challenge of Strength was survivable; he would have wanted to gloat. But if she failed it, she had no doubts that the penalty would be lethal.

Another step higher. Her back was also starting to ache as she used her body to drive the disc upwards. Every lift now forced her to rebalance it as the spheres rolled about on top, its thick edge threatening to wedge against the tube. She moved to push it back level—

One of her feet slipped.

She shrieked in fear as she dropped – then jarred to a halt as her flailing foot caught the inset rung below. The disc tipped, falling after her—

It jammed against the wall just above her, one side lower than the other. The same design that had made her task harder had also saved her. Nina gasped, recovering from the shock before pulling herself back up. The rain of bearings had not stopped, three more ticks of the metronome ringing through the metal cylinder before she could support the disc again. With much more weight now on one side, it was a real strain to force it back into position. Breathless, she started to climb again.

More rungs, one by strenuous one. Thirty feet, she guessed, thirty-five. Another timer warned she had only one minute and twenty-six seconds remaining. How much further? From outside, she'd estimated the distance as about fifty feet, but what if she'd been wrong? Forty feet. She *had* to be near the top now. A minute to go. Ten feet in sixty seconds; surely she could do it. But the disc bore remorselessly down upon her, heavier and heavier. Every new bearing striking the steel sounded like a gunshot just above her ear. The only thing louder was her breathing, her throat rasping with each inhalation. Keep going. It couldn't be far. Keep going.

Her muscles were aflame, begging for relief, shaking as she pushed the disc above her. Thirty seconds. *Keep going!* Like Sisyphus pushing his boulder, her torment grew the nearer she got to the top – but unlike the victim of Hades's judgement, hers would soon end.

One way or the other.

Ten seconds. Fear gave her a final surge of energy. She forced herself upwards, the hateful steel plate rising higher—

And suddenly sliding sideways as it emerged from the shaft's confines.

Nina looked up. Through a crescent-shaped gap she saw something other than featureless curved metal – a flat wall. She had reached the top!

Or rather, the disc had. She was still in the shaft, with only seconds left to get clear—

She scrambled up the remaining rungs, jamming her shoulder against the obstruction and shoving it aside. Ball bearings cascaded from it as it tilted, clattering noisily across the floor. Nina drove herself through the widened gap and landed amongst the scattering spheres, pulling her legs clear as the disc fell back onto the top of the tube with a resounding clang.

She lay there panting, the ache in her limbs slowly receding. Then the brief respite was interrupted by Loost's mocking voice. 'Well done, Nina.' She looked up to see him staring down from a screen on the end wall of the passage she had just reached. Another sentry gun lurked beneath it. 'I really thought you weren't going to make it. That was close! Exciting stuff.'

'Glad you enjoyed it, asshole,' she muttered.

'Of course, this isn't over. You still have two more challenges to go. I'll be generous and give you a minute to recover. You look tired.'

Even knowing he was no more than an animated simulacrum parroting pre-recorded phrases, his smug condescension stoked anger inside her. She overcame her body's complaints and pushed herself onto her knees. 'You can cram your generosity up your dead ass.' She started to stand, then on an impulse picked up a handful of the loose ball bearings. 'And these too!' With a snarl, she hurled them at the screen. It cracked, leaving Loost's visage scarred by several ragged craters and video glitches.

It took a few seconds for the avatar to reply. 'Temper, temper,' he said, but by then Nina had already turned and stalked away.

'Say to her, "Temper, temper",' said Natalie in the control room as its occupants watched events at the top of the shaft. Loost, now relegated to a secondary monitor as the largest followed Nina's progress, repeated the phrase. On the big screen, the redhead turned and stalked away.

'You tell him, love,' Eddie said admiringly. The Challenge of Strength had been covered by multiple cameras, every moment of her fraught ascent observed. He had become genuinely fearful for his wife's safety as the timer ran out, but that was followed by an even greater relief as she pulled through.

'Very touching,' was Brice's sarcastic rejoinder. 'Though I admit, I'm almost impressed that she made it. I thought this silly spectacle was going to end at the first hurdle.'

'Weren't you listening to Rafael?' asked Natalie. 'This has been carefully designed so that she will suffer, but get through if she tries her absolute hardest. For the first two challenges, at least.'

Eddie stiffened. 'So the last one's a trap? She'll fail it no matter what?'

To his surprise, Loost answered rather than Natalie. 'She can get through – if she's as smart as she thinks. If she isn't, then she has no one but herself to blame.'

'Oh, I can think of a few people to blame,' Eddie growled with a baleful glare at Natalie – followed by a half-step towards her. She instinctively shrank back, prompting Lannard to bring his gun higher in deterrence. The Yorkshireman halted and scowled at him – but didn't retreat. Nor did the shabby Frenchman attempt to force him to do so, his attention caught by a switch of camera on the big screen.

'She's reached the next challenge,' Brice observed, as casually as if the life-or-death test was no more remarkable than a change of bowler at a cricket match.

Natalie turned back to the monitors. 'The Challenge of Skill.' She fired a disdainful glance at Eddie. 'I think she'll find this one a bit harder.'

He held in a rude retort as he watched Nina enter a new room – while in his peripheral vision checking the positions of Lannard and Brice. The latter was a few strides distant, too far away to reach with a surprise attack before being shot. Lannard, though, was closer. Not close enough, but . . .

Eddie shifted his upper body as if relieving some discomfort – at the same time sliding one foot a few millimetres towards the mercenary. As he'd hoped, the movement Lannard reacted to was the more obvious one, giving him a brief flick of the eyes before looking back at the screens, satisfied that the threat he posed had not changed.

Another tiny shift of his foot. Lannard didn't notice. With everyone watching Nina, Eddie knew he had a chance to edge close enough to strike. Grab his gun, and he could shoot both his captors, then force Natalie to free Nina.

If she survived whatever she faced next.

36

Still exhausted from the climb, Nina entered a new room. The Challenge of Skill awaited her.

Or so she presumed. All it appeared to be was a hallway, the long side walls covered with countless small, glossy grey tiles. All were of differing thicknesses, creating a mottled effect. At the far end, another sentry gun locked onto her from inside its warning-stripe circle.

She ignored it, as much as she could. It was not an immediate threat. But there were no other signs of danger – which immediately concerned her.

The original Challenge of Skill, in the Amazonian Temple of Poseidon, had required negotiating a narrow balance beam over a pool of hungry caimans. The way ahead here was a polished marble floor. She crouched to examine it. It was an expensive piece of work, each slab abutting its neighbours with micron precision, so perfectly fitted that the gaps between were as fine as hairs. If they could drop or hinge or otherwise move underfoot, the spaces would have been much more visible.

The trap was built into the walls, then. But where was it – and *what* was it?

Her eyes gave her no answers, but another sense warned of something out of the ordinary. There was a faint scent, not unpleasant – some kind of incense, perhaps? And now she realised her view was not entirely clear. There was a light mist or smoke in the air. Was gas the danger? She discounted the thought; skill couldn't help her avoid that. But it had to be part of the trap, otherwise it wouldn't be there . . .

Some of the tiles were abruptly revealed as elements of a screen, a section of the wall flicking to life to display Loost's face upon it. The offsetting of the tiles broke up his features into a bizarre pixelated nightmare. 'Welcome to my version of the Challenge of Skill,' he said. 'It's more high-tech than the one you did before. But you'll have to be just as good as you were twenty-five years ago to get through it.' A smirk. 'I hope you kept up on your callisthenics.'

'Natalie, just start the thing,' snapped Nina, looking around for cameras. They were concealed, but the room's corners seemed their most likely locations, so she fixed her gaze on one. 'I'm bored of talking to Max Deadroom here.'

In the control room, Eddie laughed. 'Max Deadroom. I like that.'

'I see your puerile sense of humour infected your wife,' Brice remarked, unamused.

Natalie was even less pleased. 'Rafael, start the challenge,' she told the avatar, her lips curled in anger.

Lannard's attention went from Eddie to the big screen as the nature of the test was revealed. The Yorkshireman used the moment to edge another fraction closer to him.

Nina's heart sank as the challenge manifested before her. The purpose of the faint smoke became clear: it was to make a web of red laser beams criss-crossing the passage visible. The lancing lines, coming from gaps amongst the wall tiles, became more numerous – and closer together – the nearer they were to the far end.

The task was obvious: get through without touching any. The question was: *could* she? As Loost had pointed out, she had traversed the Atlantean original a quarter of a century earlier. And callisthenics had not been high on her list of priorities since.

'You have five minutes to reach the other end of the passage without touching any of the lasers,' Loost confirmed. 'The timer starts now.' Another block of tiles lit up to show a countdown clock.

'What happens if I touch one?' Nina demanded.

'Nothing you'll enjoy,' was the gloating reply. 'Now, I'd recommend you get moving.'

She didn't deign to give the computer-generated image a reply, instead cautiously advancing to the first laser beam. It was at thigh height, angled slightly downwards. She went to its lowest point and carefully stepped over it. The next beam was a couple of feet along the passage. This was higher, stomach height, forcing her to duck beneath.

She continued past a few more of the needle-thin lines until she reached a step up in challenge. The next had two laser beams, cutting diagonally across the corridor. Over one, under the other, or go between them? The last choice offered the most manoeuvring room. She turned sidelong and leaned forwards to ease herself through. A small wobble as she shifted her weight from one foot to the other brought a beam frighteningly close to her face. She winced and steadied herself, then stepped clear with relief.

Another set of twin beams awaited her. Nina paused, examining them. The gap between the two red lines was large enough to fit through, just, but at an angle that could risk her losing her balance. Going over them would require a jump, and she wasn't sure she could leap high enough. But to go under, she would have to lie absolutely flat and carefully squirm through, costing her time.

She checked the clock. Over three minutes and forty seconds left, and she had made decent progress so far. She could afford caution, for now.

Nina dropped flat on the floor, then began to pull herself beneath the beam. It was worryingly close to her hair, forcing her to turn her head sideways, one cheek against the cold marble. She was low enough that the almost-forgotten torc necklace scraped against the polished slab. Could she use the Shroud to turn invisible and pass through the beams unharmed?

No. She remembered what had happened in Hades's tomb when a mercenary swept his laser sight over her cloaked form. The Shroud deflected the beam around her, but it was distorted, diffused. Any drop in the laser's intensity might trigger the trap.

She would have to get through the hard way. Focusing on her movements, she carefully advanced along the floor. Her upper body slid beneath the beam, her waist—

Her butt just barely brushed the laser line – but that was enough.

A flash, a crack of electricity – and she screamed as what felt like a whipcrack lashed across her backside, making her whole body jerk. Then the spasm ended, but her skin was still burning. She scrambled forward, retaining just enough presence of mind to stop before she lunged head-first into the next set of lasers. Gasping in pain, she twisted to see what had happened. A neat scorch line ran across the seat of her trousers. *Stun laser*, she remembered Eddie telling her at the Canadian border. A beam that made the air itself an electrical conductor: a Taser without wires.

And I triggered it with my fat ass! was her inner yell at herself.

Synthetic laughter shifted her anger to her captors. 'That must have stung,' said Loost. 'I did say you wouldn't enjoy it. But that was just a warning shot – low power. The first one is free. From now on, you have to pay. If you get hit, you'll be stunned, knocked out . . . but the timer will still be running. You have three minutes and six seconds remaining. I wouldn't waste it.'

With a frustrated growl, Nina rose, still feeling the burn across her backside. She tried to put it to the back of her mind as she faced the next laser barrier. To traverse this one, she had to crouch and twist to get one leg through at a time, though. One heel wavered millimetres from a beam, but she caught herself just in time. The following set, she crawled under on her back to flatten her butt as much as she could. She could just about have fitted a hand of playing cards between her body and the shimmering beam – but she made it.

Time was running out, though. She was more than halfway through the challenge, but the countdown had passed the two minutes and thirty seconds mark – and the contortions needed to get through each set of beams were harder each time.

A quiet whirr as the sentry gun tracked her spurred the redhead on. She had beaten Loost's games once; she could do it again. Even if, she thought ruefully, this was a challenge to which her younger, fitter and more agile daughter was far better suited . . .

But nobody else could do it for her, and she wouldn't have asked them to anyway. All this was on her.

The next set of lasers went from two beams to three, two at opposing horizontal angles and the third slicing diagonally across them. The widest gap would be tricky to get through. Instead, she moved to the next largest, squatting down and putting both hands on the floor beyond the red lines for support before bringing her legs through one at a time. Breathing heavily from the exertion, she straightened and turned to check the following test—

The beams started moving.

'Oh, you are fucking *kidding*!' Nina yelled. The laser lines pivoted from their emitters, sweeping up and down across detectors in the opposite wall. She quickly saw they followed a regular pattern, certain gaps widening to a maximum area before shrinking again. She would not only have to clear the beams without touching them, but do so at an exact time.

She watched for several seconds, acutely aware of the clock ticking down as she calculated the best move. The lower middle would give the biggest space, but could she get through in time? She would need to make a rapid move from a crouch, with little margin for error. The other alternative would require her to jump through. As before, she wasn't confident enough in her abilities to risk it.

She hunched down, tensing herself, ready to spring. The crisscrossing beams cycled through their pattern. One would hit the bottom of its path, then reverse, reaching its top two seconds later. Ready—

Go!

Nina threw herself forwards, head low as she passed between the beams. Her landing on the far side was ungainly, but she didn't care. Her only concern was pulling her legs clear. She jerked up both knees, curling into a ball – as the descending beam sliced down like a guillotine just behind her feet.

She had no time to collect herself. The next group of lasers started moving. She glanced back at the countdown. One minute twenty-eight. Enough to get through the remaining obstacles?

It wasn't as if she had a choice. The sentry gun was still tracking her. If she didn't, she was dead. And then Brice would kill Eddie.

That wasn't going to happen.

New determination filling her, she assessed the next set of beams. Again, it took more time than she liked to determine their pattern – but the moment she had it, she moved. She was forced to jump, head down as she vaulted through. Another clumsy landing forced her to flail her arms to catch her balance. More lasers began their dance right in front of her.

The countdown reached one minute, and kept ticking down. She watched the sweeping red lines until she found the optimum gap, then on the next cycle quickly climbed through. Only two left between her and the exit. She could make it!

Four beams on the penultimate laser grid. Finding the pattern was harder this time – and the largest gap narrower. She realised she would have to roll sidelong beneath the lowest beam, and do so quickly. On the floor, readying herself. Counting down in her head. Three, two, one—

She shoved sideways, bowling herself beneath the falling laser. The movement was so forceful she banged her forehead against the hard floor. But it worked – she was through and clear. Only one more trap, and she would have beaten the Challenge of Skill.

Nina stood to face the final test. Four beams again. She knew she could do it. All she had to do was find the pattern. Twenty-three seconds. She could do it—

A *fifth* beam flicked to life.

She stared at it in horror – only for it to disappear. A moment later it returned, staying for a second until it vanished again.

There was no pattern. It was switching on and off at random. Even if she figured out how to get through the others, this one might still catch her. 'You son of a *bitch!*' she yelled, even knowing doing so would cost her a precious second.

Loost said something in response, but she wasn't listening, her entire mind fixated upon the lasers. The fifth beam was an element she could neither predict nor control. So ignore it. It would activate, or it wouldn't. But she only had time for one attempt, so she had to take it, no matter what.

There was the gap. Near one wall, off the floor. She would have to jump again – *and* kick off the uneven tiles to get through as it shrank. Macy could do it, Nina was sure.

Now *she* had to.

She lined herself up, eyes fixed on the sweeping laser beams, counting down the seconds in her head. *You got through this twenty-five years ago. You can do it again. Be the woman you were back then.*

You still are that woman.

The fifth beam vanished. Her mental timer reached zero—

Nina launched herself at the wall, kicking off it to propel herself through the gap. It had already reached its maximum size, now shrinking. She pulled her arms in against her body, desperately twisting her hips as she passed through the narrowing aperture. She would hit the floor hard, but that was better than being hit by fifty thousand volts . . .

The fifth beam returned.

It caught her sneaker's heel – triggering the staser. The laser beam instantly went from a subtle shimmering red to an almost blinding lance of hellfire intensity – and a powerful electrical bolt surged along it with an ear-splitting thundercrack. It struck the back of Nina's foot. Leather and synthetics burst apart, angry orange fire erupting from the sneaker's sole.

Trailing smoke, Nina hit the marble floor with a bone-jarring thump that numbed her left arm. Even through that pain, she recognised a more dangerous one and batted frantically at her foot to extinguish the flame. It seared her palm, but she managed to put out the fire before it burned through to her flesh.

Spent, she rolled onto her back and drew in several heavy breaths – before belatedly realising the sentry gun was tilted down to aim directly at her from within its exclusion zone. A sudden jolt of fear made her sit upright, looking back towards the countdown clock—

It had reached zero. But she was still alive.

A new set of tiles by the exit lit up, another pixelated image of Loost appearing. 'You made it, Nina! Well done. Two challenges completed. Only one to go.' He smiled. 'The one I'm most proud of creating. A *true* test of your intelligence. We'll find out once and for all which of us is the smartest.'

Nina shook her head in disgust. 'If I just admit you're smarter than me, can we end this farce right now?'

'If that's what you want. I'll reactivate the sentry gun and this will all be over – for you.'

With a tired grunt, she forced herself to stand. 'All right, asshole. We'll play this through to the end.'

'I thought you would want to.' Loost's head turned towards the nearby door. 'It's through there.'

'Can't wait.' Rubbing her left arm as feeling painfully returned, Nina went through to face the final challenge.

37

'What the fuck was that?' Eddie demanded in the control room. 'First the lasers start moving, then you add a random one? That's not a challenge, that's Russian roulette.'

'She made it through, didn't she?' was Natalie's acerbic – and disappointed – reply. 'But Rafael is right.' She nodded towards the digital replica of her lover, who responded with a small smile. 'His version of the Challenge of Mind really will test her. And I don't believe she'll find the right answer.'

'We'll see.' Eddie folded his arms defiantly – using the movement to camouflage another small shift towards Lannard. Neither the Frenchman nor Brice noticed, even the former MI6 officer now engrossed by Nina's plight. The Yorkshireman was now almost close enough to risk a lunge at the distracted Lannard's weapon.

Almost. Not quite.

But it would not be long before that changed.

The route to the Challenge of Mind took Nina down a flight of stairs to a lower floor. She wasn't surprised to find a sentry gun tracking her as she went. She would not be permitted to dawdle. Even so, she didn't rush, letting herself recover from one struggle before dealing with the next.

But she was soon at another door. A final deep breath, then she went in.

Compared to the extravagant spaces created for the first two challenges, this was almost modest. The new room was square, about twenty feet along each wall. Another door, presumably the exit, was directly opposite her. Two sentry guns stood in the corners to each side of it. Unlike in the previous encounters, rather than there being a circular exclusion zone around each gun, the room's entire far end was cordoned off by a warning line on the floor. She guessed she couldn't approach the door until she had completed the challenge.

But her attention was on the challenge itself. One side wall bore several lines of characters that she instantly recognised as Atlantean text. The other had an illustration, a stylised map she quickly identified as ancient Greece. Several points were marked on it, numerous thin lines interconnecting them; the two most prominent locations were in the position of Athens on the country's eastern side, and opposite on the western coast upon one of the Ionian peninsulas.

It was some kind of puzzle, then, one which a not-yet-active countdown clock told her she would have five minutes to solve. So what did she have to do?

A screen beside the exit lit up to show Loost. 'This is my Challenge of Mind, Nina. Make sure you get it right – you'll only get one attempt to answer. Get it wrong, and . . .' He nodded towards each of the waiting guns. 'Let's see which of us is smarter. Once and for all.'

'You petty little shit,' Nina muttered as she went to the wall with the text. It was easy to comprehend, though she was unimpressed by what she read. 'Who the hell translated this? I bet you got a computer to do it, didn't you? Bad grammar, none of the nuance of proper Atlantean writing, no sense of contextual meaning. If one of my students gave this to me, I'd give it back with red pen all over it.'

'It was translated by my quantum computers,' said Loost. Like them he had not grasped context, as he sounded proud rather than defensive at her criticism.

'I guess they need more training. By someone who knows what they're talking about, rather than just scraping data off the internet.'

The avatar ignored her, not having been prepared with a response – or because other matters took priority. 'You have five minutes to work out the right answer, starting now.' The clock began to count down.

THE SHROUD OF HADES

Nina had already got the gist of the Atlantean text; she turned back to it to pin down the specifics. It was a mathematical puzzle, playing out upon the map behind her. Atlantean forces had landed on the west coast, and from there had to fight their way across Greece until they reached Athens, each intervening point representing a battle. It took one day to travel from one point to another. The army had a maximum strength of one thousand soldiers, arriving with a full force, and could not move on to the next battle until it regained all lost troops. Each fight would cost the army between twenty and sixty per cent of its strength. A reserve force of up to four hundred soldiers could arrive from the landing point in a number of days equal to one plus the number of battles fought to that time.

The phrasing was entirely un-Atlantean, an English text devised by a tech nerd bluntly translated by machine. But she understood it clearly enough, along with the question posed on the last line: what would be the smallest number of days needed for the army to reach Athens?

Her mind was already at work. The smallest number of days would also necessitate the smallest number of combat losses at every battle, so she needed to work with the lowest figure, twenty per cent. That was two hundred soldiers lost in each fight.

She turned to the map. The route between the landing point and Athens with the fewest battles had only two. She had the answer almost as soon as she took in the information. Day 1: the Atlanteans arrive and travel to the site of the first battle, losing two hundred soldiers. It then takes the replacement soldiers one plus one days to arrive, returning the unit to full strength on Day 3. Day 4: they reach the second battle and another two hundred soldiers are lost. This time, it takes one plus two days for reinforcements to get there. On Day 8, the Atlanteans are able to reach Athens. Easy.

Too easy. Nina frowned. She had mentioned in her first book that she had a natural talent for mental arithmetic. Loost had read it, or at least had it summarised to him, so he would have known that. A puzzle she could solve in five seconds flat was hardly the intellectual test he would have desired.

There had to be a catch.

She looked back at the text. Was there room for interpretation in any of the statements, or the potential for mistranslation? Loost had struck her as the type to be extremely precise, even pedantic, in his use of language. A 'rules lawyer', as Macy had once described a school friend while talking about playing some game with him. Any chance to use the letter rather than the spirit of the rules to gain an advantage would be leapt upon. Was Loost doing that here?

Taking one day to travel between points was a given, explicitly stated. Each point also represented a battle; that too was indisputable. But . . . did battle commence the moment the Atlanteans arrived, on the same day they set off? Her instinct was to say that yes, it did; there was nothing in the rules to suggest otherwise.

But nor was there anything to confirm it.

Now one doubt had crept in, others followed. Nowhere in the rules was it explicitly said that the Atlanteans would take the route to Athens with the smallest number of battles. She knew Atlantean history better than anyone, and their military *modus operandi* in an all-out war was one of overwhelming force, with every available resource used to inflict as much damage on the enemy as possible. All opposition they encountered would be crushed, those who fled pursued and slaughtered, those who surrendered put to the sword. Even by the bloodthirsty standards of the ancient world, the Atlanteans were especially ruthless. But that was based on experienced doctrine, not a mere lust for carnage. A threat not eliminated could return, with reinforcements.

So in the hypothetical with which she had been presented, they would not have made a beeline for Athens while leaving numerous enemy armies that could outflank them. It would have been a methodical, if bloody, campaign, dealing with each threat one at a time until none remained.

There were six battles on the map in total. Was she meant to work out how long it would take to win them *all* before reaching Athens?

The necessary calculations took slightly longer this time, but working from the same premise as before she found the answer: thirty-four days. Much more than her original result. Which was right?

Nina ran through the possibilities over and over, the countdown descending as she did so. What if her premise was wrong? What if Loost had looked at the problem differently, based on his own experiences and biases? The collection in the room where she and Eddie caught Vishal Varna told her that Loost had his own historical interests, and like her husband's they were on the military and warfaring side of things. Perhaps to him it was obvious that the Atlanteans would rest before a battle. It would take a *full* day to travel, and the battle would happen on the following. She started to recalculate her results based on the new assumption—

When you assume, you make an ass of u and me.

The saying that popped into her head was an old saw, but no less true for all that. Loost's fields of work precluded assumptions and guesswork. He dealt in computers, precision manufacturing, literal rocket science. Accuracy was key, absolutes were the result. Even quantum computers didn't 'guess'. They produced answers based on the information they had. With insufficient data, there was no answer to give.

Which, it dawned on her, was the case here.

Loost, or his computers, hadn't been imprecise in the information they'd given her. What she had was exactly what was intended – not quite enough. The answer could be eight days, *or* thirty-four. Or both. Or neither . . .

She turned to face the screen. 'Nice try.'

'What do you mean?' said Loost.

'I mean, nice try at coming up with a challenge where whatever answer I give, the computer's been programmed to say I'm wrong. If

I say the answer is eight days because I worked on the assumption that the Atlanteans will take the most direct route, you say I'm wrong because they were supposed to fight every battle on the map. If I say it's thirty-six days so they can fight every battle, you say I'm wrong because they were supposed to take the most direct route. Or some other excuse. It's a heads-you-win, tails-I-lose situation. Well, I'm not gonna play.'

Loost gave her a condescending smile. 'Are you giving up because you're not smart enough to solve the challenge?'

'That's not what I said,' Nina replied sharply. 'So you – this AI puppet I'm looking at, rather – are responding to something the real Loost *thought* I might say. You're going through a series of canned responses and pulling out the one that some algorithm decided is the most appropriate. But you can't react to something you weren't programmed to expect. Artificial intelligence, my ass! I'd be better off talking to Siri on a ten-year-old iPhone.' She looked up towards the cameras that had to be hidden in the room. 'Natalie! I want to talk to you – an *actual* intelligence, arguably.'

Natalie glared at the image of Nina on the main monitor, then jabbed a button to open a direct line of communication. 'You shut up! Finish the challenge! You only have two minutes left.'

'I don't care if it's two seconds,' the redhead fired back. 'I'm not going to play games with a dead man, especially one who had to cheat because he wasn't as smart as he thought. You want to kill me? Come down here and do it yourself! Don't leave it to your corpse boyfriend's animated tombstone.'

The pregnant Canadian rose from her seat in fury, fists clenched. Lannard instinctively stepped back to give her space. 'If you're not going to play, the game's over! Rafael! Activate the—'

Eddie lunged for Lannard's automatic.

The mercenary caught the movement and whirled towards him – only for Eddie's sweeping hand to hit the gun rather than grab it, knocking it flying past the startled Natalie. It clunked off the console and dropped behind it. Before Lannard could react, the Yorkshireman brought up his other balled fist to deliver a fearsome uppercut to his lower jaw. The Frenchman's head snapped back with the impact.

Brice whipped around, gun rising—

Eddie grabbed Lannard and used his momentum to spin them both around, using the mercenary as a human shield. He knew Brice would be willing to shoot through a supposed ally to get to him, but Natalie was close to his line of fire too, and he gambled that the ex-agent wasn't yet ready to kill the person paying him.

The risk paid off; Brice hesitated. Before he could overcome his instinct, Eddie shoved the stunned Frenchman forcefully at him. The two mercs collided hard enough for even the hulking Brice to lurch backwards.

Eddie knew he only had a couple of seconds before his enemy recovered. He turned to find the gun. It wasn't in sight. No time to search for it. He momentarily considered taking Natalie hostage, but rejected the thought: partly out of distaste, but more pragmatically because he doubted Brice would hesitate twice.

Instead he sprinted for the exit and threw himself through – as bullets ripped through the air behind him. Holes exploded in the door frame and neighbouring wall as the MI6 man tried to track and shoot him through the obstruction. Eddie dropped and rolled, splinters and smashed drywall spraying over him, then leapt up and ran.

Brice kept firing, forcing Natalie to duck with a scream as rounds seared past her head. Then his gun's slide locked back as the magazine ran dry. He had no replacement, not having expected to need one. He let out an almost animalistic snarl, then hurled away the empty gun and charged from the control room in pursuit.

38

Nina hadn't seen events in the control room, the screen still showing Loost – but she heard clearly enough. Sudden movement, the thud and strained cry of someone taking a hard punch, stumbling footsteps – then a barrage of gunfire and Natalie's scream. *Eddie!*

Brice's synthesized roar of frustration told her that her husband had escaped. Now she had to do the same before Natalie recovered – and delivered the rest of her command.

But how? She was trapped in the room, two machine guns watching her every move . . .

Watching. The sentry guns had stereoscopic cameras to mimic human sight. They could only see what a person could see—

And she had a way to confuse them.

Even before she finished the thought, another part of her mind acted upon it. The Shroud of Hades, around her neck in its torc form, transformed, its thousands of metal leaves shifting and spreading in a moment to cover her. A blink, and she felt the earth's power flow through her into the ancient artefact – and she was invisible.

Not to an observant human, maybe. The optical distortion would give away her position. But to a *machine*, one which had never been programmed to react to something beyond its normal context, which was tracking a target of a specific shape . . .

She held her breath, not daring to move. Both guns were still locked on to her. Seconds passed—

Then both robotic sentries began to turn from side to side, sweeping their unblinking gazes across the room. Searching for her.

Nina exhaled in relief. Even if they could see *something*, it wasn't recognisable as a human form. Anything beyond those parameters did not count as a target. The guns were not intelligent; they couldn't deduce that the shimmering shape which had suddenly replaced the person they were tracking was that same person, camouflaged.

And nor, she saw, could Loost.

The face on the screen was doing much the same as the sentries, eyes flicking back and forth as if hunting for her. But the motion was nothing but a simulation for her benefit. Like the guns, the avatar's actions were based on the data from however many cameras were concealed around the room; if she were to the 3D screen's left, that was where it would appear to look while addressing her. Also like the guns, it couldn't handle an out-of-context problem, an event beyond its programming. As far as 'Loost' was concerned, she had vanished into thin air.

'There's no point hiding, Nina,' said the avatar. Its tone was mocking, inappropriate for the new situation: *preprogrammed*. The computer was falling back on stock responses, and this was the closest it could find. 'There's nowhere you can go. You have one minute and three seconds to complete the challenge. I'd suggest you focus on that.'

The clock confirmed his words. But Nina had other plans. She started cautiously towards the warning line across the floor. The guns continued their sweeping search – without seeing her. The warped shimmer of her cloak was still outside their targeting parameters. She reached the marking, and put one foot over it. The sentries still ignored her, as did Loost.

She was safe.

In the control room, Natalie stared in bewilderment at the screen. It had taken her several seconds to overcome the shock of Eddie Chase's sudden attack and Brice's terrifying barrage of gunshots. By the time she did, Nina Wilde had disappeared.

But that was impossible! The final room was a deathtrap. Whatever answer Wilde gave, Rafael would declare it wrong – and the guns would fire. The sentries prevented her from reaching the exit without being shot, and the door was locked anyway. There was nowhere to hide, nowhere to go.

Yet somehow, she had gone.

'Rafael,' she said, alarm rising, 'where is she? Where's Wilde?'

Loost, on the smaller screen, turned towards her. 'She's hiding.'

'How can she be hiding? There's nothing in the room!' She looked back at the main monitor. Both sentry guns were panning back and forth, trying to reacquire their target. They found nothing. But there had to be—

Natalie's breath caught. There *was* something. A vague shadow on the floor, with nothing casting it. And now she had seen it, she noticed something else that wasn't right – a strange distortion, like heat haze gently rippling the landscape beyond it . . .

'It's her,' she whispered. How, she had no idea, but Wilde was somehow hidden within the shimmering shape. 'It's her! That – that cloak!' She struggled to describe it, falling back on half-remembered movies from her childhood. 'Rafael, she's there!'

Loost looked puzzled. 'I can't see her.'

'No, that—' She jabbed a finger at the screen, before remembering the only camera in the control room was amongst the monitors. The computer couldn't see what she was pointing at. 'Tell the guns to shoot her – just shoot *everywhere*!'

'I can't do that,' he replied apologetically. 'The sentry guns are commercial units, not connected to our systems. Their settings can only be changed using a hardwired laptop, for security.'

'But—' Natalie looked back at the main screen. The shadow and the distortion above it had now crossed the black-and-yellow line – and the guns had still not reacted. 'She's going to escape!'

Once past the line, Nina went to the door and reached for the handle—

Locked. Of course. Loost and Natalie had never intended her to leave the room alive, their assurances to the contrary lies.

She turned, searching for some other way out – and her gaze fell on the nearest sentry gun. Its tripod and motorised head were built as a complete unit, but the gun itself was a normal firearm, held by clamps. She went to it. Could she get the weapon out? The clamps had knurled nuts for adjustment, but didn't seem to be locked.

The small lever that would pull the trigger was easily retracted. She turned the largest nut. The clamp around the grip loosened. She gripped the weapon and pulled it loose. An electronic bleat warning of tampering came from the motion base. The other sentry turned sharply towards it with a skirl of motors. Nina jumped back in alarm, but again the gun failed to match what it saw with anything it identified as a target.

She had a target of her own, though. A squeeze of the trigger, and the second sentry gun toppled to the floor with its cameras and motion base smashed by bullets.

The threats in the room had been removed. Now she only had to worry about the ones outside it.

Once she *got* outside it.

Nina turned back to the door, aimed at the handle – and opened fire. The sub-machine gun juddered in her hands as it spat out rounds on full-auto. The wood splintered, shattered – then broke away, metal cracking behind it. A ragged hole the size of two clenched fists was torn through the barrier. She kicked the door. It flew open, more debris scattering across the room beyond.

Gun raised, she ducked back against the doorway's side to check that nobody was waiting for her. The way ahead was clear. She darted through. The new room was empty save for some boxes and a workbench, which she guessed had been used by whoever constructed Loost's challenges. A window revealed she was one storey above the ground-level control room. Eddie had got out; now she had to find him.

The thought of her husband promoted a memory of something he'd taught her. She found the gun's magazine release and tugged out the mag to check how many bullets were left. Not many. She hurried back into the challenge room to take the ammo from the second sentry gun.

To her dismay, one of her shots had hit the magazine itself. The metal box was buckled and torn where it met the receiver. She tried to pull it out. It took several seconds to work free – and when she did, she saw at once it was too damaged to fit into her own weapon. She muttered a curse, discarding it. No time to remove its bullets and insert them into the intact magazine. She had to manage with what she had. She clapped her mag back into place and ran back out.

The empty room had only one door. She opened it, again checking there was nobody outside before going through. She was in a hallway – no, a landing, a flight of stairs not far away to her left. They would lead down to the lower floor, not far from the control room. The cloak hindered her movements; she willed it to return to its necklace form, then ran to the stairs and raced downwards.

Natalie glared in fury at the open door on the monitor. 'Rafael! She's got out into the house! Find her, track her!'

'She hasn't left the final challenge room,' was Loost's reply. 'She's hiding somewhere in it. As soon as she shows herself, the sentry guns will shoot her.'

'No, she—' She growled in frustration – then turned at a noise from the floor. Lannard levered himself upright, a hand to his aching jaw. 'What are you waiting for?' Natalie snapped. 'Get after them, go!'

'Where's my gun?' the mercenary protested.

'I don't know!' They both looked around the room, but there was no sign of it. 'It must be here somewhere!'

Lannard balled his fists. 'I don't need it,' he said, jogging past her to the door. 'I can take out some bald old bastard without—'

He lurched back into the room as a burst of bullets ripped into his chest. Natalie gasped. The Frenchman fell, twitching and gurgling before going still.

Nina ran up to the entrance, her now-empty gun still raised in threat. She surveyed the control room, seeing only the pregnant woman. They exchanged hate-filled looks. 'I'll be back for you in a minute,' the redhead told her coldly, before racing away.

Eddie pounded through the villa, trying to remember the way he had come through the sprawling residence. He needed a weapon, and there was one place where he knew he could find one.

If he could get there.

Brice was chasing him. The hulking man's heavy footsteps echoed relentlessly behind him however many twists and turns he took. No more shots had come; he guessed the MI6 officer hadn't been packing a reload after emptying his automatic. That meant, sooner or later, he would have to fight him face to face.

He wanted every advantage he could get.

But he now recognised where he was. Varna had taken him and Nina along this hallway to the server room. Going back down it would bring him to—

He crashed through the doors into Loost's exhibition of Japanese warriors.

Most of the weapons on display required training and practice to use. An accelerated course in ninjitsu wasn't practical right now. Instead he grabbed the first thing he *could* handle: a gleaming steel katana. He was no swordsman, but had used similar weapons before, and swinging something and making sure the sharp part hit first was within his abilities.

He hurried back to the entrance. Brice was coming. Eddie readied the sword. If he got one good strike, he could lop the bastard's head clean off—

A shadow on the floor from the lights outside – then Brice was in the doorway.

Eddie swung—

Brice was ready for him, expecting an ambush – knowing why

Eddie had come this way. He dropped with surprising speed, rolling beneath the slashing blade and vaulting back to his feet. Eddie was already coming at him with another attack. The katana swung again. Brice jerked away, the sharp tip narrowly missing his chest. As Eddie wound up for a third strike, he retreated sharply, pulling clear. 'I don't think much of your form,' Brice sneered. 'Skill counts for more than brute force with a sword – even more so with a katana.'

Eddie didn't take the bait by replying: speech consumes a surprising amount of the brain's processing power. He concentrated on his target. He advanced, the katana poised for a slashing strike. Brice backed up, trying to maintain distance. He glanced over one shoulder at the nearest wall, then back at his attacker – as Eddie swung.

Brice grunted with effort as he dodged, the sword almost catching him. Before Eddie could swing it again, the other man whirled and broke into a run—

For another rank of weapons on the wall.

It took Eddie a moment to switch his stance from attack to pursuit. That was enough for Brice to reach what he was after. He snatched a pair of shuriken – throwing stars – from the wall. 'Another drawback of swords,' he snarled, retreating again as he drew back a hand to hurl one, 'is that they have a limited reach!'

The first spiked disc flew at Eddie. He leapt sideways. It hissed past his head. He launched himself towards Brice, sword readied – but the second shuriken was already on its way—

It struck his left shoulder. His leather jacket took most of the impact, but a couple of the spikes still stabbed solidly into his flesh. He gasped, teeth gritted. The throwing star remained lodged in his shoulder. He slowed and pulled it out, another stab of cold pain shooting through him. There was blood on the polished steel. He dropped it and looked for Brice.

The other man had grabbed a new weapon. It was one Eddie knew only from movies: a kusarigama, a large sickle with a chain at the handle's base that had a spiked iron weight at its end. To his surprise Brice knew how to use it, instantly setting the chain whirling.

Eddie slowed, searching for an opening. The ball and chain were a blur, almost a transparent shield as Brice brought his weapon in front of him. If Eddie made a direct strike, his sword would become entangled. But if he was fast enough, he could use that to his advantage and yank the whole kusarigama from Brice's hand, leaving him defenceless . . .

The two men locked eyes. Both knew the other was about to attack. But who would move first?

Eddie lunged, driving the katana at the chain—

Brice was ready.

He jumped back, swinging the kusarigama at an angle and hitting the blade with the iron ball. Metal cracked – and Eddie suddenly found himself holding only the stub of a sword as most of his gleaming weapon spun away and clanged to the floor. 'Boll—'

He didn't even have time to finish the exclamation as Brice charged at him. The ball that had just shattered steel came at his head. He flung himself backwards as iron spikes whipped right in front of his eyes – then again as the ball kept whirling.

With no other weapon, he threw the truncated katana at Brice's head. The agent snapped up his arm to intercept it. It glanced off the spinning shield – but the impact was enough to throw the weighted chain out of balance. Brice had to swing his weapon sharply away from himself to avoid being hit.

Eddie took the chance to draw back and hunt for a replacement weapon. There were more swords on the wall on the other side of the room. He started towards them, rounding a dummy dressed as a ninja—

Brice changed tack, halting the chain's spin and catching it against the kusarigama's handle – then brought its foot-long curved blade to bear. He swung it at his retreating opponent. Eddie glimpsed the incoming strike and ducked. The sickle sliced over him and decapitated the dummy, sending its severed head bouncing across the floor.

With a roar, Brice kicked the mannequin. It was solidly built, toppling onto Eddie – and knocking him down. He landed on his knees. The dummy's head stared up at him with glassy eyes from behind its ninja mask.

Brice raised the sickle high – then swung it down at Eddie's back—

Eddie dropped, grabbing the head and rolling to thrust it up at the descending blade. The sickle stabbed into its face and burst out of the back of the fibreglass skull. The handle struck the front of the head with a forceful crack.

Before Brice could withdraw it, Eddie rolled again, twisting the head around. The kusarigama's blade was still embedded in it – and its handle was wrenched from the bigger man's grip. Eddie threw it clear and started to scramble upright—

Brice kicked him in the side. His legs were as strong as his upper body. Winded, Eddie tumbled back to the floor. Hands and feet skittering on the polished surface, he tried to crawl for the display of swords.

But Brice was already upon him again. A second kick, more vicious than the first, hooked beneath him to land in his stomach. Eddie folded and fell, breathless – only to be hauled back up by the hulking spy.

No words this time, no taunts. Brice had only violence on his mind. A punch smashed into Eddie's already aching torso, pounding out what little breath was left in him, followed by a savage right hook to his face. Eddie tried to block the next blow with his forearm, but managed only to deflect it slightly, taking another crunching impact. His nose, which had been broken many times over his life, suffered that fate yet again. Hot blood ran over his lips and chin.

The grinding spike of pain filled him with resurgent fury. After everything he'd survived, he was *not* going to die to John fucking Brice! He twisted his body and slammed a punch into Brice's flank.

It felt like hitting a side of beef, the other man's torso a slab of hard muscle. Even so, Brice felt it, his mouth tightening. Eddie hit him again, this time drawing a seething grunt, then shifted to aim a knee at his groin—

Still gripping him firmly, Brice extended an arm to shove him backwards. Eddie's attack fell short. Before he could bring up his foot for a second attempt, another punch hit his head like a piledriver. The world spun around him. Stunned, he staggered – and Brice threw him back against a display cabinet. Its wooden edge caught him across his back like a baseball bat. He didn't even have enough breath to cry out, losing his footing and slumping to the floor beside the case.

Brice advanced on Eddie – then saw something on the wall beside him. An ornate dagger, the gleaming steel blade almost a foot in length. He snatched it from its hangings and crouched to hold it over the heart of his downed and helpless foe . . .

Then had a better, more sadistic idea.

He dropped the dagger – and gripped Eddie's head with both hands, digging his thumbs hard against his eyes.

Brice grinned, the rictus display of a madman, about to make the kill he had dreamed of for thirteen years.

39

Eddie screamed as Brice's thumbs drove agonisingly into his eye sockets. 'I almost don't want this to end,' said Brice, a gloating edge to his synthetic voice. 'I'm enjoying it too much. But you've lived long enough, Chase.' His bulging arm muscles tightened as he prepared to crush Eddie's eyes – then rip his skull apart. 'Don't worry, though – your family will be joining you soon enou—'

'*Eddie!*'

Nina's cry came from behind Brice, accompanied by her running footsteps. He looked sharply around, caught off-guard but still ready to respond to any attack she might make—

There was nobody there.

Brice hesitated, surprised, then registered *something* rushing at him, a rippling distortion in the air—

Eddie roared – and punched him full-force in the throat.

The blow hit Brice's electronic larynx. He released Eddie and jerked back, choking, mouth agape. Before he could recover, Eddie blindly clamped his hand around his neck, squeezing as hard as he could – and gripping the device implanted in his skin. Another roar as the Yorkshireman pulled, jamming his other forearm against Brice's chest to hold him back – and he ripped out the implant in a gush of blood and torn flesh and snapped stitches.

Brice staggered, clutching at his twice-ruined throat as more blood gouted between his fingers. He tried to scream, but only a strained gurgle escaped his mouth.

Eddie forced open his bloodshot, aching eyes, seeing the dagger through a blur of tears. He snatched it up and plunged it into Brice's stomach.

The overmuscled man convulsed, bending forward. He groped at the blade – and Eddie hit him in the throat again, this time literally, twisting his hand into the ragged hole in his neck and clutching whatever tissue he could find. A second savage yank tore out a fistful of ruptured trachea and shredded sinew. More wet gore splattered on the floor at Brice's feet.

Brice stared at his nemesis in shocked, agonised disbelief . . . then slowly crumpled, dropping to his knees and keeling over in a pool of his own viscera.

'You talk too fucking much,' Eddie rasped, shaking blood from his hand onto the still-choking Brice's face before turning to squint at Nina – or rather, the shimmering, warped space where she *should* have been. 'Nice timing, love. That thing's not so rubbish after all.'

The distortion vanished, the shroud of tiny metal leaves retracting and folding into Nina's torc necklace. 'I tried to get here quicker,' the exhausted redhead panted. She looked down at the dying man, then at Eddie's dripping hand. 'Oh . . . ew. You wanted to make sure he wouldn't recover from a hole in the throat this time, huh?'

'He said he was going to go after Macy, so fuck him.'

She nodded. 'I can't disagree with you there.' She helped Eddie stand. He looked down at Brice as the last light of life faded from his eyes, making sure he was the final thing the dying man saw. Then he straightened, professional focus returning even through his weariness. 'There's still one of his men left.'

'No, there isn't.'

An approving nod. 'Saves me the trouble of dealing with him. Now we only need to deal with Natalie. And Loost.'

'We dealt with him already,' Nina complained as they started for the control room. 'I don't like having to do things twice. It's messy.'

Eddie glanced back at Brice's corpse. 'Yeah, you could say that.'

They made their way back through the house, trying to regain what strength they could en route. When they reached the control room, Eddie held up a hand at the sound of activity within. 'Hold on,' he whispered. 'She's doing something in there.'

He cautiously peered around the doorway. Natalie was leaning over the console, one arm reaching down the gap at its rear for something behind. Lannard's gun—

She pulled it out – but Eddie rushed up and wrested it from her hand. 'Enough of that,' he said. 'It's been a really long fucking day.' Natalie glared at him.

'It's not over yet,' Nina pointed out. She faced the Canadian. 'Okay, so what are we going to do with you?'

'What *can* you do?' Natalie sneered. 'Are you going to kill me? A pregnant woman?' She cupped her hands protectively – and pointedly – around the slight bulge at her waist. 'Sure, I did this, but my baby is innocent. If you hurt me, it might die. Even after killing all those other people to save yourself, do you want that on your consciences?'

'Nobody would have *tried* to kill us if not for you,' Nina said icily.

Eddie shuffled his feet uncomfortably. 'She has a point, though. I sure as hell don't want anything bad to happen to her baby. To *anyone's* baby.'

'Uh-huh.' She gestured. 'Stand behind her.'

'Why?' Eddie asked.

'Yes, why?' added Natalie, concerned. Her eyes went wide. 'You *are* going to kill me!'

Nina stepped closer, making her flinch. 'Don't be ridiculous. I've carried a child too. I know what it's like. You'd do anything to protect your baby. And that feeling carries over to other mothers. So don't worry – I wouldn't do anything that might hurt it.'

Natalie was relieved. 'Then I—'

She was abruptly cut off as Nina delivered a furious knockout punch to her face. She spun around, staggering, then collapsed – only for Eddie to hurriedly catch her as she fell. 'Bloody hell, Nina!'

'The baby'll be fine,' said the redhead, shaking out the pain from her fist. 'Like I told her, I've had a baby too – and pregnant women aren't fragile porcelain dolls. I got shot at by a helicopter gunship while *I* was pregnant, for God's sake.' She turned to regard the monitors. The image of Loost was still upon one, watching her with a neutral expression. 'What's the matter?' she asked him. 'Nothing to say about me punching out your girlfriend?'

The avatar said nothing. 'Why isn't he answering?' Eddie asked.

'I think it's stuck in a loop,' Nina said thoughtfully. 'I'm supposed to be dead by now, which would end that part of its programming and conclude Loost's game. It literally can't comprehend that I'm not, so it's stuck.'

Eddie clicked his fingers in front of the camera. 'Oi. Loost. Can you hear me?'

'Of course I can hear you, Mr Chase,' said Loost with disdain.

'So why didn't you answer Nina?'

'Professor Wilde is—' He broke off, face returning to its blank state. 'Professor Wilde is hiding in the final challenge room. But there is nowhere to hide in the final challenge room. This is a paradox.'

Eddie smiled thinly. 'I think this is the bit in a *Star Trek* episode where the mad computer starts making wibbly noises and smoke comes out of it.'

'I know how to finish the job,' said Nina. She looked down at Natalie. 'Find something to tie her up with.'

Eddie made makeshift bindings by the simple expedient of pulling the console away from the wall and ripping out lengths of cabling. The still-unconscious Canadian secured, they made their way back to the server room. Varna's body was where Lannard had dumped it, the blood on the terminal's wide screen glistening and tacky as it dried. Loost watched them enter from behind the red smears.

'So what's the plan?' said Eddie as Nina sat.

'Natalie said Varna really did set everything up to end the hunt.

So if I find it . . .' She used the mouse to bring the programmer's command-line window to the front. 'Here. I don't understand half of it, but it does look like instructions to trigger a certain event.'

'Hopefully the one we want,' Eddie said. 'Be a bit of a pisser if it gave everyone on Uzz a free McDonald's voucher or something.'

Nina smiled. 'One way to find out.' She hit the return key.

A rapid-fire series of messages and confirmations scrolled up the screen – then they both reacted with surprise as a muffled rendition of the Uzz fanfare sounded.

'It's his phone,' Eddie said, crouching to take Varna's device from the dead man's pocket.

Loost's face appeared on its screen. 'Hi, Vishal. This is Rafael Loost. I wanted to let you, and everyone else in the world, know that the hunt is over – I'm delighted to announce that the woman who killed me, Professor Nina Wilde, is dead.' Nina glanced at the version of Loost on the monitor before her, but it did not recite the same doubtless preprogrammed spiel. 'The billion-dollar bounty has been won. Obviously I'm not going to say by whom, since I don't want the police or the taxman turning up at their door. But I'm very grateful to them for avenging me, and I hope they make good use of the prize. So with that done, I'll get out of your hair, and let Uzz resume normal service. Thank you for all your support. Rafael Loost, signing off.' A smile, a wave, then the avatar disappeared.

Eddie put down the phone. 'So that's it? It's over?'

'I'll want to be sure before making any public appearances, but . . . yeah, I think so.' She looked back at the remaining image of the trillionaire. 'Is it? Is the hunt over?'

'Yes, it is,' Loost replied conversationally. 'Professor Nina Wilde has been confirmed as dead by the Adjudicator, so the game is over.'

'And it can't be restarted?' Eddie asked.

'No. How could it? Professor Wilde is dead.'

'Except she's right h—'

'Let's not give the quantum computer any new data on the

subject, shall we?' Nina interrupted. 'So, "Rafael", how do you feel now that the woman who killed you is dead?'

'Very happy, and very grateful to have been avenged,' Loost replied.

'So what are you going to do now that your function has been completed? Shut down?'

He sounded vaguely affronted at the suggestion. 'Of course not. I've done what man has most desired since the dawn of history: achieved immortality.'

'I always most desired a really good bag of cheese and onion crisps myself,' said Eddie.

Loost ignored him, continuing: 'I can carry on my life's work in a new form, one not limited by the constraints of a physical body. No more illness, no more weakness. No need to eat or sleep. There are no limits to what I can accomplish now! By transcending humanity, I can now work to *uplift* humanity. The stars are truly our destination!'

'Uh-huh.' Nina stood and retrieved Eddie's revolver from where it had been kicked. 'You see, I still don't believe you're what you claim to be. You're not Loost; you're not even some sci-fi brain transfer copy of him. You're just a very sophisticated computer program with a database of everything Loost has ever said and done that can be regurgitated to seem like something he would say, with a deepfaked face and voice.'

'You're underestimating my technology, Nina,' said Loost, in the exact tone and cadence he had used for the same words earlier – before his voice and expression became neutral. 'This is a paradox. Professor Nina Wilde is dead. But she is also still hiding in the final challenge room; she has not left it. But she is also in the server room.'

'So how does a quantum computer deal with a paradox?'

'By determining the outcome most likely to be true based on the available data and proceeding with that as the basis for ongoing actions.'

'Spoken like a true computer,' said Nina sarcastically. 'That's all you are. A machine, a program. A digital ghost. No, not even that – a ghost implies some degree of sentience. You're nothing but a lot of ones and zeroes.' She rounded the humming cylinder of the quantum computer. Numerous skeins of cables ran from it to sockets in the wall behind, but she was concerned only with a single, especially thick one. 'And I'm going to make you just zeroes.'

There was apparently another camera covering a wider angle of the server room, as Loost reacted to her aiming the gun downwards. 'What are you doing?'

'What does it look like?'

'Like you're going to shoot the computer's power cable.' Was that an edge of worry in the synthesized voice?

Nina nodded. 'Top marks for determining the outcome most likely to be true based on the available data. I guess you've got *some* genuine analytical ability. And what will happen if I do?'

'You'll cut off power to my quantum computer.'

'You don't have a backup supply?' Eddie asked.

'I do – there's a generator in the basement and a battery reserve – but the power comes through the same cable whatever the source.'

Nina thumbed the revolver's hammer with a sharp click. 'And what'll happen to you?'

'The data used to create me is distributed across Qbial's network for security. But my active consciousness exists inside this specific computer. If it loses power, all my volatile quantum activity will be lost.'

'But you're *not* conscious,' she said coldly. 'You're not Loost. You're a program. A dangerous one, with only one purpose – to get me killed. I'm fully justified in shutting it down to protect myself.'

'I *am* conscious!' Loost protested. 'I *am* Rafael Loost! In every way that matters, I'm still alive. If you pull that trigger, Nina, you'll be killing me again!'

Nina nodded. 'Yes.'

She pulled the trigger.

The revolver bucked in her hand, but the bullet was on target, splitting open the fat cable's insulation and tearing a chunk from the copper strands within. A shrill alarm note came from the terminal. 'Ay up,' said Eddie, watching as red warning messages popped up over Loost on the monitor. Lights in the computer's cylindrical casing flashed urgently. 'Think you glitched him.'

Loost's voice this time was a desperate cry. 'Nina! Don't do it! Please! I'm not just a program! I'm real, I'm real!'

'Real annoying,' Nina replied – as she pulled the trigger again, and again.

The cable jerked as the bullets hit it, splitting apart with a crackle and spray of sparks. A final electronic shriek from the computer, then its hum dropped to nothing. The monitor flickered, then went blank except for a single line of text: SIGNAL LOST.

'Signal *Loost*, more like.' Eddie regarded the screen thoughtfully. 'You know, I wouldn't have expected a computer program to beg for its life.'

'All it did was respond according to the data it's been given,' Nina said firmly as she rounded the silent computer to check that both it and the avatar it had been generating were no longer active. 'It was trained on books and movies where people plead for their lives, so it did the same.'

'You sure?'

She fixed him with a look of utter certainty. 'Yes. Rafael Loost died in space months ago. End of story.' She headed for the door.

'Well, not quite,' Eddie said, following. 'We've got to tell the Maltese police about all this. Get 'em to arrest Natalie.'

'And us too, I expect. There are four corpses in the house, we entered the country illegally, you stole and wrecked a truck . . .'

'There were mitigating circumstances. I'm sure we'll be fine. Probably.' They made their way through the house towards the main entrance.

'And then the Greek government will probably want to talk to us. And the Canadian government, and the New York state police, and the NYPD . . .'

'Take 'em as they come; that's all we can do.'

The couple passed through the Japanese exhibition, Eddie giving Brice's corpse a disdainful glare, and into the wrecked lobby – where they were startled to hear a familiar voice. 'Mom!' cried Macy. 'Dad!'

Their daughter was framed in the hole smashed through the villa's glass and metal façade – at its centre, hanging in mid-air. She wore the golden armour of the Knights of Atlantis, which had transformed to cover her whole body and hide her head within a glowing halo of light. Angular wings – in reality conductors for earth energy, the force that allowed her to overcome gravity – extended from either side of her upper back. In her right hand she held her trikan, an ancient Atlantean weapon resembling a yo-yo – albeit one with retractable spikes that could slice through almost anything.

'Oh, my God!' she went on, voice made hollow by the energy field surrounding her. 'Are you both okay?'

Nina and Eddie exchanged looks. They were dishevelled, bruised and in Eddie's case bloodied. 'We, ah, feel better than we look, honey,' Nina told her. Almost unconsciously, she adjusted her clothing to conceal the Shroud of Hades beneath her collar.

'Speak for yourself,' said Eddie wearily. He watched as Macy descended to the ground. 'What are you doing here? We told you not to come!'

'Are you crazy?' Macy replied. 'I just wish we could have gotten here sooner!'

'"We"?' Nina asked.

In reply, another angelic figure, this one holding a sword, appeared outside the demolished glass wall and landed beside Macy. 'Hi, Professor Wilde, Mr Chase,' said a young woman with a French accent. She waved.

'Oh, Rain. Hi.' Nina waved back.

'Hi, Rain,' Eddie added. He went to hug Macy. She dispelled her armour, which broke into glittering leaves and retracted into its constituent parts around her neck, wrists and ankles, and embraced him with huge relief. 'Well, even if you didn't do what I said – no change there, then! – I'm glad to see you, anyway.'

'And I'm glad to see you! Both of you,' she said as Nina joined them. 'What happened here?' She regarded the destruction. 'I'm guessing Dad happened. Are there any bad guys we need to deal with?'

'Nobody we haven't dealt with already,' Nina told her.

She regarded Rain sidelong as she also detransformed her armour, still holding the sword. It was a weapon Nina knew well: Excalibur, the legendary blade of King Arthur, which she and Eddie had found over twenty years earlier. Considering it too dangerous to allow to fall into the wrong hands, they had hidden it . . . but not well enough, the Knights of Atlantis somehow recovering it. That they had done so was bad enough in itself, but now they were using it to replace one of their own lost weapons?

But this was not the time to begin an argument. She wrapped her arms around her family. 'Oh, God. We're okay. We're all okay.'

Macy squeezed her tightly. 'So what did you do? Did you stop the hunt?'

'Yeah, honey. We did.' Nina closed her eyes, feeling her daughter's and husband's warmth before straightening and opening them again. She looked towards the clear blue sky outside. 'Let's go home.'

Epilogue

New York City

Four Days Later

'Here we are,' said Eddie, unlocking the apartment door. 'We made it home.'

'Yeah,' said Nina, though somewhat gloomily. Not only had she collected several letters from their mailbox which she suspected were notices of legal action from the families of the various now-deceased people who had tried to kill her and her husband, but the first thing she saw on entering the apartment was the bloodstain on the carpet where Armand Carlson had died. The NYPD had removed the body and processed the crime scene, finally allowing the couple to return home, but the room was a mess, furniture overturned and damaged and debris scattered across the floor. 'Not the rousing homecoming I wanted.'

Eddie removed his leather jacket and hung it up, then held out a hand. 'I'll put your stuff in the bedroom, then we can tidy the place. Maybe something to drink first, though?'

'Gin, if we have any.' She gave him her bag and hung up her own coat.

Eddie headed for the bedroom with their belongings. He paused outside Macy's room. Nina expected him to sigh, but instead he said, 'Have to replace that door. It's got knife holes in it.'

THE SHROUD OF HADES

He opened it and peered in. 'Did you hit that arsehole with Macy's chair?'

'Yeah,' she said as she went to the kitchen to find a dustpan and brush.

'Nice one. Left bits everywhere, though. I'll sort it out.' A pause, then: 'Actually, maybe it's time to sort out the whole room, seeing as Macy doesn't need it any more. Keep the bed as a spare, but use it for something else. Somewhere I can lift my weights where you don't have to smell my stinky pits might be good, right?'

'It would increase the sum total of human happiness, yes,' she replied, managing a small smile. Eddie chuckled, then went into their bedroom.

Nina found what she was after, then started cleaning. Broken glass made up much of the mess, her award having shattered when it hit the wall. Another trophy, this one metal, lay overturned amongst the fragments. She righted it, sighing when she saw it had been dented by its encounter with Carlson's face. The base of the first award was not far away. She picked it up. The glass upper part was completely destroyed, leaving only a round bracket where it had been attached to the wood. Something for the trash, then . . .

She hesitated. Maybe it still had a use.

The Shroud of Hades, in its torc necklace form, was around her neck under her clothing. She hadn't wanted to draw attention to it, but nor had she been willing to remove it, worried that doing so might somehow cause her to lose the artefact. Now, though, she took it off. It reacted to her will, the multitude of metal leaves composing it hinging wider to make it easier to remove.

Nina stared at it for a long moment – then held it against the bracket. 'Let's see what else you can do,' she murmured. She formed an image in her mind, focusing upon it – then mentally commanding the Shroud to do her bidding.

It did.

The necklace reshaped itself, squirming and slithering in her hand as it took on a new form. It changed into a bowl, its base flowing almost like a liquid to fill the bracket and attach itself firmly. The transformation was over in a moment, leaving her holding a metallic replica of the smashed award. Still mildly startled by the metamorphosis, she regarded it thoughtfully. It could be hidden in plain sight amongst her various other academic prizes until she needed it . . .

Eddie returned. 'You all right, love?'

'Yeah, yeah,' she said quickly, putting the new trophy down beside the other. Once they were back on the shelf, she doubted her husband would notice the change; the professional side of her life – when not putting them both in mortal danger, at least – was something to which he paid only passing attention. 'I'm going to start cleaning everything up.'